D0564080

ART BALTAZAR

DREW AND JOT™

DUELING DOODLES

Ross Richie CEO & Founder
Joy Huffman CFO
Matt Gagnon Editor-in-Chief
Filip Sablik President, Publishing & Marketing
Stephen Christy President, Development
Lance Kreiter Vice President, Licensing & Merchandising
Arune Singh Vice President, Marketing
Bryce Carlson Vice President, Editorial & Creative Strategy
Scott Newman Manager, Production Design
Kate Henning Manager, Operations
Spencer Simpson Manager, Sales
Elyse Strandberg Manager, Finance
Sierra Hahn Executive Editor
Jeanine Schaefer Executive Editor
Dafna Pleban Senior Editor
Shannon Watters Senior Editor
Eric Harburn Senior Editor
Chris Rosa Editor
Matthew Levine Editor
Sophie Philips-Roberts Associate Editor
Amanda LaFranco Associate Editor
Jonathan Manning Associate Editor

Gavin Gronenthal Assistant Editor
Gwen Waller Assistant Editor
Allyson Gronowitz Assistant Editor
Jillian Crab Design Coordinator
Michelle Ankley Design Coordinator
Kara Leopard Production Designer
Marie Krupina Production Designer
Grace Park Production Designer
Chelsea Roberts Production Design Assistant
Samantha Knapp Production Design Assistant
José Meza Live Events Lead
Stephanie Hocutt Digital Marketing Lead
Esther Kim Marketing Coordinator
Cat O'Grady Digital Marketing Coordinator
Amanda Lawson Marketing Assistant
Holly Aitchison Digital Sales Coordinator
Morgan Perry Retail Sales Coordinator
Megan Christopher Operations Coordinator
Rodrigo Hernandez Mailroom Assistant
Zipporah Smith Operations Assistant
Sabrina Lesin Accounting Assistant
Breanna Sarpy Executive Assistant

kaboom!™

DREW AND JOT: DUELING DOODLES, December 2019. Published by KaBOOM!, a division of Boom Entertainment, Inc. Drew and Jot is ™ & © 2019 Electric Milk Creations, Inc. All rights reserved. KaBOOM!™ and the KaBOOM! logo are trademarks of Boom Entertainment, Inc., registered in various countries and categories. All characters, events, and institutions depicted herein are fictional. Any similarity between any of the names, characters, persons, events, and/or institutions in this publication to actual names, characters, and persons, whether living or dead, events, and/or institutions is unintended and purely coincidental. KaBOOM! does not read or accept unsolicited submissions of ideas, stories, or artwork.

BOOM! Studios, 5670 Wilshire Boulevard, Suite 400, Los Angeles, CA 90036-5679. Printed in Canada. First Printing.

ISBN: 978-1-68415-430-2
eISBN: 978-1-64144-547-4

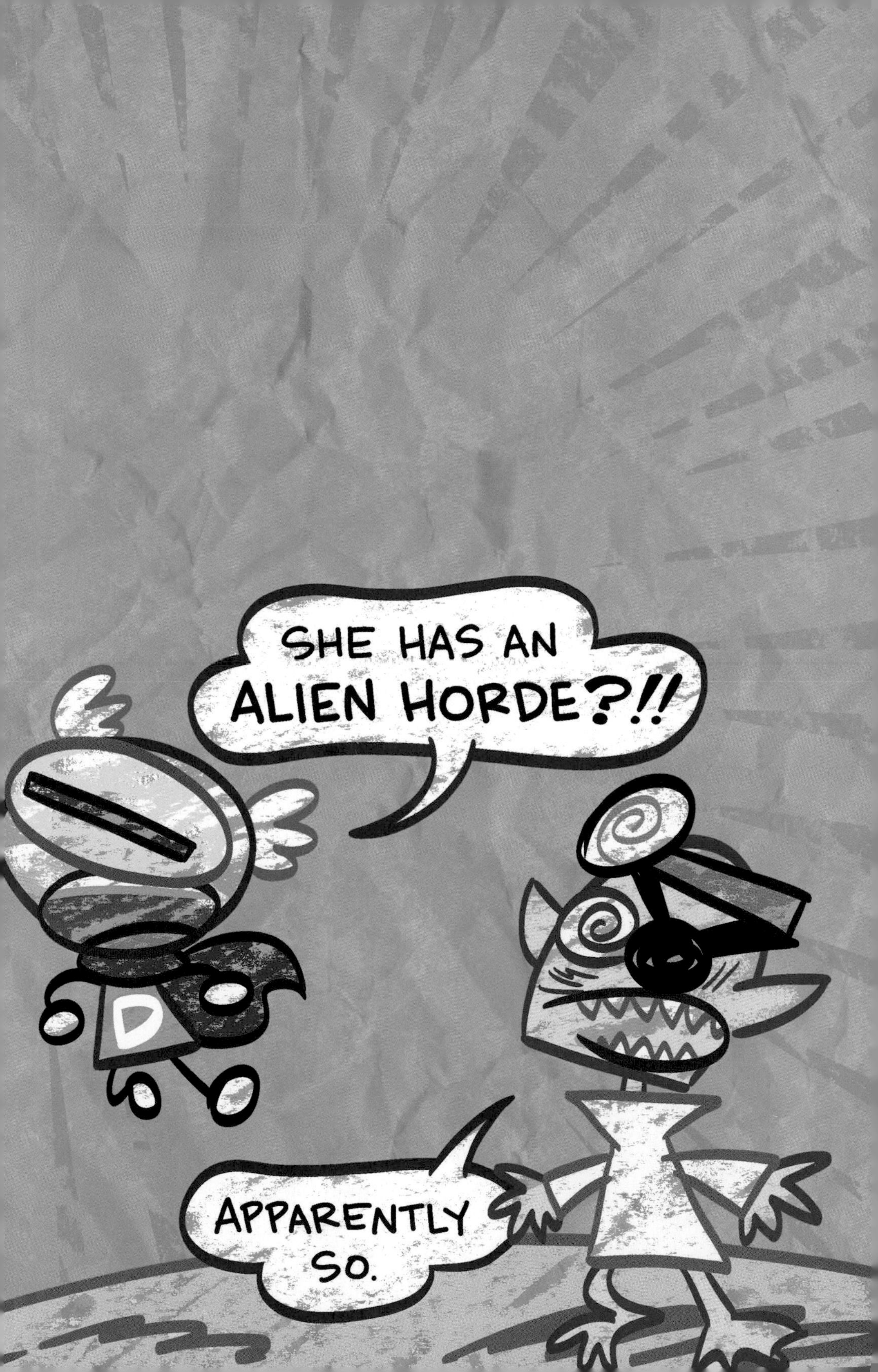
SHE HAS AN ALIEN HORDE?!!
APPARENTLY SO.

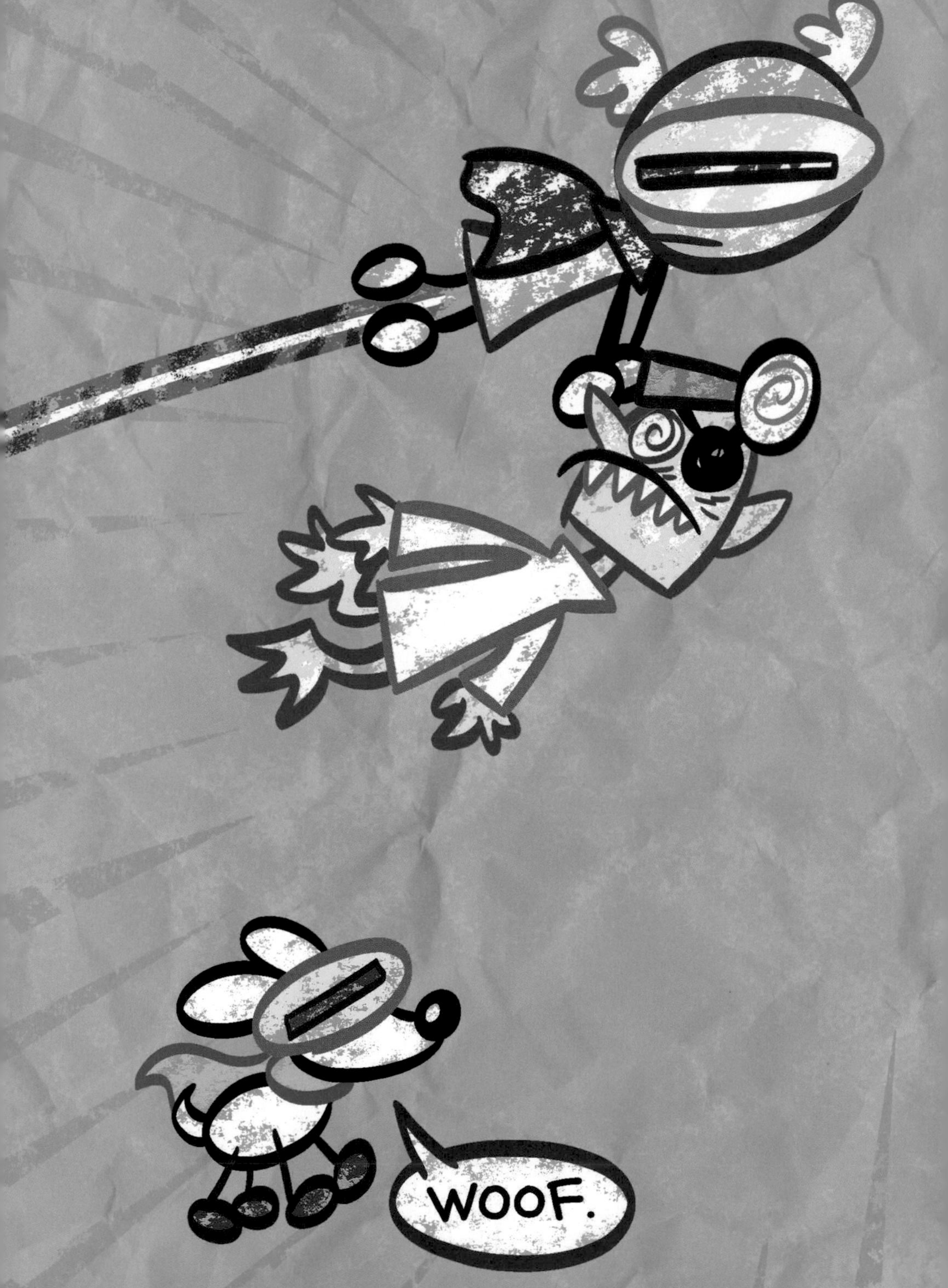
WOOF.

DREW AND JOT

BOOK ONE
DUELING DOODLES

BY
ART BALTAZAR

DESIGNER
JILLIAN CRAB

EDITOR
CHRIS ROSA

CREATED BY
ART BALTAZAR

SPECIAL THANKS
WHITNEY LEOPARD

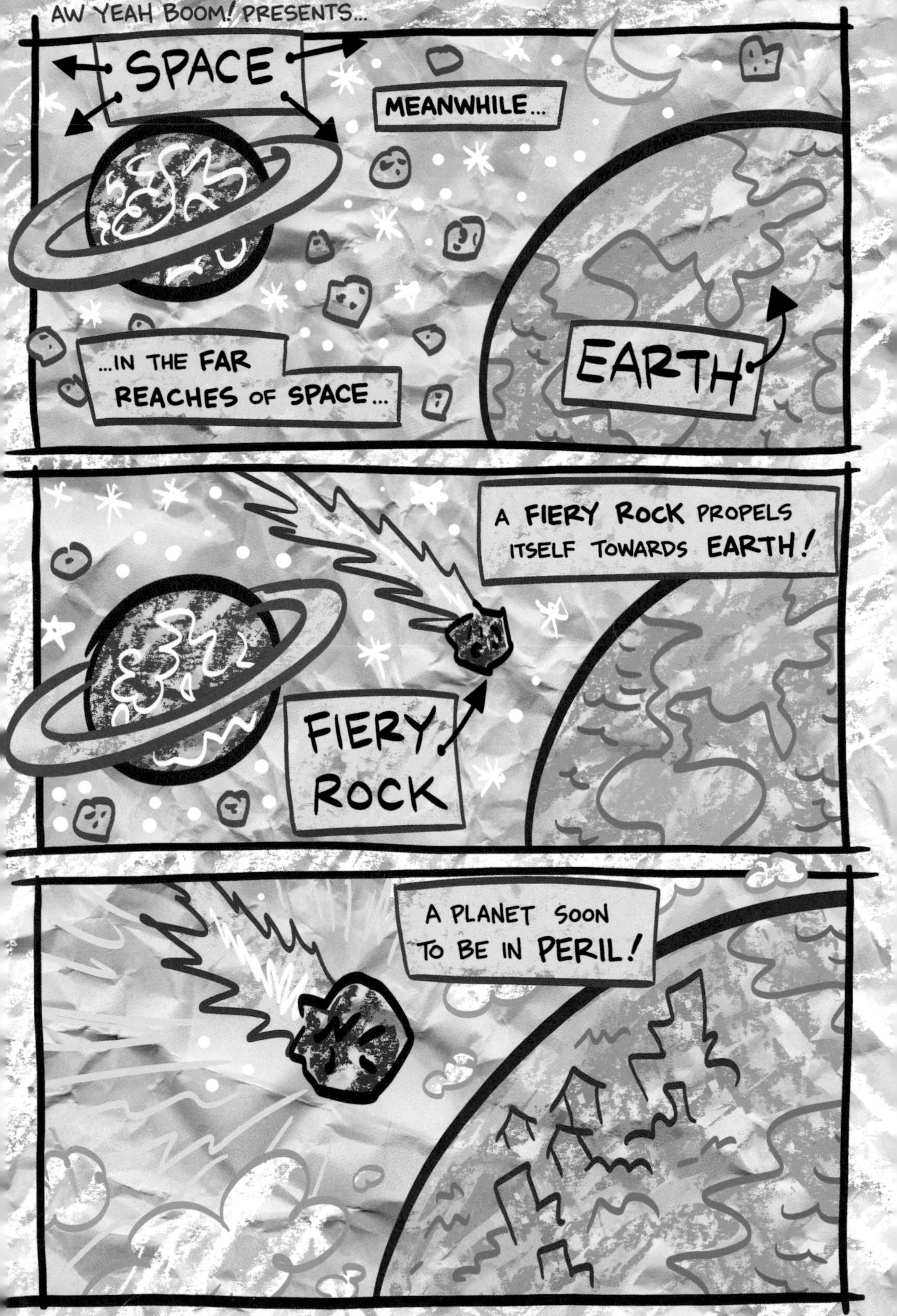
AW YEAH BOOM! PRESENTS...
SPACE
MEANWHILE...
...IN THE FAR REACHES OF SPACE...
EARTH
A FIERY ROCK PROPELS ITSELF TOWARDS EARTH!
FIERY ROCK
A PLANET SOON TO BE IN PERIL!

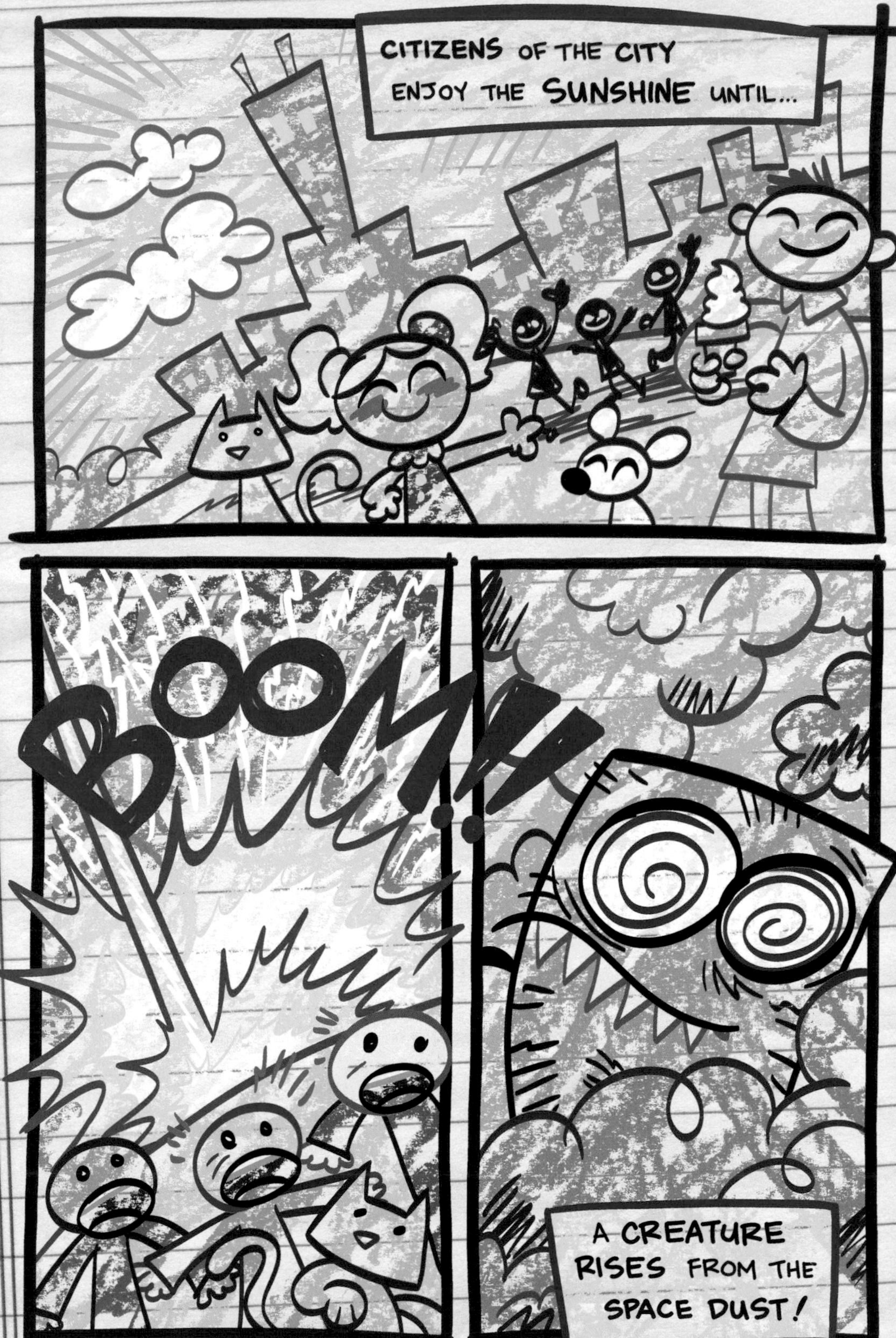
CITIZENS OF THE CITY ENJOY THE SUNSHINE UNTIL...
BOOM!!
A CREATURE RISES FROM THE SPACE DUST!

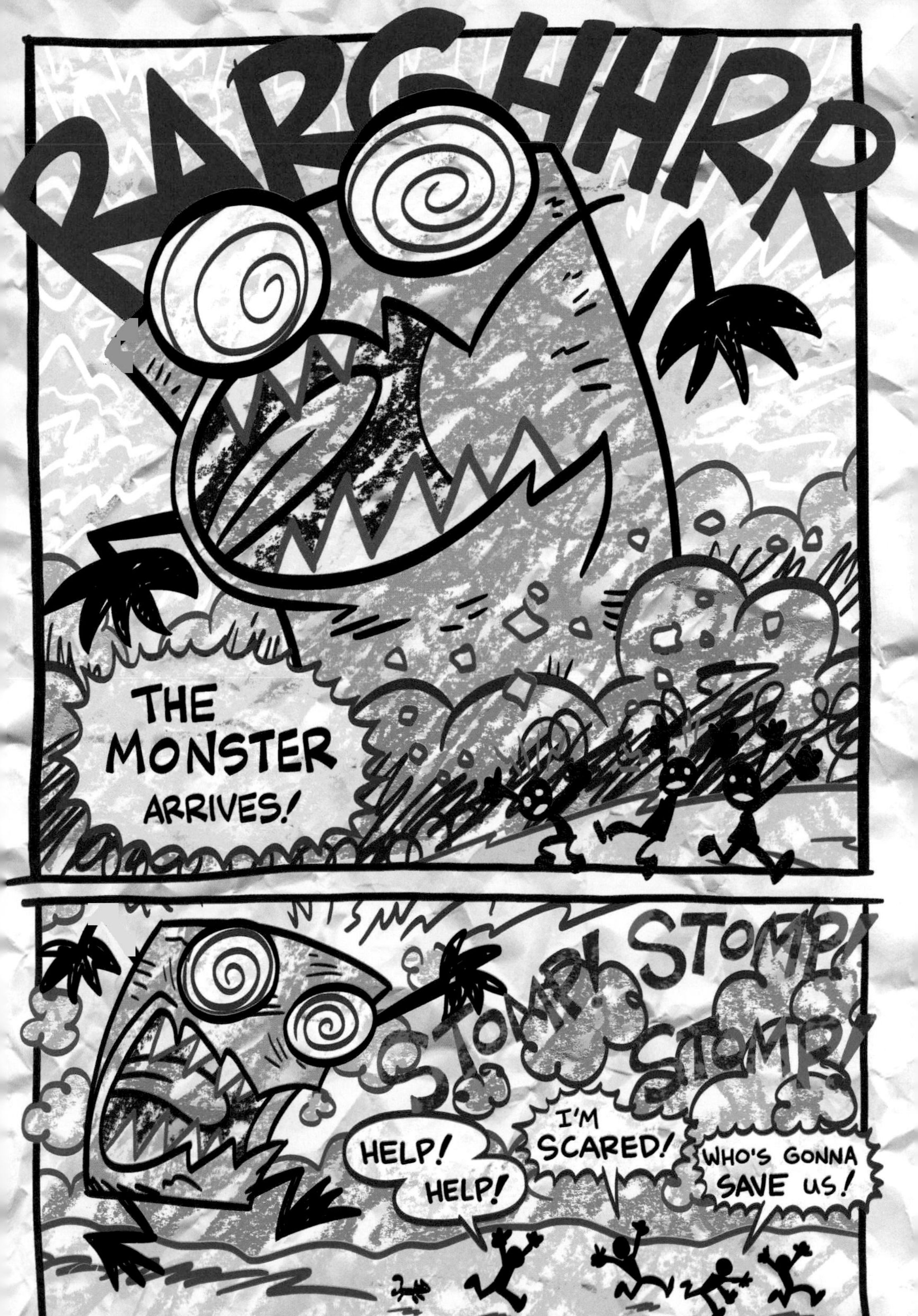
RARGHHRR
THE MONSTER ARRIVES!
STOMP! STOMP!
STOMP!
HELP! HELP!
I'M SCARED!
WHO'S GONNA SAVE US!

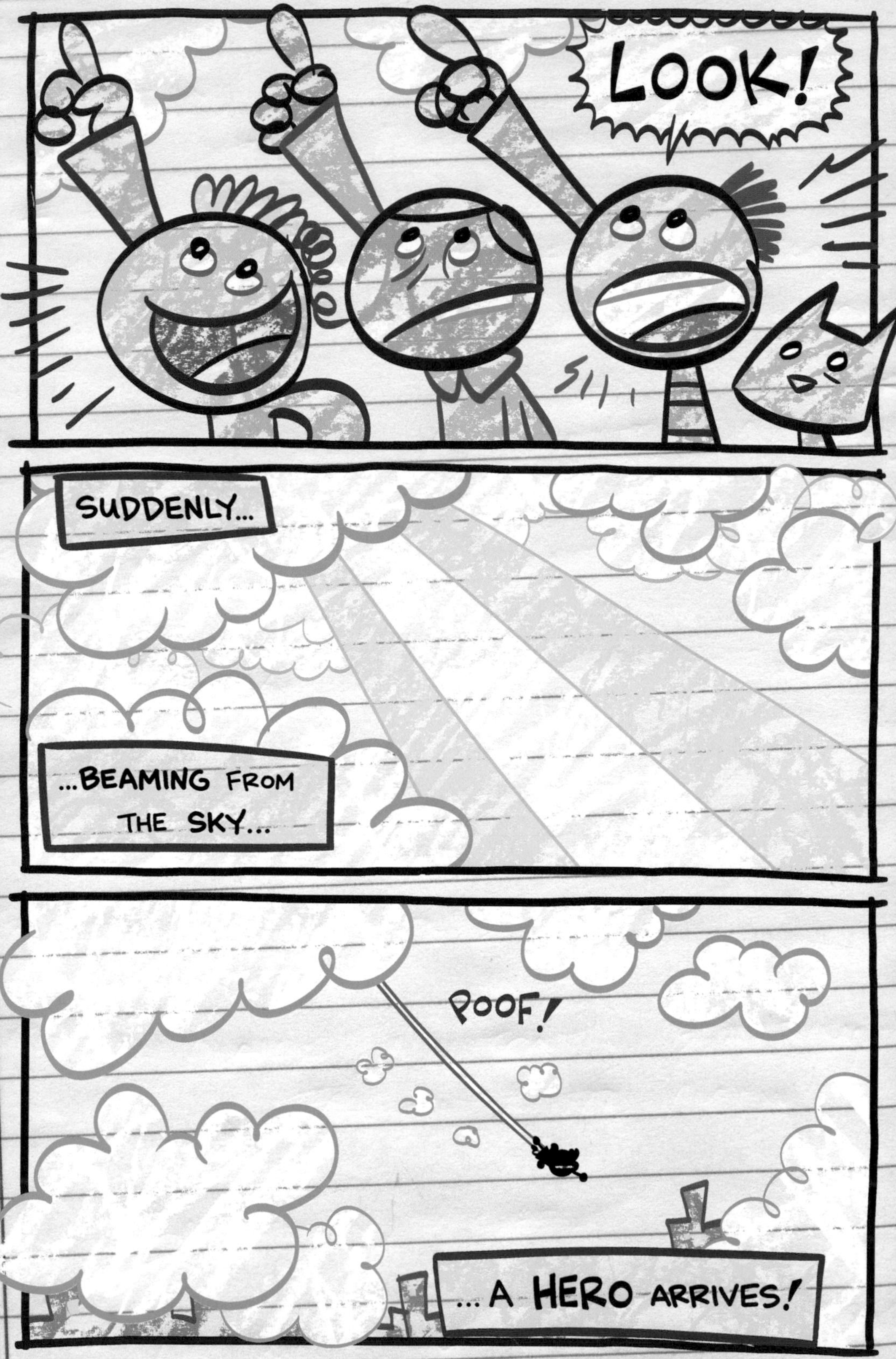
LOOK!
SUDDENLY...
...BEAMING FROM THE SKY...
POOF!
... A HERO ARRIVES!

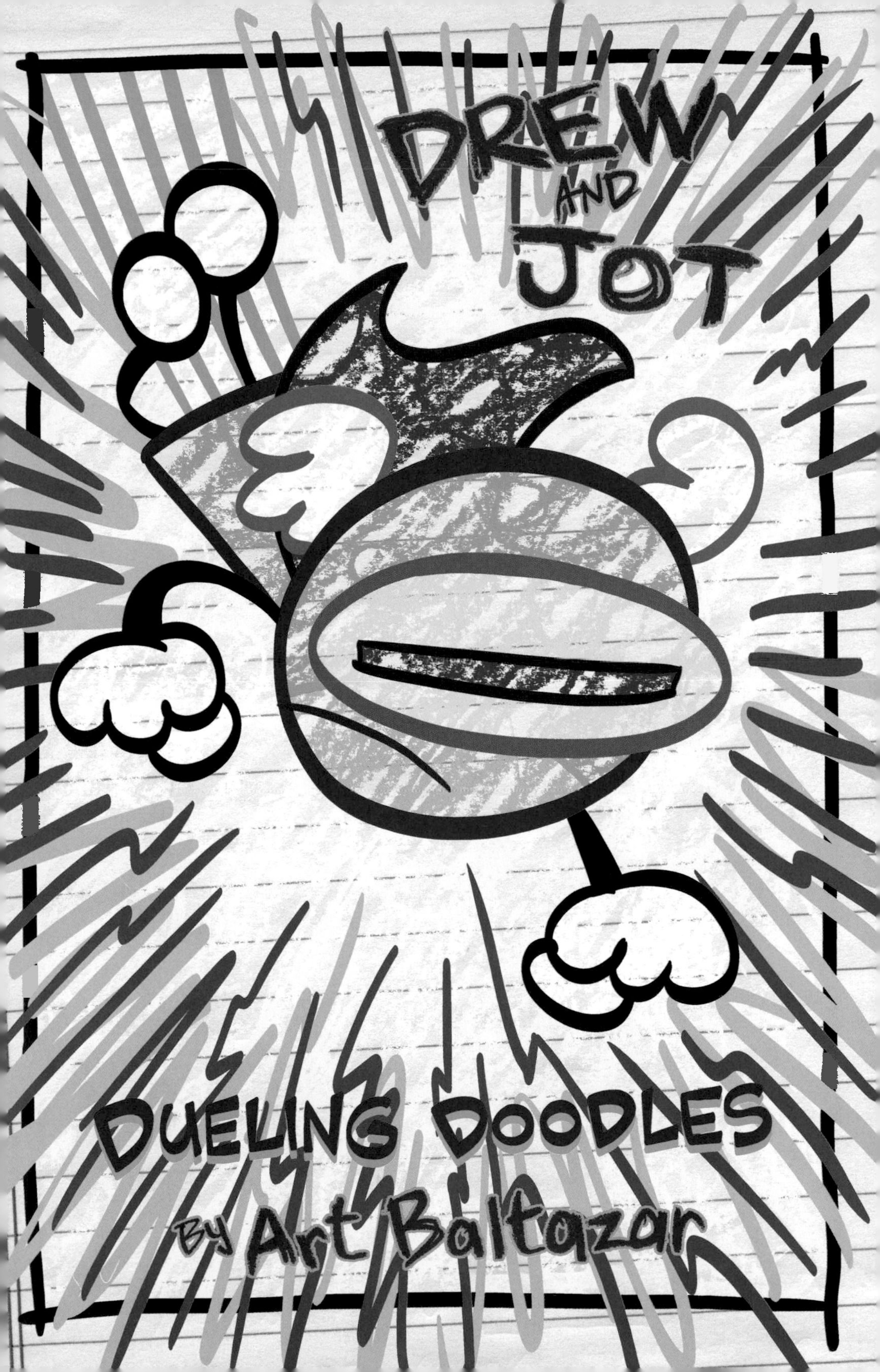
DREW AND JOT
DUELING DOODLES
By Art Baltazar

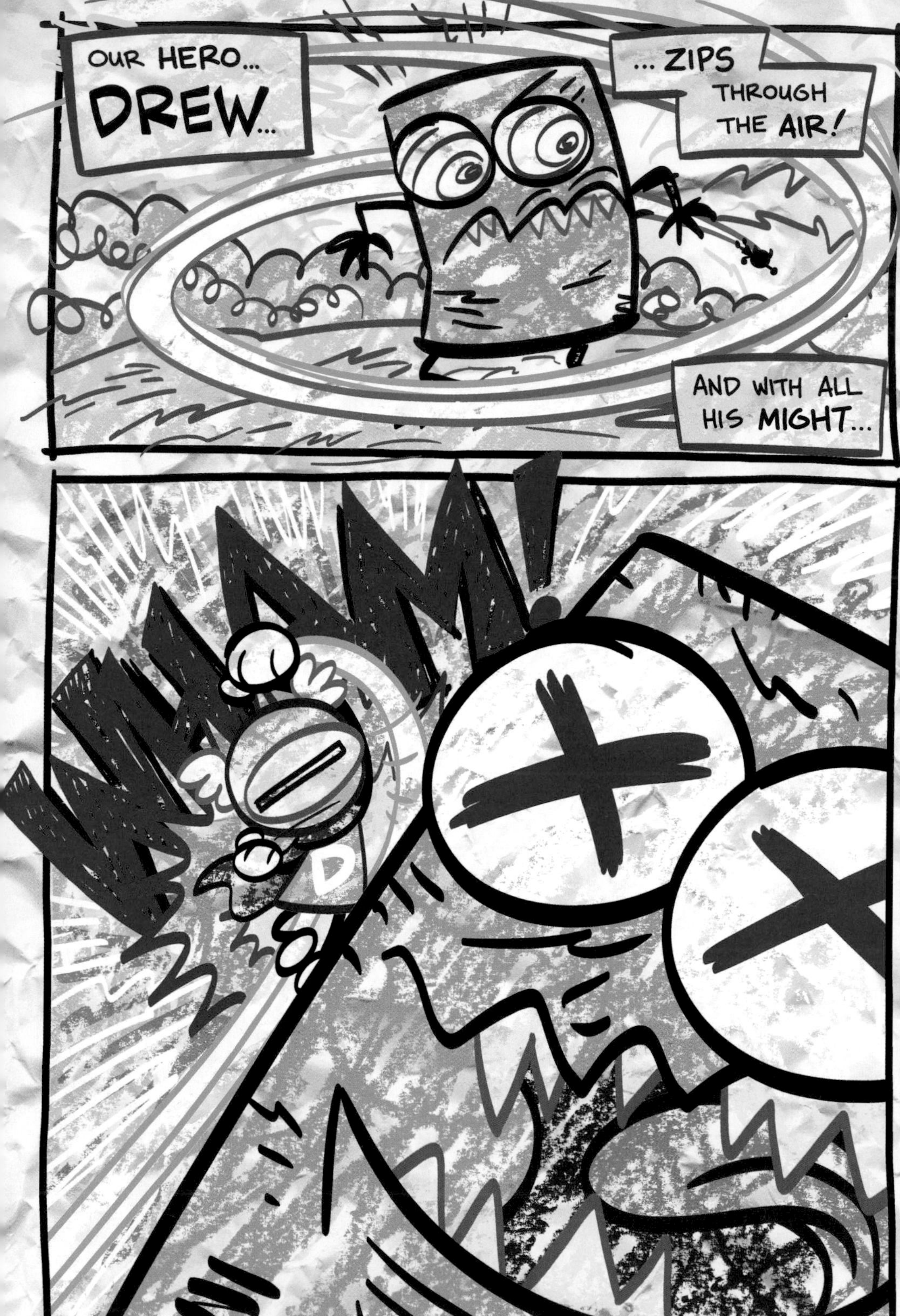
OUR HERO... DREW...
... ZIPS THROUGH THE AIR!
AND WITH ALL HIS MIGHT...
WHAM!

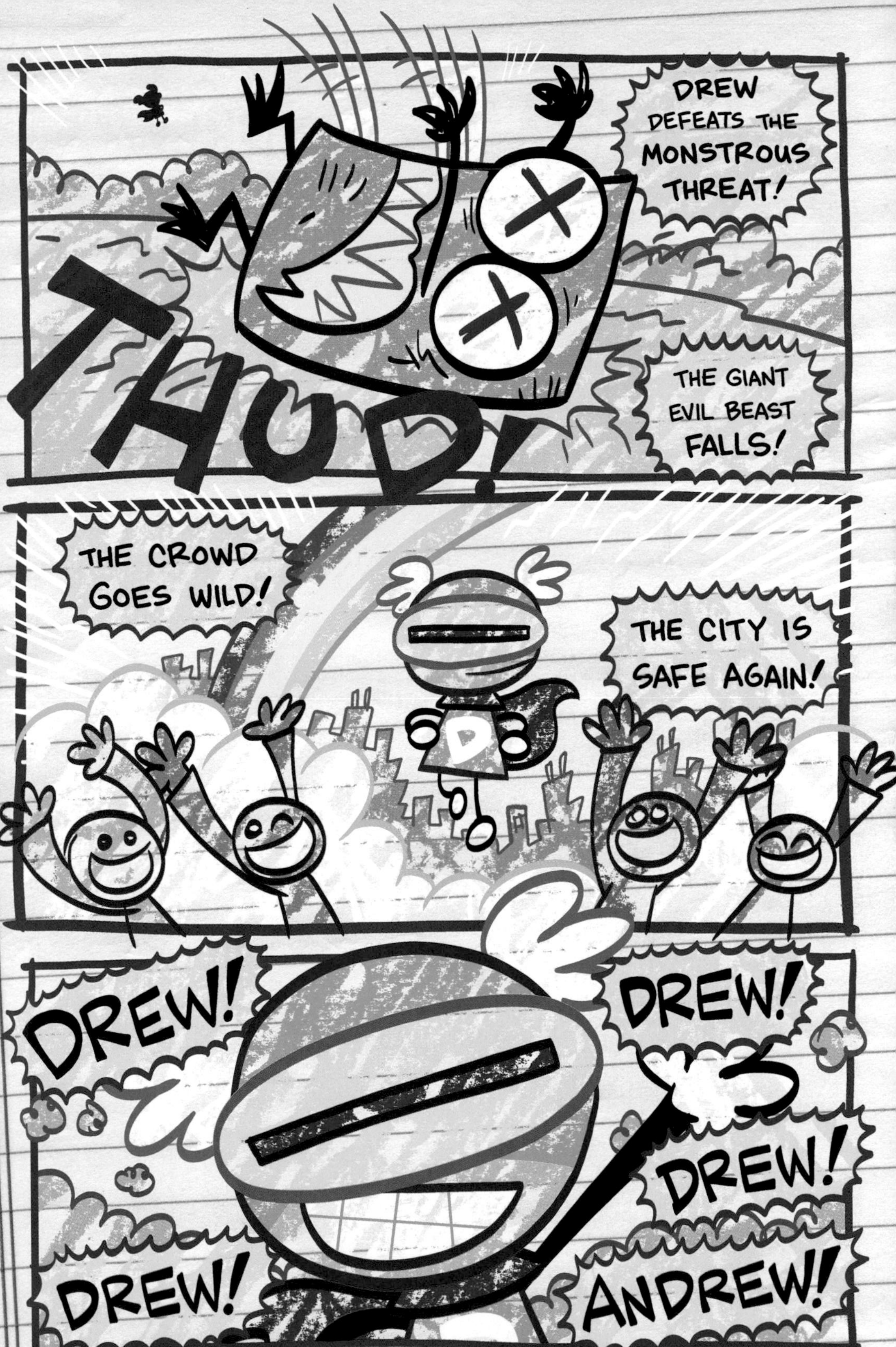
DREW DEFEATS THE MONSTROUS THREAT!
THUD!
THE GIANT EVIL BEAST FALLS!
THE CROWD GOES WILD!
THE CITY IS SAFE AGAIN!
D
DREW!
DREW!
DREW!
DREW!
ANDREW!

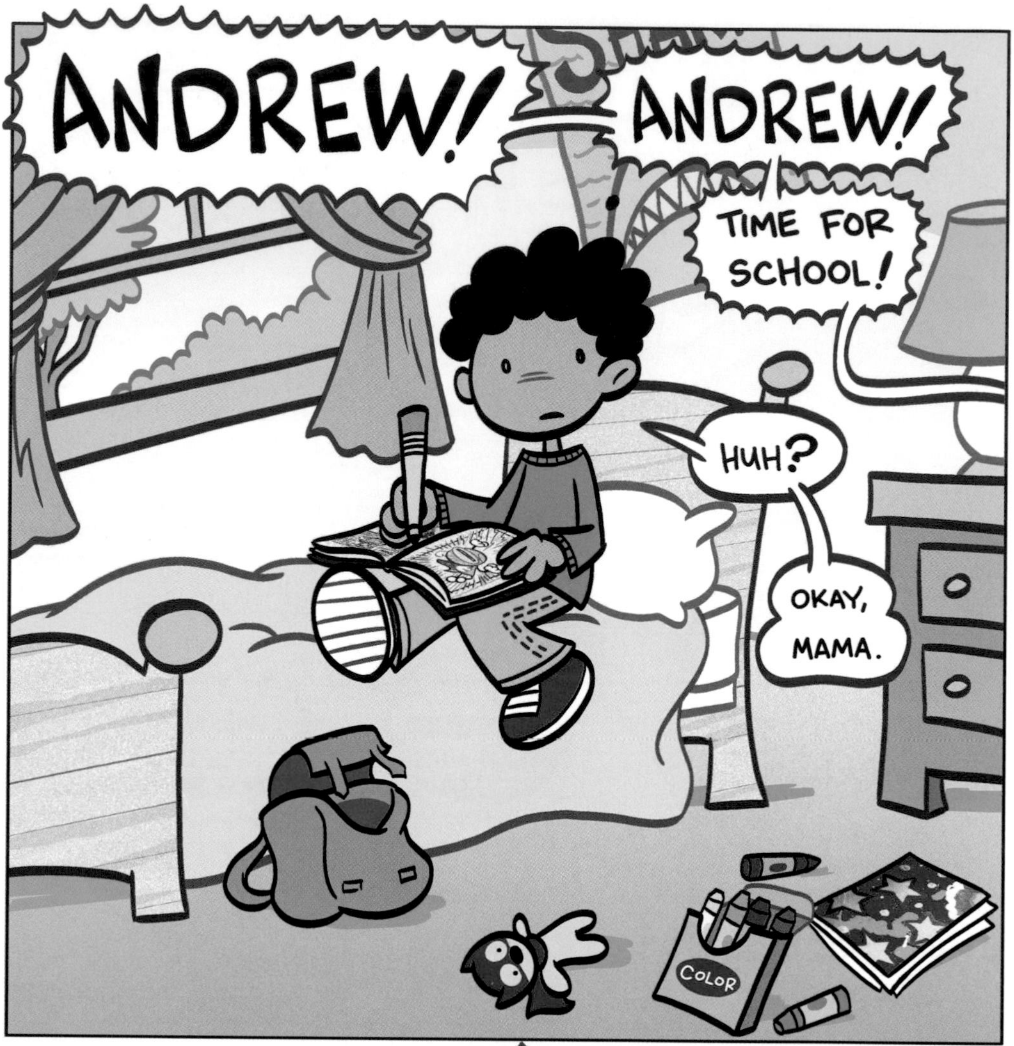
ANDREW! ANDREW!
TIME FOR SCHOOL!
HUH?
OKAY, MAMA.
COLOR

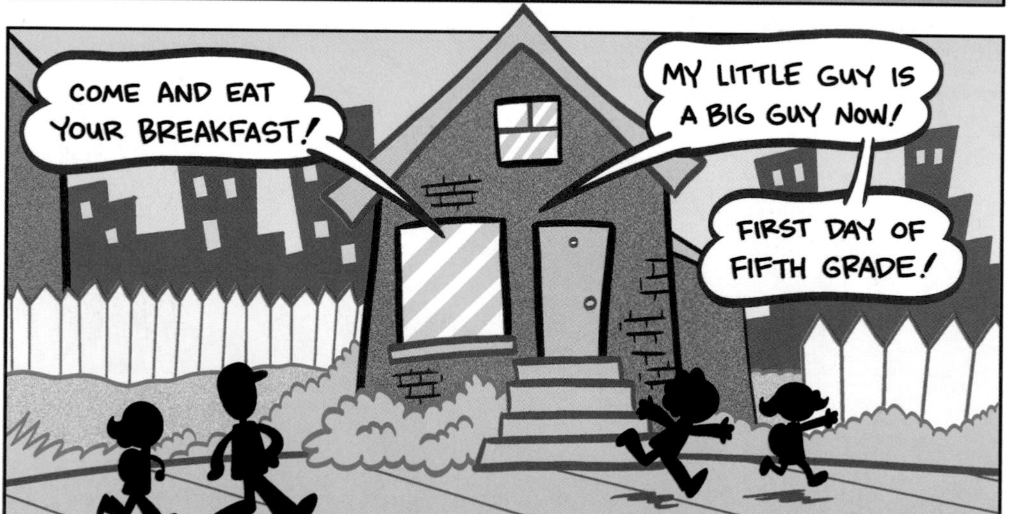
COME AND EAT YOUR BREAKFAST!
MY LITTLE GUY IS A BIG GUY NOW!
FIRST DAY OF FIFTH GRADE!

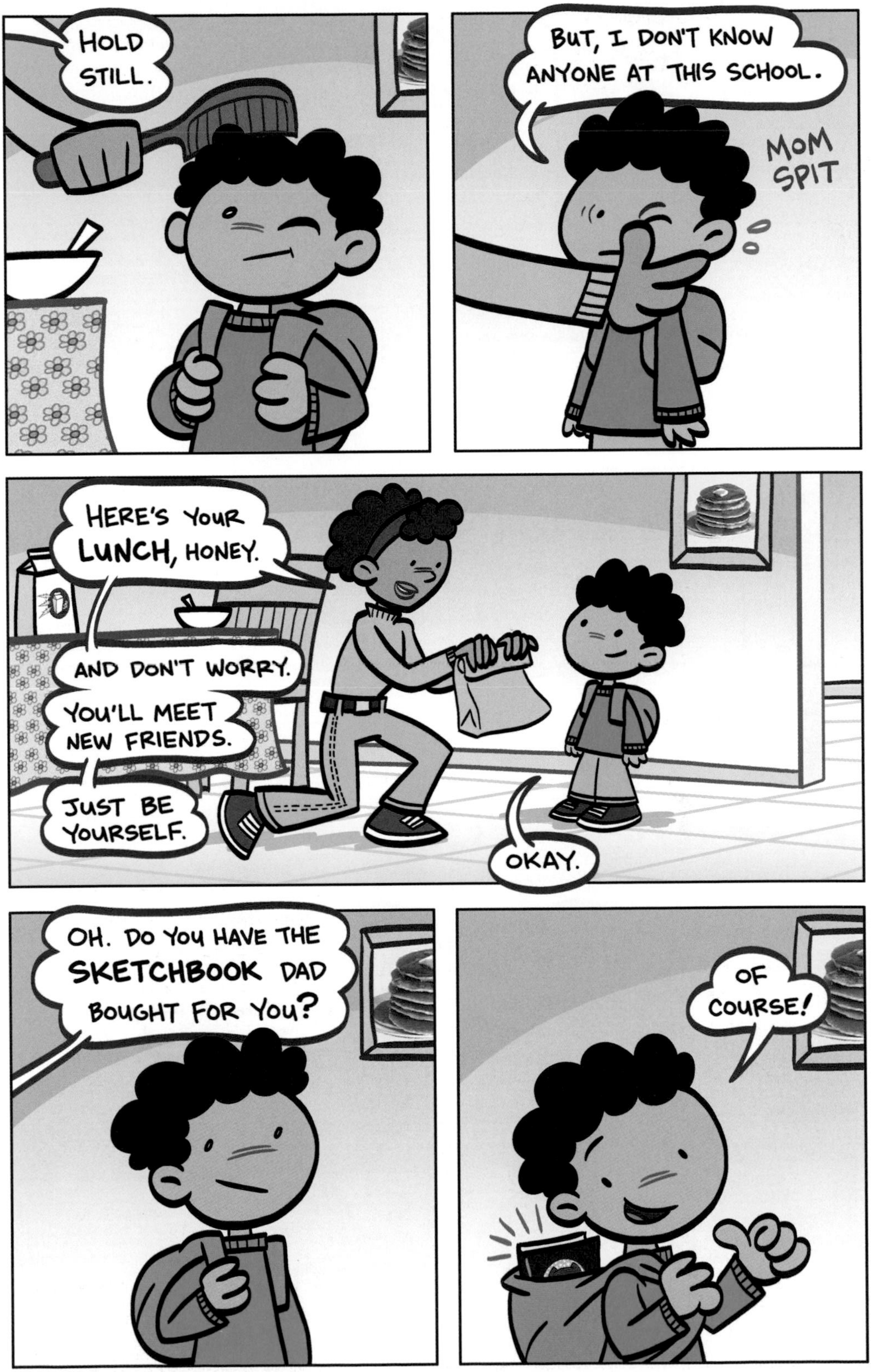
HOLD STILL.
BUT, I DON'T KNOW ANYONE AT THIS SCHOOL.
MOM SPIT
HERE'S YOUR LUNCH, HONEY.
AND DON'T WORRY.
YOU'LL MEET NEW FRIENDS.
JUST BE YOURSELF.
OKAY.
OH. DO YOU HAVE THE SKETCHBOOK DAD BOUGHT FOR YOU?
OF COURSE!

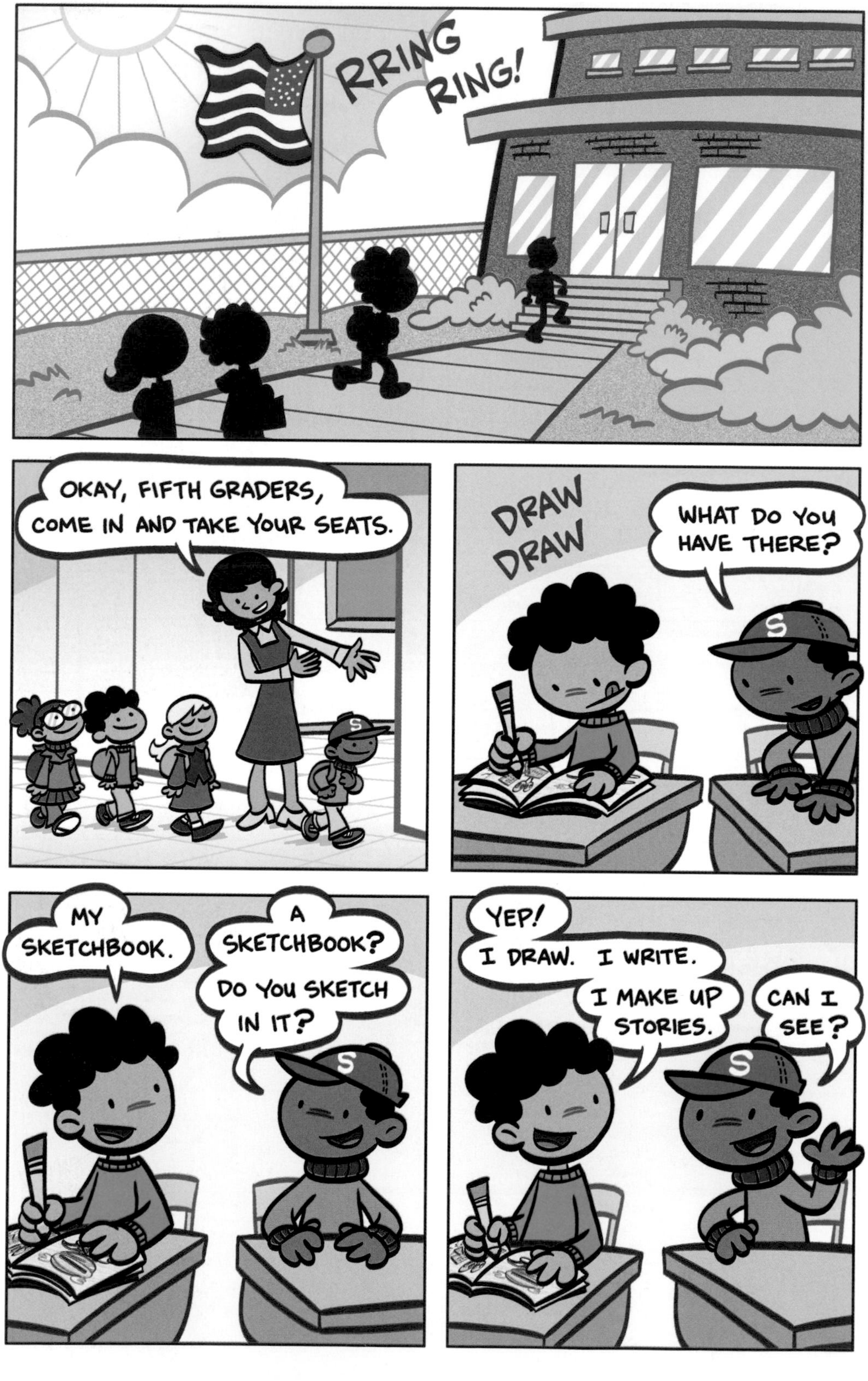
RRING RING!
OKAY, FIFTH GRADERS, COME IN AND TAKE YOUR SEATS.
DRAW DRAW
WHAT DO YOU HAVE THERE?
MY SKETCHBOOK.
A SKETCHBOOK?
DO YOU SKETCH IN IT?
YEP!
I DRAW. I WRITE.
I MAKE UP STORIES.
CAN I SEE?

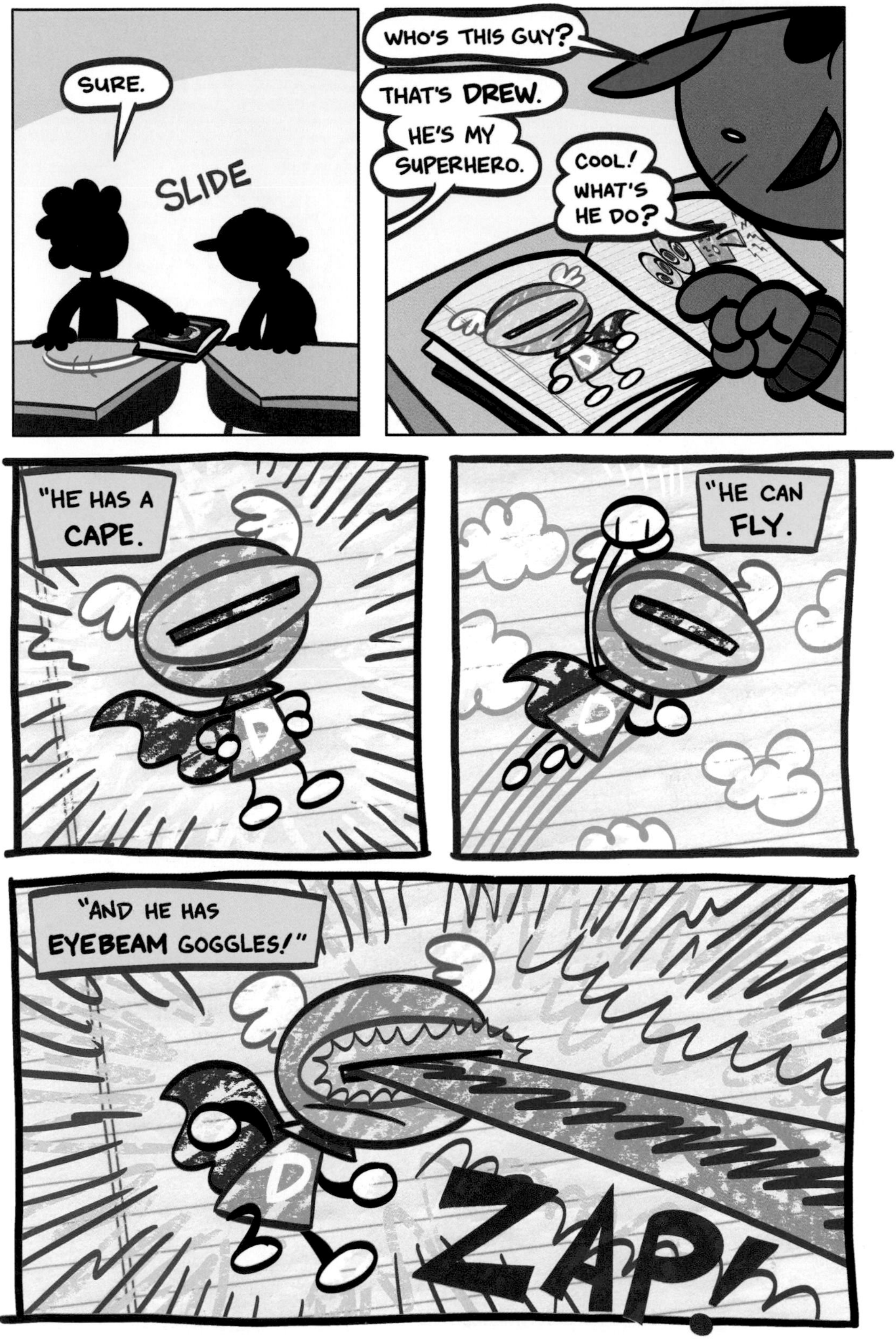
SURE.
SLIDE
WHO'S THIS GUY?
THAT'S DREW.
HE'S MY SUPERHERO.
COOL! WHAT'S HE DO?
"HE HAS A CAPE.
"HE CAN FLY.
"AND HE HAS EYEBEAM GOGGLES!"
ZAP!

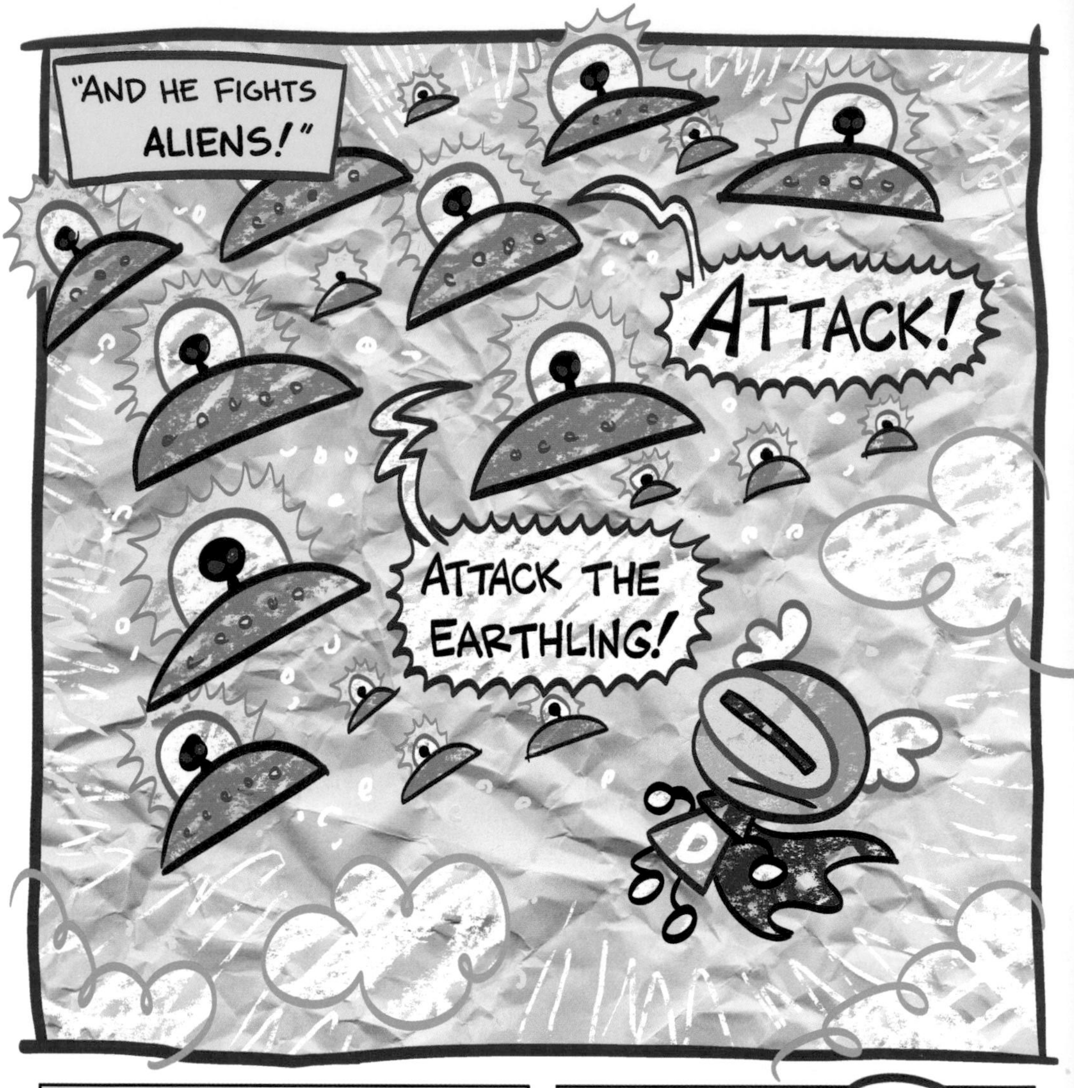
"AND HE FIGHTS ALIENS!"
ATTACK!
ATTACK THE EARTHLING!

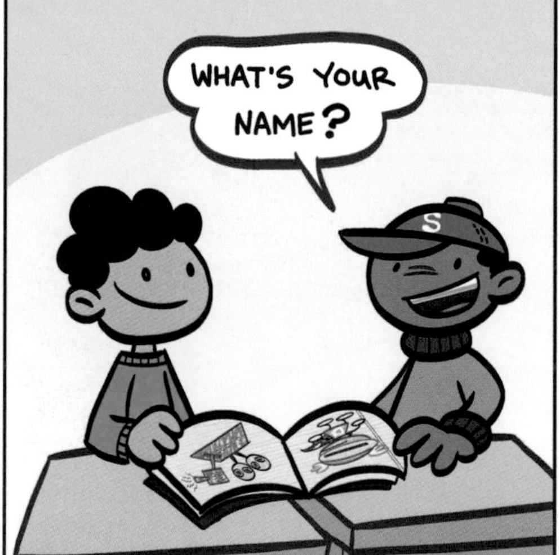
WHAT'S YOUR NAME?

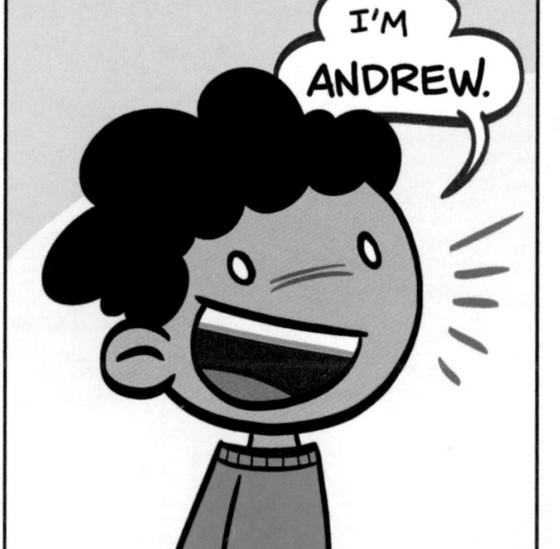
I'M ANDREW.

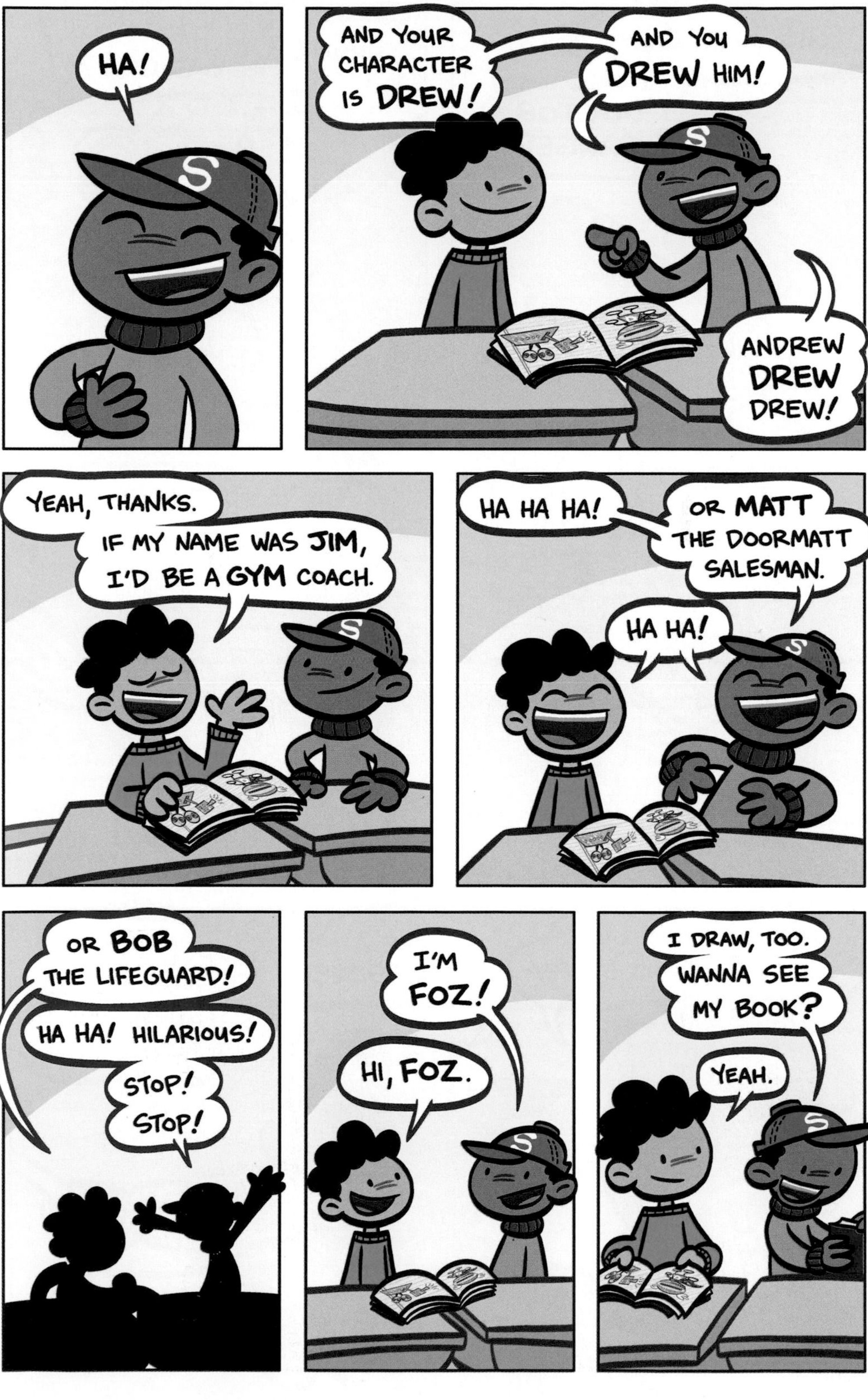
HA!
AND YOUR CHARACTER IS DREW!
AND YOU DREW HIM!
ANDREW DREW DREW!
YEAH, THANKS.
IF MY NAME WAS JIM, I'D BE A GYM COACH.
HA HA HA!
OR MATT THE DOORMATT SALESMAN.
HA HA!
OR BOB THE LIFEGUARD!
HA HA! HILARIOUS!
STOP! STOP!
I'M FOZ!
HI, FOZ.
I DRAW, TOO. WANNA SEE MY BOOK?
YEAH.

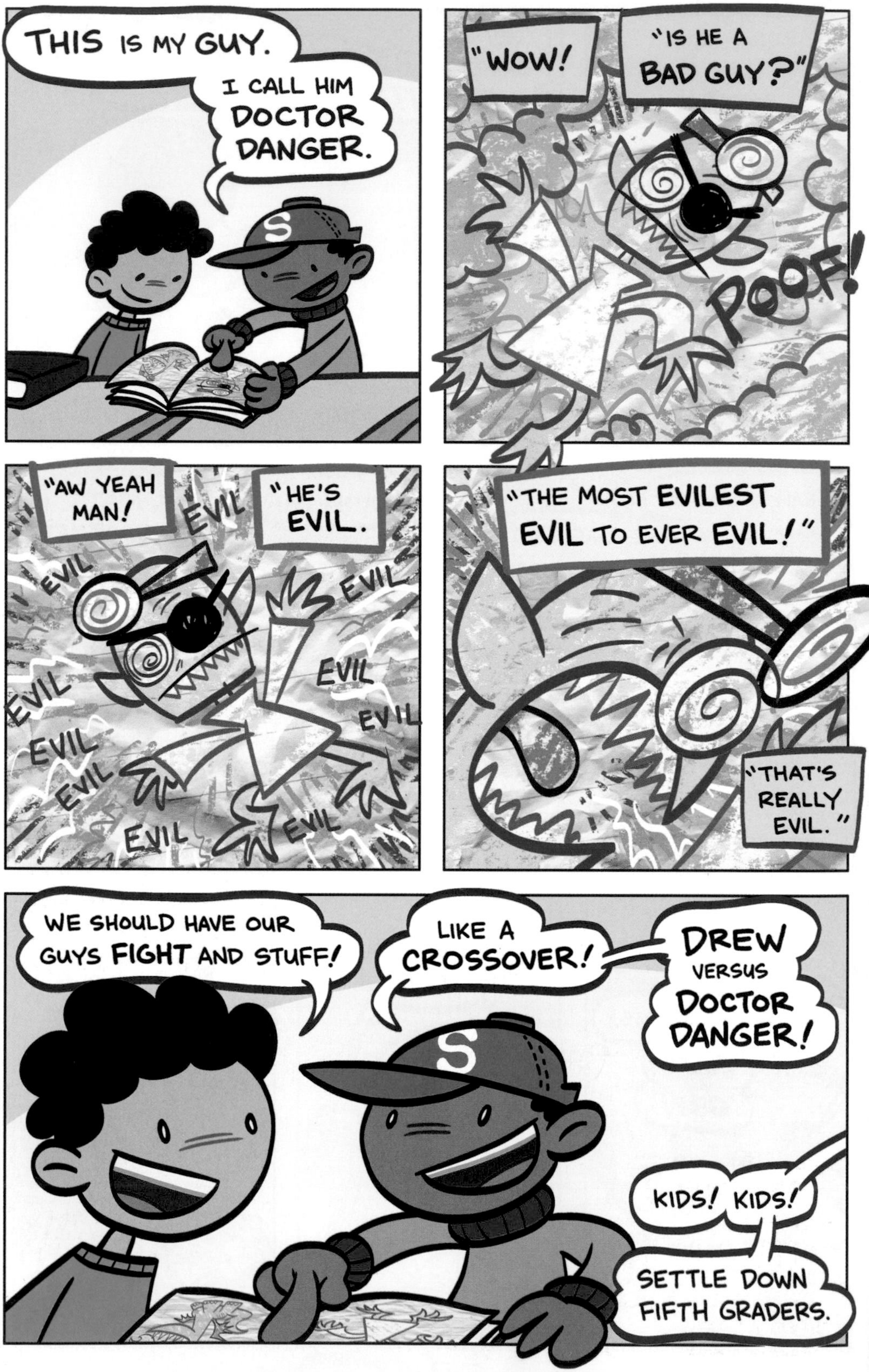
THIS IS MY GUY.
I CALL HIM DOCTOR DANGER.
"WOW!
"IS HE A BAD GUY?"
POOF!
"AW YEAH MAN!
"HE'S EVIL.
EVIL EVIL EVIL EVIL EVIL EVIL EVIL EVIL EVIL EVIL EVIL
"THE MOST EVILEST EVIL TO EVER EVIL!"
"THAT'S REALLY EVIL."
WE SHOULD HAVE OUR GUYS FIGHT AND STUFF!
LIKE A CROSSOVER!
DREW VERSUS DOCTOR DANGER!
KIDS! KIDS!
SETTLE DOWN FIFTH GRADERS.

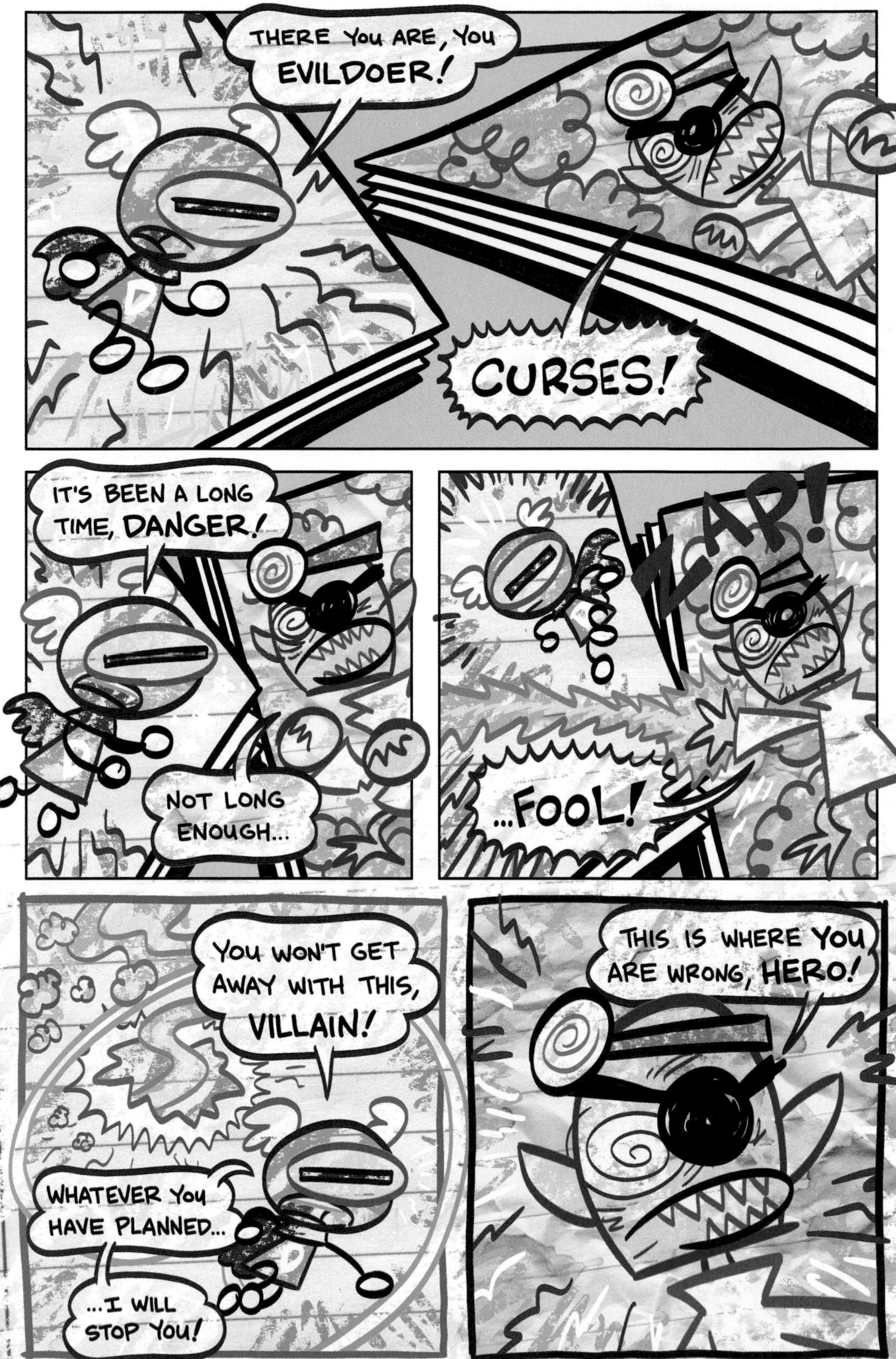

THERE YOU ARE, YOU EVILDOER!
CURSES!
IT'S BEEN A LONG TIME, DANGER!
NOT LONG ENOUGH...
ZAP!
...FOOL!
YOU WON'T GET AWAY WITH THIS, VILLAIN!
WHATEVER YOU HAVE PLANNED...
...I WILL STOP YOU!
THIS IS WHERE YOU ARE WRONG, HERO!

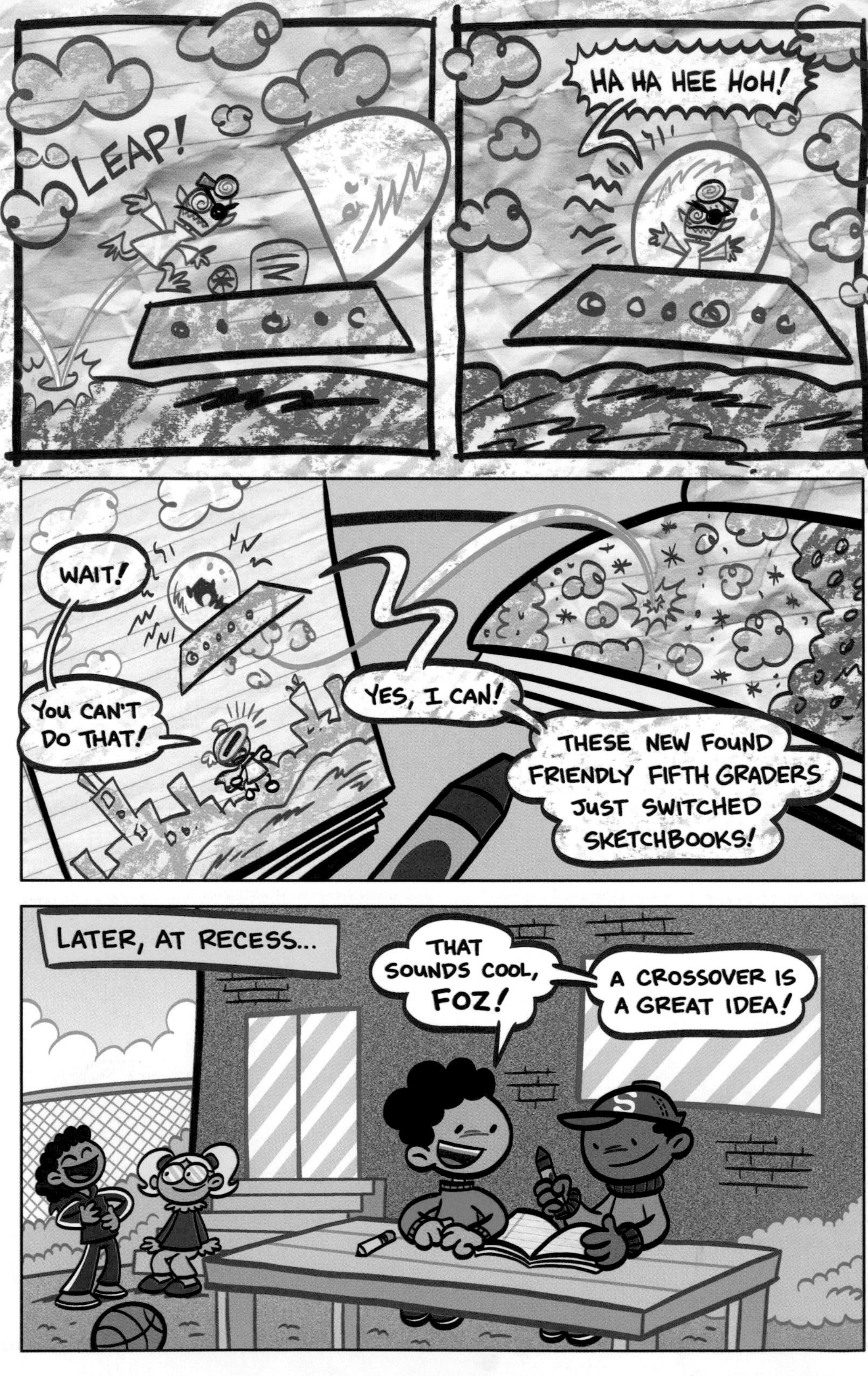
LEAP!
HA HA HEE HOH!
WAIT!
YOU CAN'T DO THAT!
YES, I CAN!
THESE NEW FOUND FRIENDLY FIFTH GRADERS JUST SWITCHED SKETCHBOOKS!
LATER, AT RECESS...
THAT SOUNDS COOL, FOZ!
A CROSSOVER IS A GREAT IDEA!

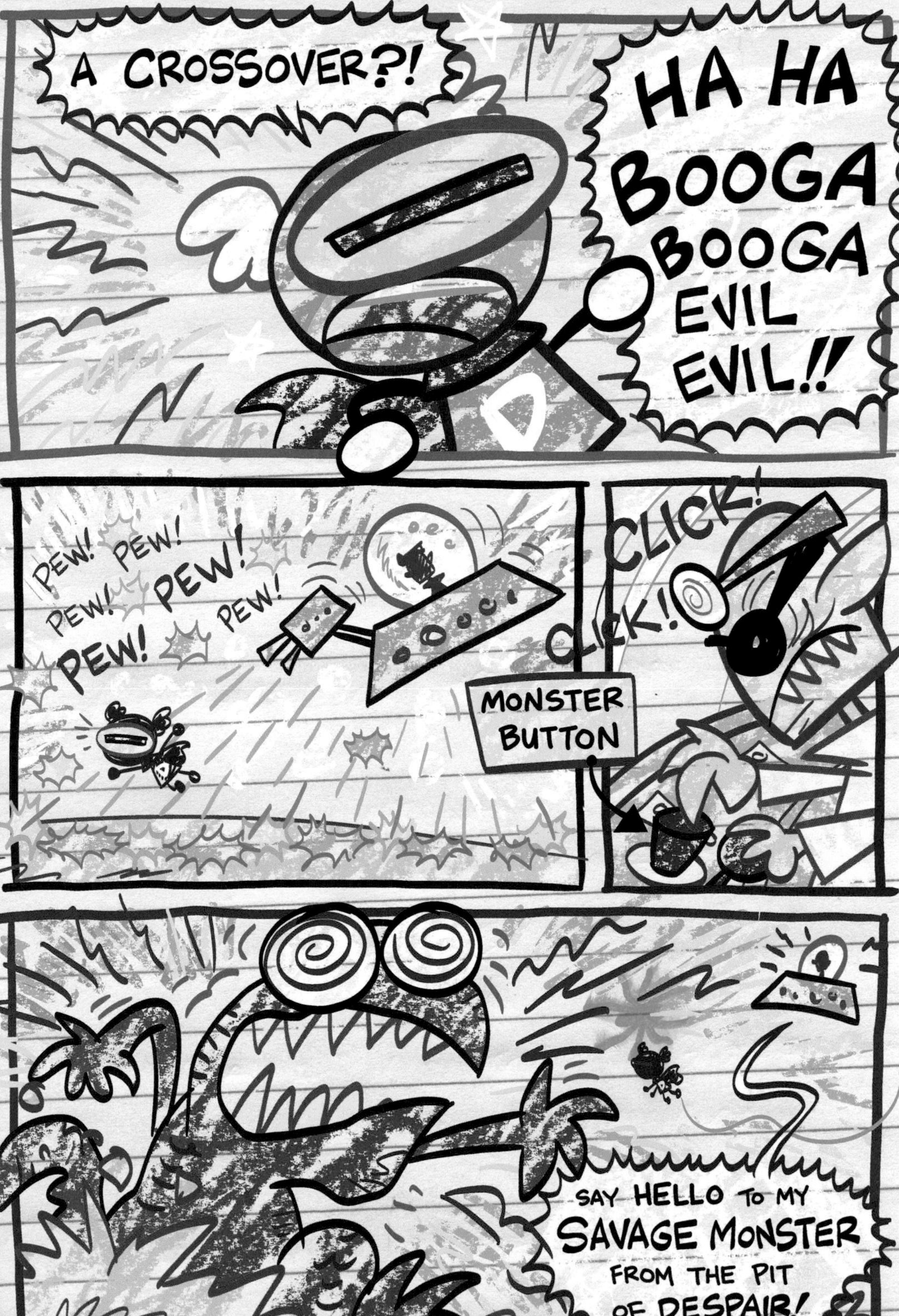
A CROSSOVER?!
HA HA BOOGA BOOGA EVIL EVIL!!
PEW! PEW! PEW! PEW! PEW! PEW! PEW!
CLICK! CLICK!
MONSTER BUTTON
SAY HELLO TO MY SAVAGE MONSTER FROM THE PIT OF DESPAIR!

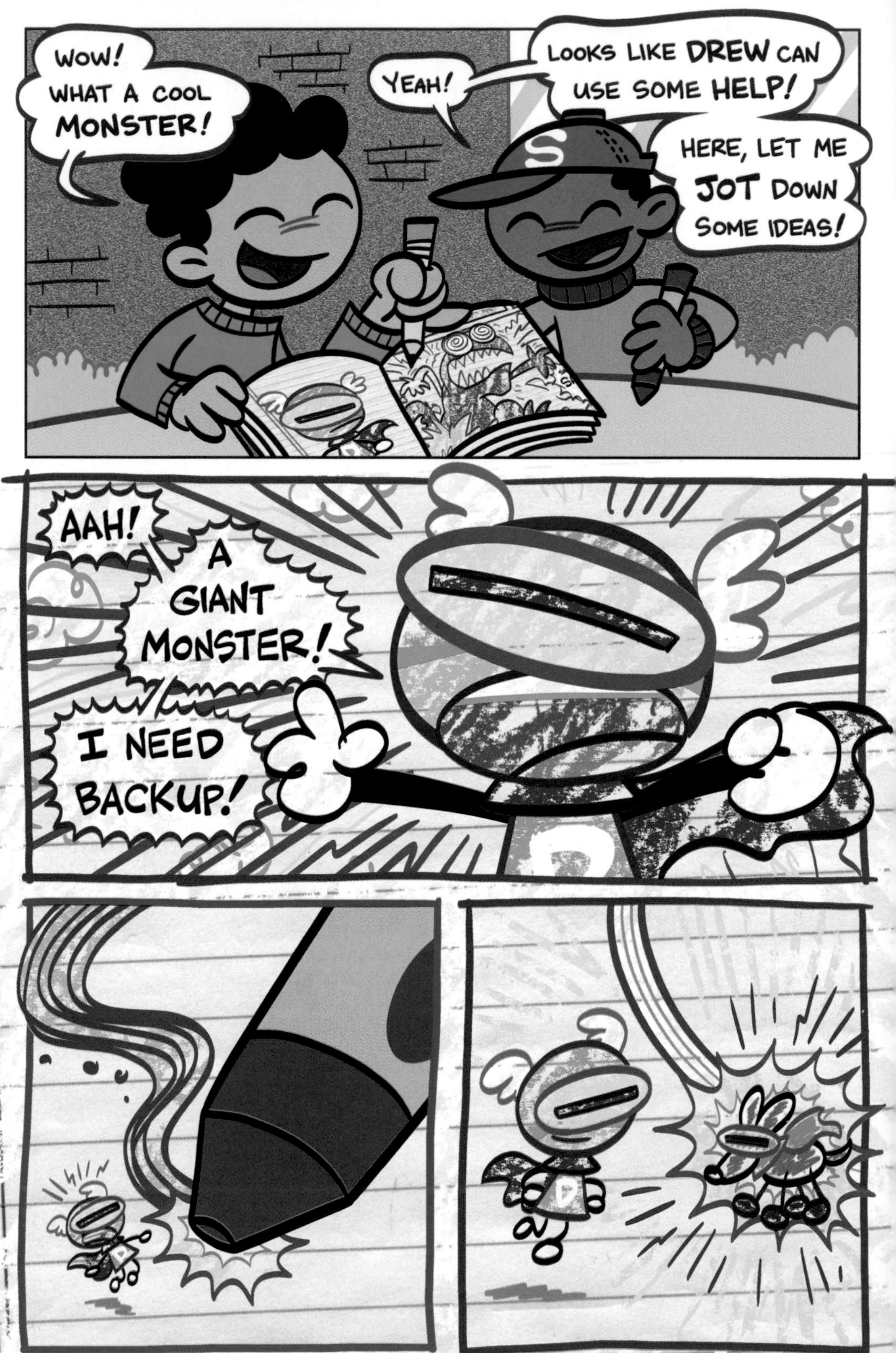
WOW! WHAT A COOL MONSTER!
YEAH!
LOOKS LIKE DREW CAN USE SOME HELP!
HERE, LET ME JOT DOWN SOME IDEAS!
AAH!
A GIANT MONSTER!
I NEED BACKUP!

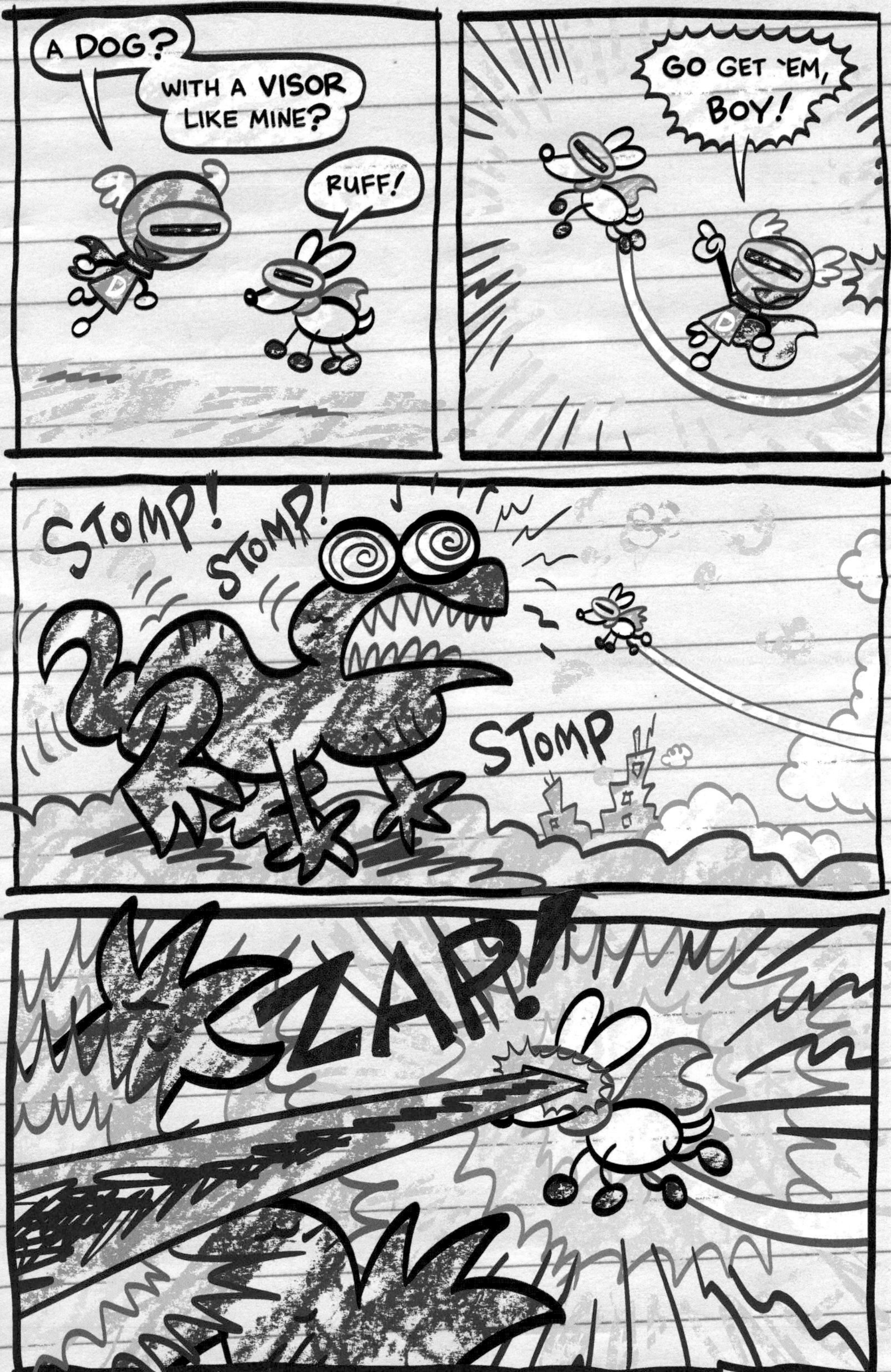
A DOG?
WITH A VISOR LIKE MINE?
RUFF!
GO GET 'EM, BOY!
STOMP!
STOMP!
STOMP
ZZAP!

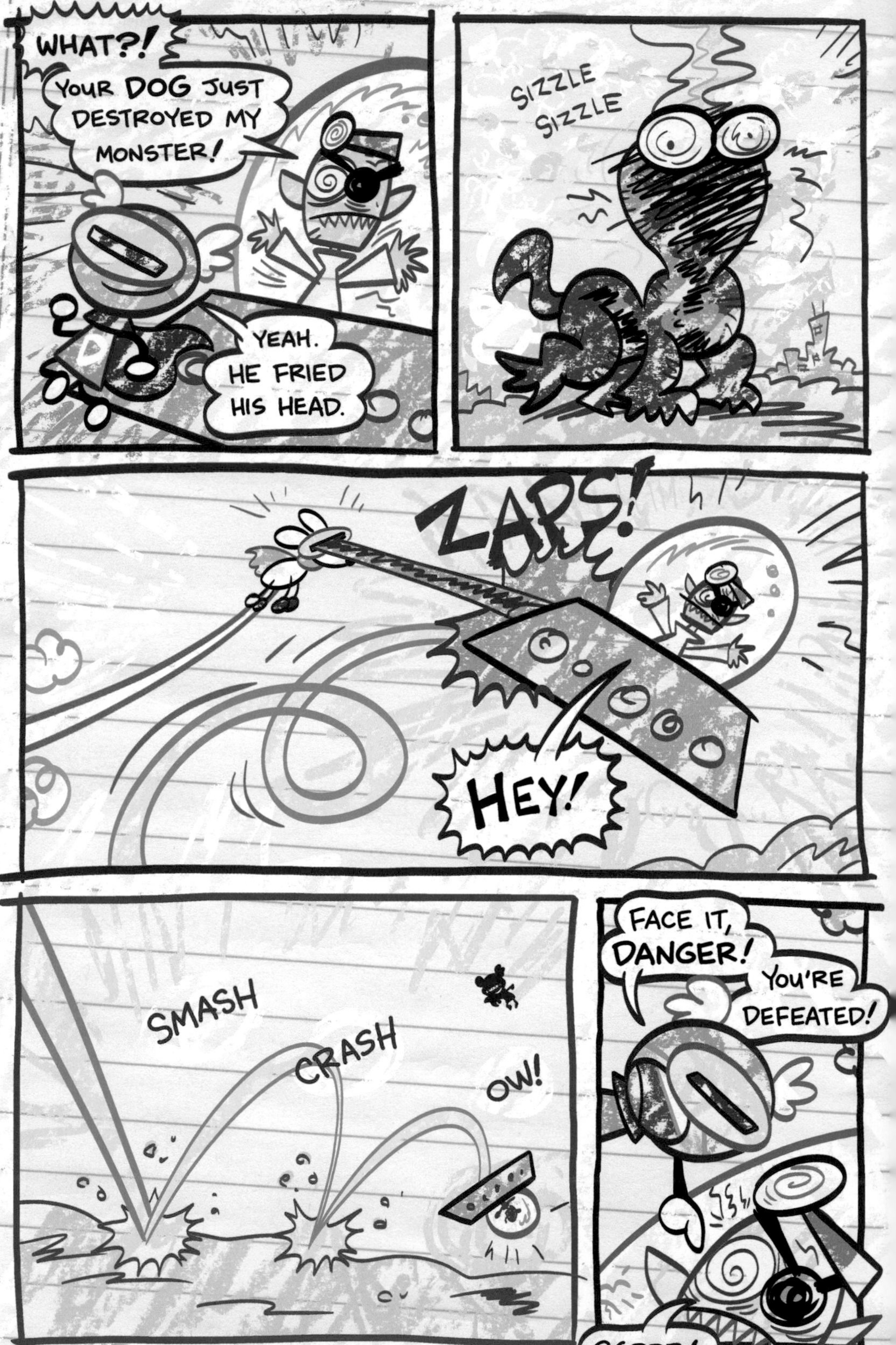
WHAT?!
YOUR DOG JUST DESTROYED MY MONSTER!
YEAH. HE FRIED HIS HEAD.
SIZZLE SIZZLE
ZAPS!
HEY!
SMASH
CRASH
OW!
FACE IT, DANGER!
YOU'RE DEFEATED!
GGRRR!

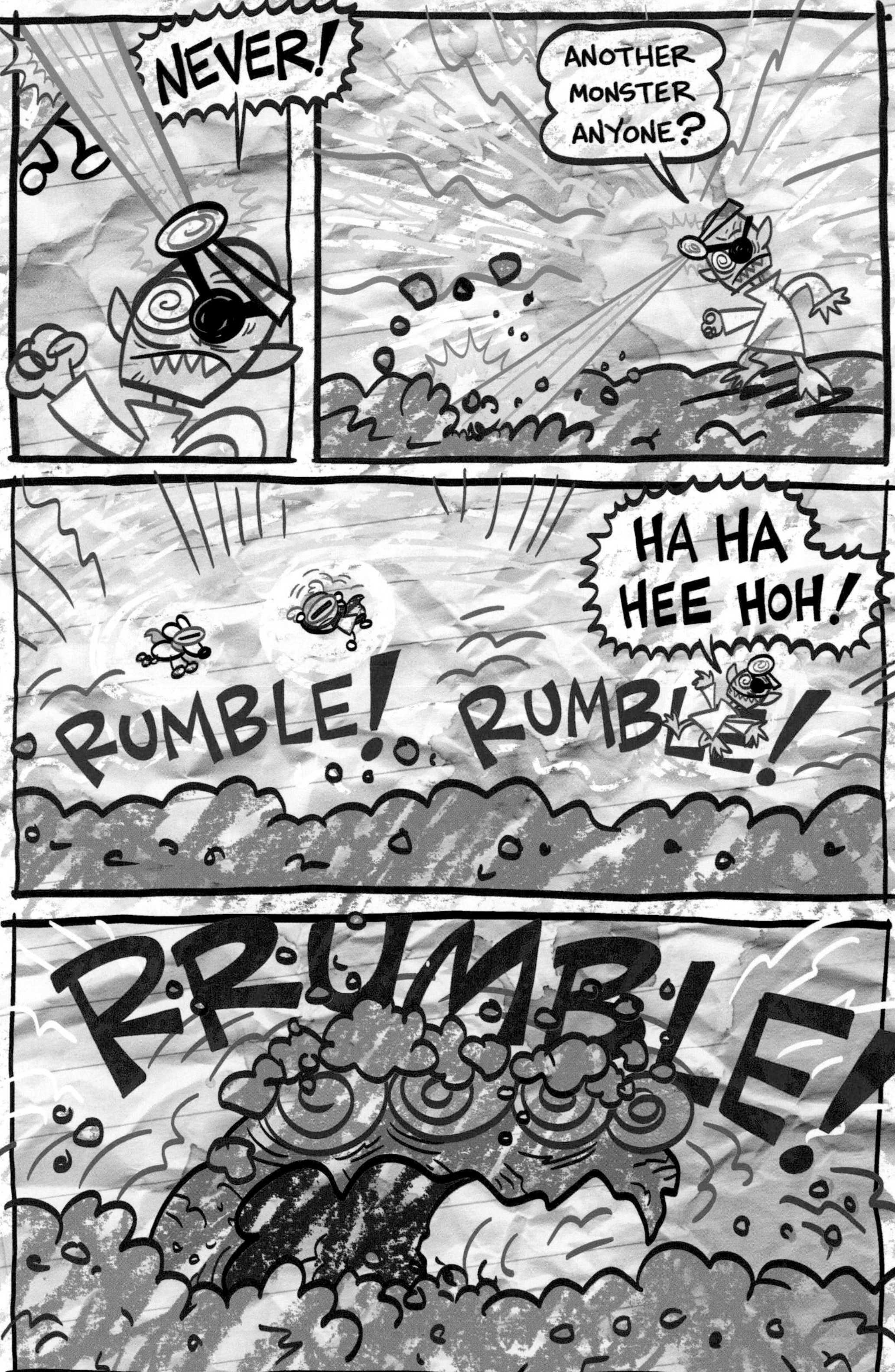
NEVER!
ANOTHER MONSTER ANYONE?
HA HA HEE HOH!
RUMBLE! RUMBLE!
RRUMBLE!

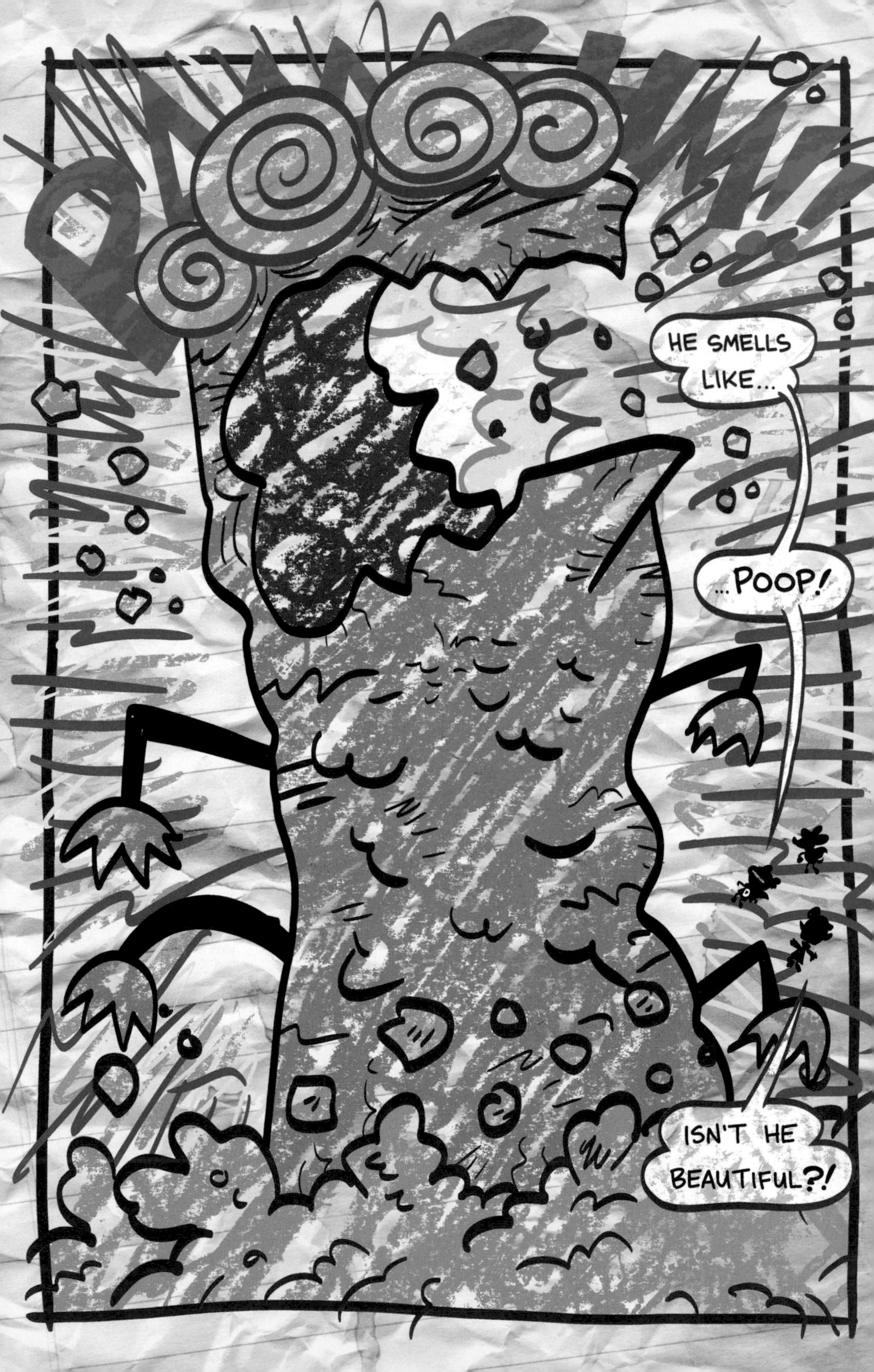
HE SMELLS LIKE...
...POOP!
ISN'T HE BEAUTIFUL?!

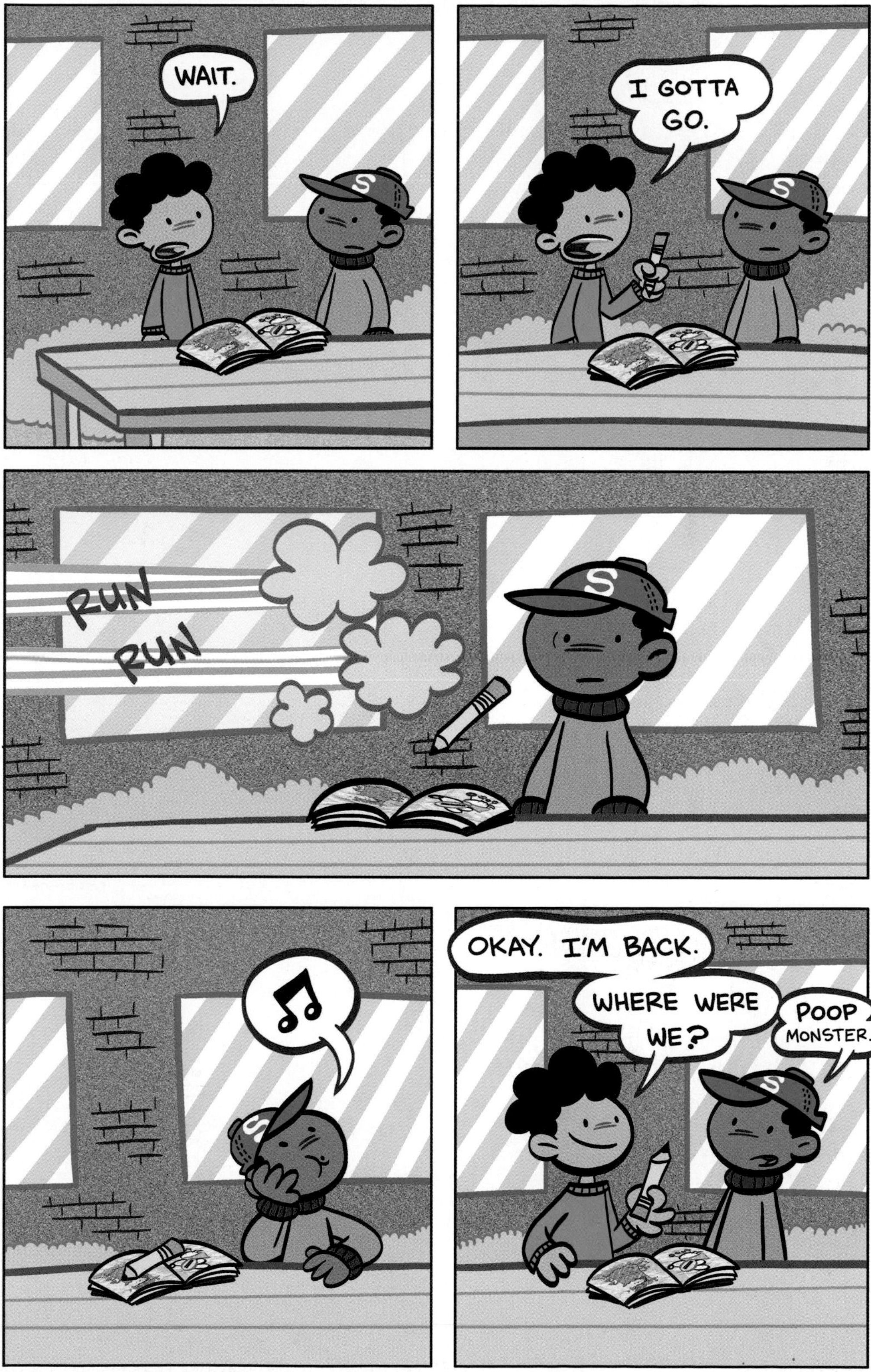
WAIT.
I GOTTA GO.
RUN
RUN
OKAY. I'M BACK.
WHERE WERE WE?
POOP MONSTER.

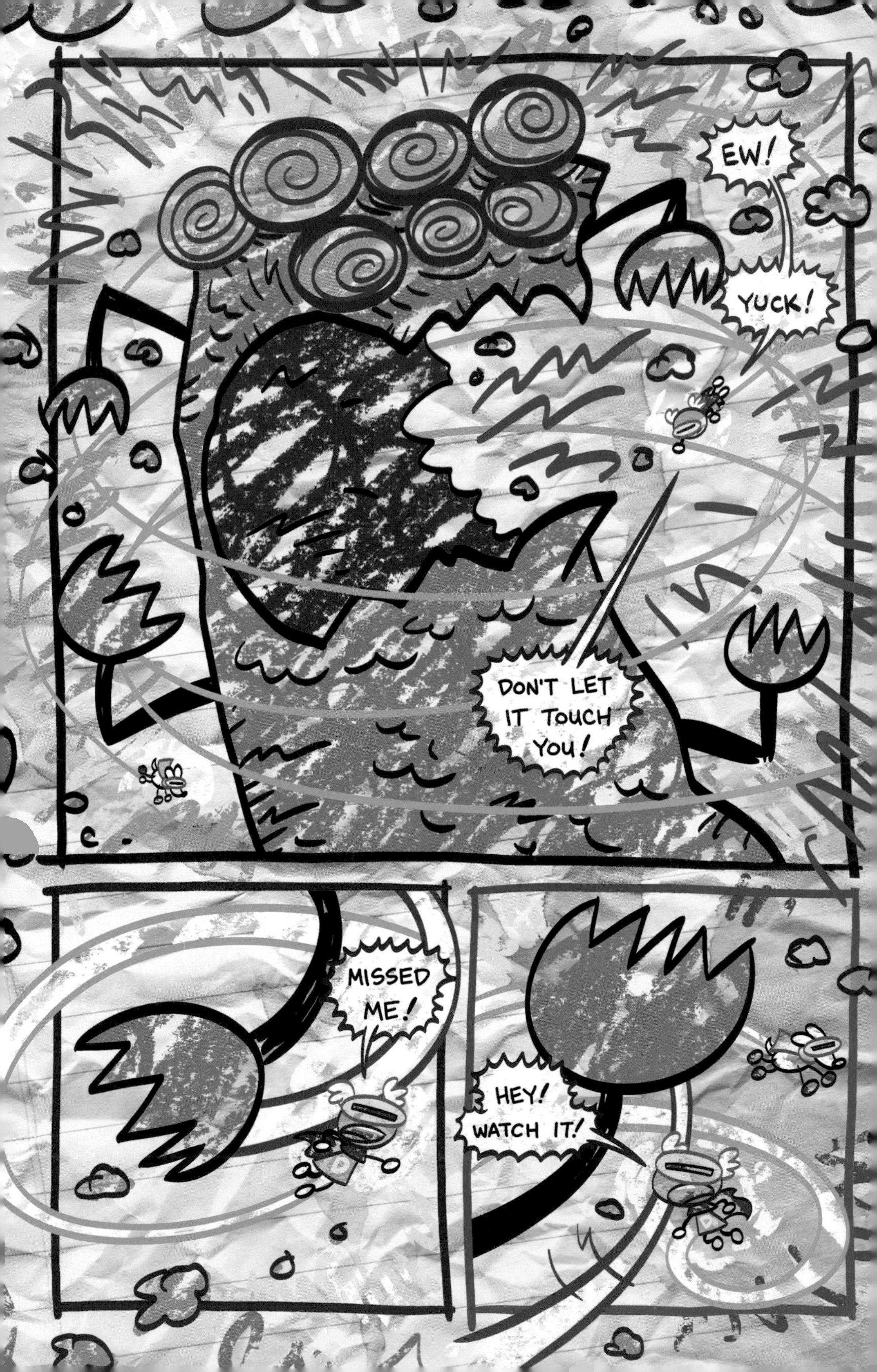
EW!
YUCK!
DON'T LET IT TOUCH YOU!
MISSED ME!
HEY! WATCH IT!

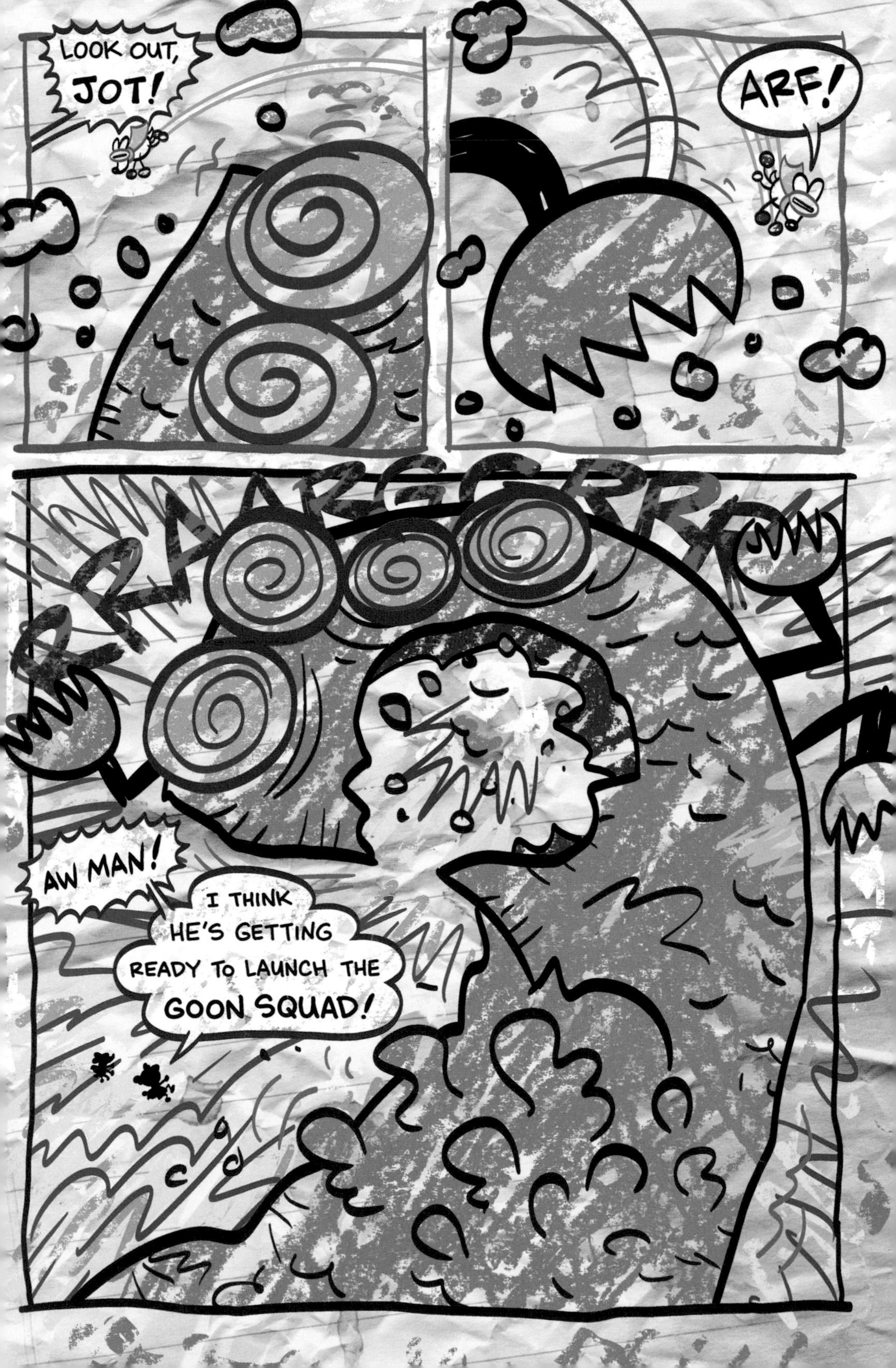

LOOK OUT, JOT!
ARF!
RAARGGRR
AW MAN!
I THINK HE'S GETTING READY TO LAUNCH THE GOON SQUAD!

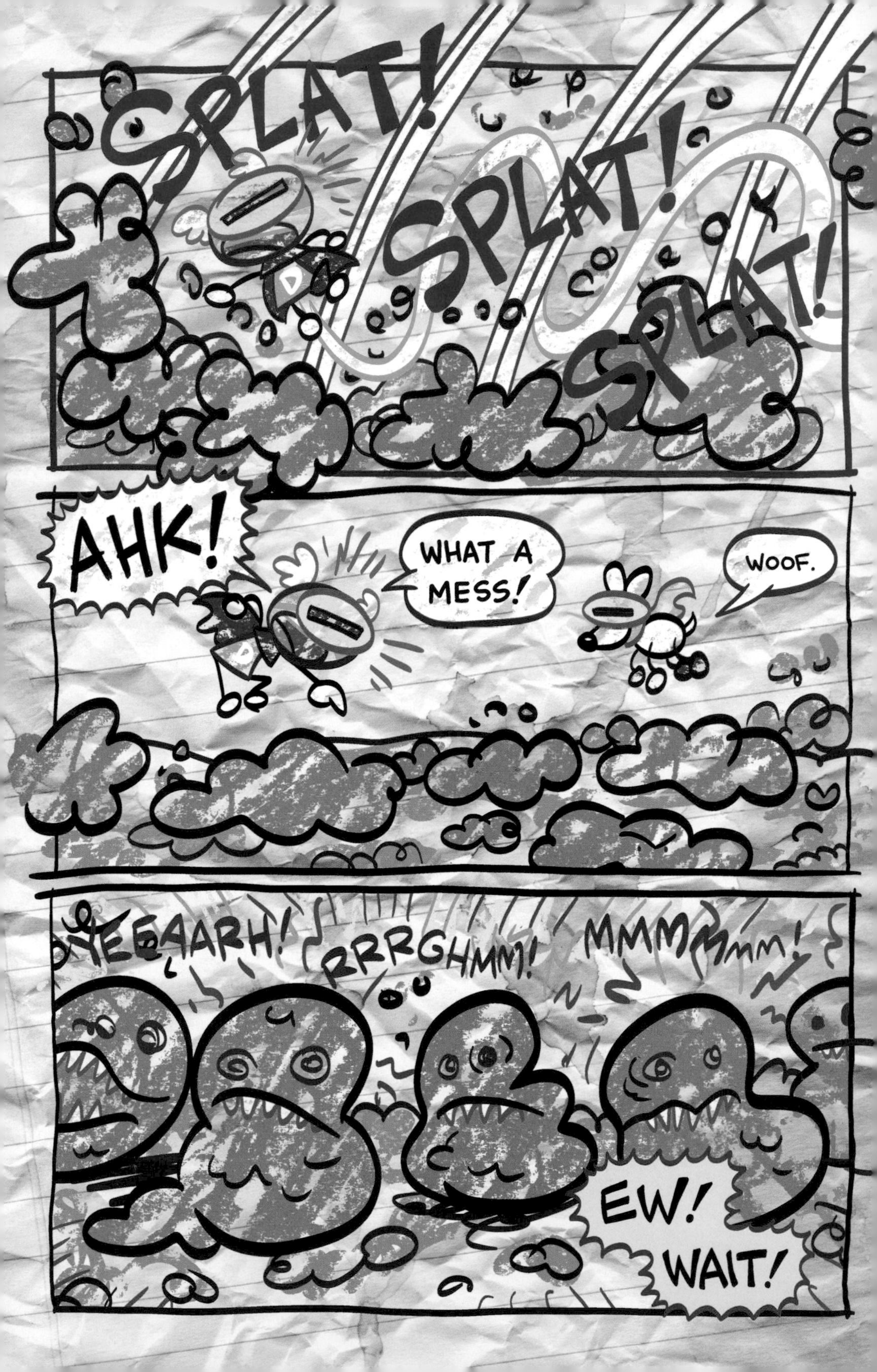
SPLAT!
SPLAT!
SPLAT!
AHK!
WHAT A MESS!
WOOF.
YEEAARH!
RRRGHMM!
MMMMmm!
EW!
WAIT!

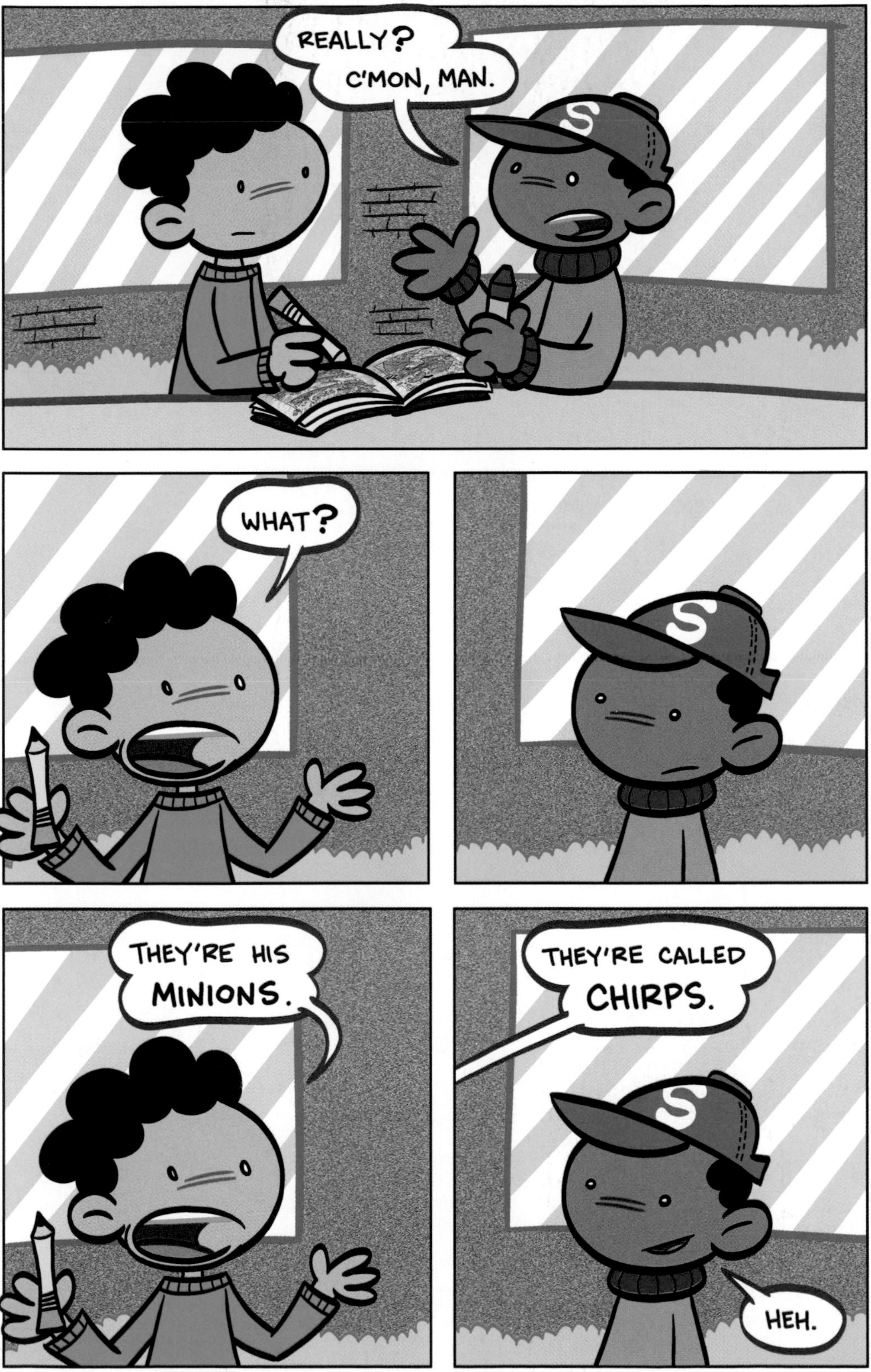
REALLY? C'MON, MAN.
WHAT?
THEY'RE HIS MINIONS.
THEY'RE CALLED CHIRPS.
HEH.

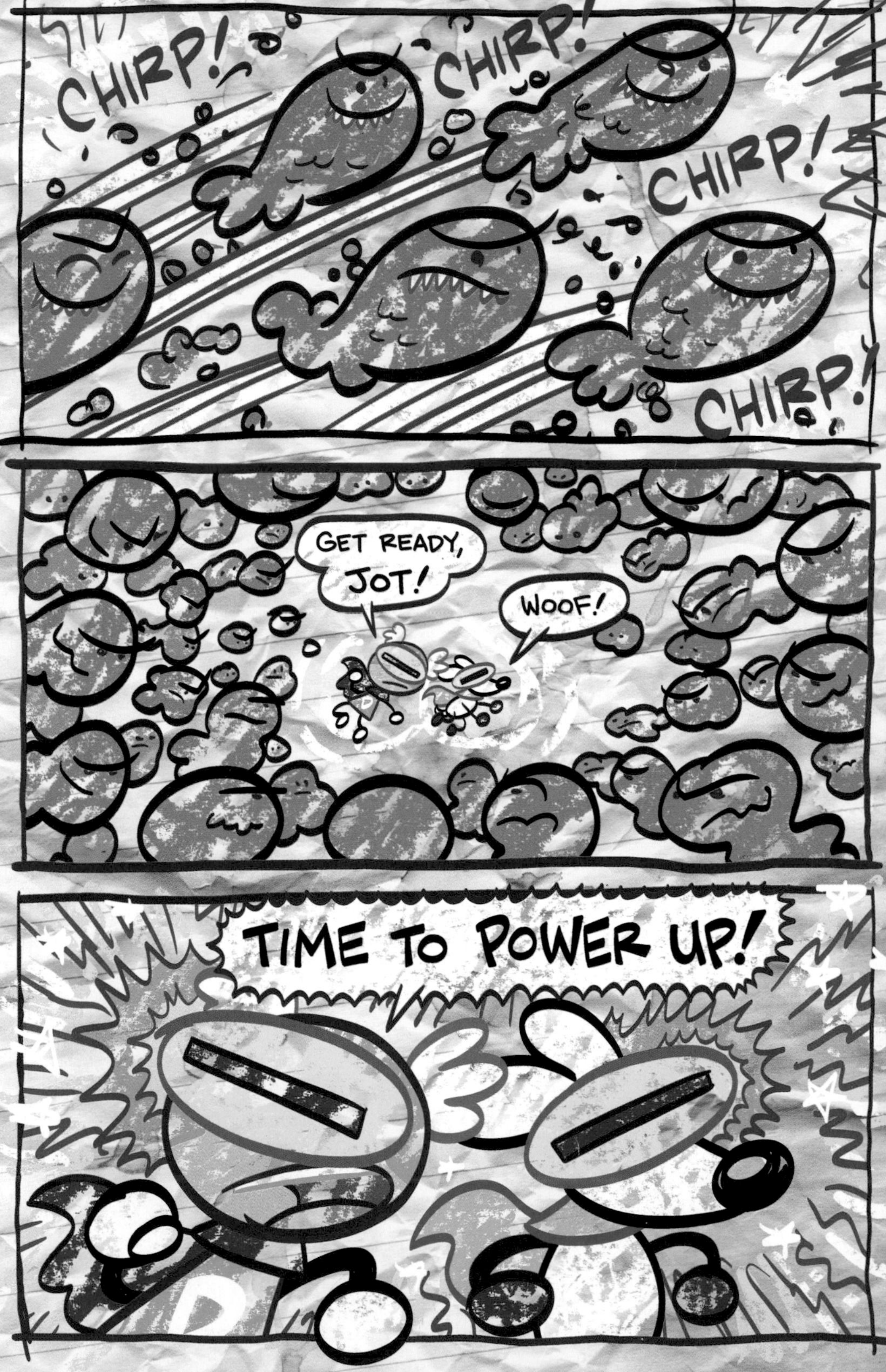
CHIRP!
CHIRP!
CHIRP!
CHIRP!
GET READY, JOT!
WOOF!
TIME TO POWER UP!

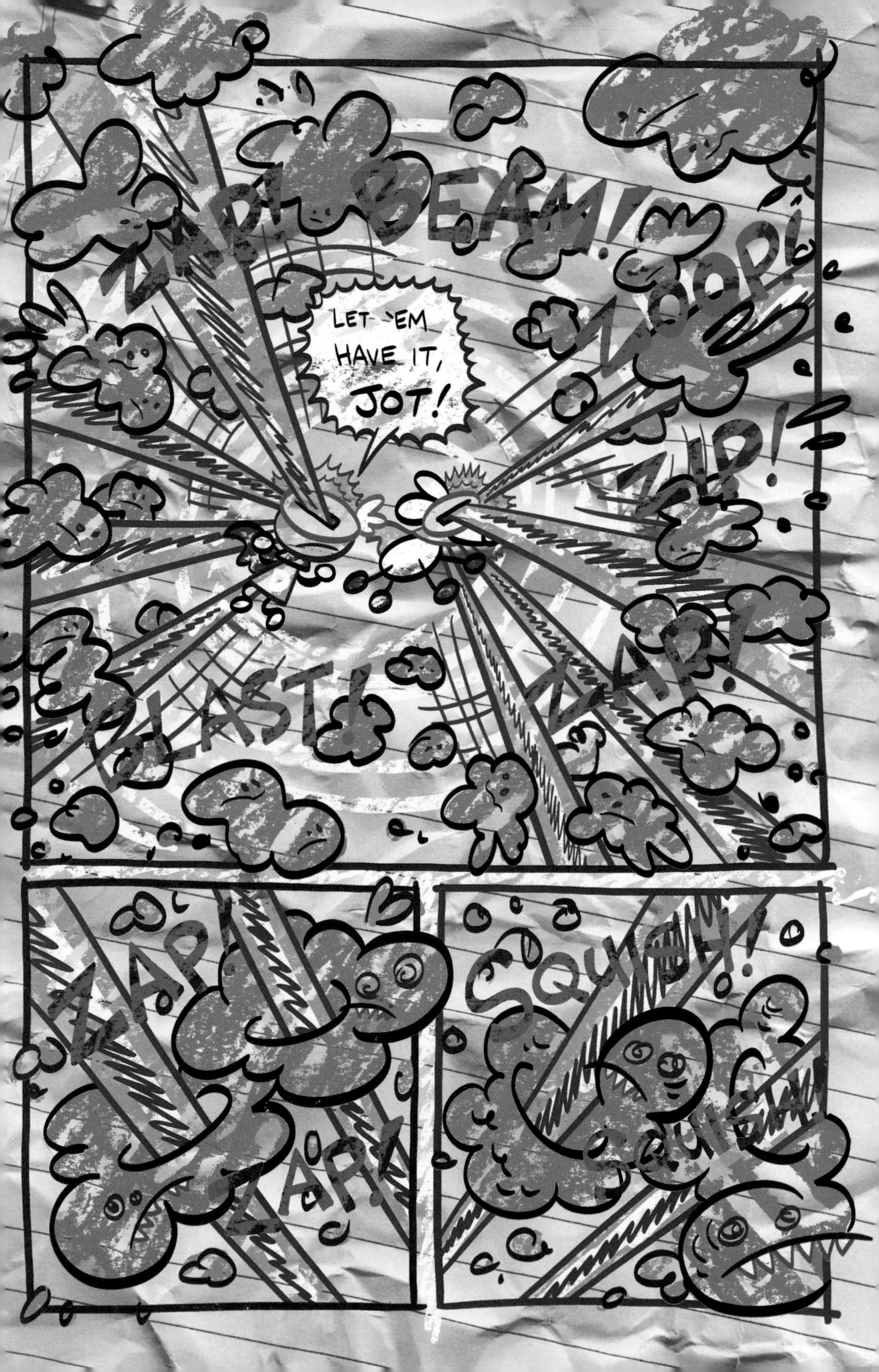
ZAP!
BEAM!
ZOOP!
LET 'EM HAVE IT, JOT!
ZIP!
BLAST!
ZAP!
ZAP!
ZAP!
SQUISH!
SQUISH!

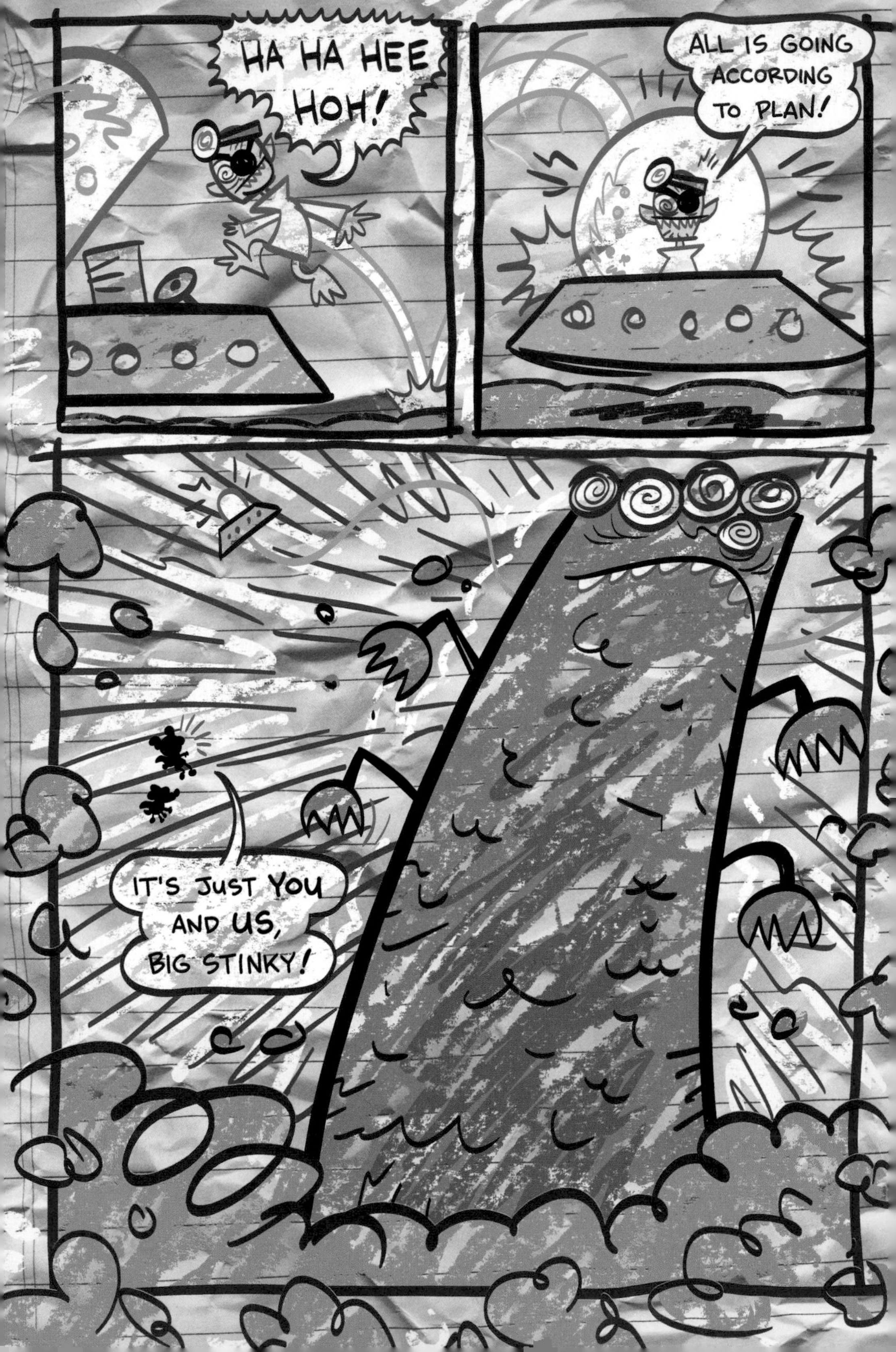
HA HA HEE HOH!
ALL IS GOING ACCORDING TO PLAN!
IT'S JUST YOU AND US, BIG STINKY!

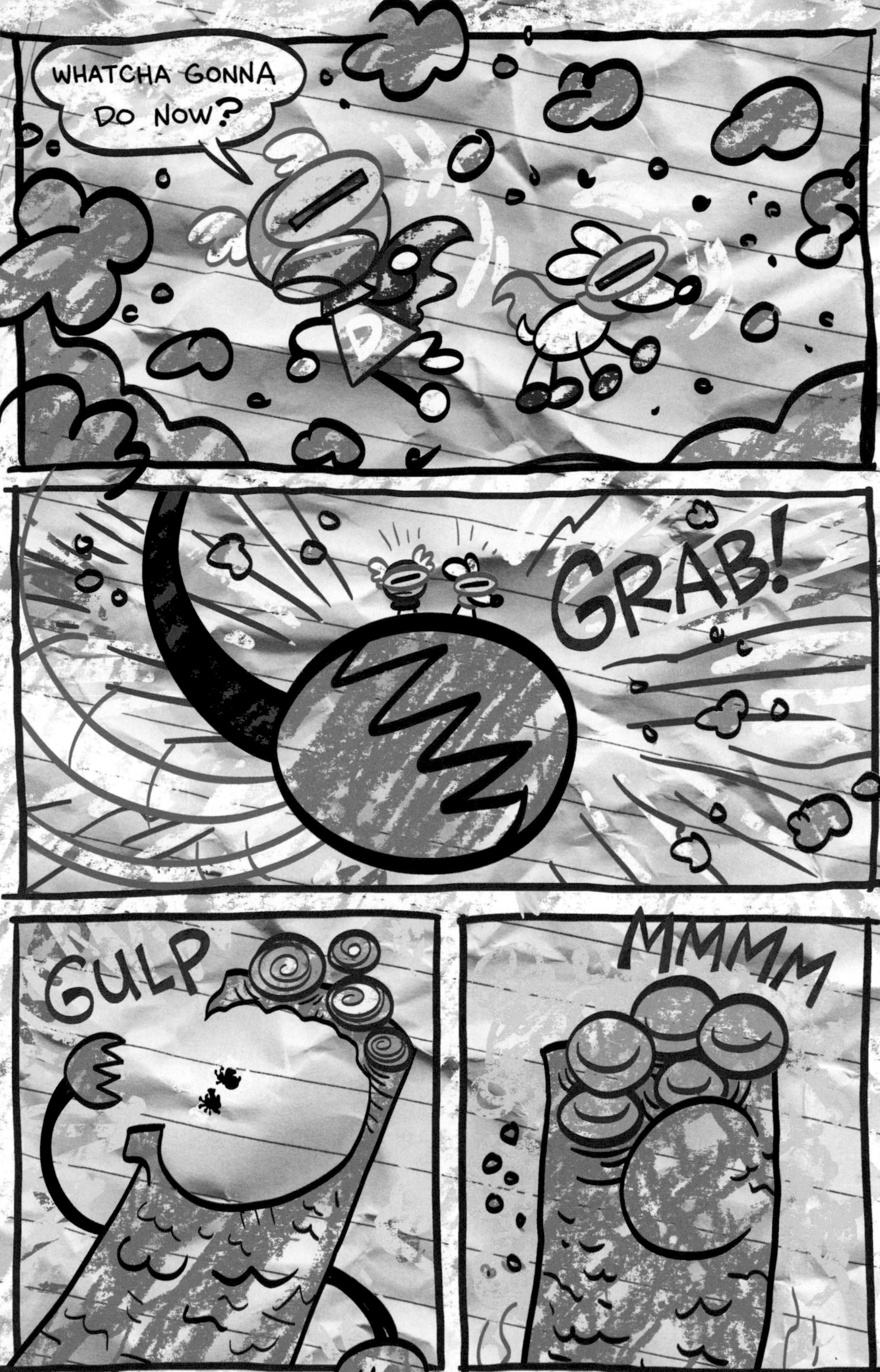
WHATCHA GONNA DO NOW?
GRAB!
GULP
MMMMM

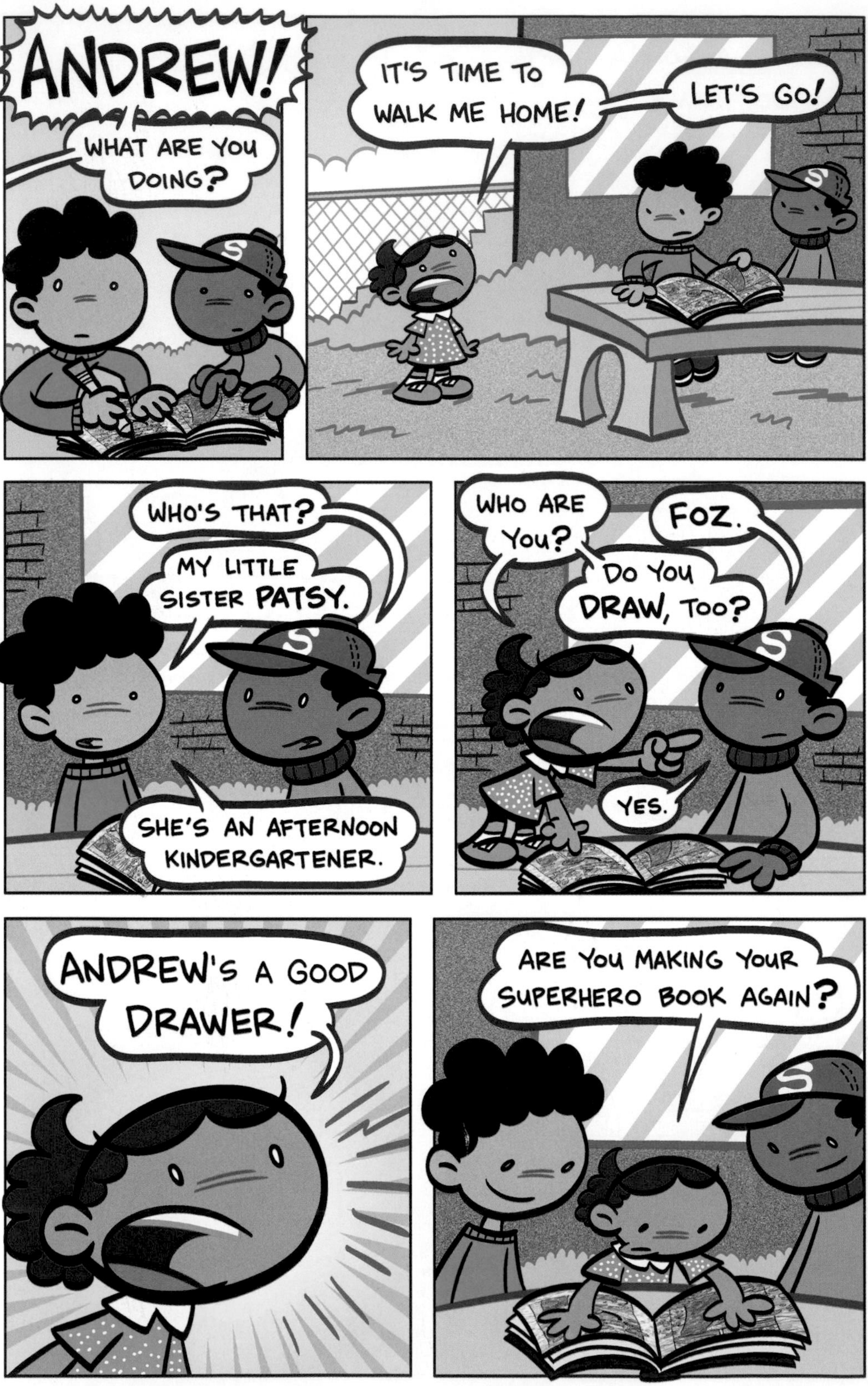
ANDREW!
WHAT ARE YOU DOING?
IT'S TIME TO WALK ME HOME!
LET'S GO!
WHO'S THAT?
MY LITTLE SISTER PATSY.
SHE'S AN AFTERNOON KINDERGARTENER.
WHO ARE YOU?
FOZ.
DO YOU DRAW, TOO?
YES.
ANDREW'S A GOOD DRAWER!
ARE YOU MAKING YOUR SUPERHERO BOOK AGAIN?

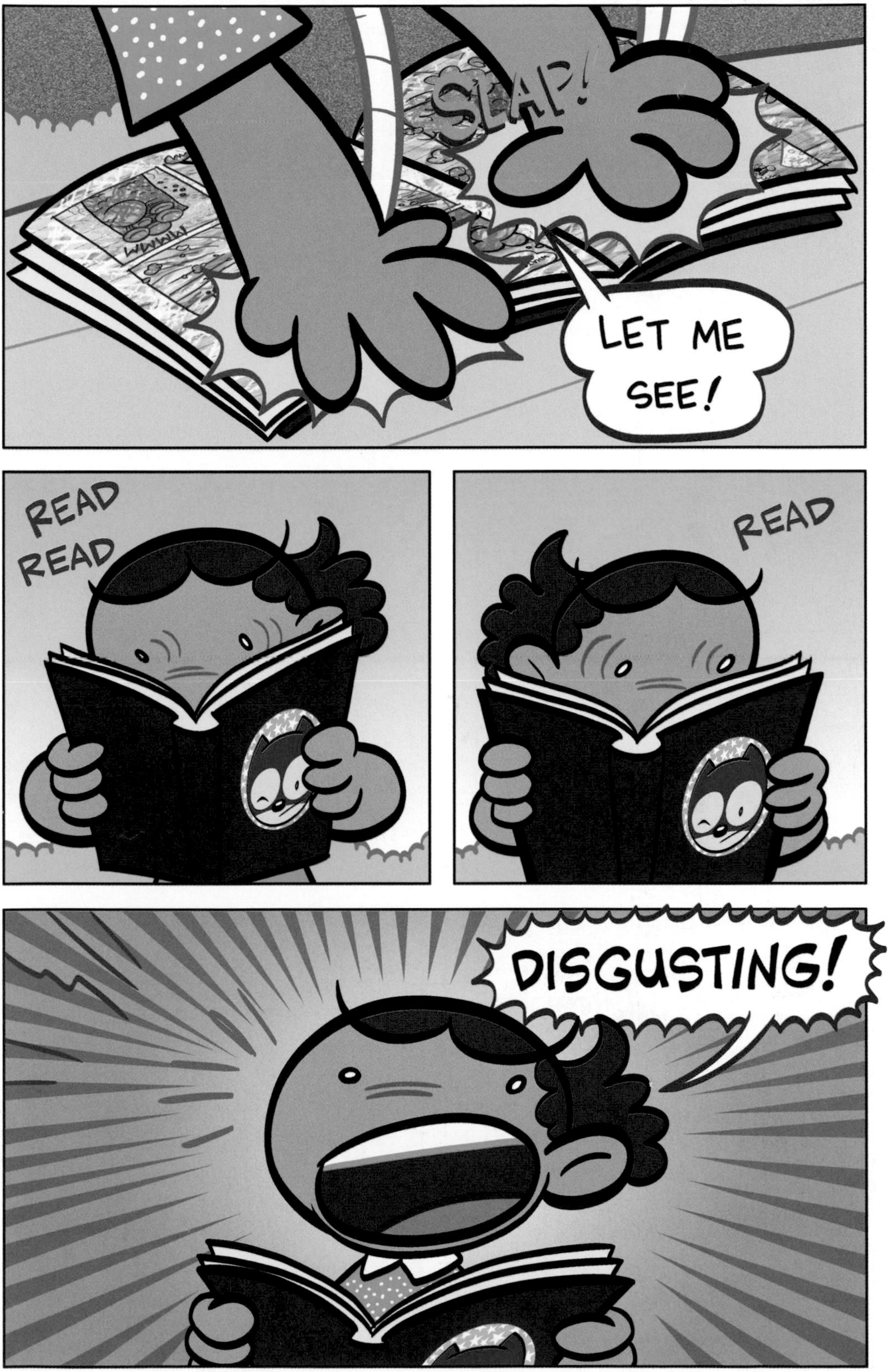
SLAP!
LET ME SEE!
READ
READ
READ
DISGUSTING!

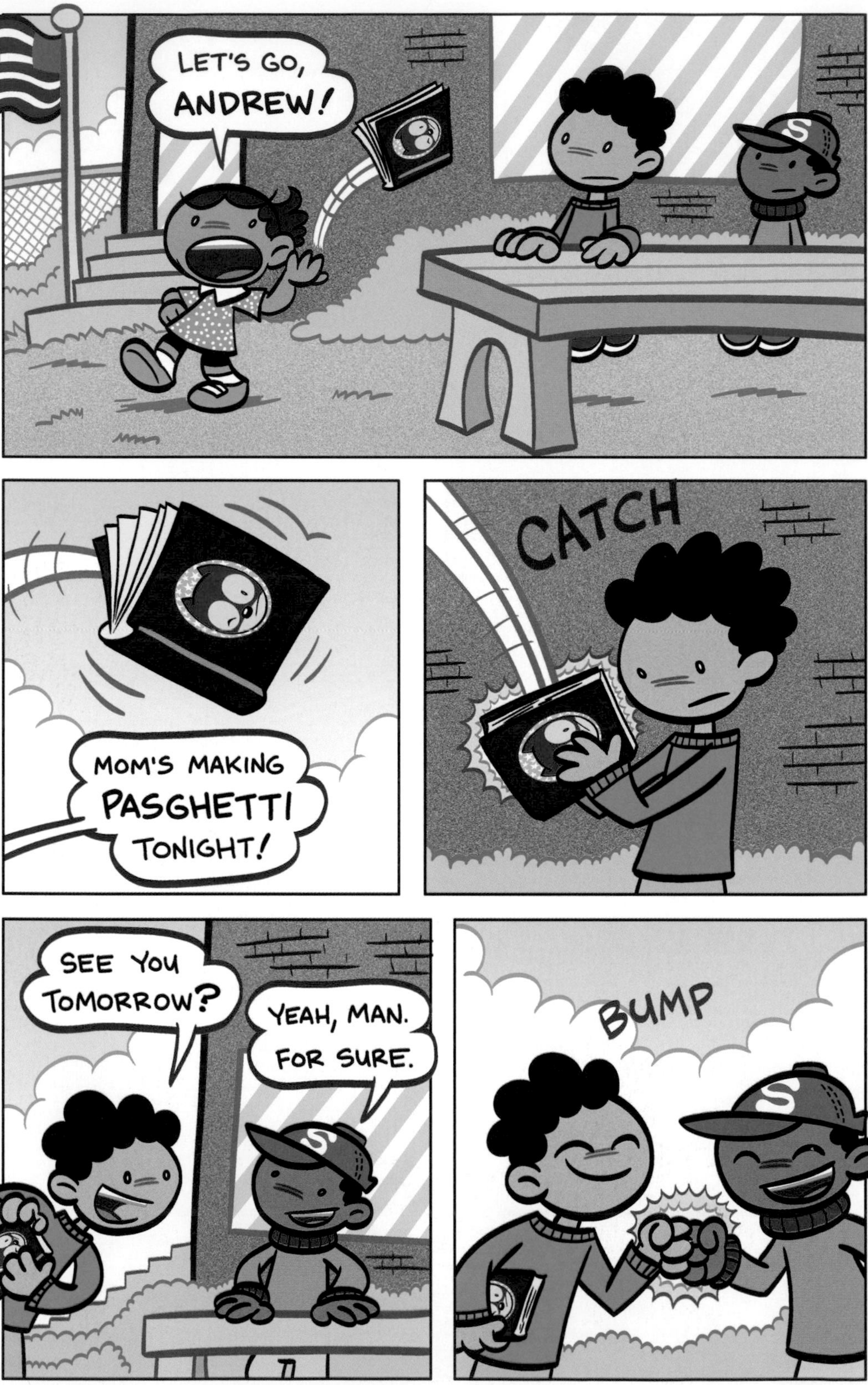
LET'S GO, ANDREW!
MOM'S MAKING PASGHETTI TONIGHT!
CATCH
SEE YOU TOMORROW?
YEAH, MAN. FOR SURE.
BUMP

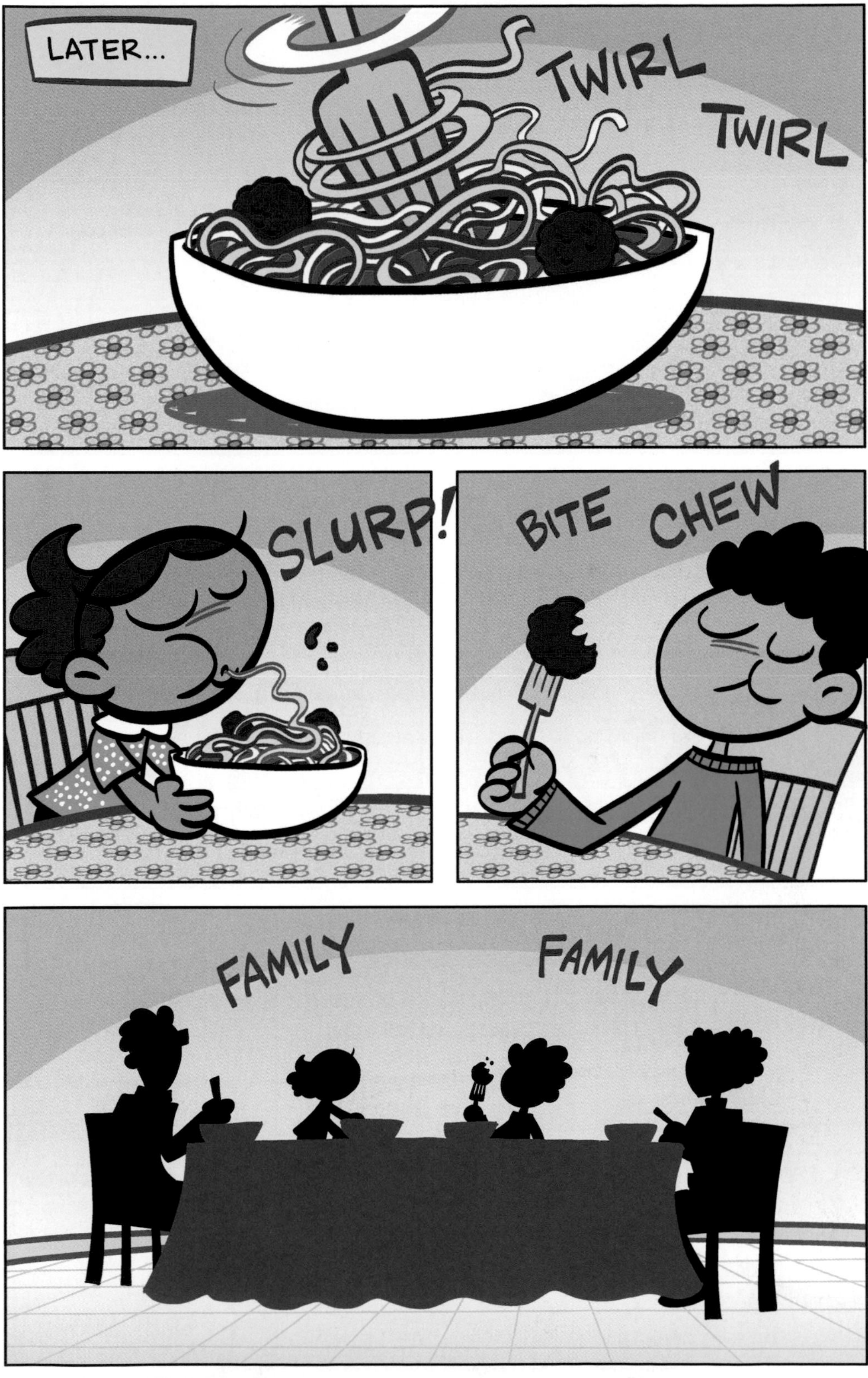
LATER...
TWIRL
TWIRL
SLURP!
BITE
CHEW
FAMILY
FAMILY

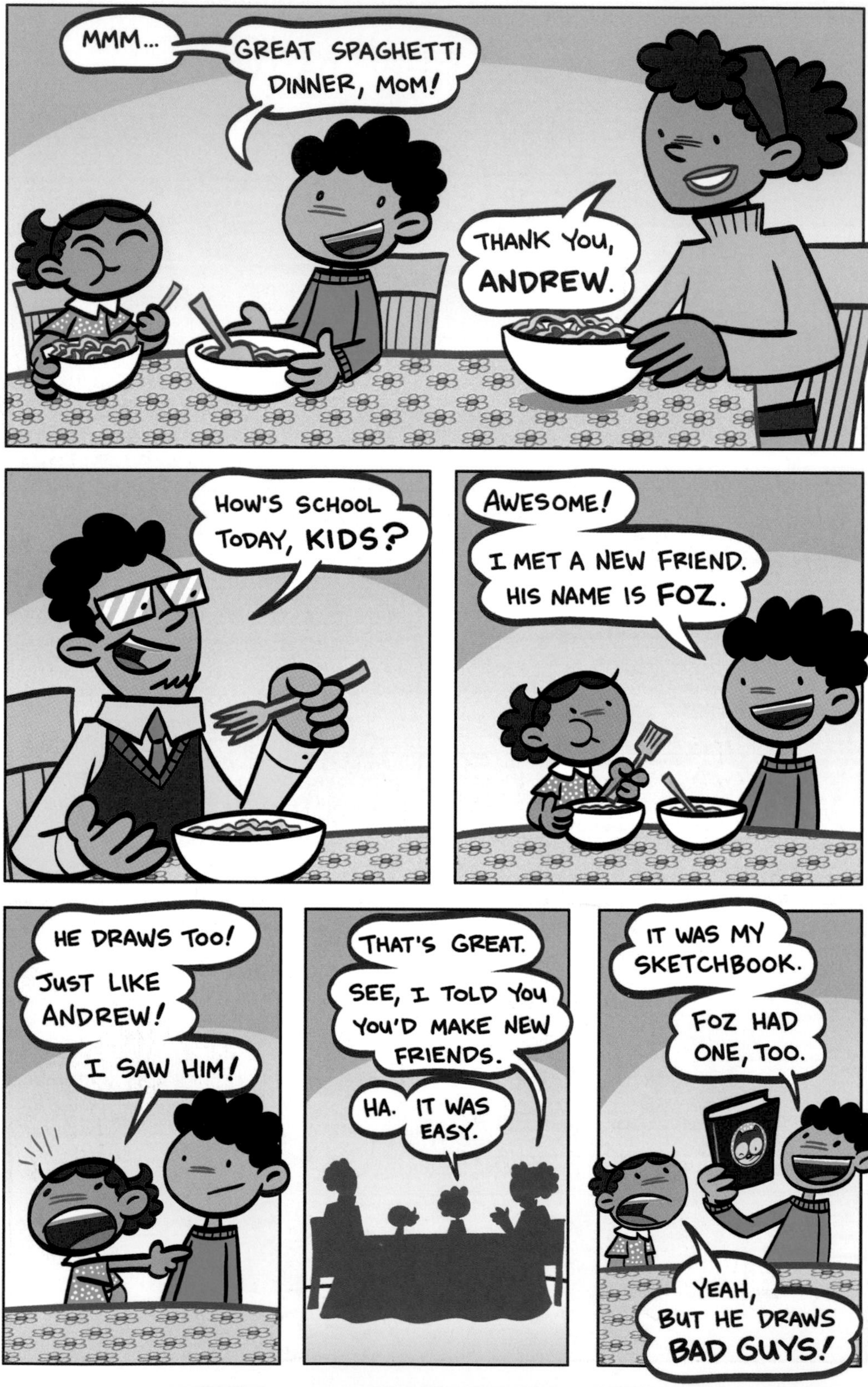
MMM...
GREAT SPAGHETTI DINNER, MOM!
THANK YOU, ANDREW.
HOW'S SCHOOL TODAY, KIDS?
AWESOME!
I MET A NEW FRIEND. HIS NAME IS FOZ.
HE DRAWS TOO!
JUST LIKE ANDREW!
I SAW HIM!
THAT'S GREAT.
SEE, I TOLD YOU YOU'D MAKE NEW FRIENDS.
HA. IT WAS EASY.
IT WAS MY SKETCHBOOK.
FOZ HAD ONE, TOO.
YEAH, BUT HE DRAWS BAD GUYS!

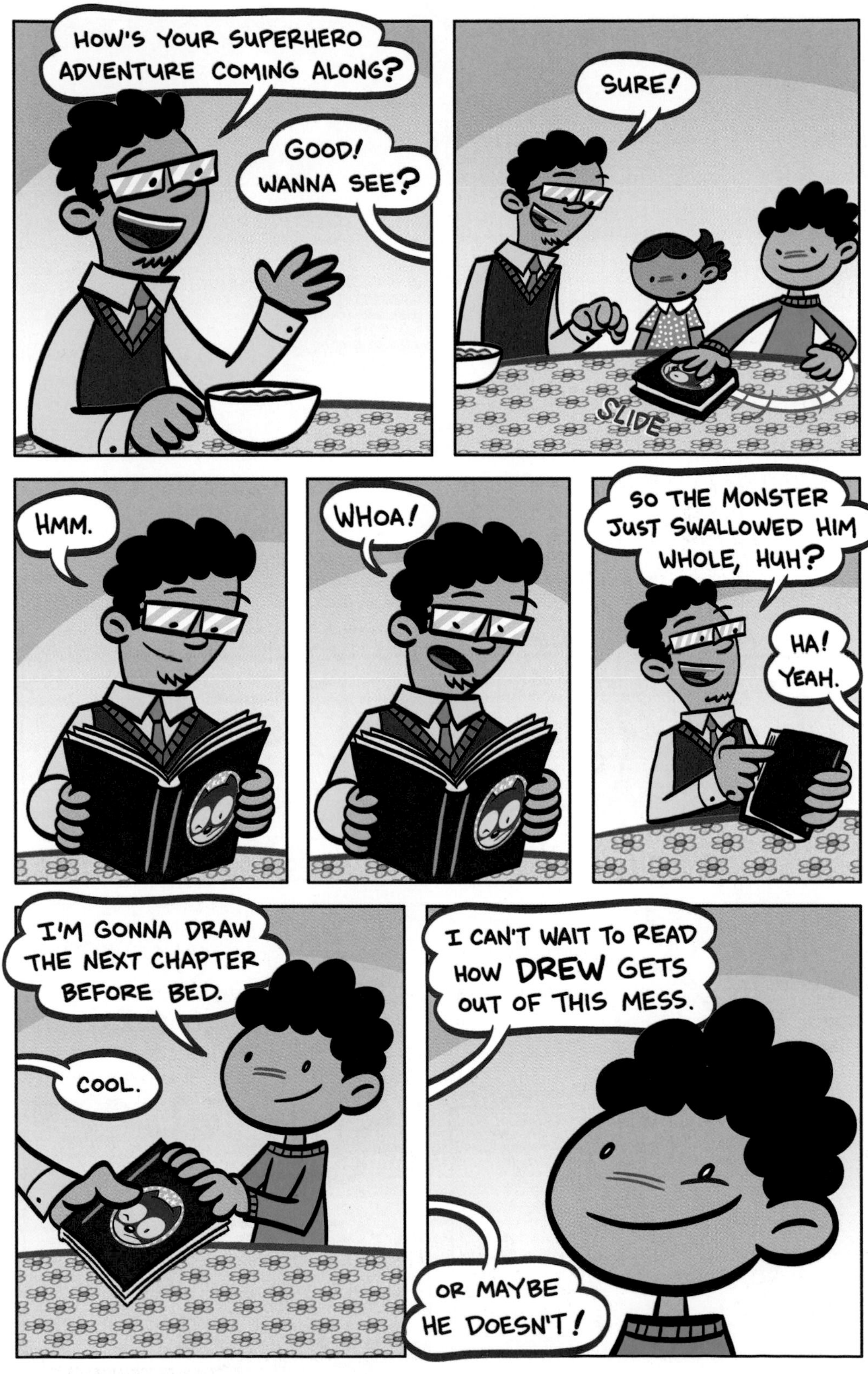
HOW'S YOUR SUPERHERO ADVENTURE COMING ALONG?
GOOD! WANNA SEE?
SURE!
SLIDE
HMM.
WHOA!
SO THE MONSTER JUST SWALLOWED HIM WHOLE, HUH?
HA! YEAH.
I'M GONNA DRAW THE NEXT CHAPTER BEFORE BED.
COOL.
I CAN'T WAIT TO READ HOW DREW GETS OUT OF THIS MESS.
OR MAYBE HE DOESN'T!

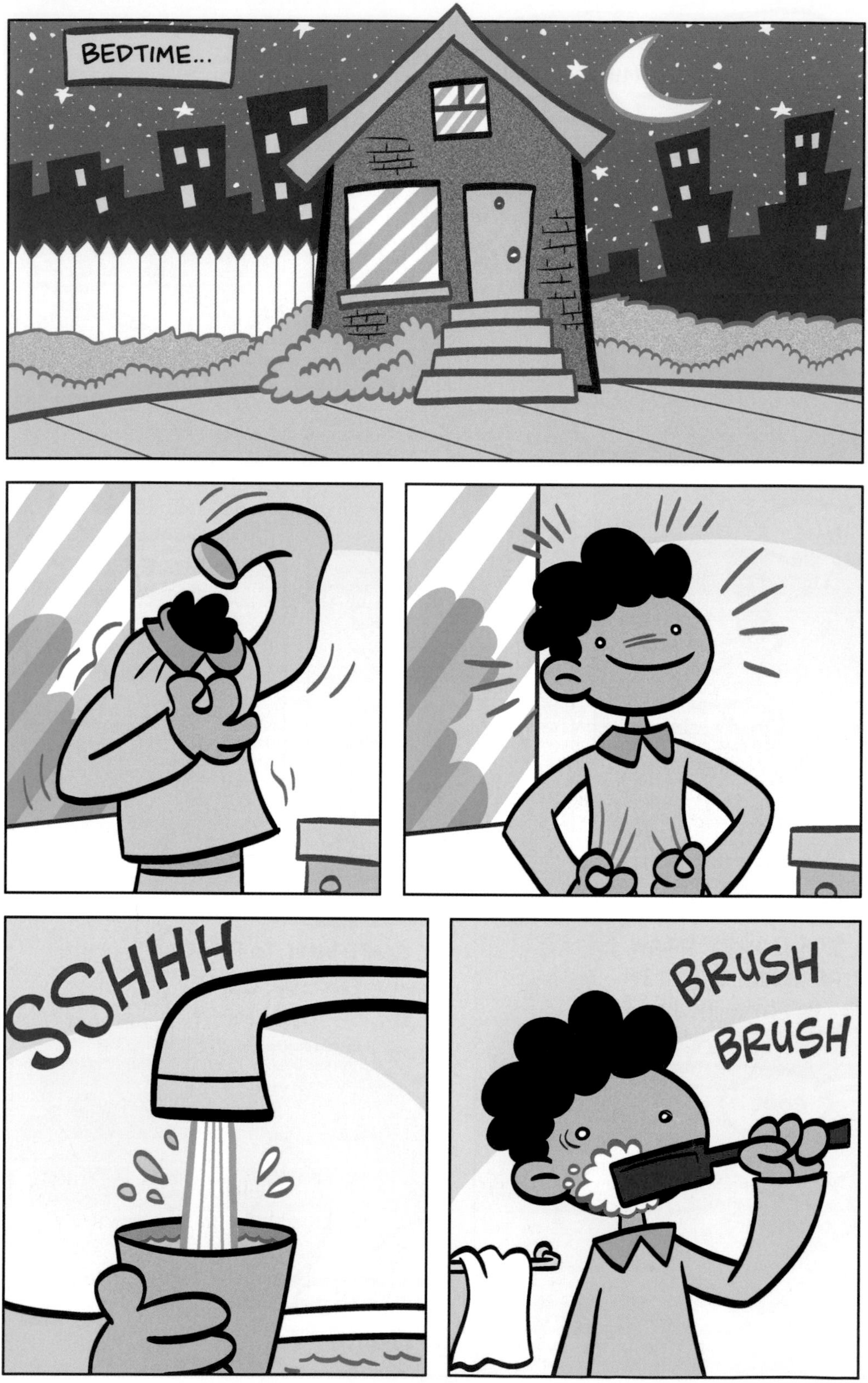
BEDTIME...
SSHHH
BRUSH
BRUSH

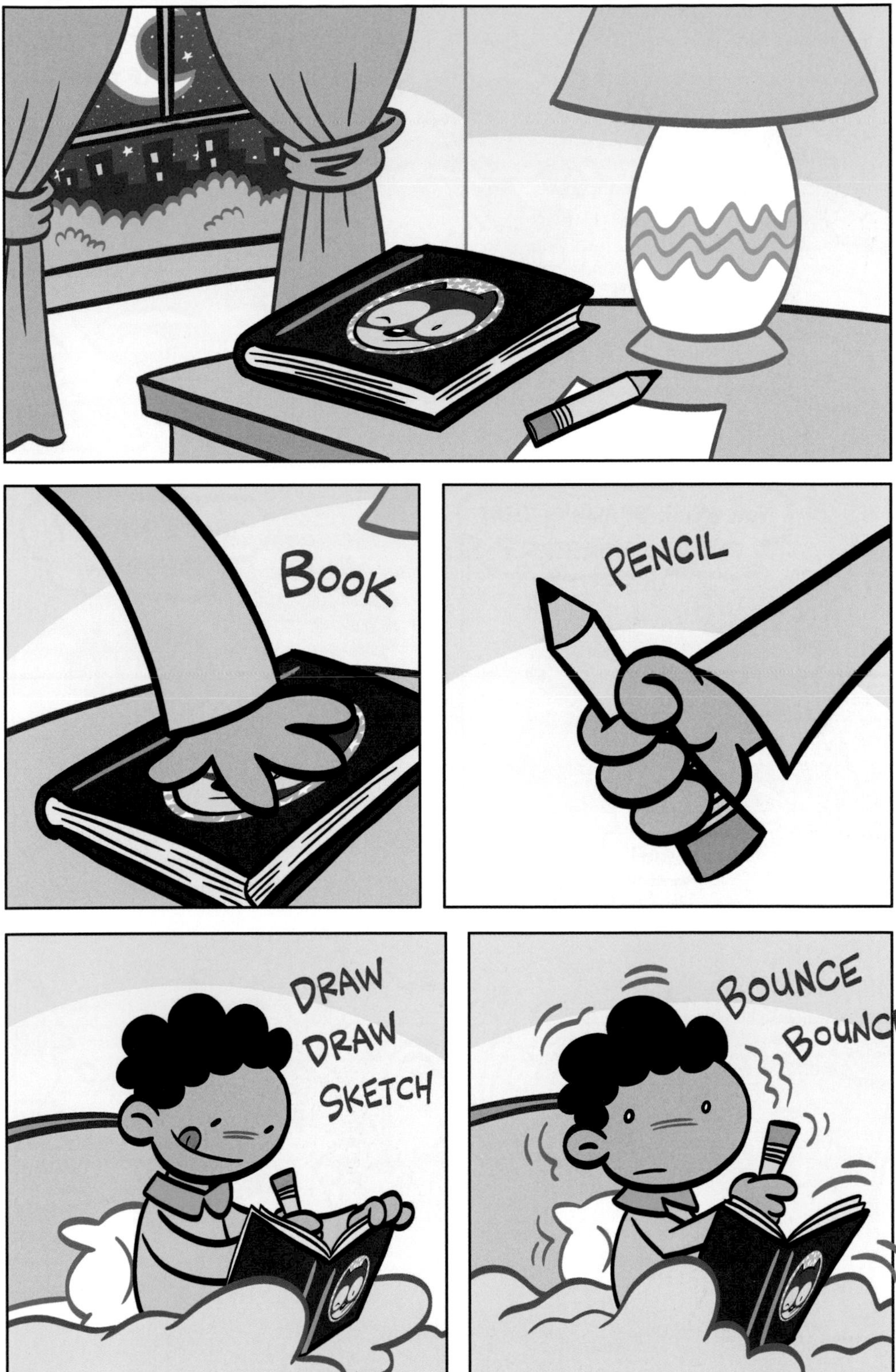
BOOK
PENCIL
DRAW
DRAW
SKETCH
BOUNCE
BOUNCE

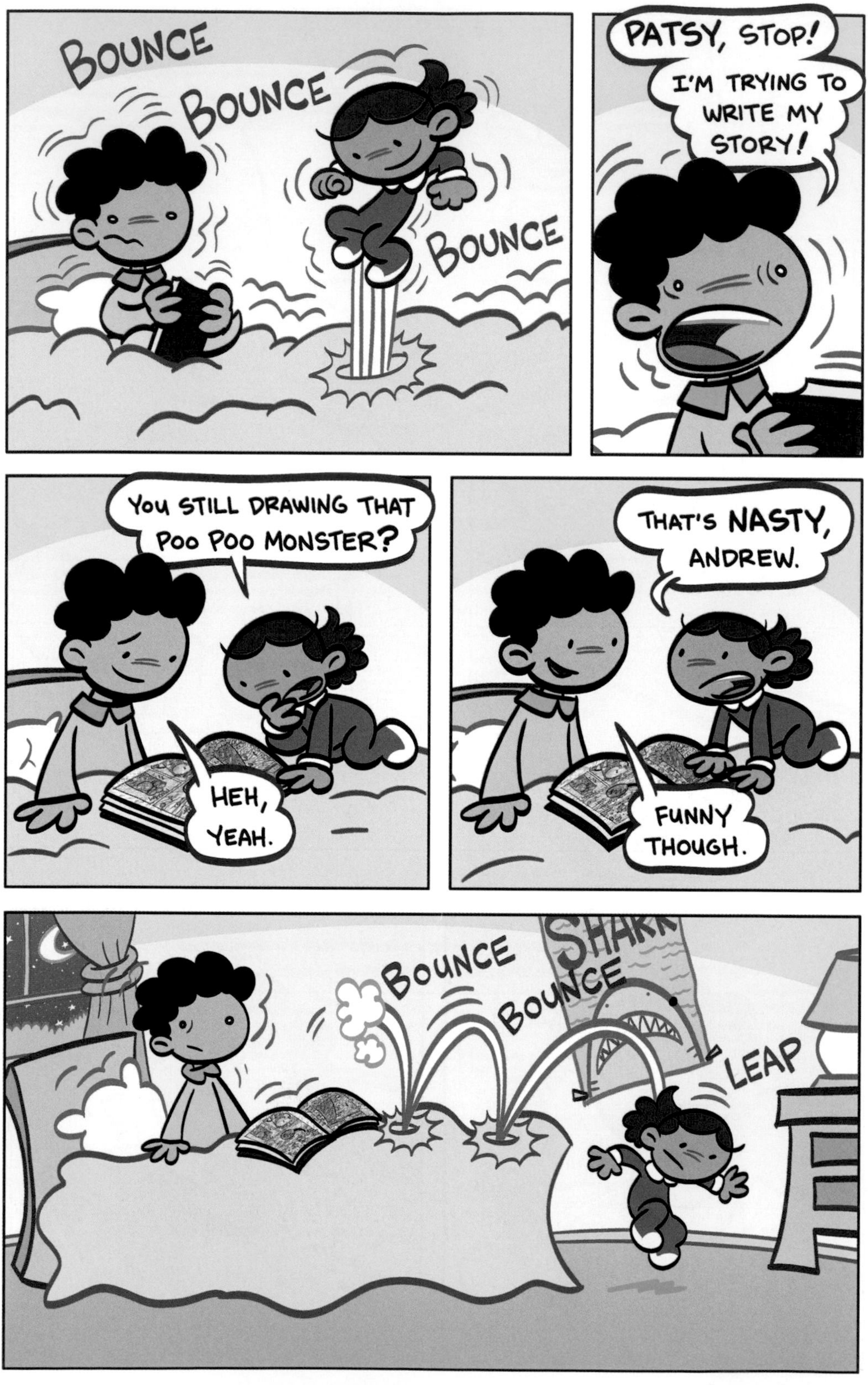
BOUNCE
BOUNCE
BOUNCE
PATSY, STOP!
I'M TRYING TO WRITE MY STORY!
YOU STILL DRAWING THAT POO POO MONSTER?
HEH, YEAH.
THAT'S NASTY, ANDREW.
FUNNY THOUGH.
BOUNCE
BOUNCE
LEAP

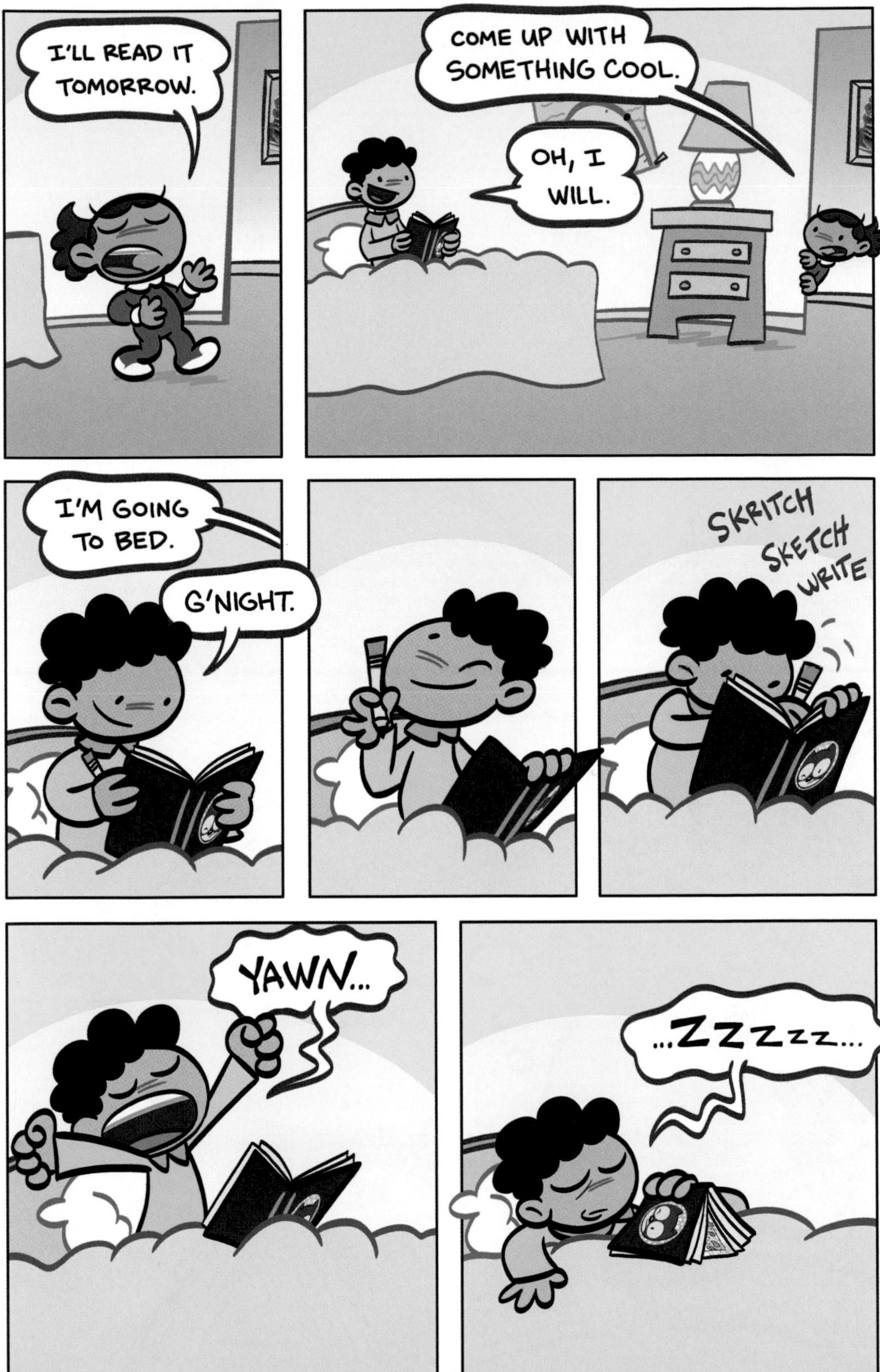
I'LL READ IT TOMORROW.
COME UP WITH SOMETHING COOL.
OH, I WILL.
I'M GOING TO BED.
G'NIGHT.
SKRITCH
SKETCH
WRITE
YAWN...
...ZZZzz...

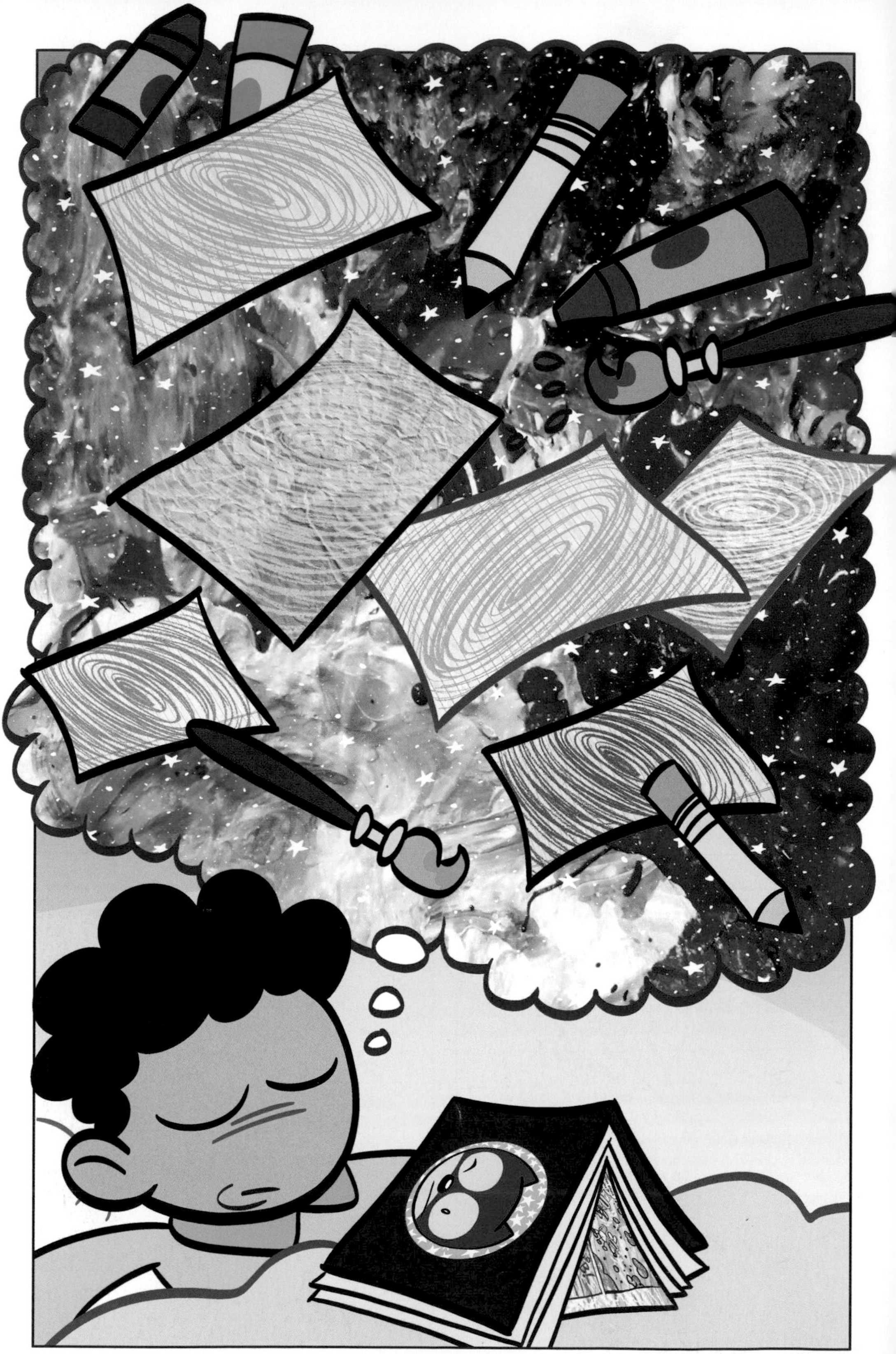

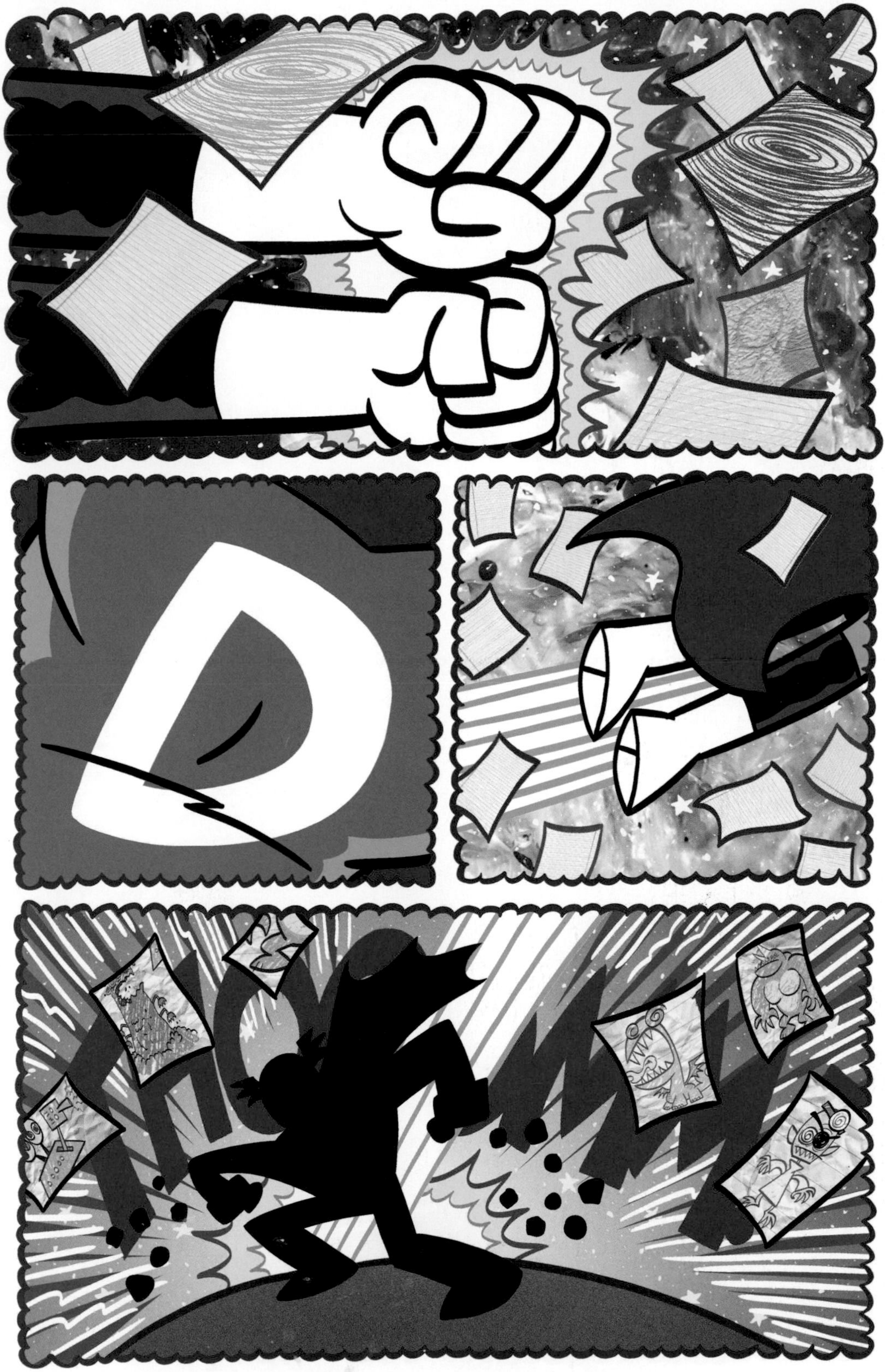

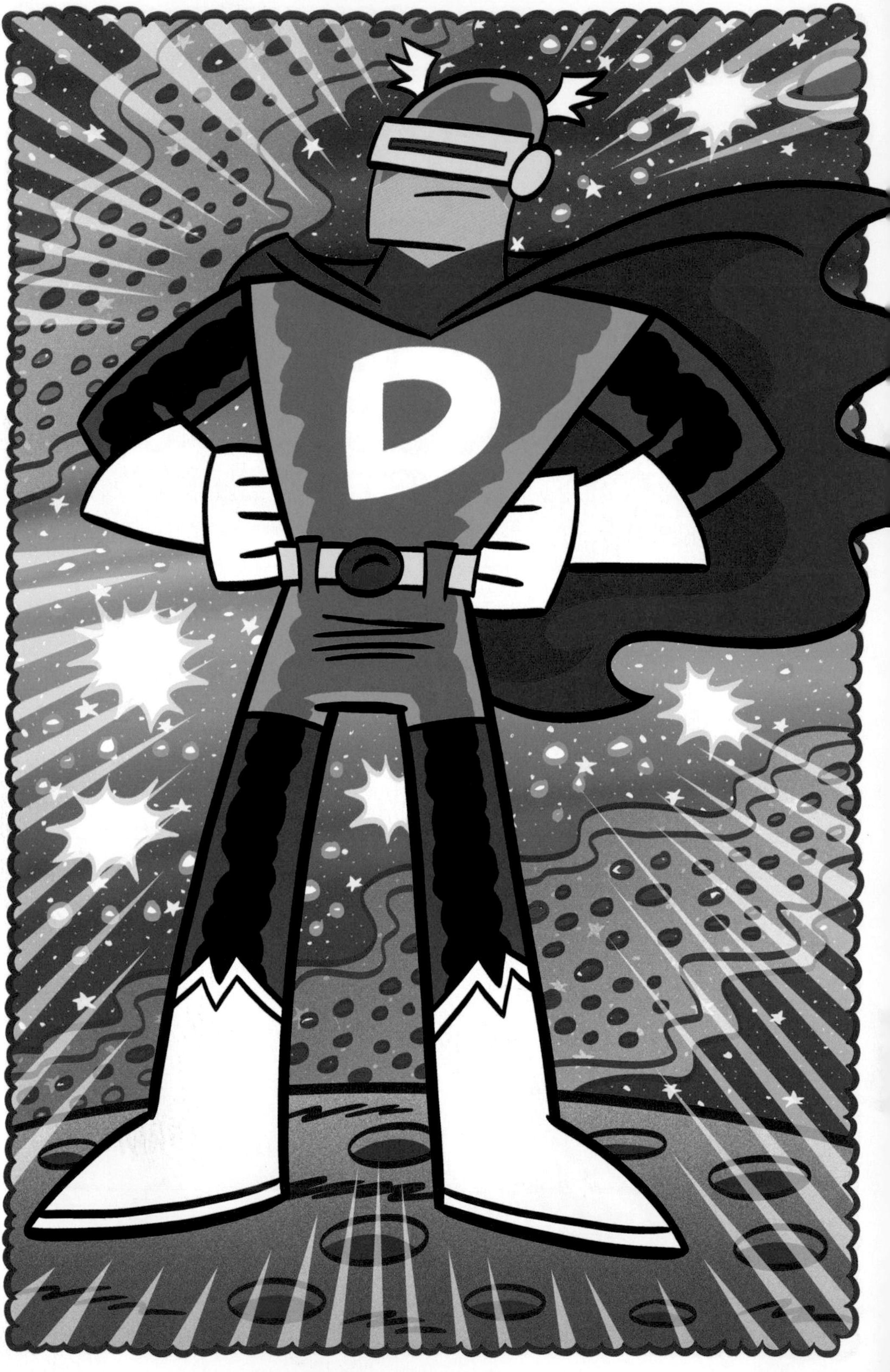

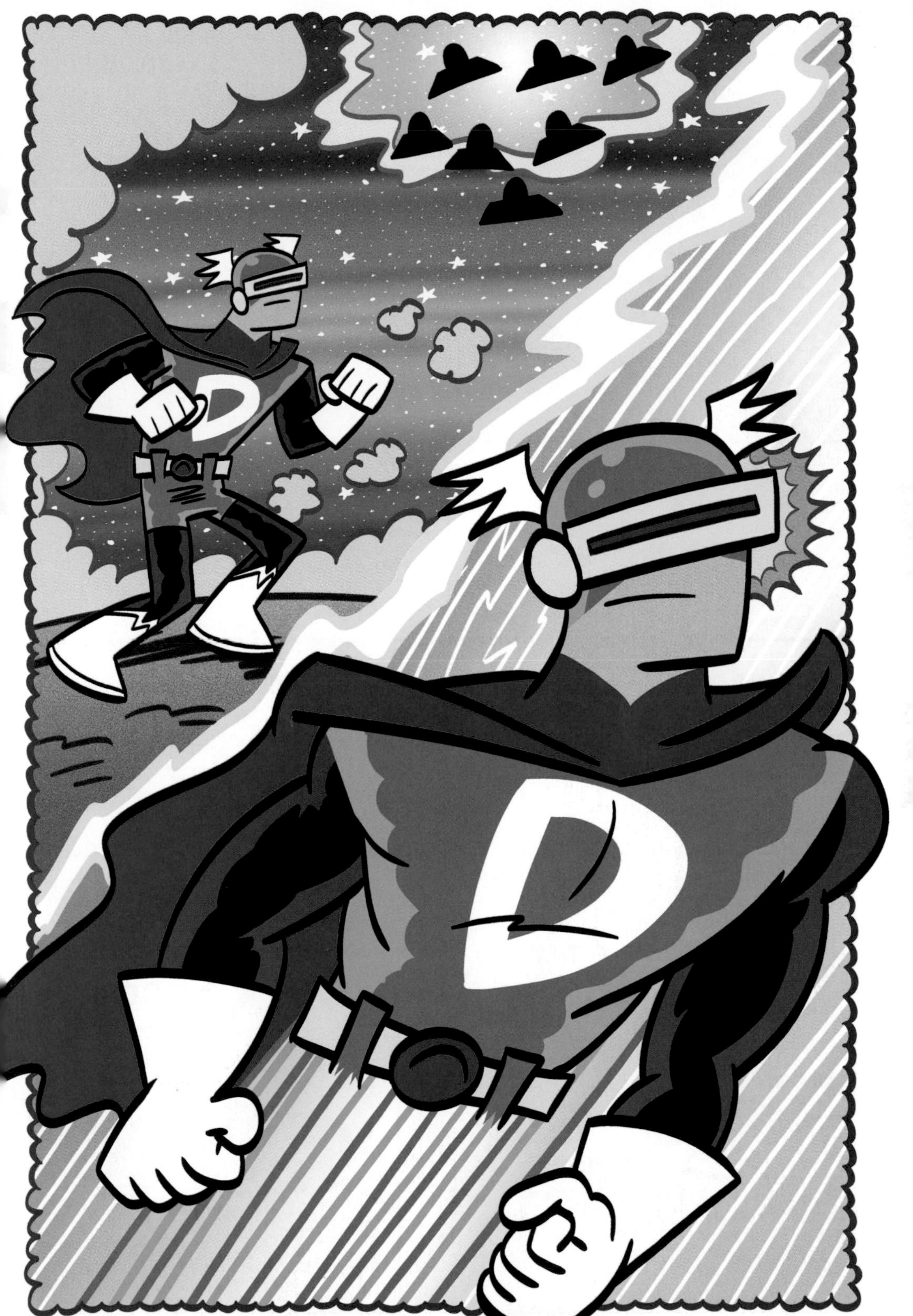

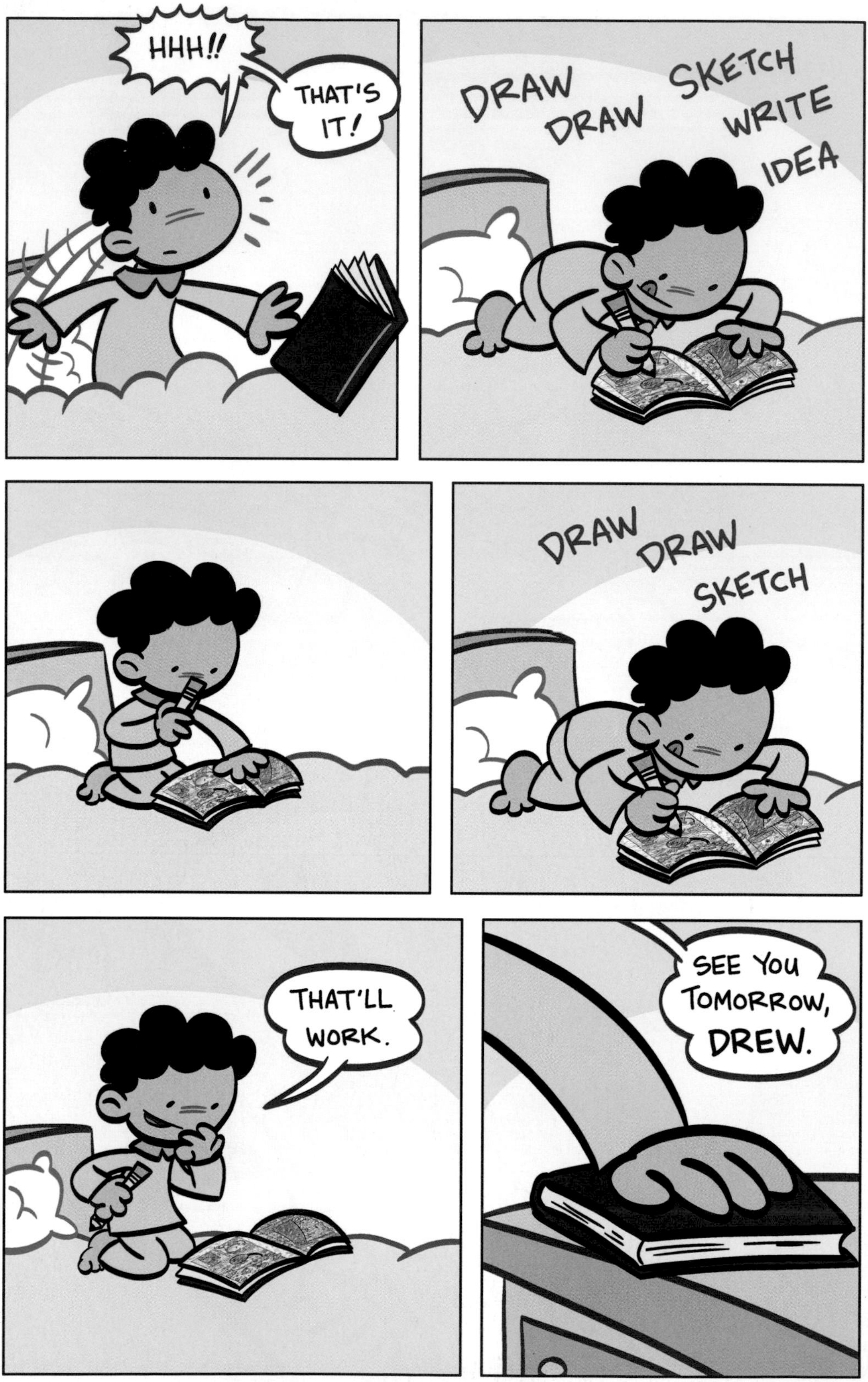
HHH!!
THAT'S IT!
DRAW
DRAW
SKETCH
WRITE
IDEA
DRAW
DRAW
SKETCH
THAT'LL WORK.
SEE YOU TOMORROW, DREW.

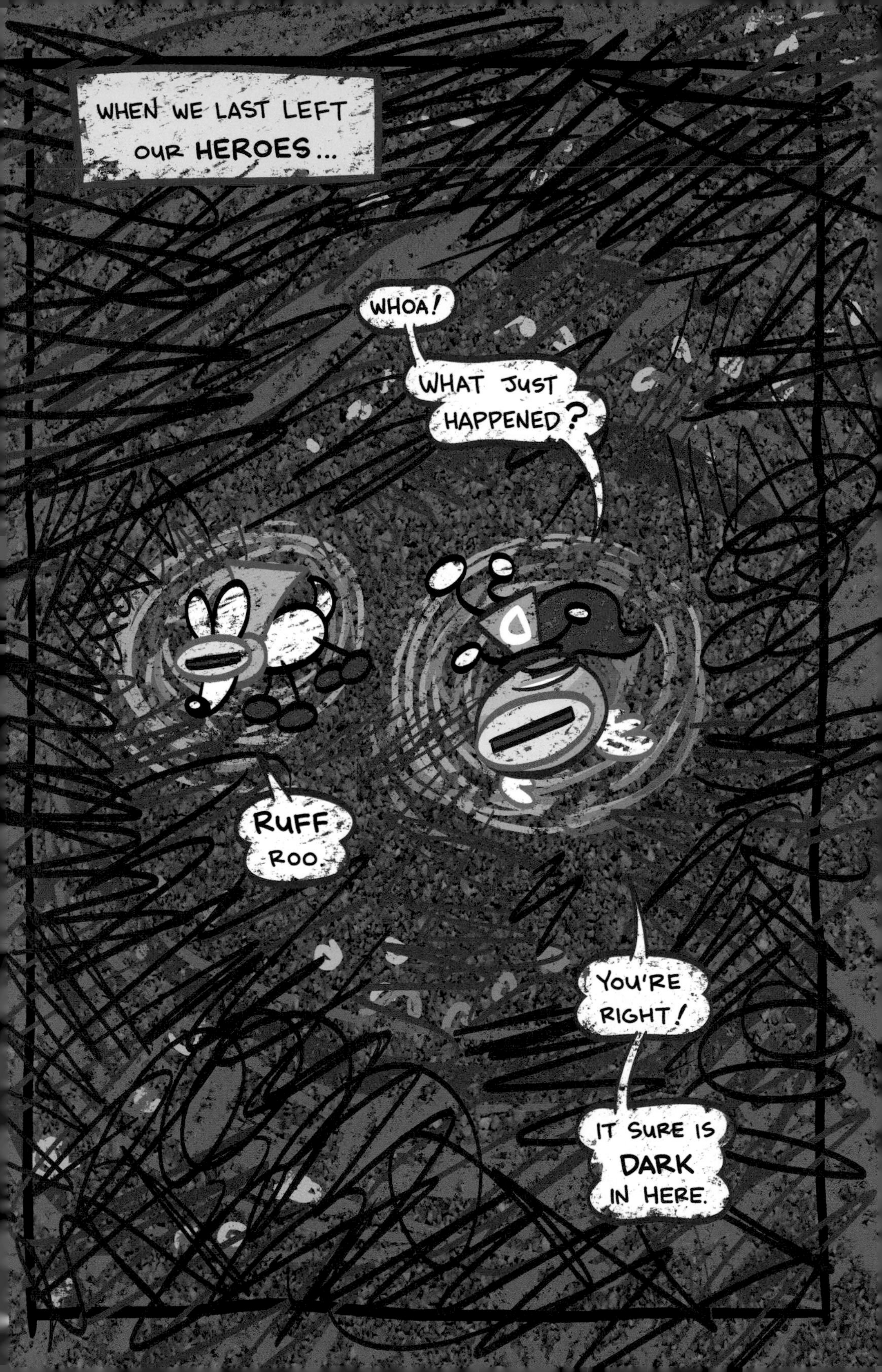
WHEN WE LAST LEFT OUR HEROES...
WHOA!
WHAT JUST HAPPENED?
RUFF ROO.
YOU'RE RIGHT!
IT SURE IS DARK IN HERE.

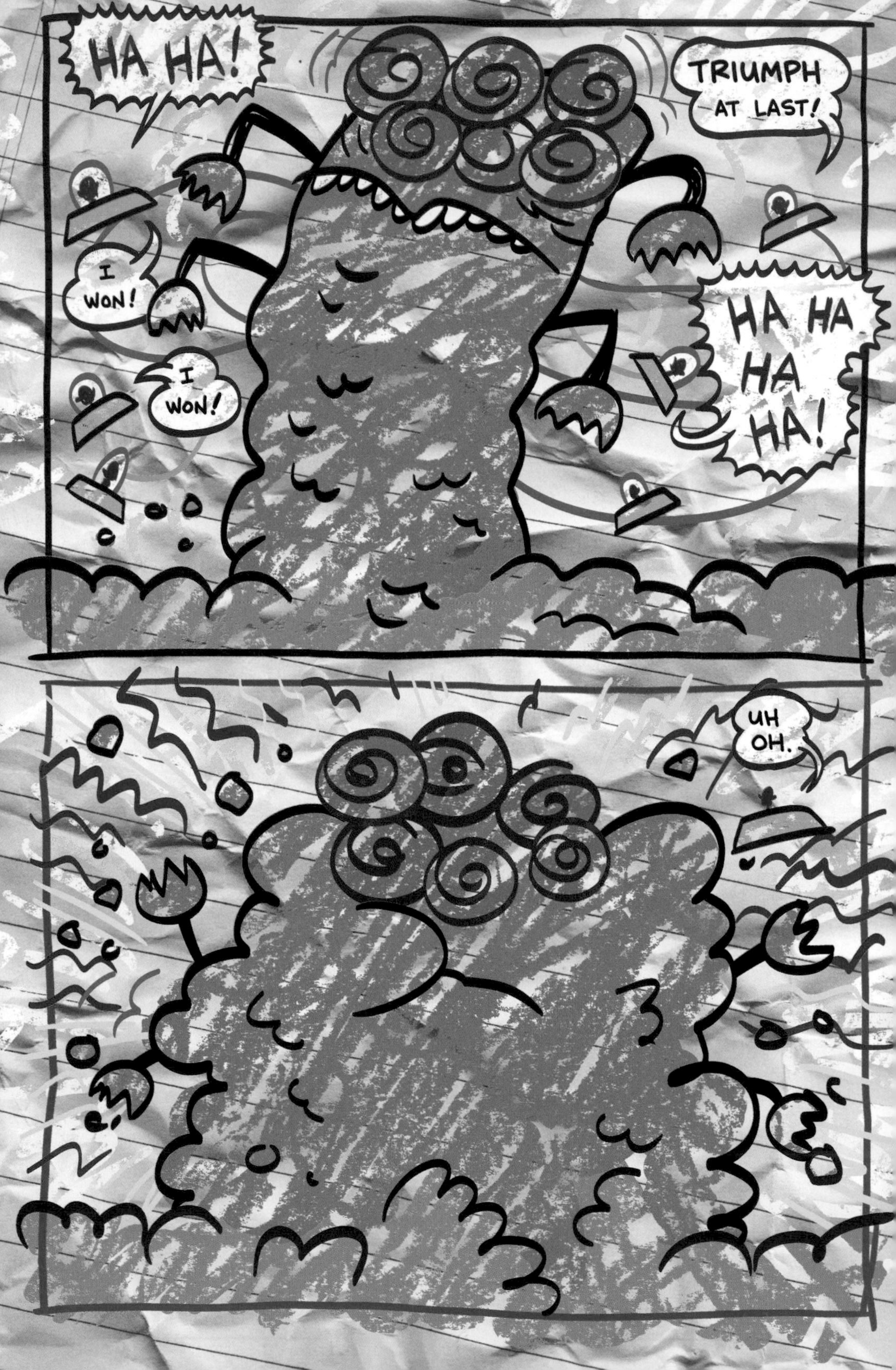
HA HA!
TRIUMPH AT LAST!
I WON!
I WON!
HA HA HA HA!
UH OH.

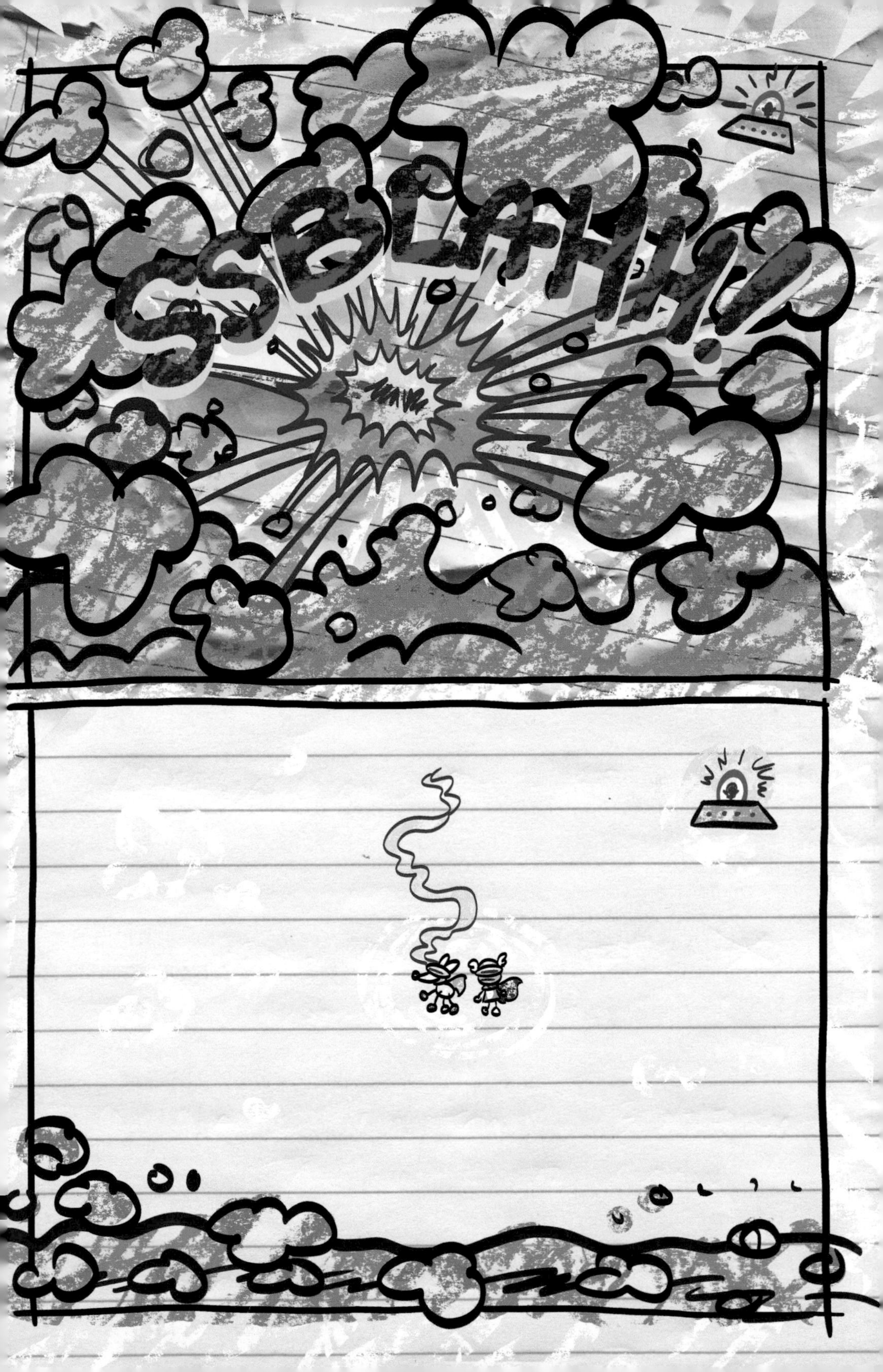
SSBLAHH!!

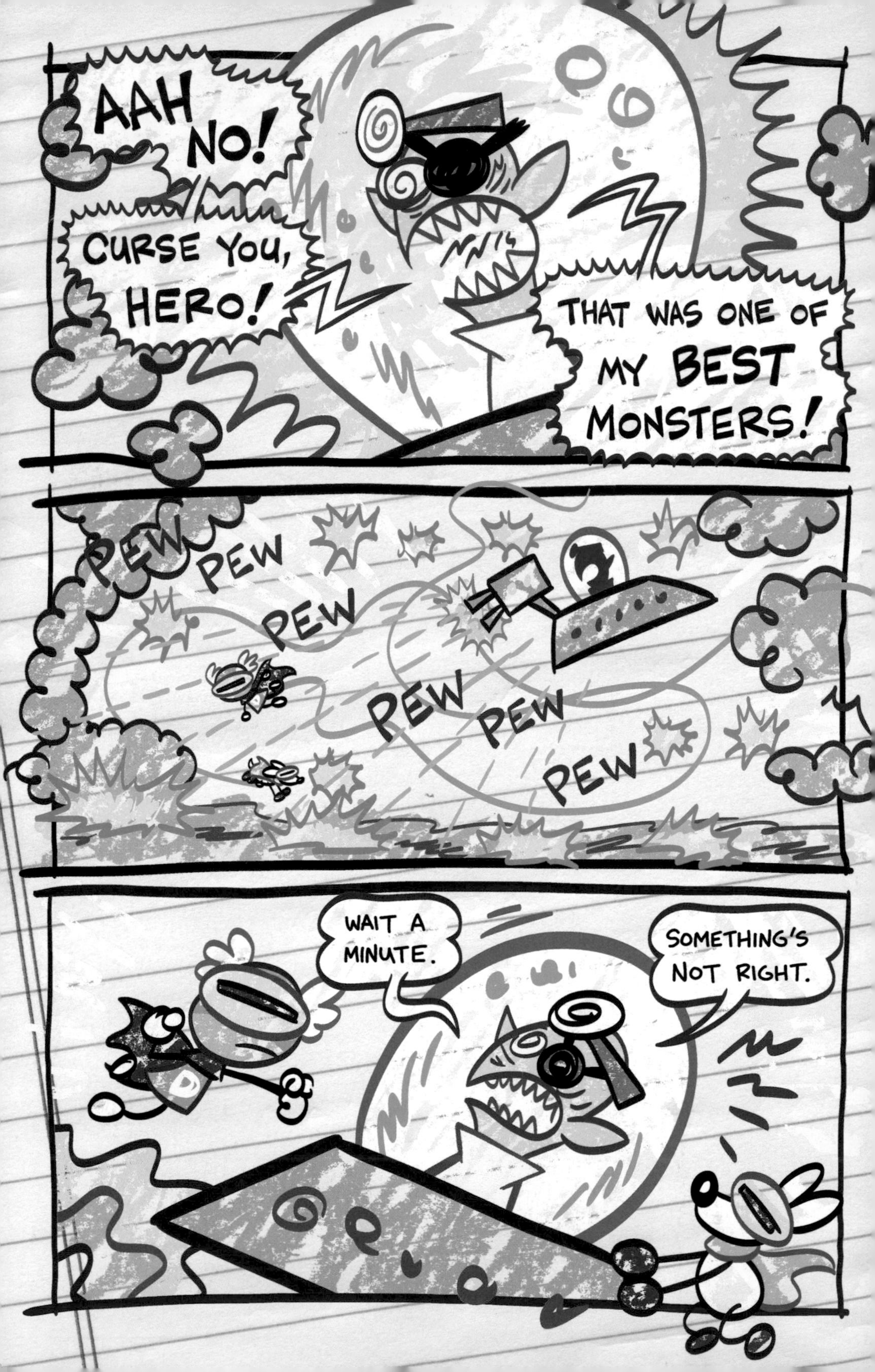
AAH NO!
CURSE YOU, HERO!
THAT WAS ONE OF MY BEST MONSTERS!
PEW
PEW
PEW
PEW
PEW
PEW
WAIT A MINUTE.
SOMETHING'S NOT RIGHT.

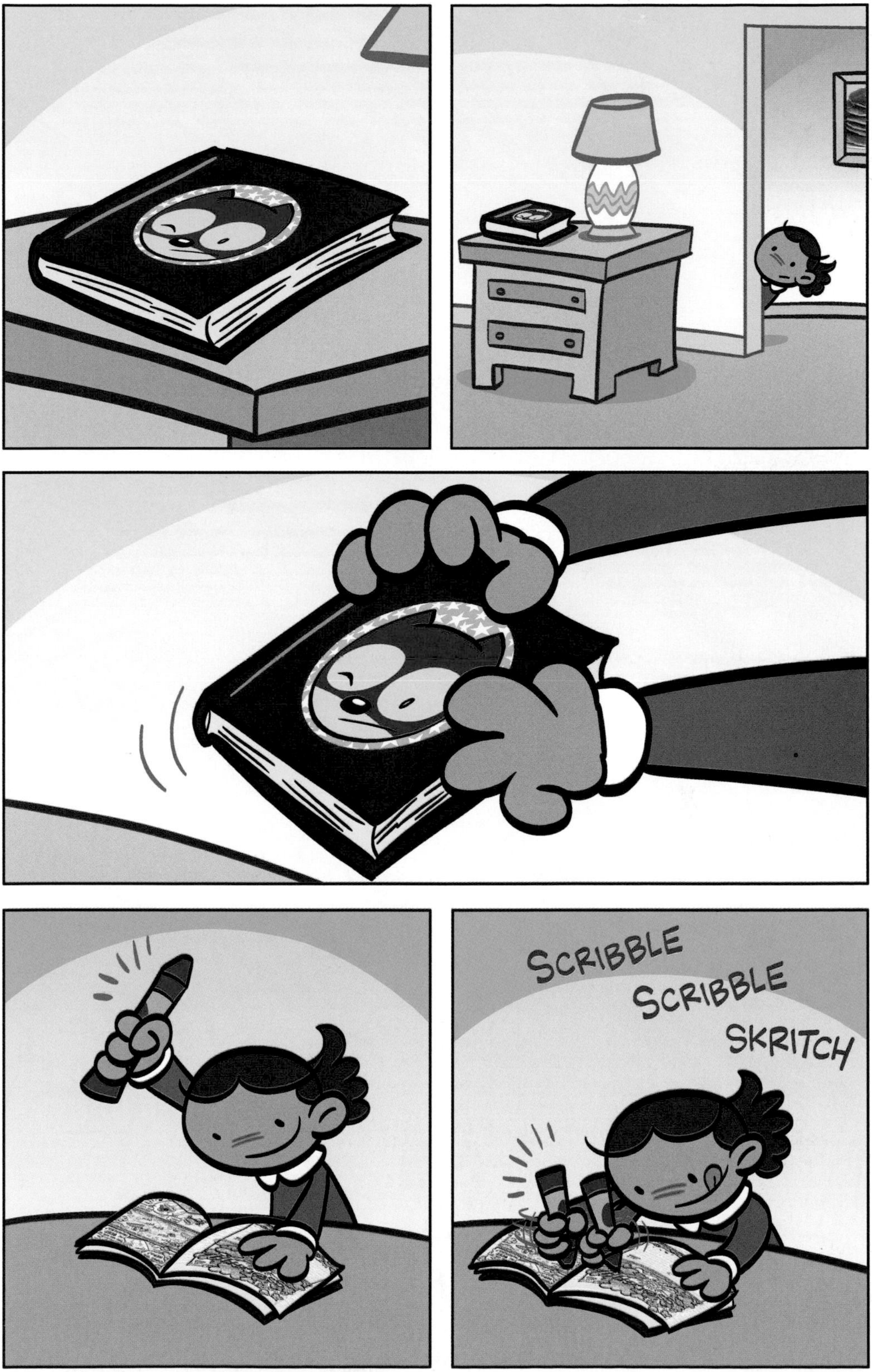
SCRIBBLE
SCRIBBLE
SKRITCH

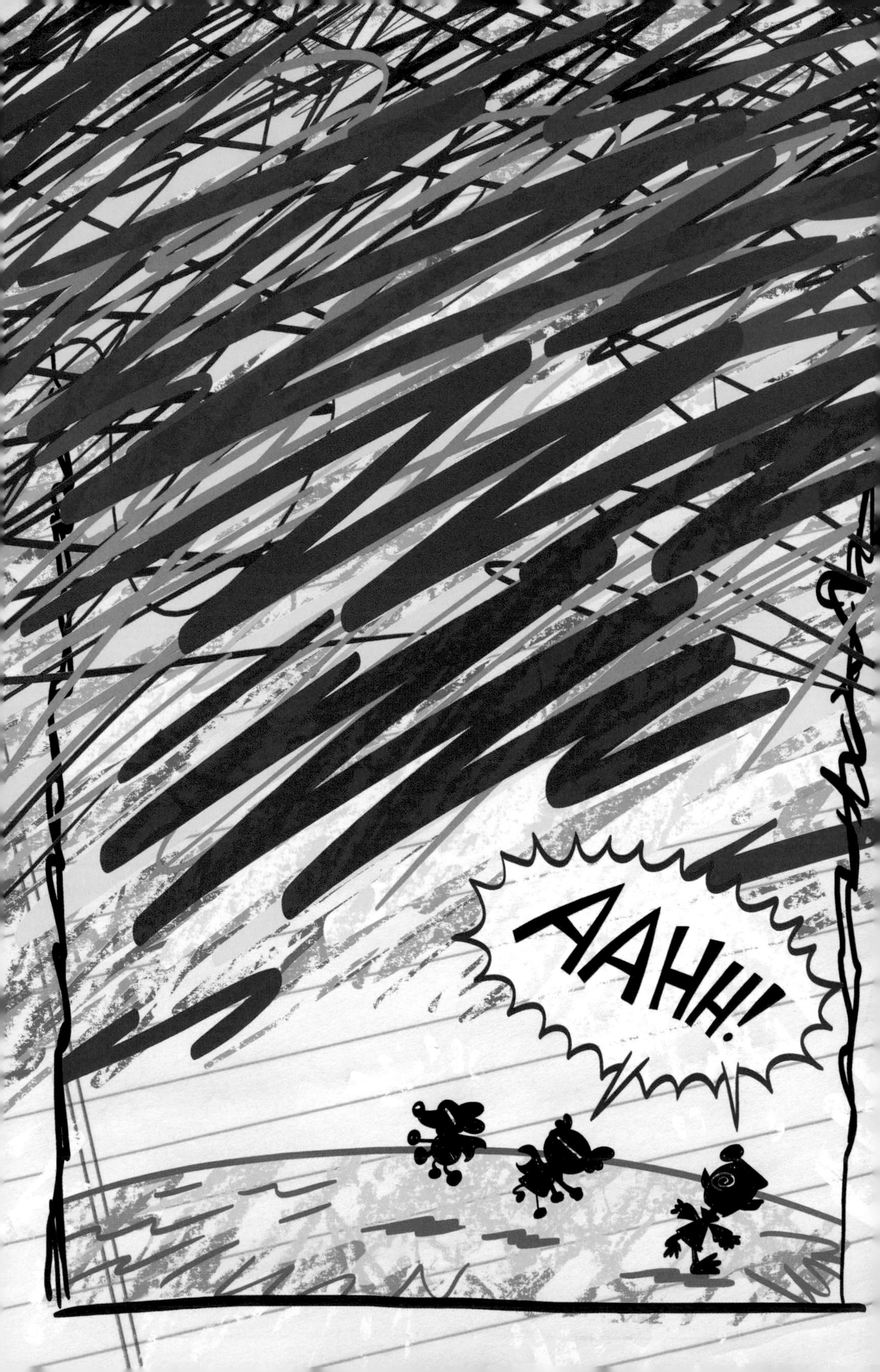
AAHH!!

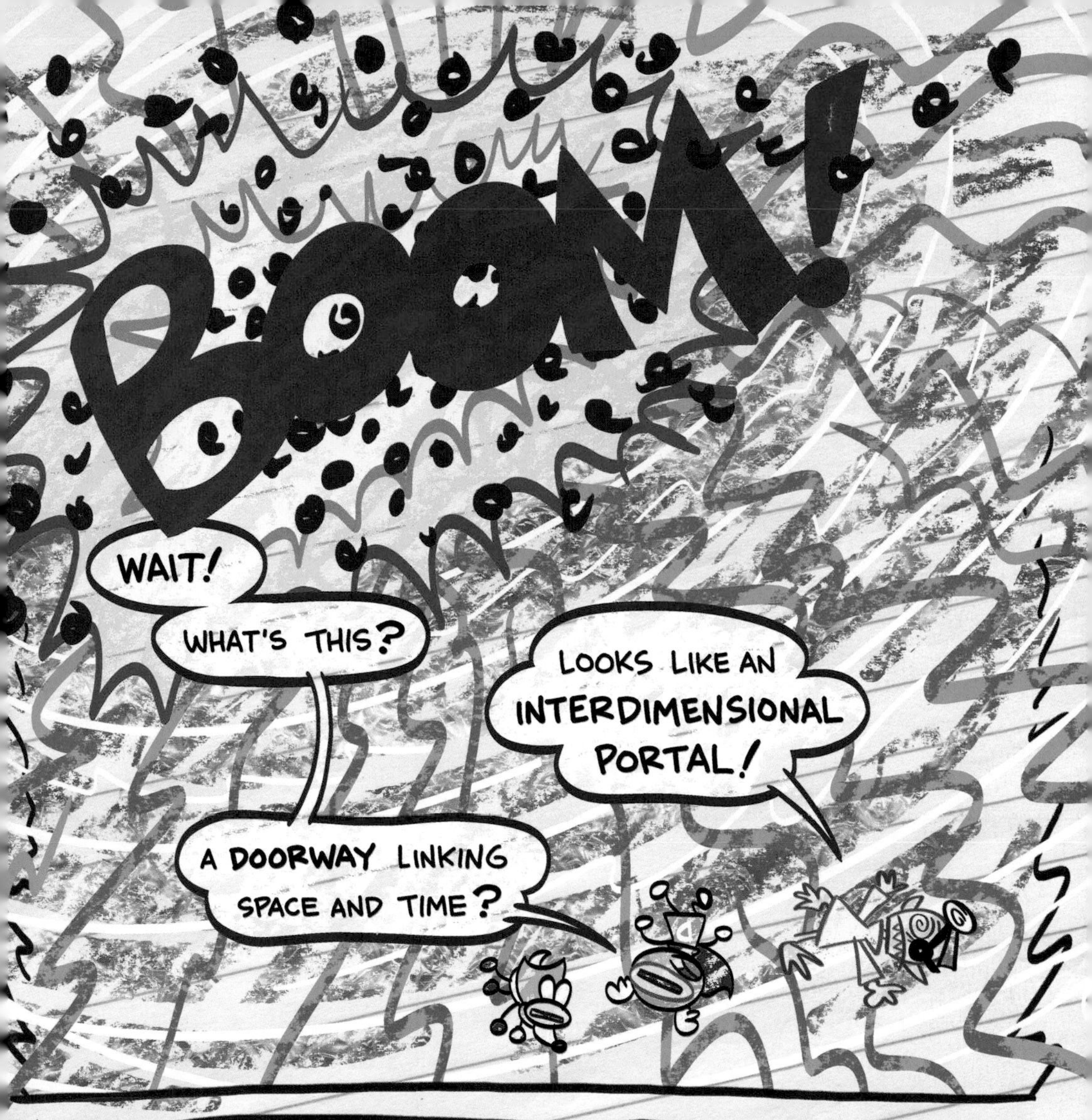
BOOM!
WAIT!
WHAT'S THIS?
A DOORWAY LINKING SPACE AND TIME?
LOOKS LIKE AN INTERDIMENSIONAL PORTAL!

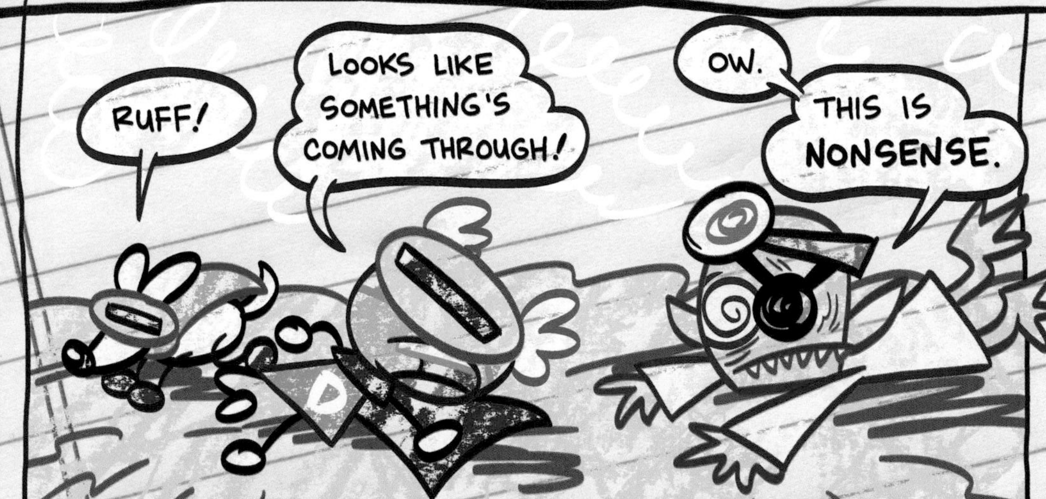
RUFF!
LOOKS LIKE SOMETHING'S COMING THROUGH!
OW.
THIS IS NONSENSE.

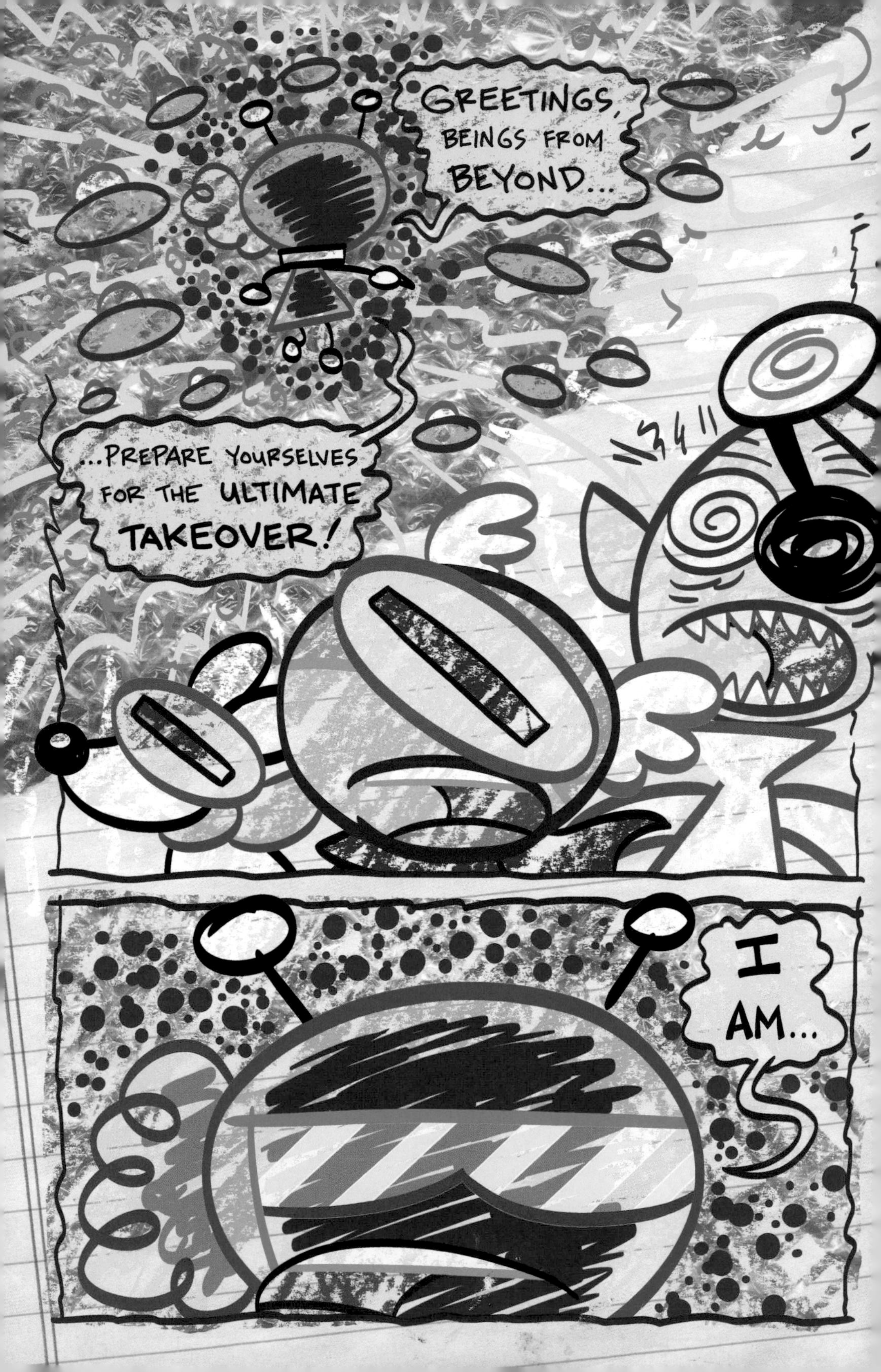
GREETINGS, BEINGS FROM BEYOND...
...PREPARE YOURSELVES FOR THE ULTIMATE TAKEOVER!
I AM...

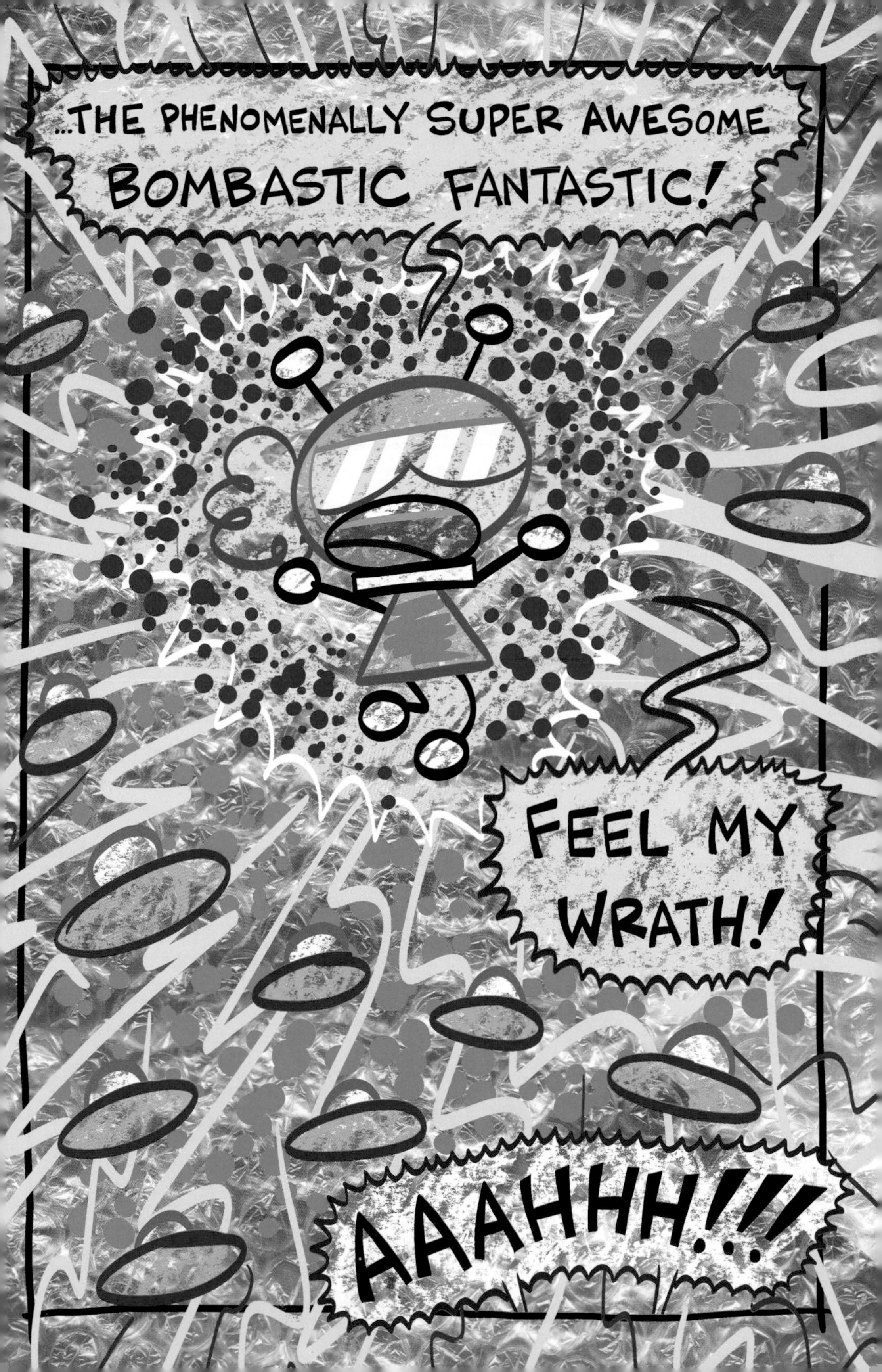
...THE PHENOMENALLY SUPER AWESOME BOMBASTIC FANTASTIC!
FEEL MY WRATH!
AAAHHH!!!

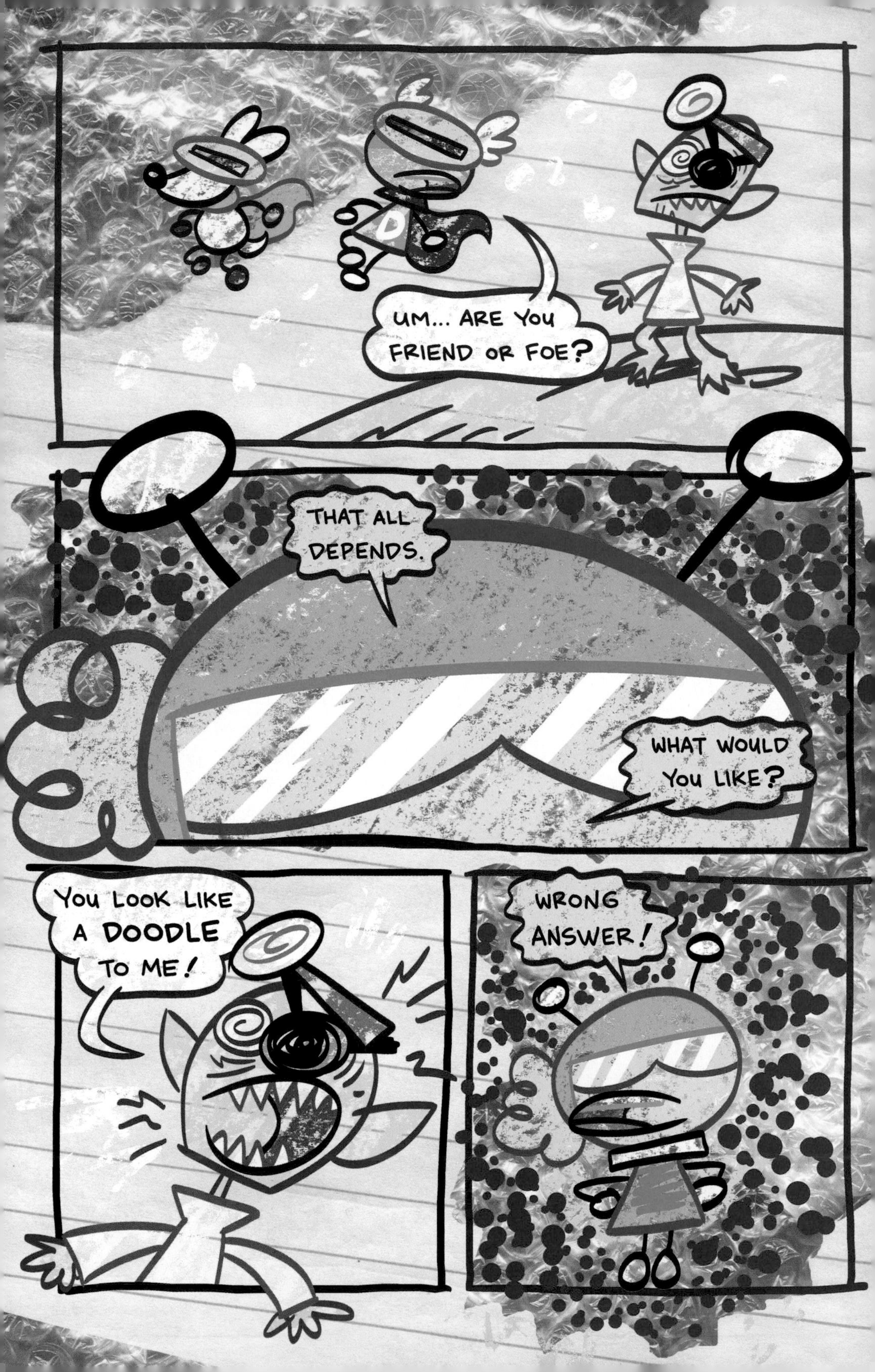
UM... ARE YOU FRIEND OR FOE?
THAT ALL DEPENDS.
WHAT WOULD YOU LIKE?
YOU LOOK LIKE A DOODLE TO ME!
WRONG ANSWER!

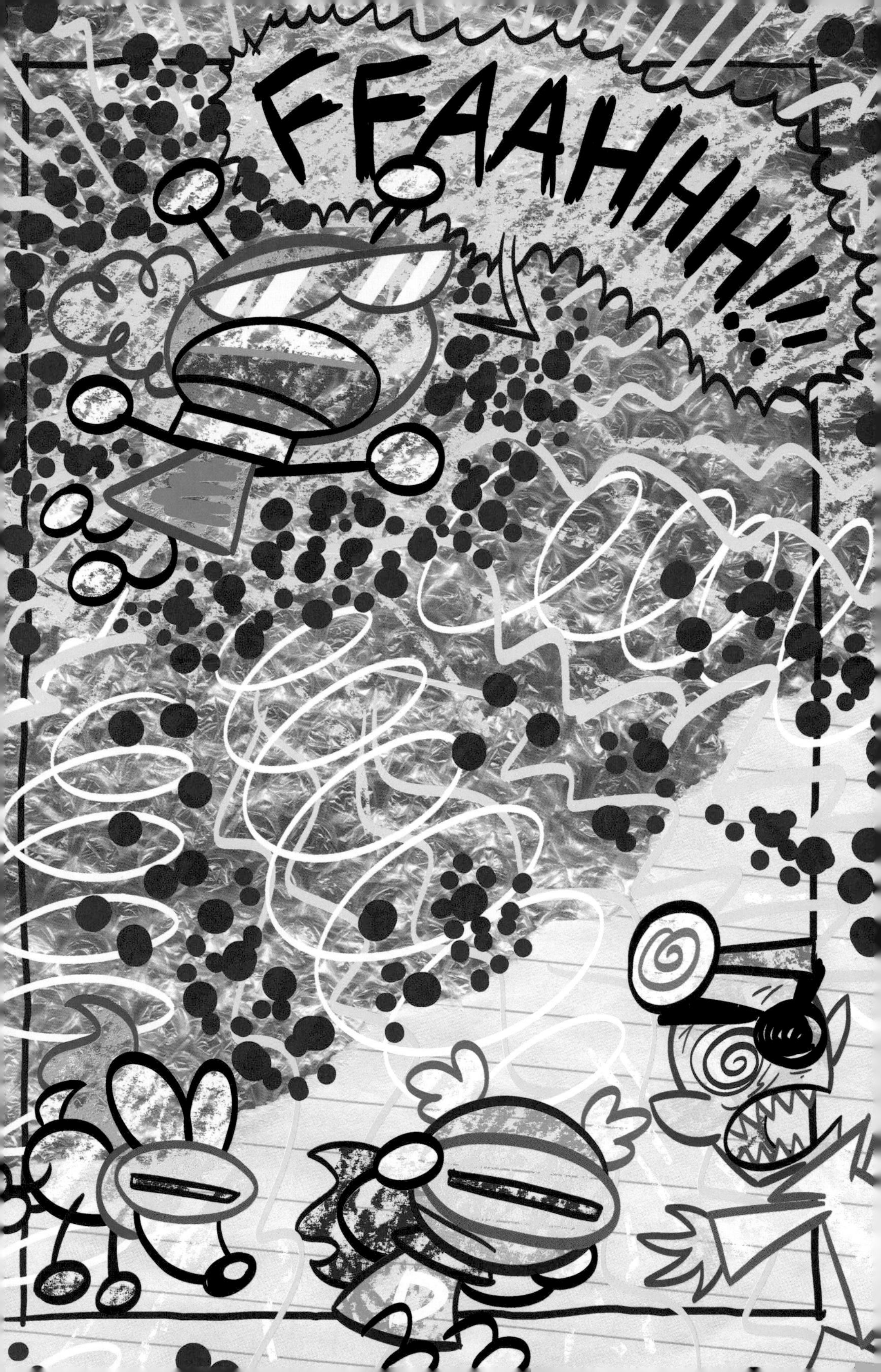
FFAAHHHH!!!

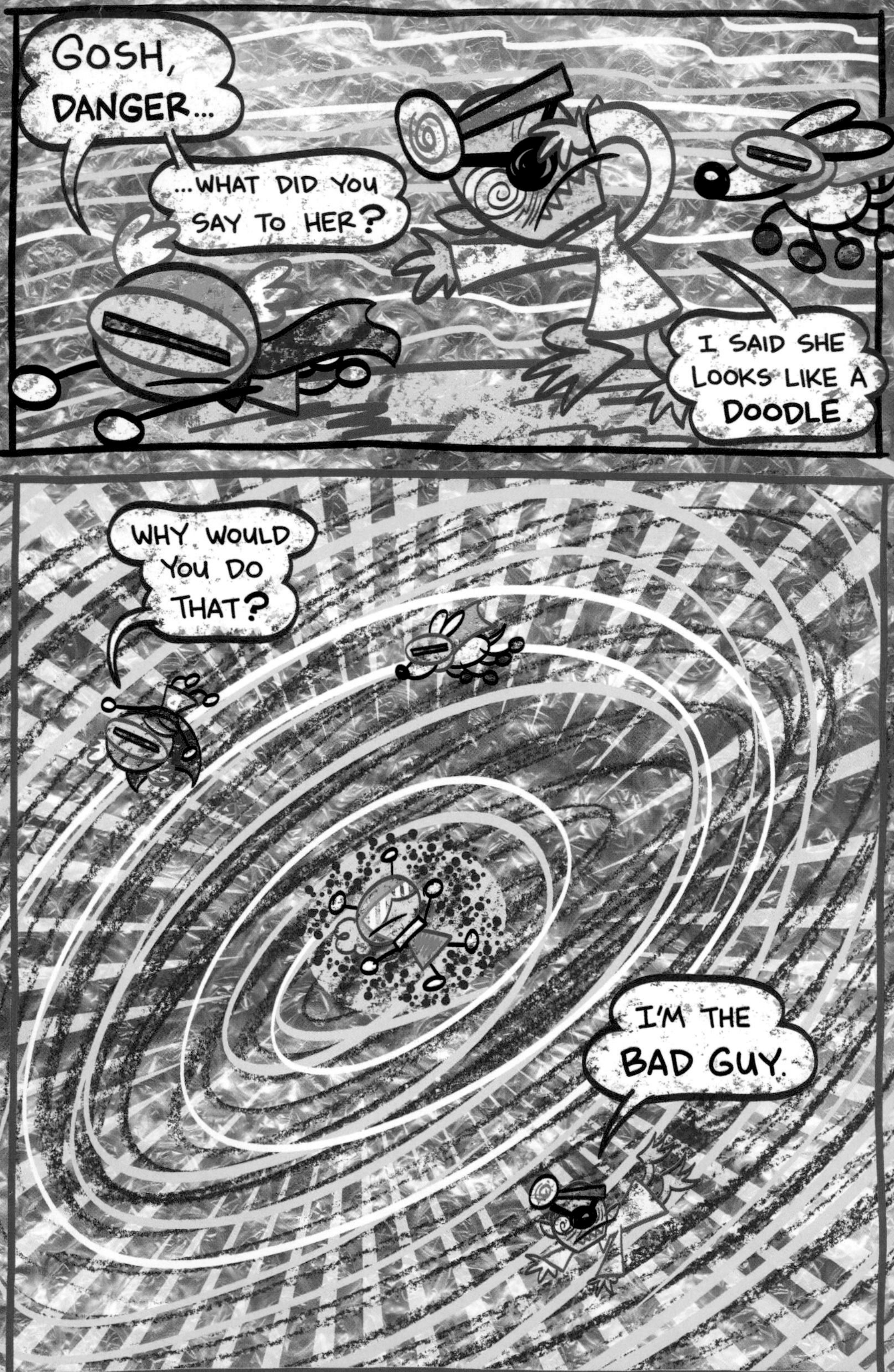
GOSH, DANGER...
...WHAT DID YOU SAY TO HER?
I SAID SHE LOOKS LIKE A DOODLE.
WHY WOULD YOU DO THAT?
I'M THE BAD GUY.

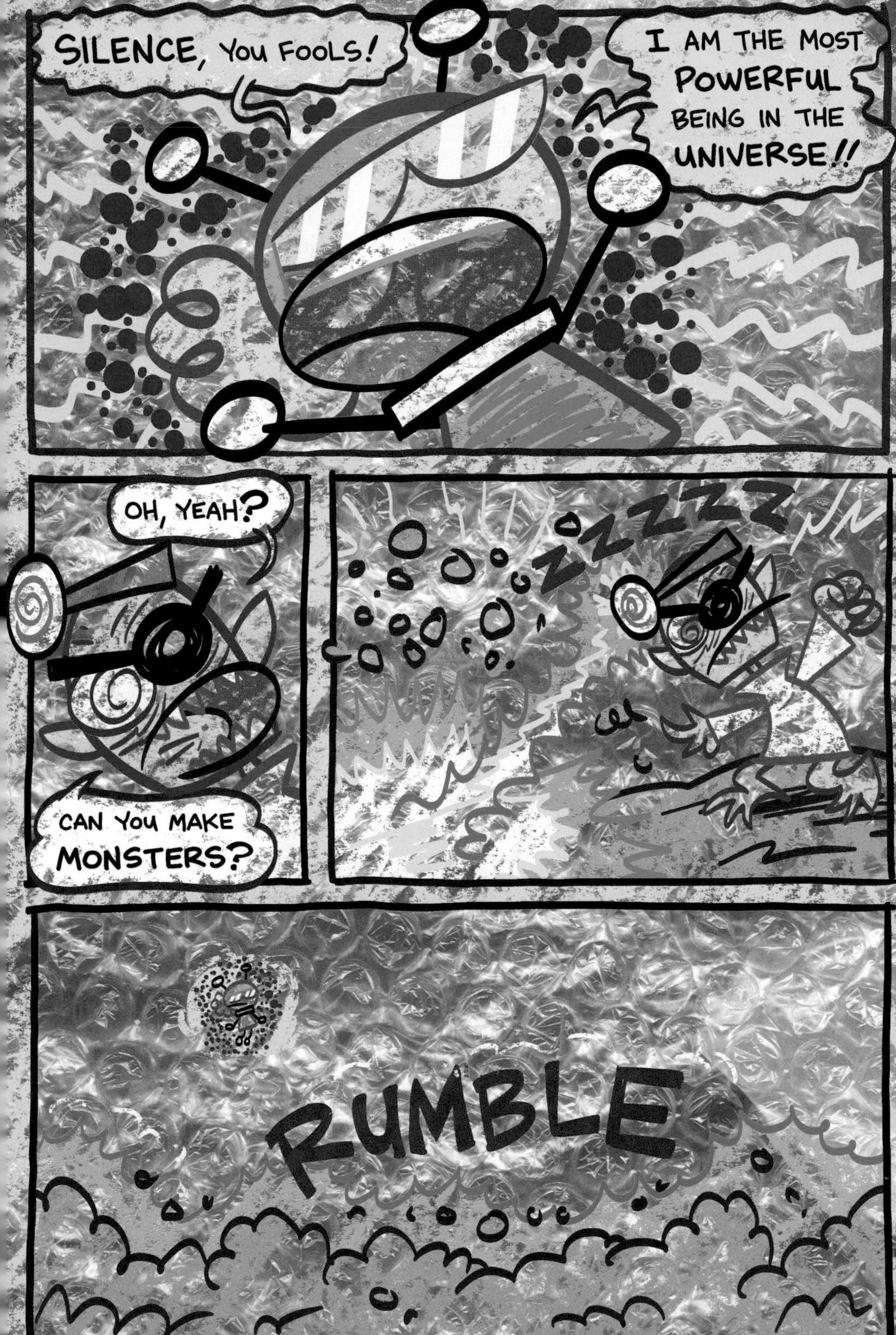
SILENCE, YOU FOOLS!
I AM THE MOST POWERFUL BEING IN THE UNIVERSE!!
OH, YEAH?
CAN YOU MAKE MONSTERS?
ZZZZZZ
RUMBLE

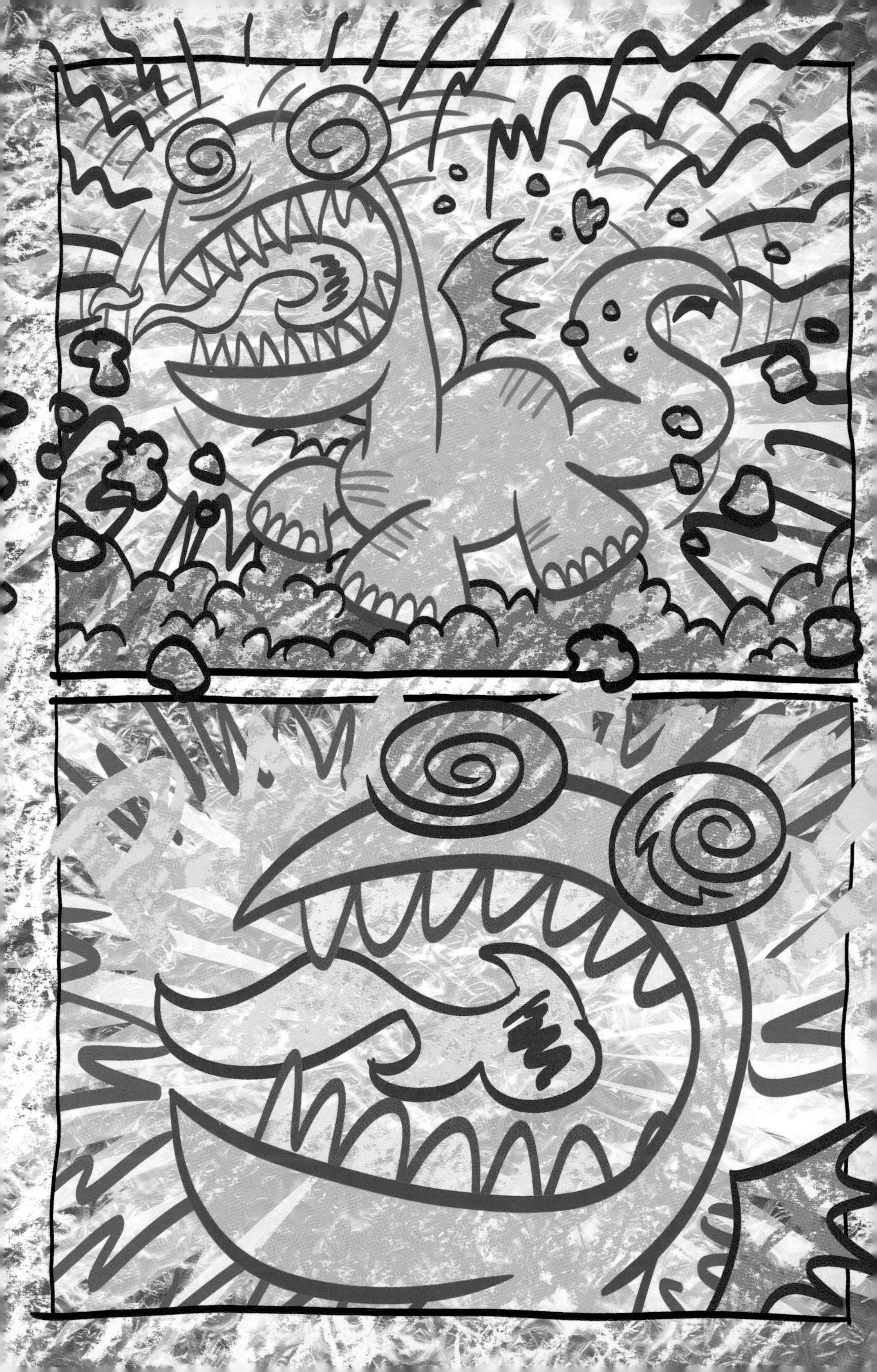

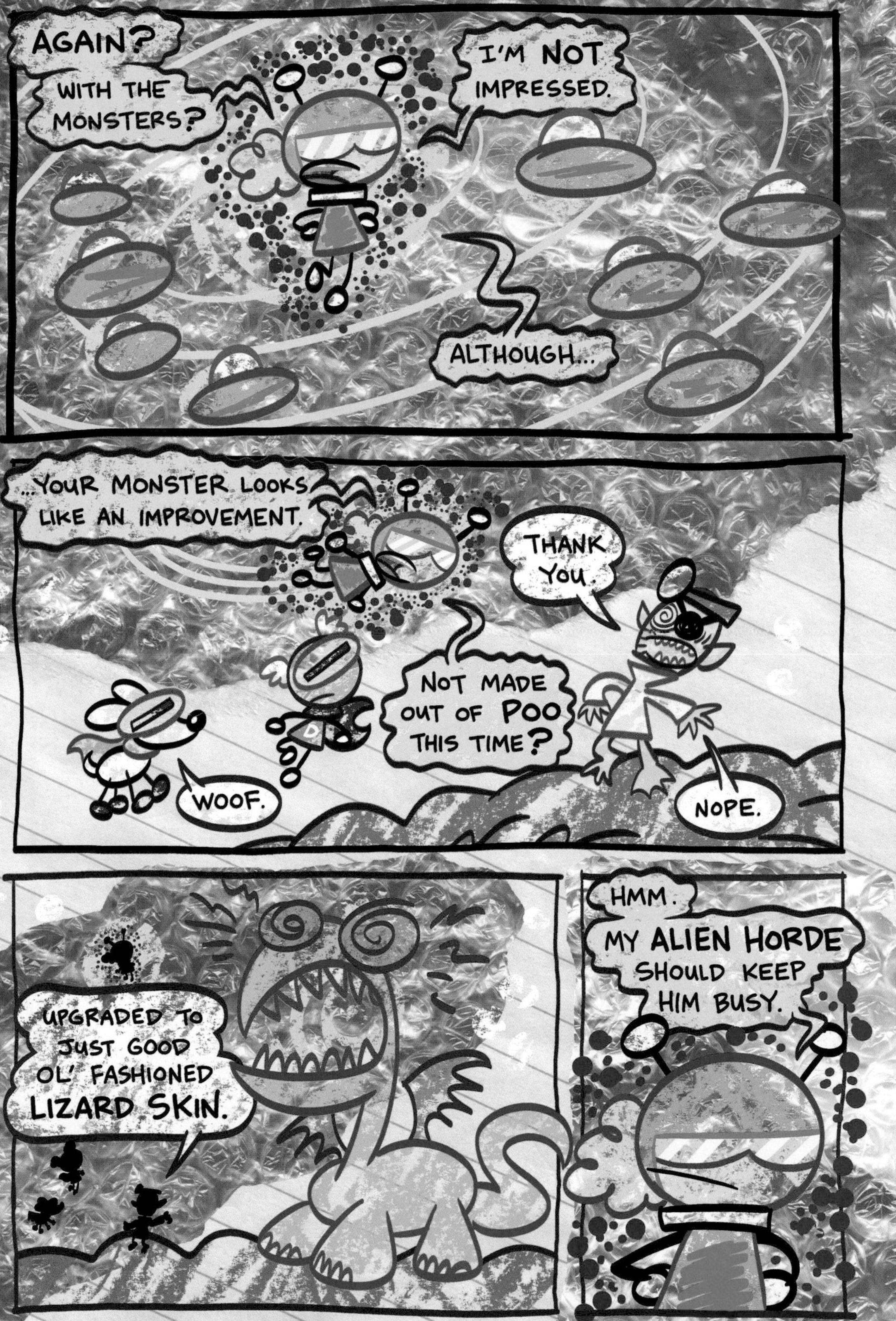
AGAIN?
WITH THE MONSTERS?
I'M NOT IMPRESSED.
ALTHOUGH...
...YOUR MONSTER LOOKS LIKE AN IMPROVEMENT.
THANK YOU.
NOT MADE OUT OF POO THIS TIME?
WOOF.
NOPE.
UPGRADED TO JUST GOOD OL' FASHIONED LIZARD SKIN.
HMM.
MY ALIEN HORDE SHOULD KEEP HIM BUSY.

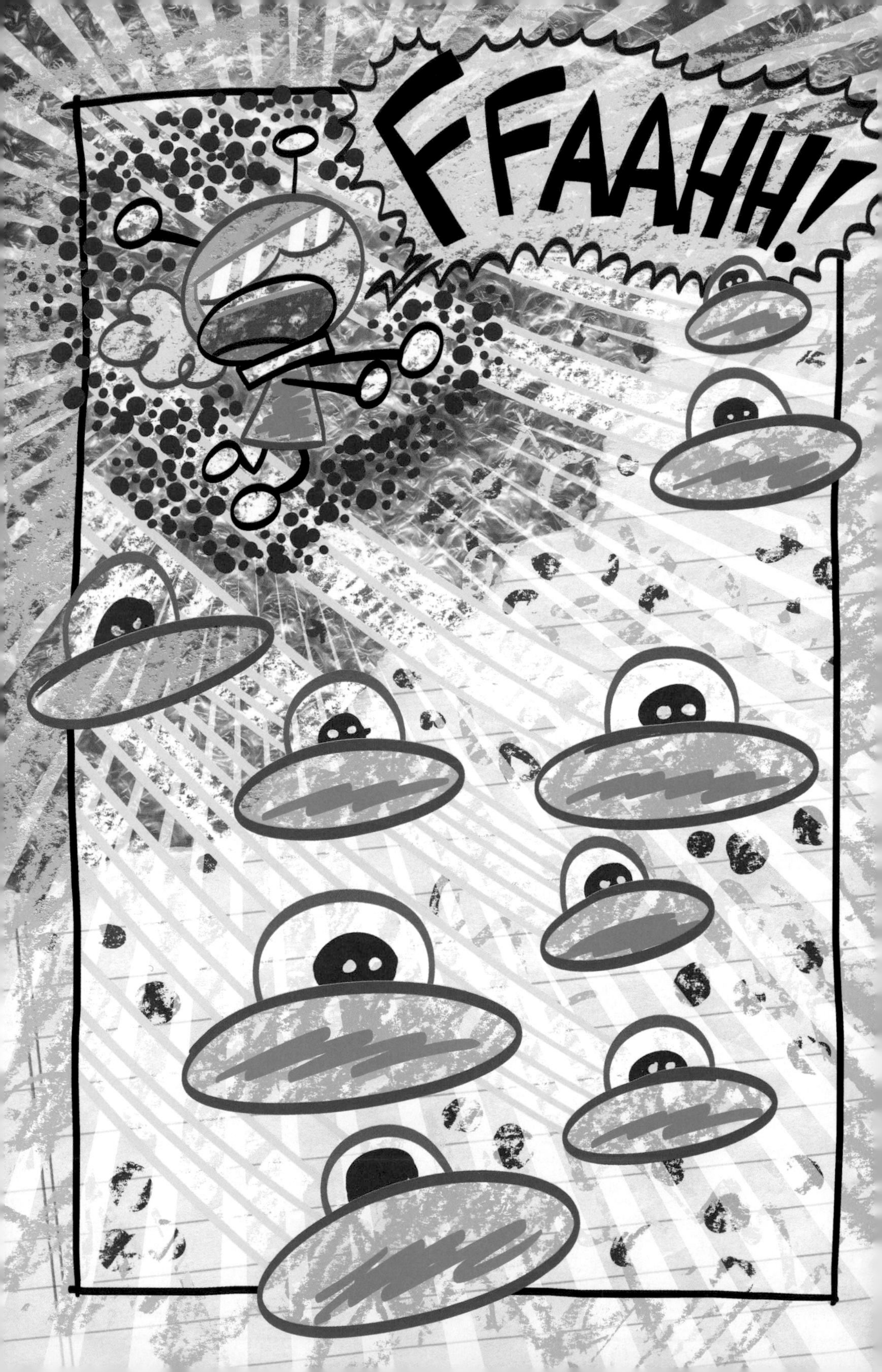
FFAAHH!!

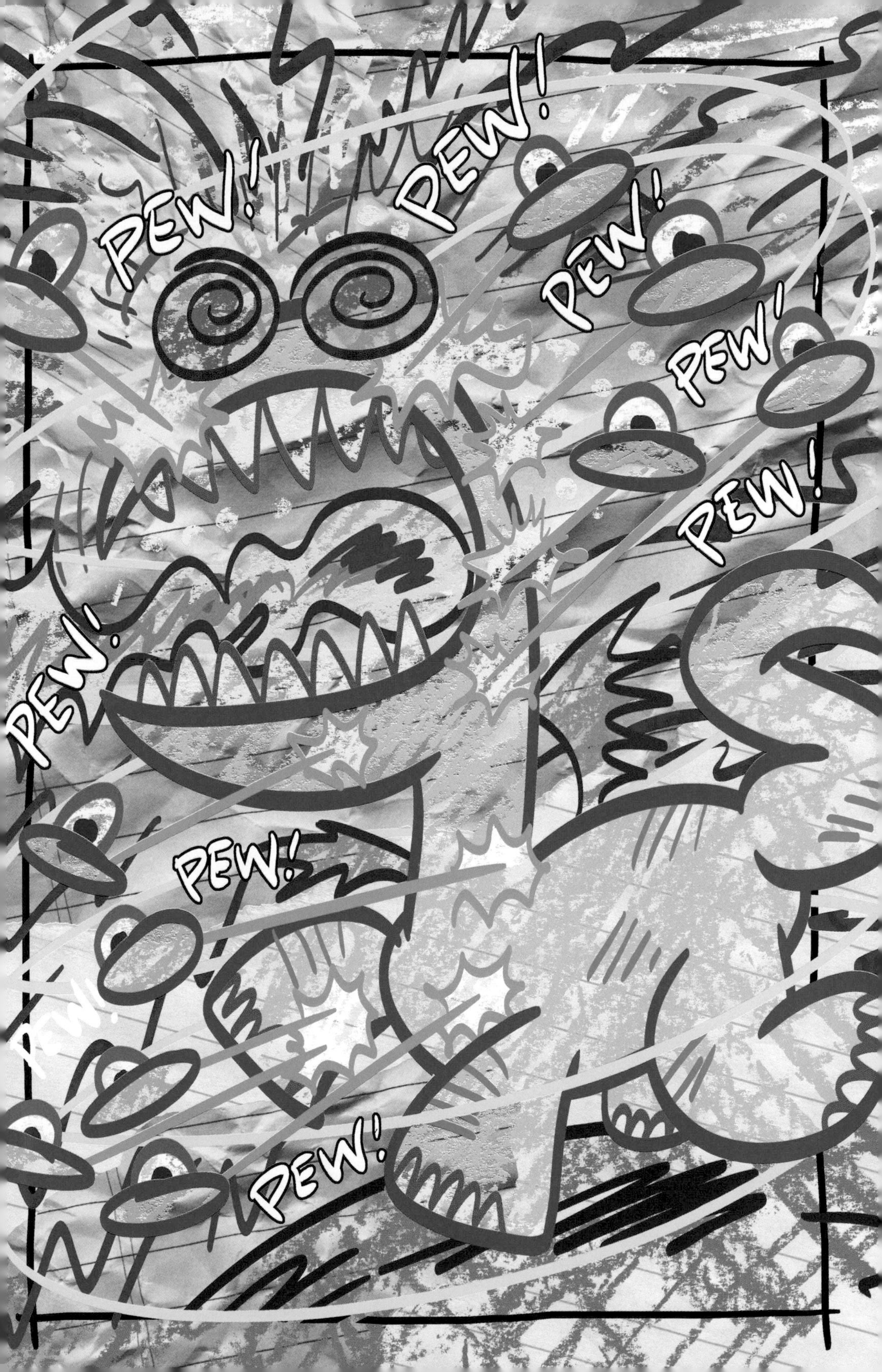
PEW!
PEW!
PEW!
PEW!
PEW!
PEW!
PEW!
PEW!
PEW!

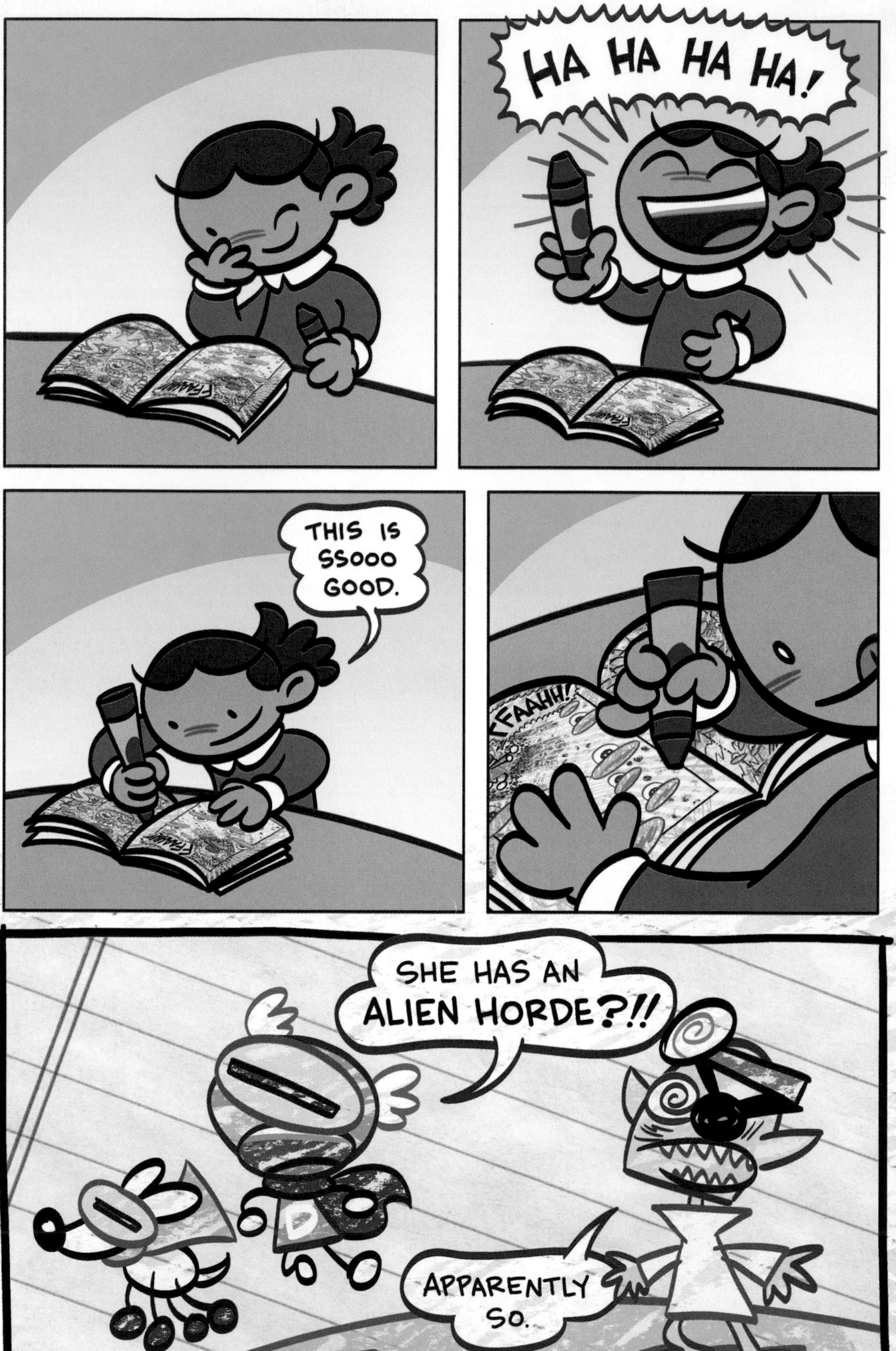
FAAHH!
HA HA HA HA!
THIS IS SSOOO GOOD.
FAAHH!
SHE HAS AN ALIEN HORDE?!!
APPARENTLY SO.

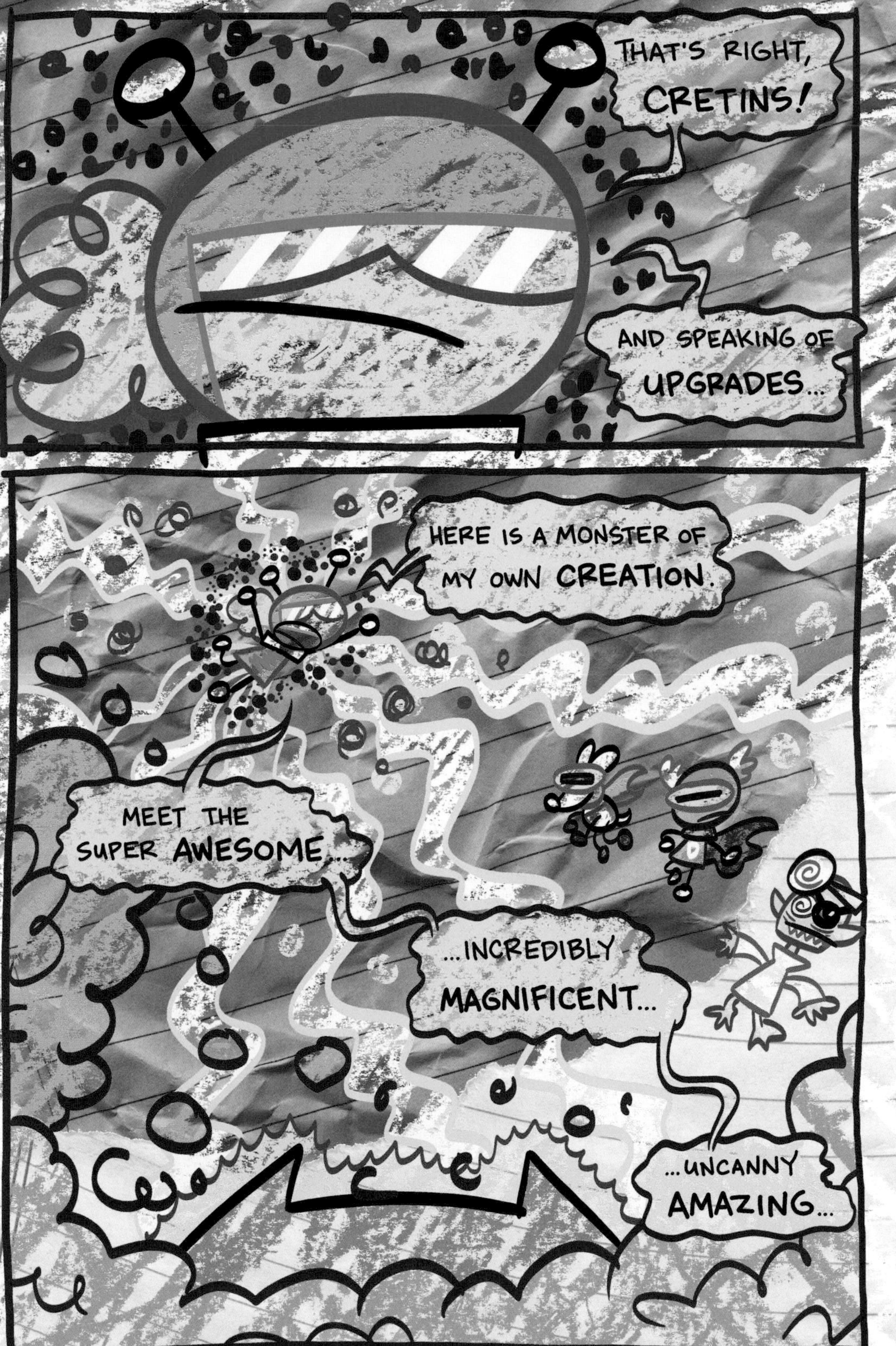
THAT'S RIGHT, CRETINS!
AND SPEAKING OF UPGRADES...
HERE IS A MONSTER OF MY OWN CREATION.
MEET THE SUPER AWESOME...
...INCREDIBLY MAGNIFICENT...
...UNCANNY AMAZING...

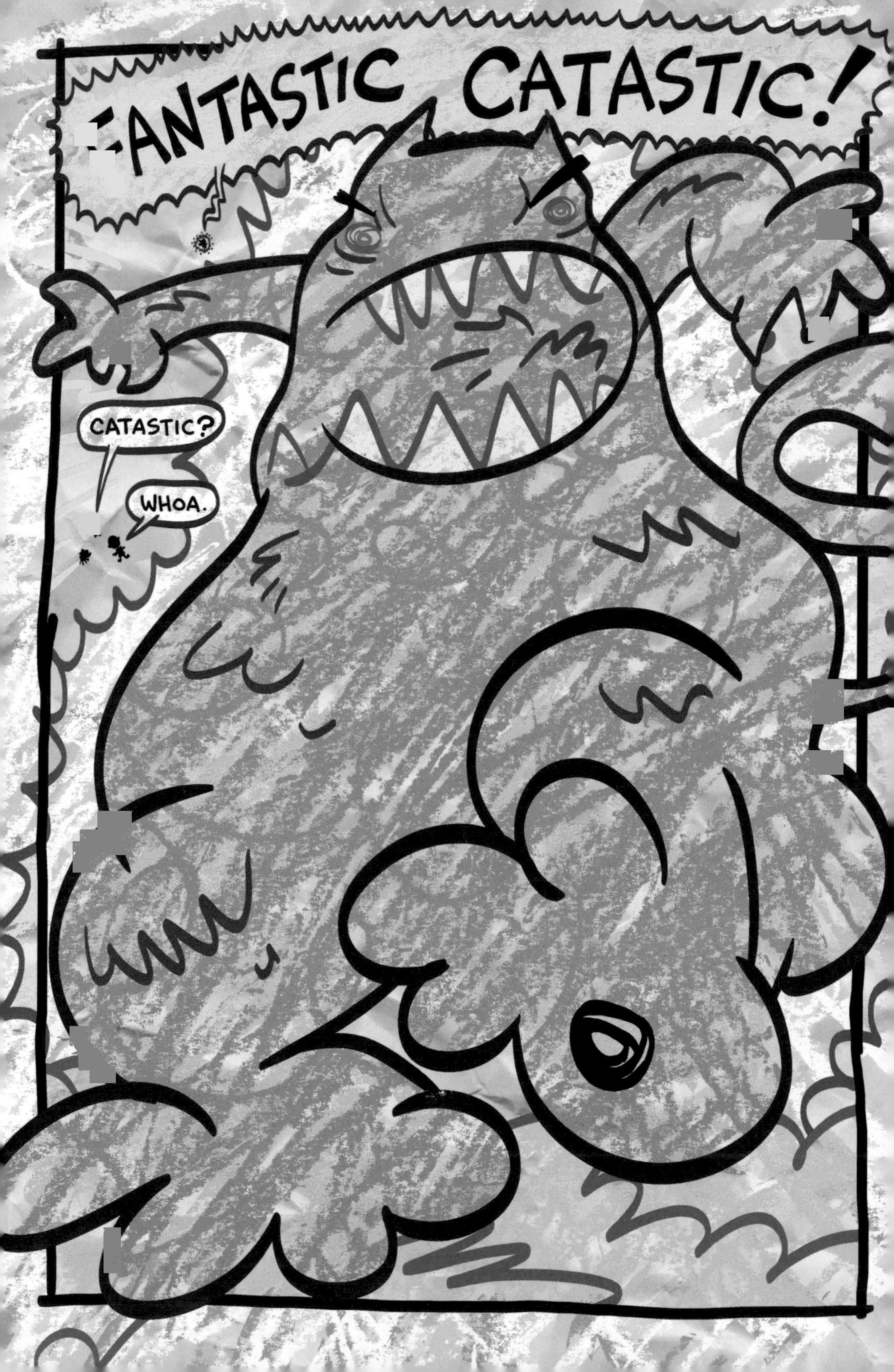
FANTASTIC CATASTIC!
CATASTIC?
WHOA.

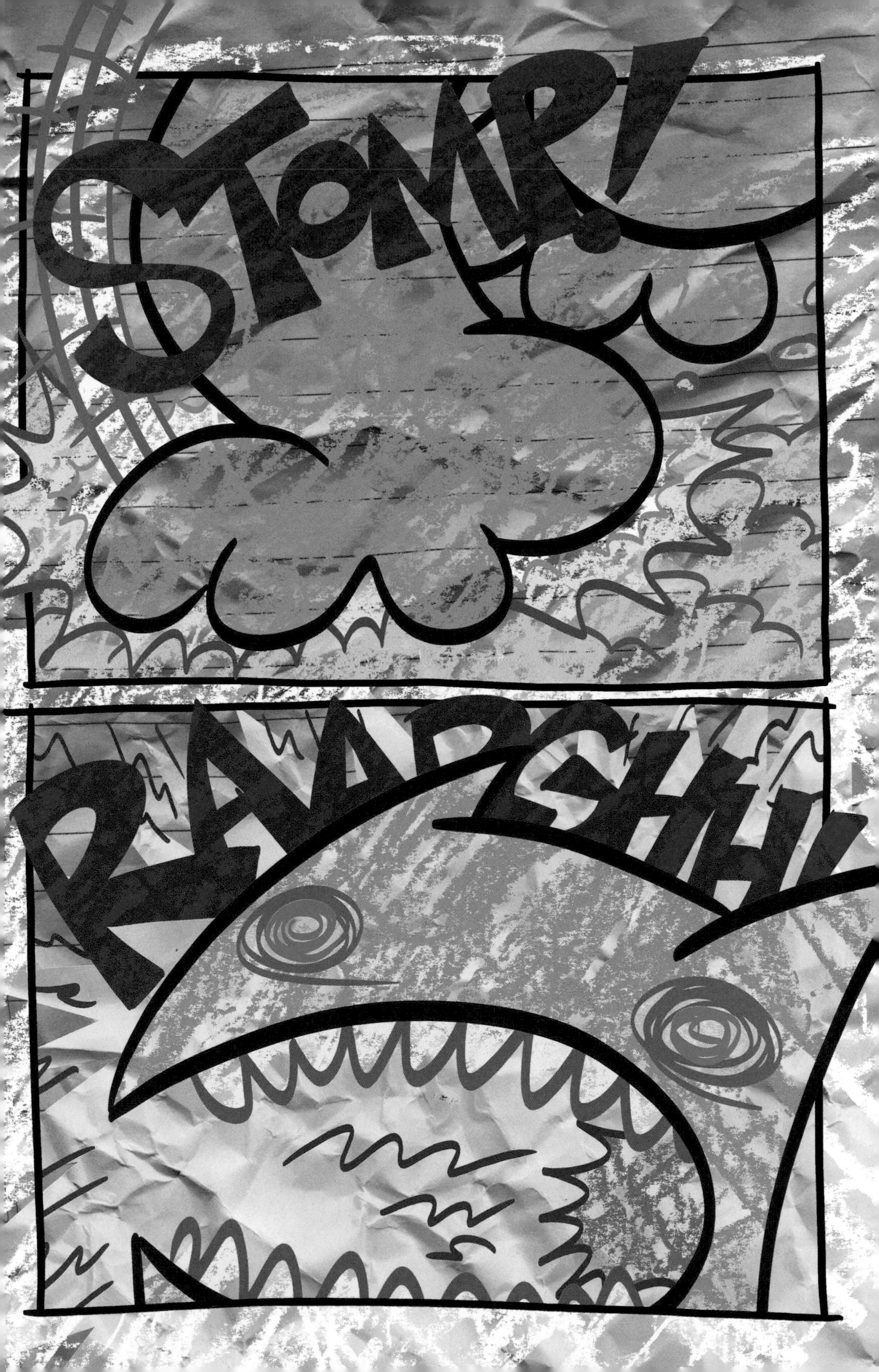

STOMP!
RAAARGH!

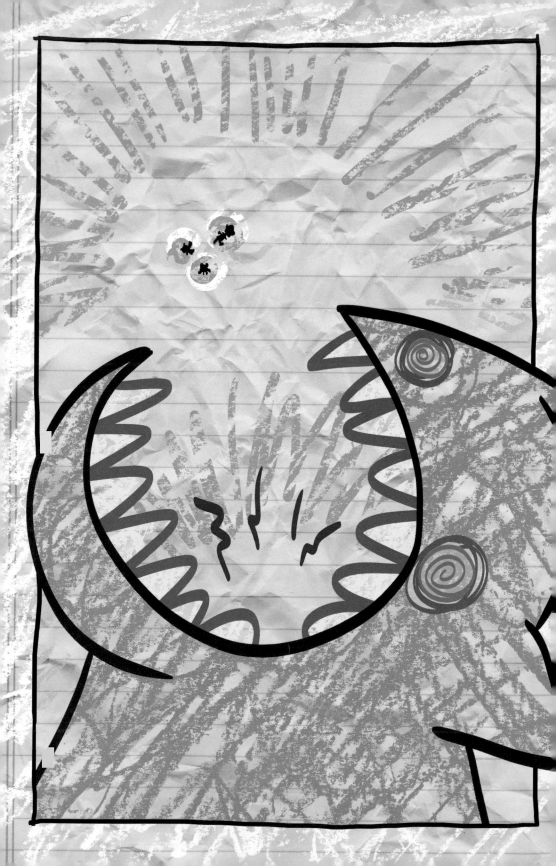

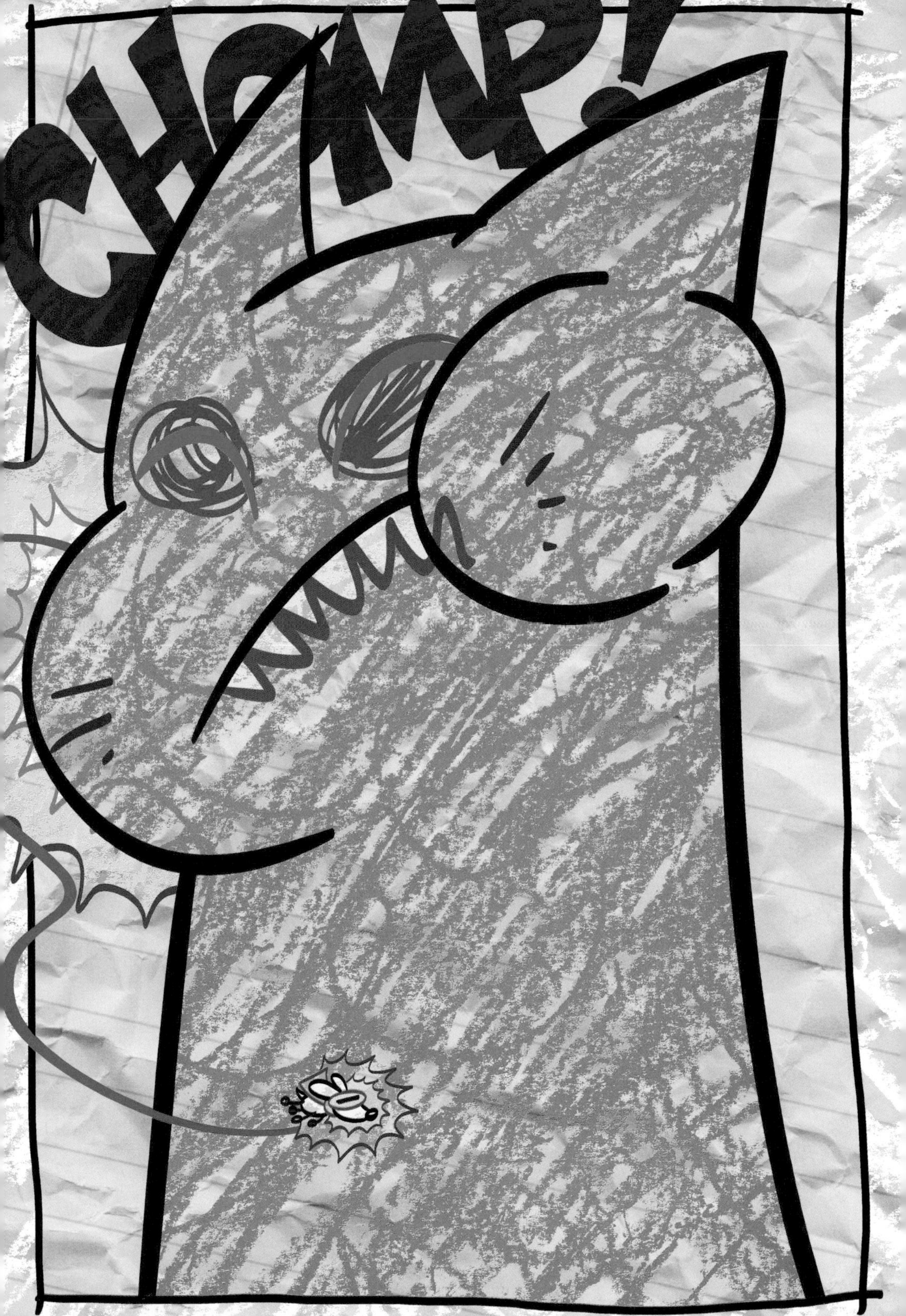
CHOMP!

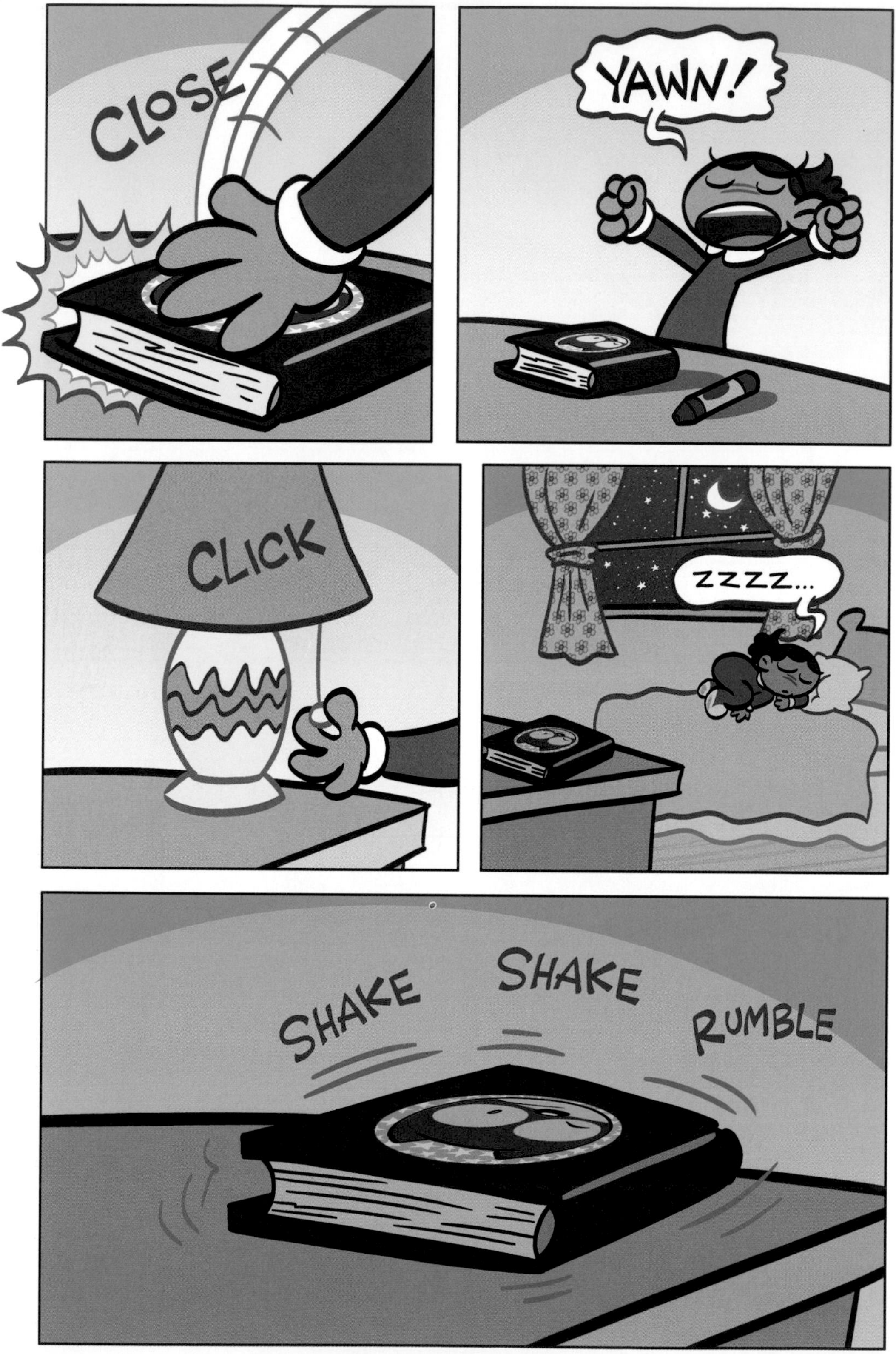
CLOSE
YAWN!
CLICK
ZZZZ...
SHAKE
SHAKE
RUMBLE

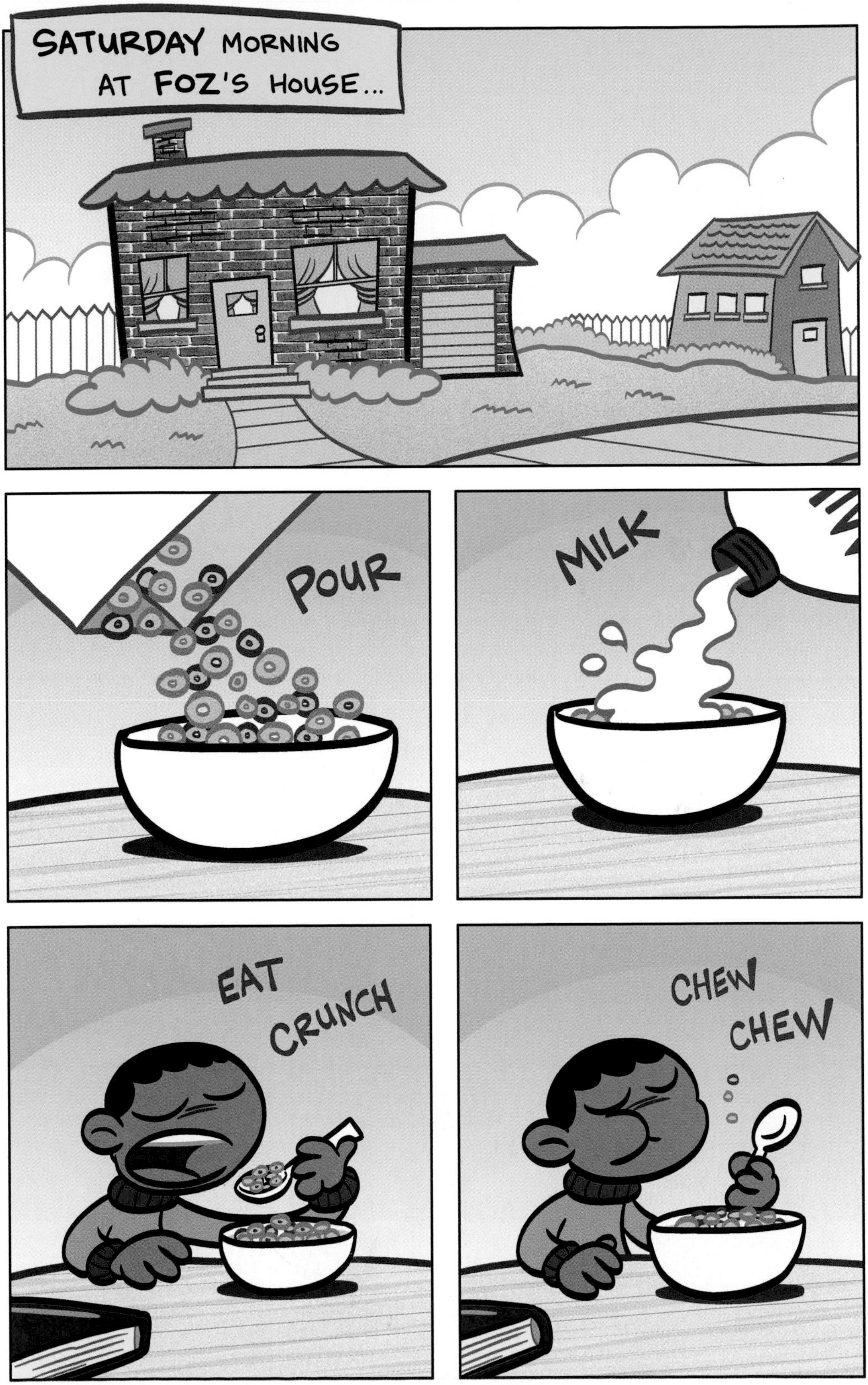
SATURDAY MORNING AT FOZ'S HOUSE...
POUR
MILK
EAT
CRUNCH
CHEW
CHEW

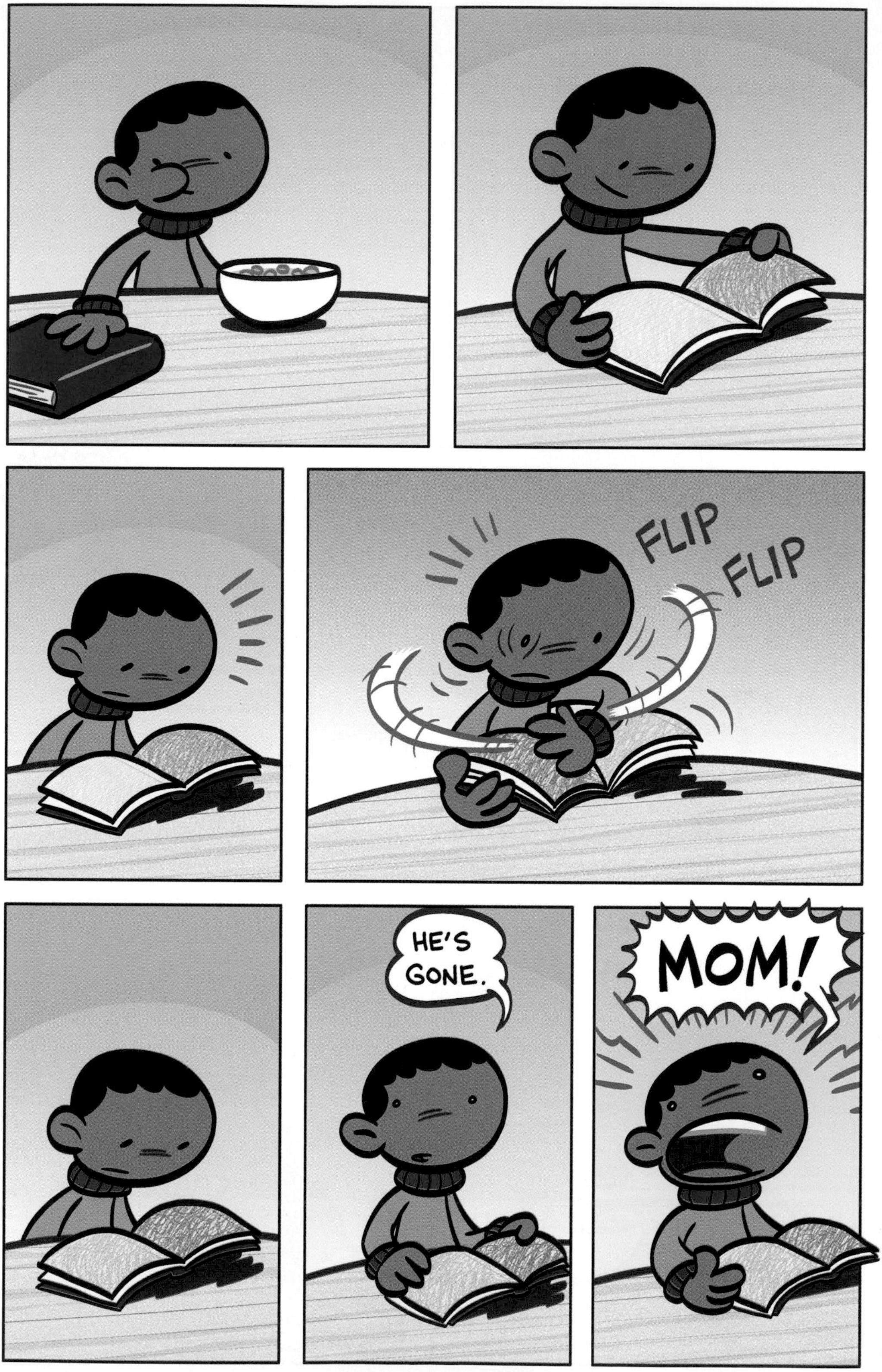
FLIP
FLIP
HE'S GONE.
MOM!

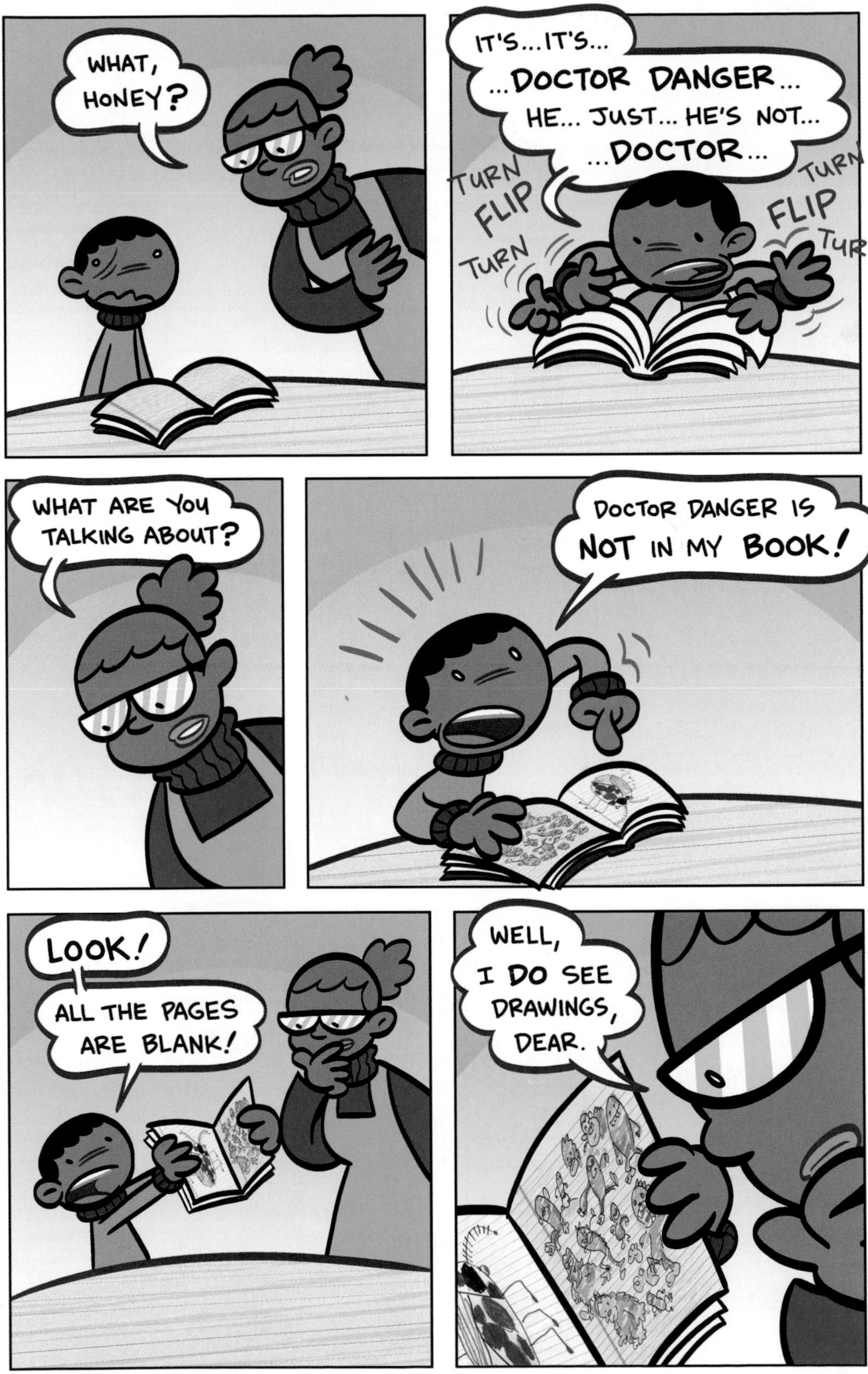
WHAT, HONEY?
IT'S... IT'S...
...DOCTOR DANGER... HE... JUST... HE'S NOT... ...DOCTOR...
TURN
FLIP
TURN
TURN
FLIP
TURN
WHAT ARE YOU TALKING ABOUT?
DOCTOR DANGER IS NOT IN MY BOOK!
LOOK!
ALL THE PAGES ARE BLANK!
WELL, I DO SEE DRAWINGS, DEAR.

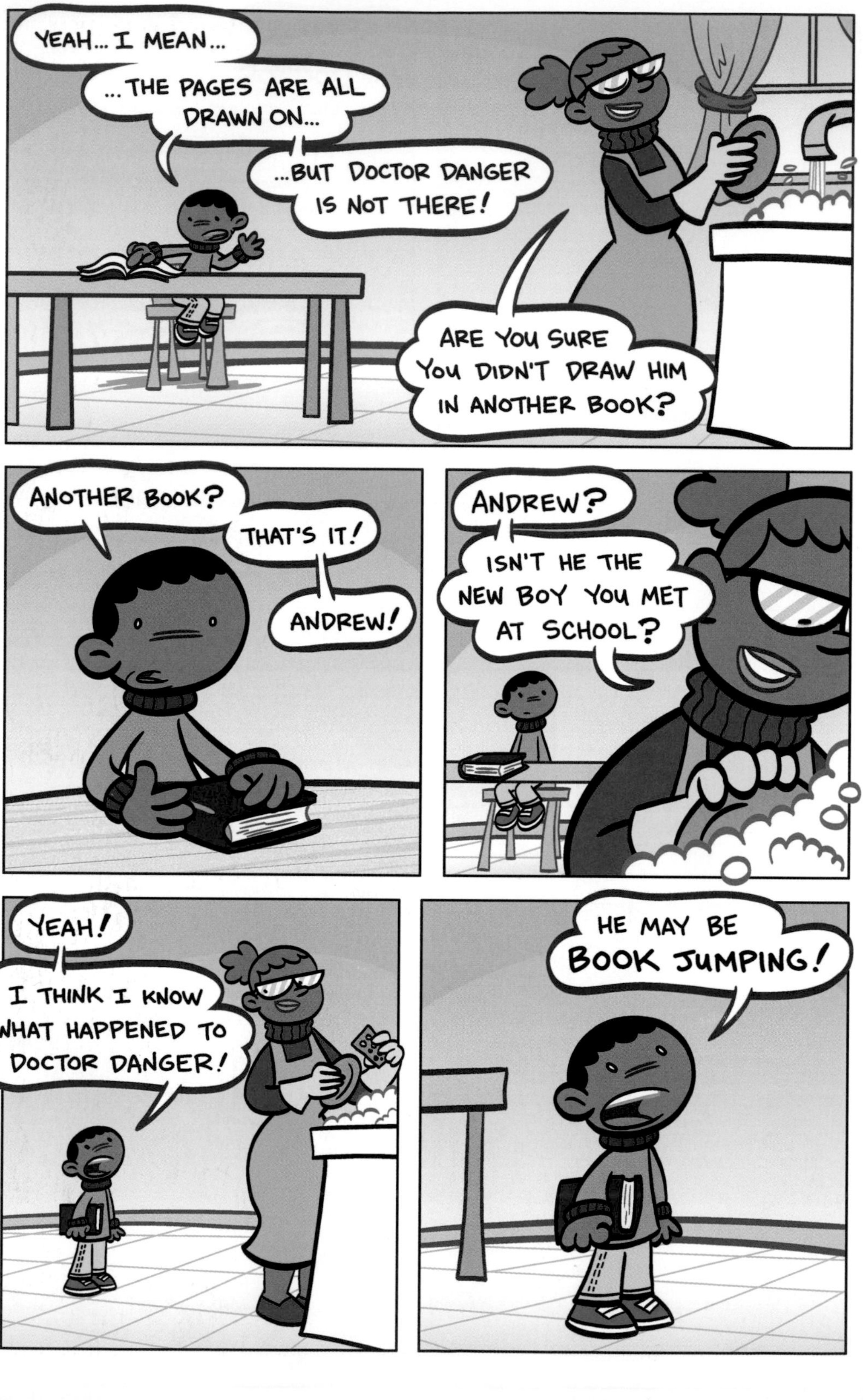
YEAH... I MEAN...
... THE PAGES ARE ALL DRAWN ON...
...BUT DOCTOR DANGER IS NOT THERE!
ARE YOU SURE YOU DIDN'T DRAW HIM IN ANOTHER BOOK?
ANOTHER BOOK?
THAT'S IT!
ANDREW!
ANDREW?
ISN'T HE THE NEW BOY YOU MET AT SCHOOL?
YEAH!
I THINK I KNOW WHAT HAPPENED TO DOCTOR DANGER!
HE MAY BE BOOK JUMPING!

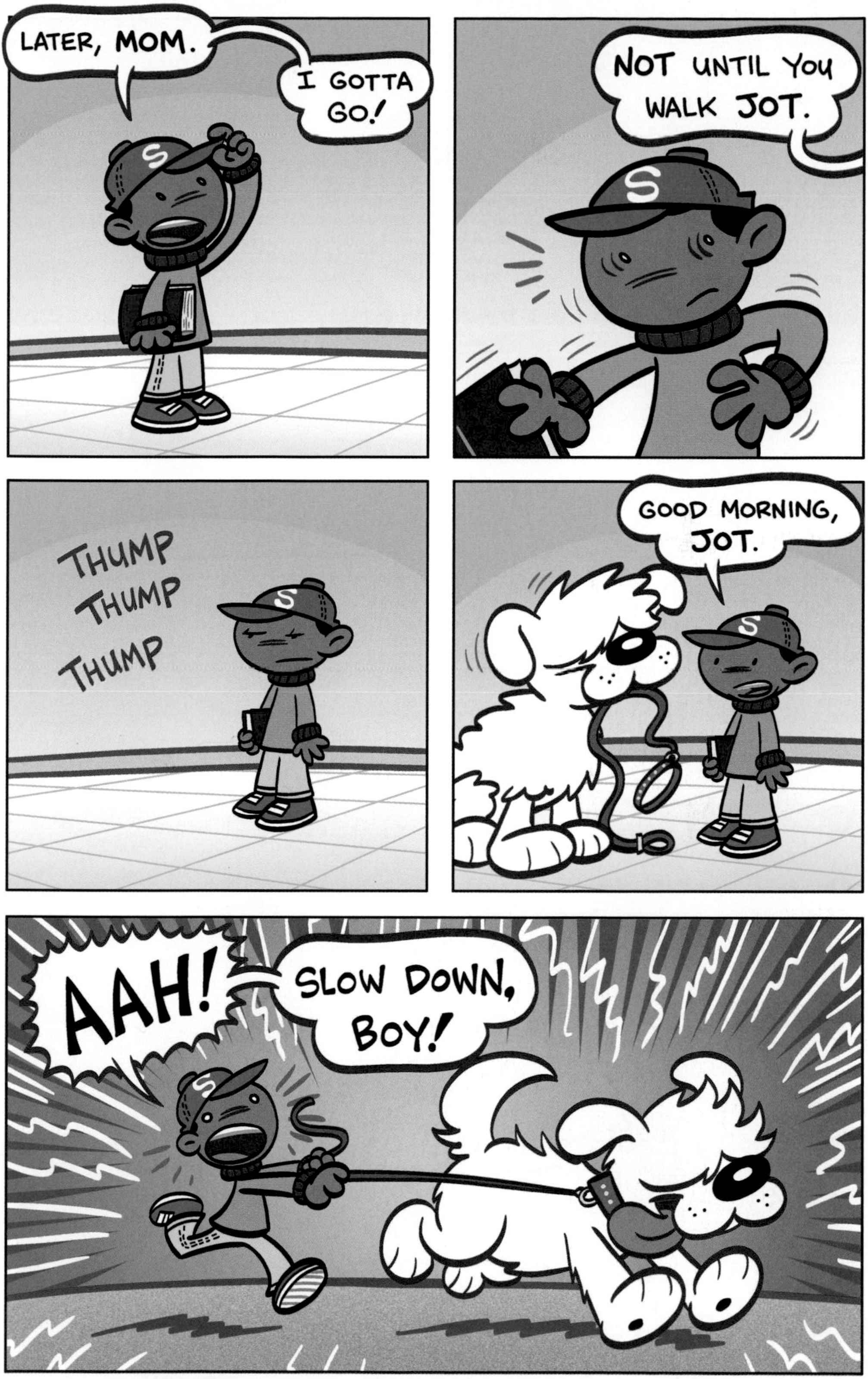
LATER, MOM.
I GOTTA GO!
NOT UNTIL YOU WALK JOT.
THUMP
THUMP
THUMP
GOOD MORNING, JOT.
AAH!
SLOW DOWN, BOY!

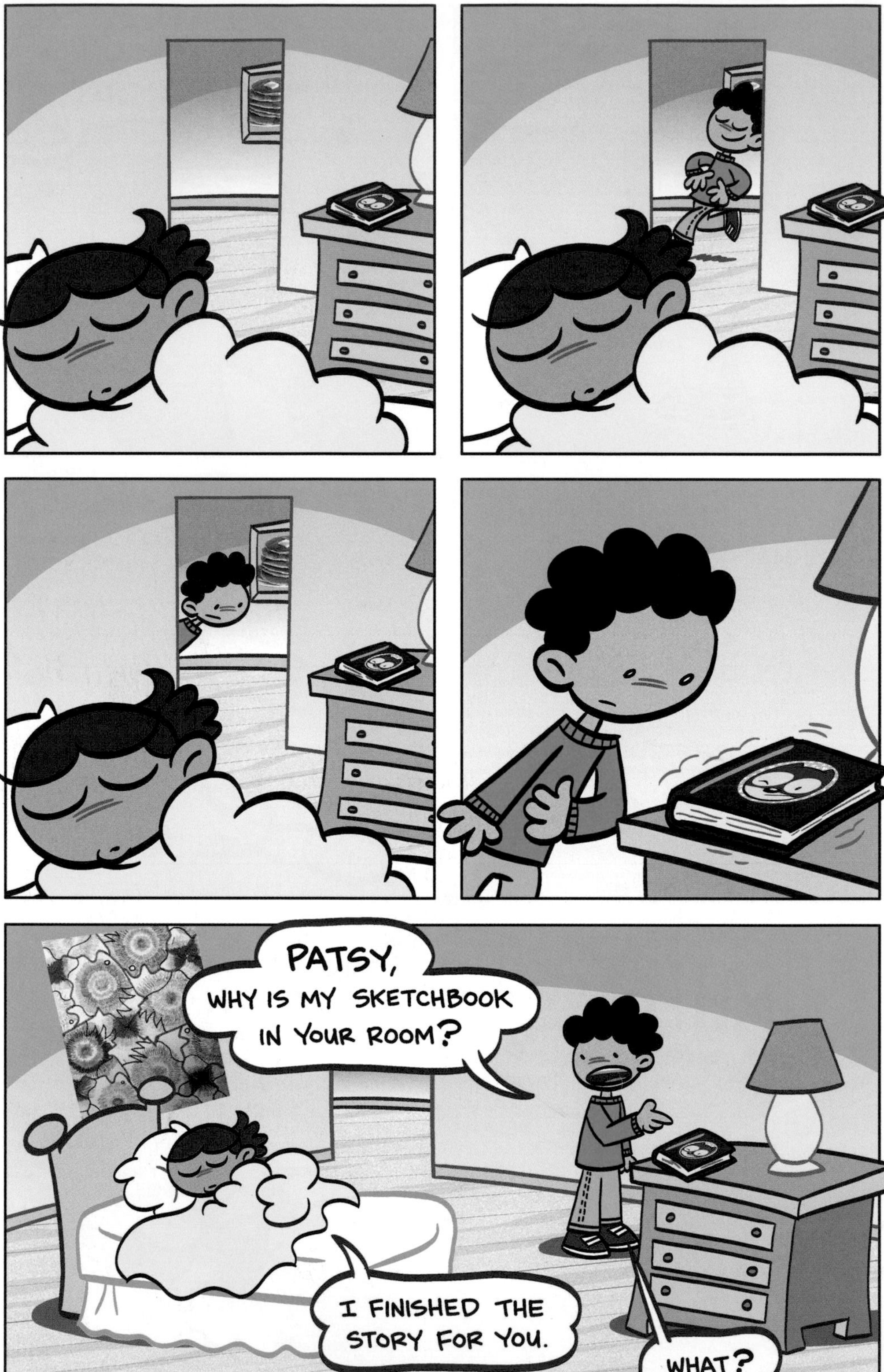
PATSY,
WHY IS MY SKETCHBOOK IN YOUR ROOM?
I FINISHED THE STORY FOR YOU.
WHAT?

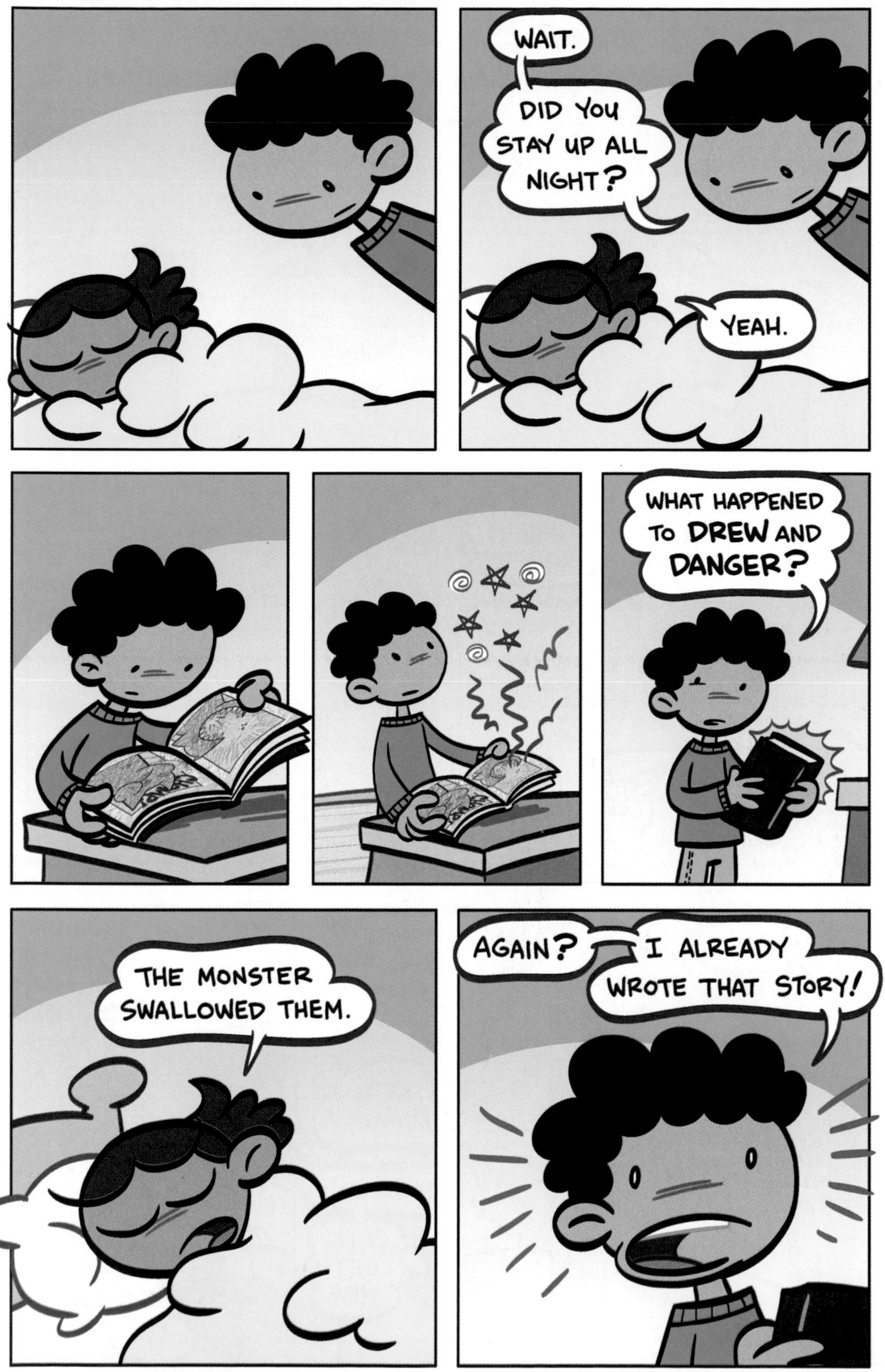
WAIT.
DID YOU STAY UP ALL NIGHT?
YEAH.
WHAT HAPPENED TO DREW AND DANGER?
THE MONSTER SWALLOWED THEM.
AGAIN?
I ALREADY WROTE THAT STORY!

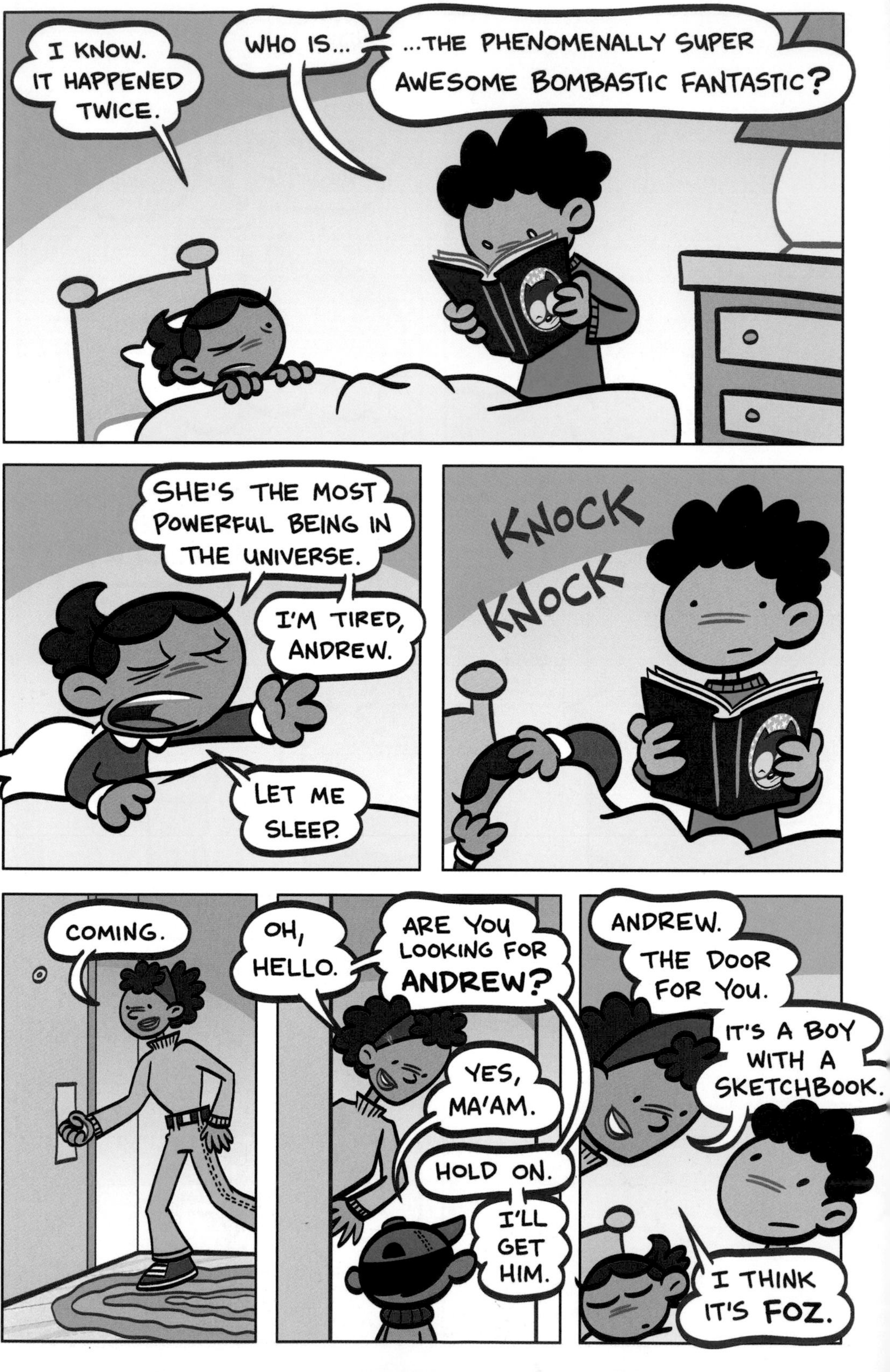
I KNOW. IT HAPPENED TWICE.
WHO IS...
...THE PHENOMENALLY SUPER AWESOME BOMBASTIC FANTASTIC?
SHE'S THE MOST POWERFUL BEING IN THE UNIVERSE.
I'M TIRED, ANDREW.
LET ME SLEEP.
KNOCK
KNOCK
COMING.
OH, HELLO.
ARE YOU LOOKING FOR ANDREW?
YES, MA'AM.
HOLD ON.
I'LL GET HIM.
ANDREW.
THE DOOR FOR YOU.
IT'S A BOY WITH A SKETCHBOOK.
I THINK IT'S FOZ.

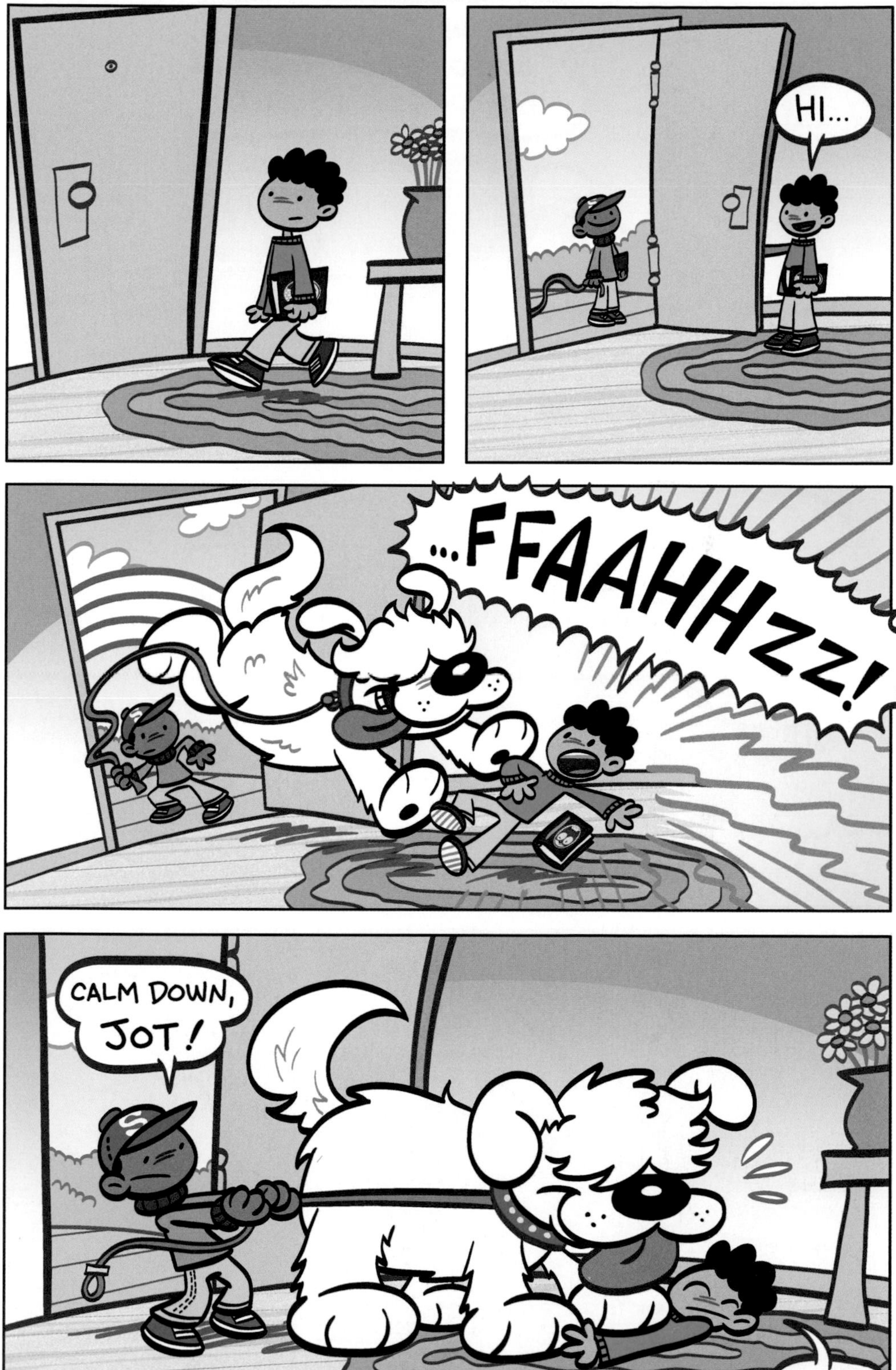
HI...
...FFAAHHzzz!
CALM DOWN, JOT!
WAIT...

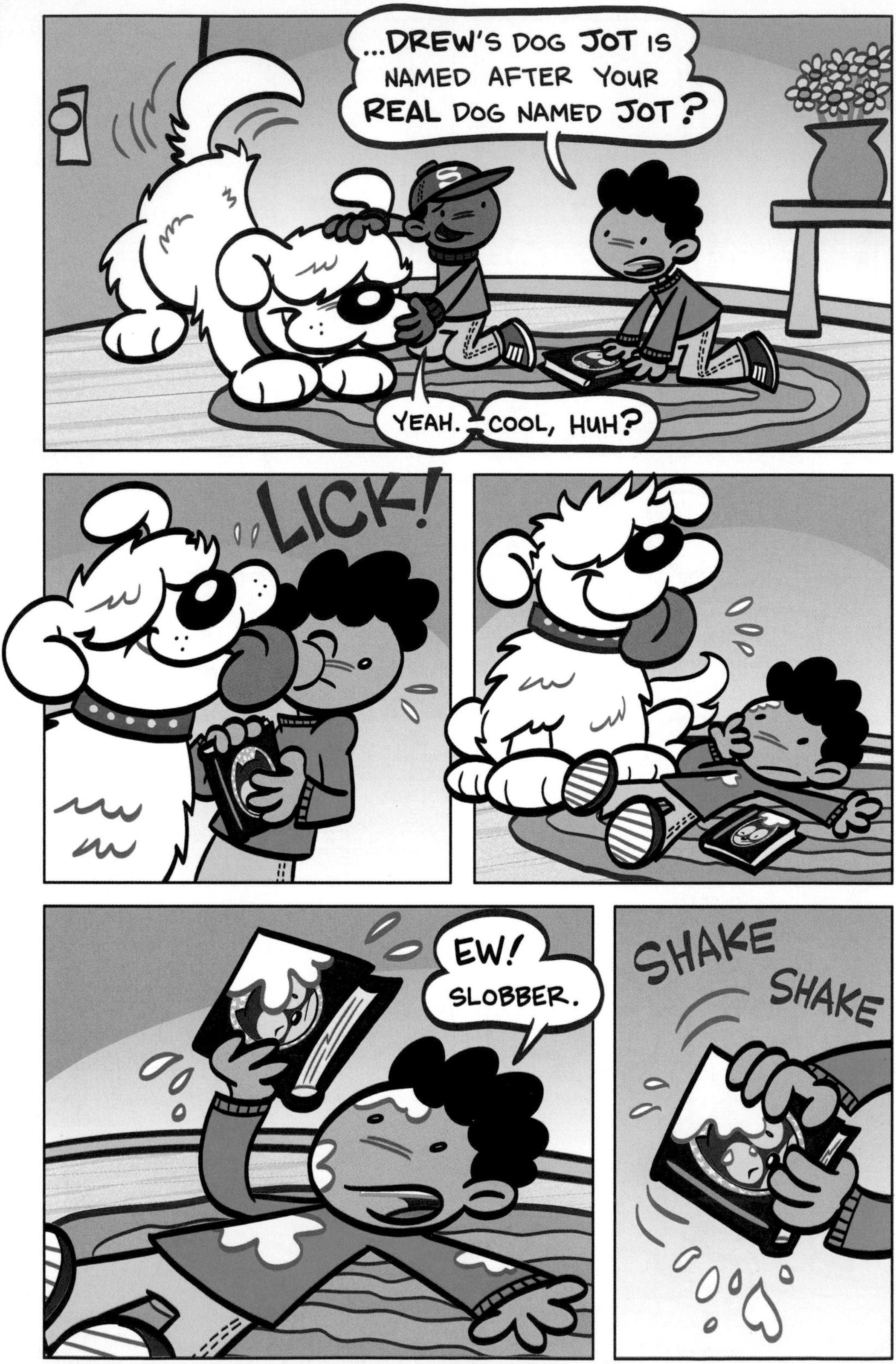
...DREW'S DOG JOT IS NAMED AFTER YOUR REAL DOG NAMED JOT?
YEAH.
COOL, HUH?
LICK!
EW! SLOBBER.
SHAKE
SHAKE

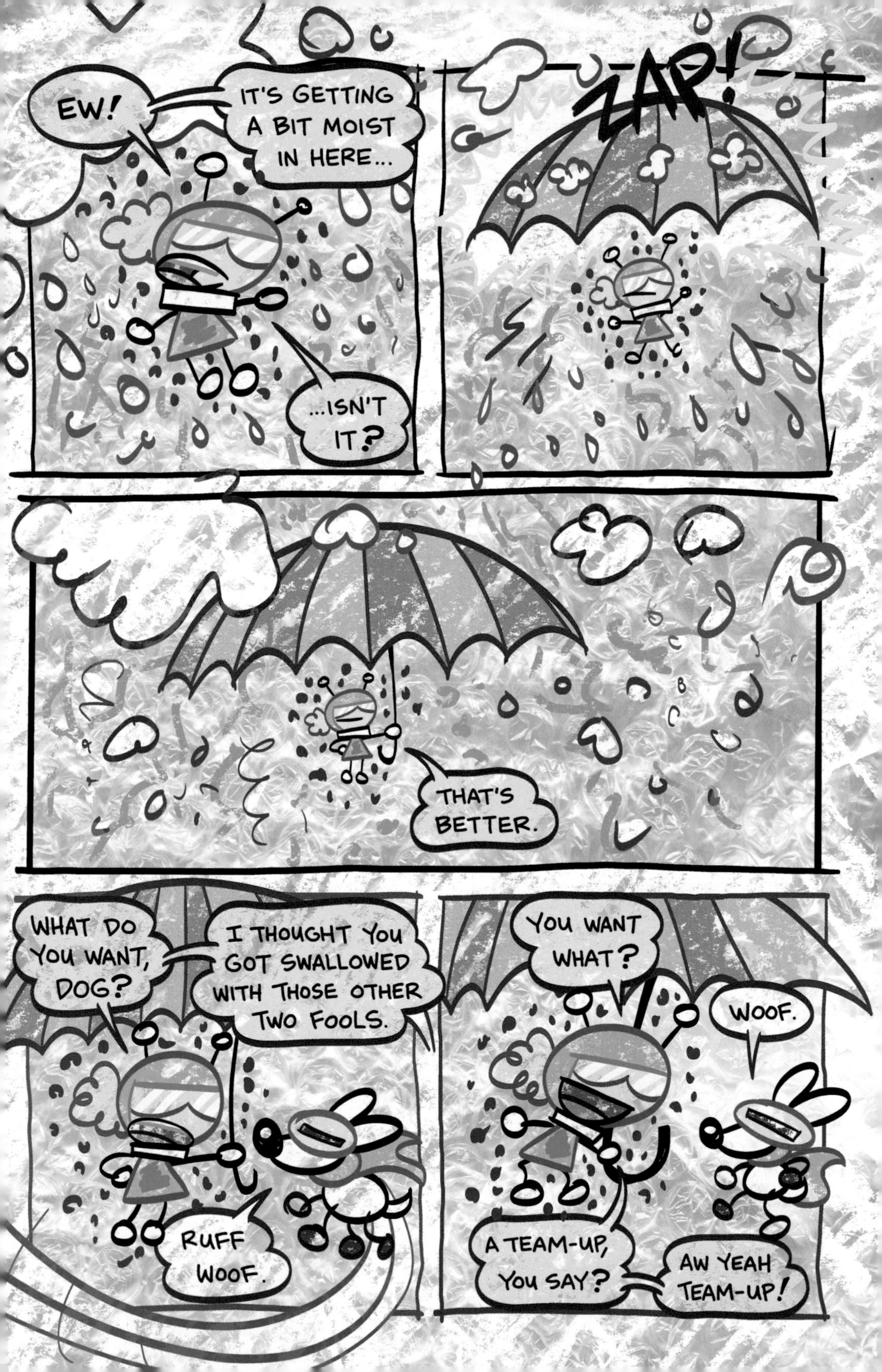
EW!
IT'S GETTING A BIT MOIST IN HERE...
...ISN'T IT?
ZAP!
THAT'S BETTER.
WHAT DO YOU WANT, DOG?
I THOUGHT YOU GOT SWALLOWED WITH THOSE OTHER TWO FOOLS.
RUFF WOOF.
YOU WANT WHAT?
WOOF.
A TEAM-UP, YOU SAY?
AW YEAH TEAM-UP!

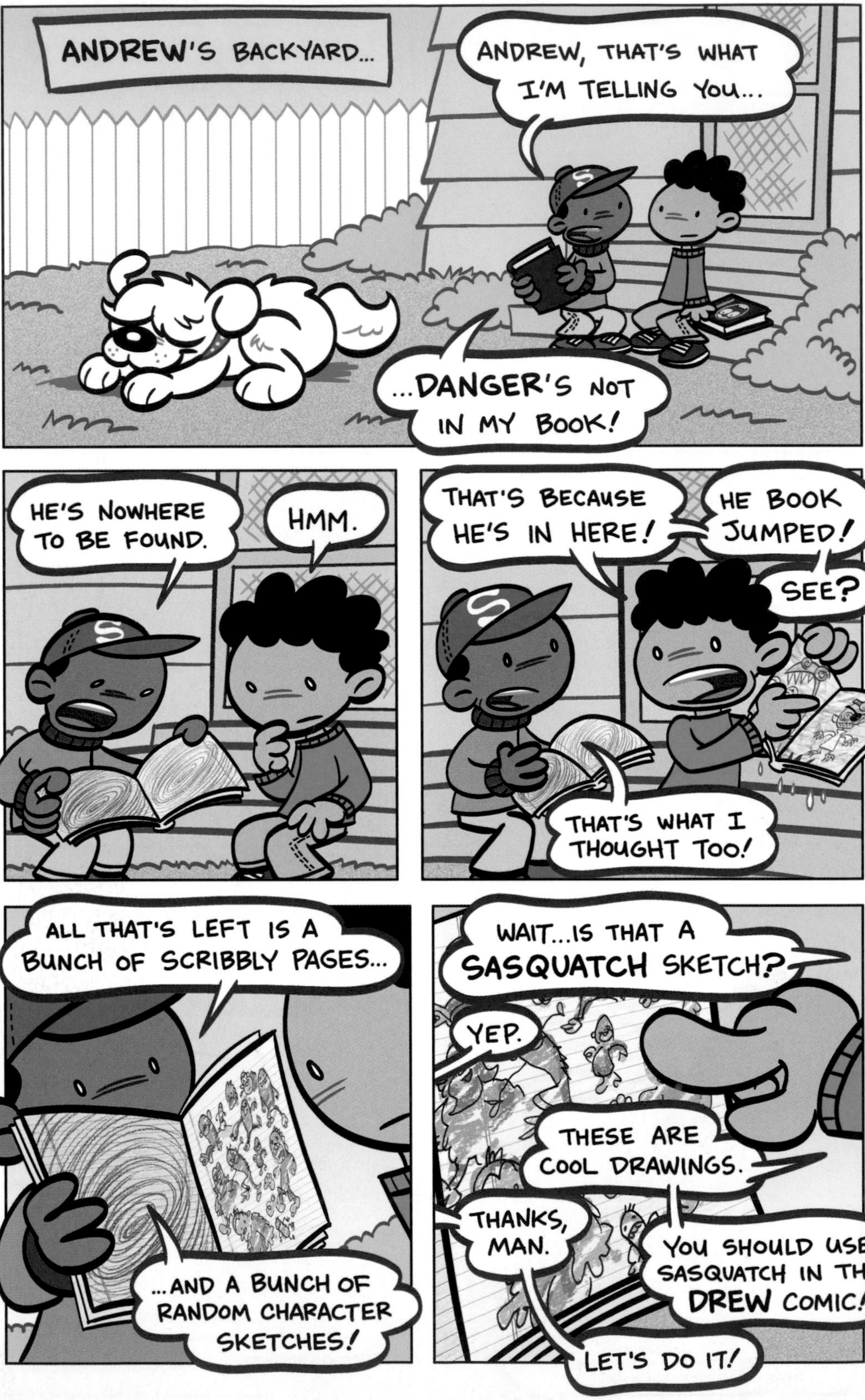
ANDREW'S BACKYARD...
ANDREW, THAT'S WHAT I'M TELLING YOU...
...DANGER'S NOT IN MY BOOK!
HE'S NOWHERE TO BE FOUND.
HMM.
THAT'S BECAUSE HE'S IN HERE!
HE BOOK JUMPED!
SEE?
THAT'S WHAT I THOUGHT TOO!
ALL THAT'S LEFT IS A BUNCH OF SCRIBBLY PAGES...
...AND A BUNCH OF RANDOM CHARACTER SKETCHES!
WAIT...IS THAT A SASQUATCH SKETCH?
YEP.
THESE ARE COOL DRAWINGS.
THANKS, MAN.
YOU SHOULD USE SASQUATCH IN THE DREW COMIC!
LET'S DO IT!

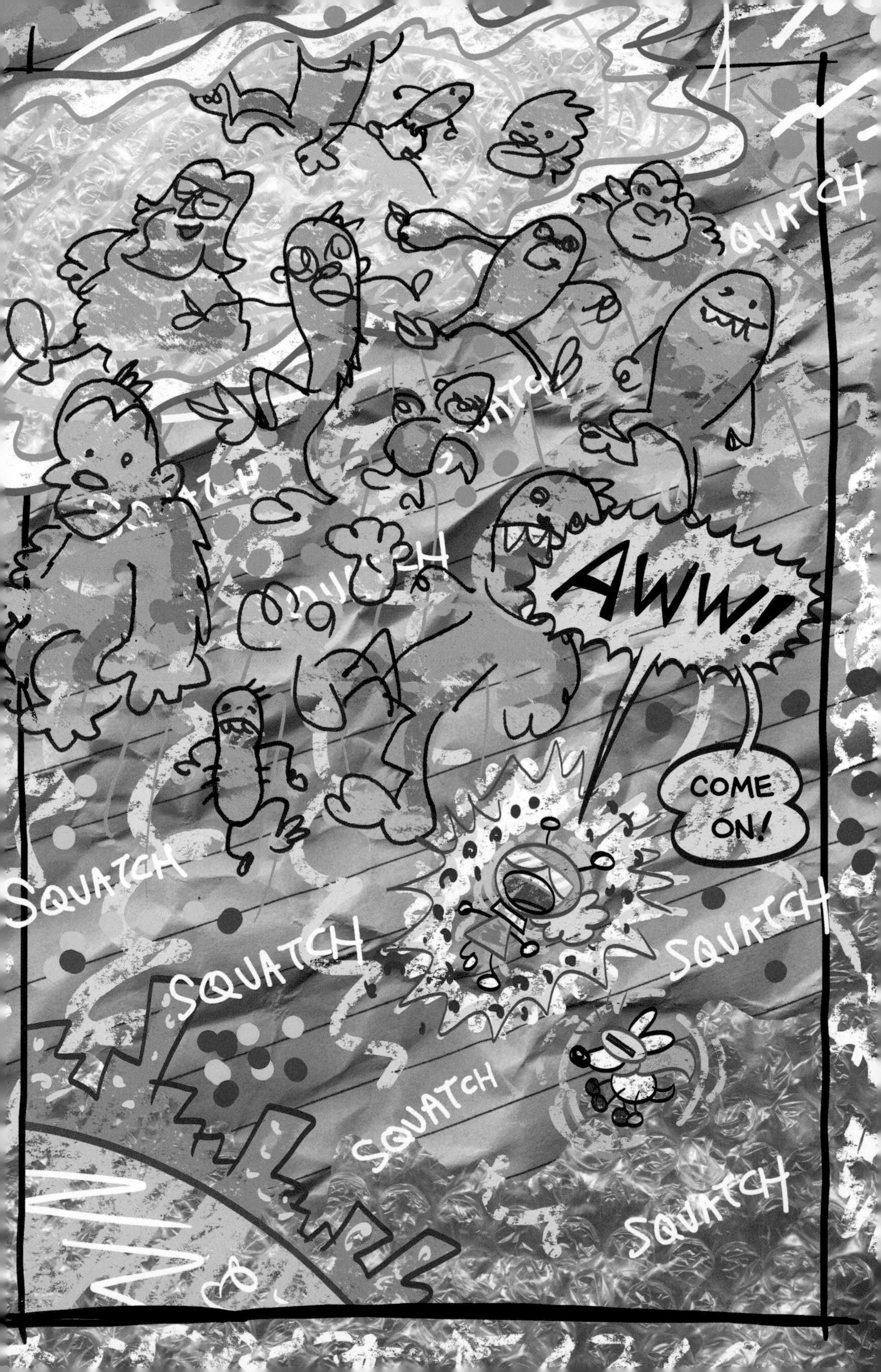
SQUATCH
AWW!
COME ON!
SQUATCH
SQUATCH
SQUATCH
SQUATCH
SQUATCH

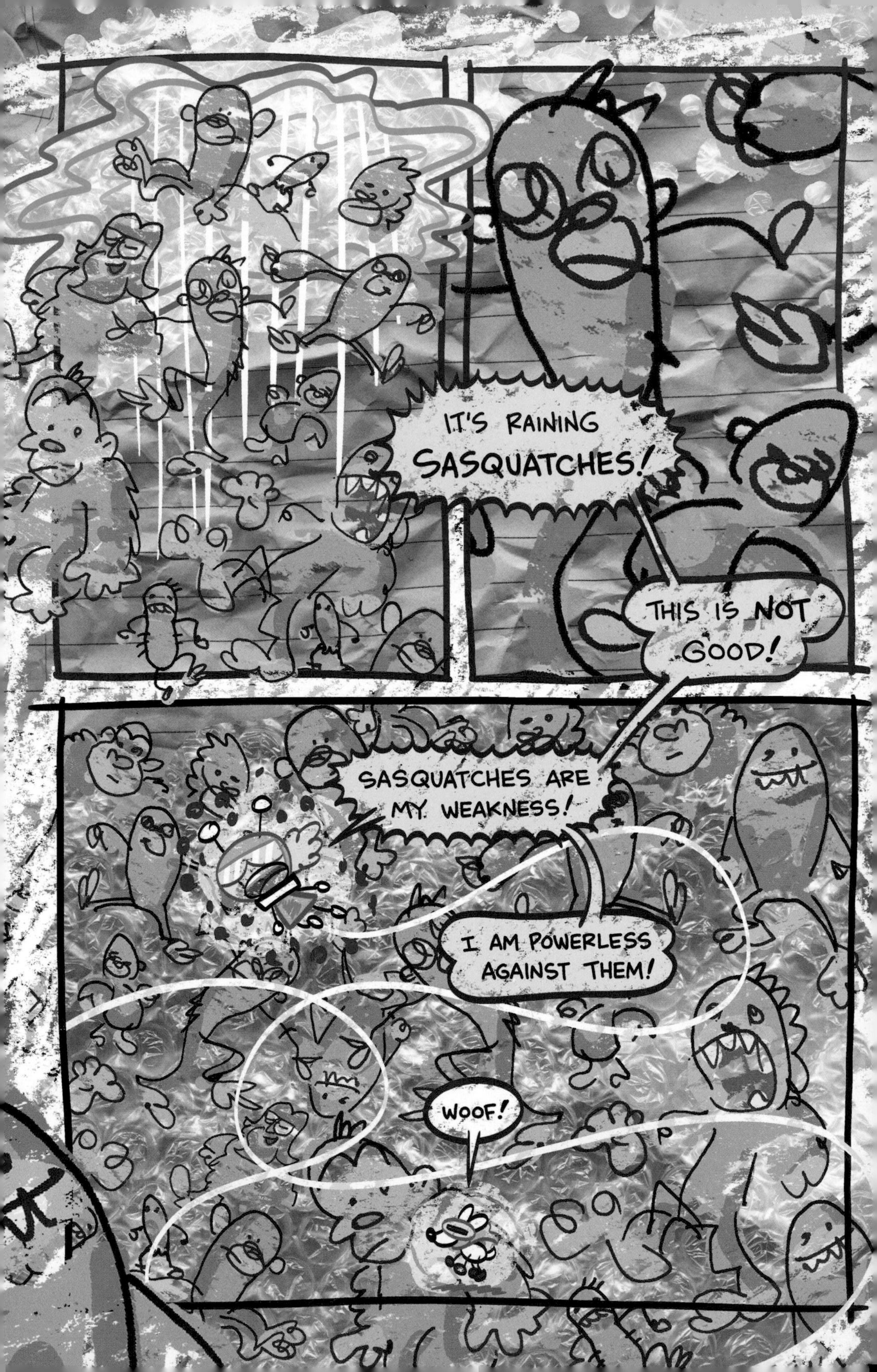
IT'S RAINING SASQUATCHES!
THIS IS NOT GOOD!
SASQUATCHES ARE MY WEAKNESS!
I AM POWERLESS AGAINST THEM!
WOOF!

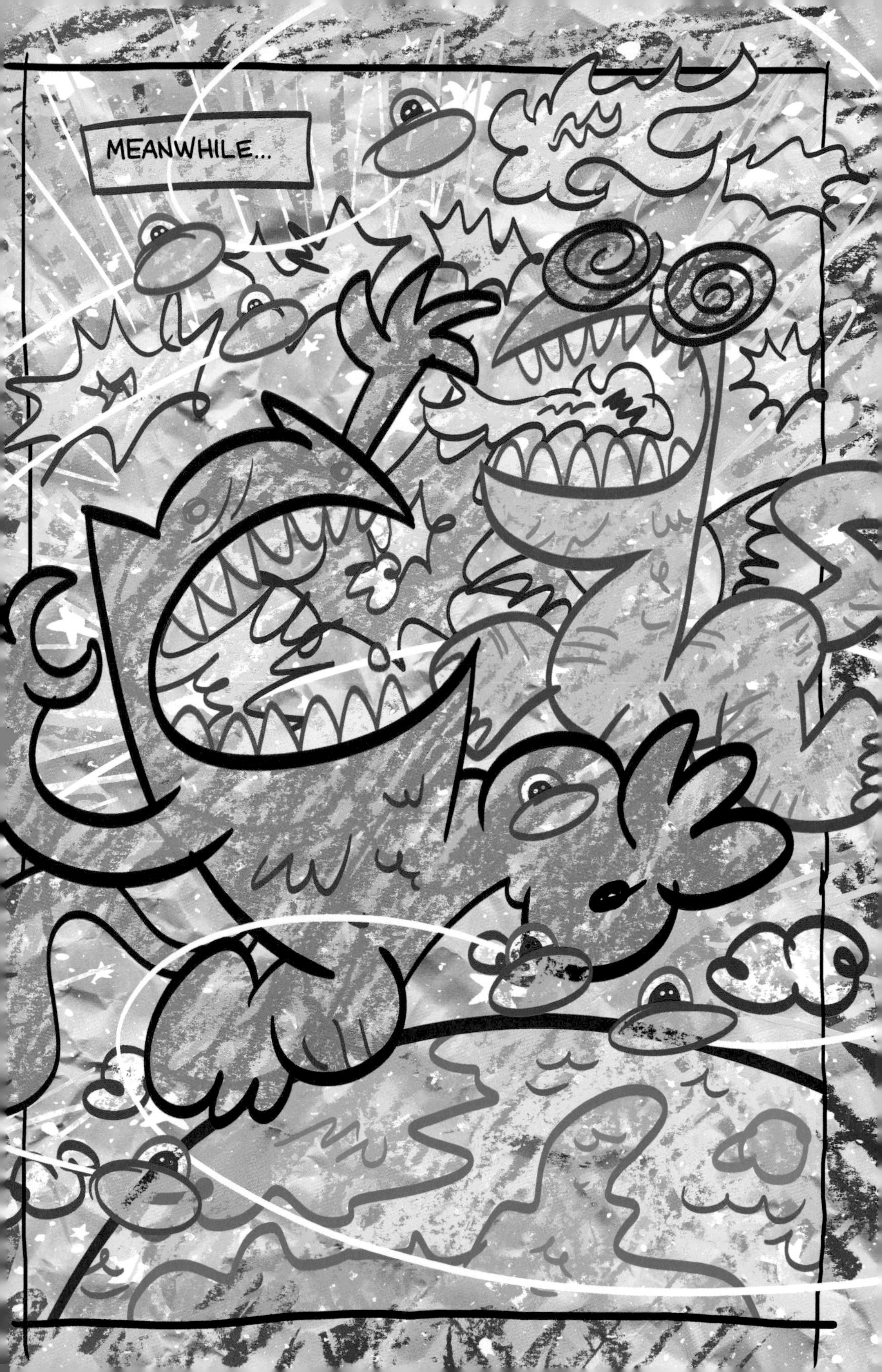
MEANWHILE...

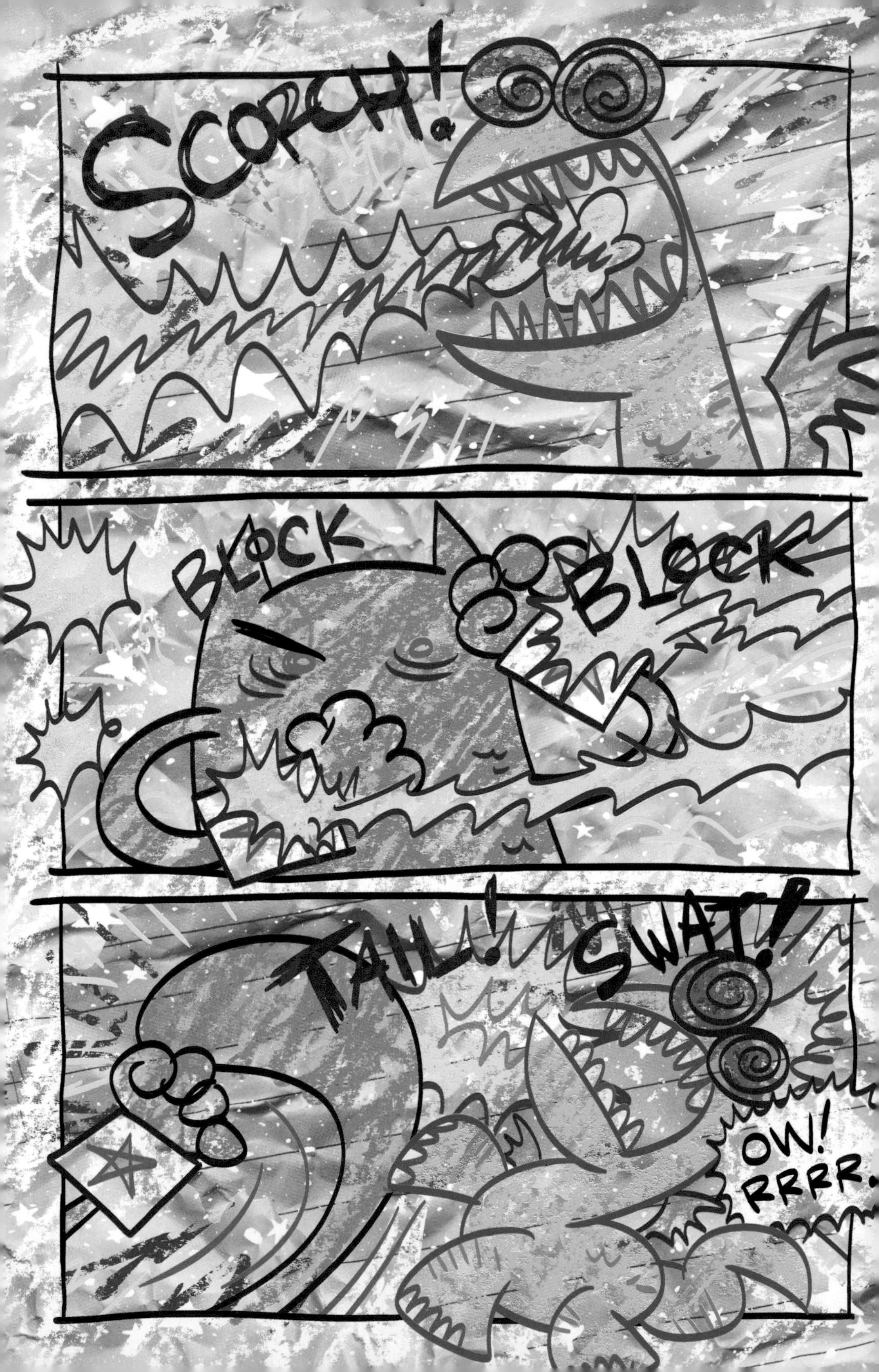
SCORCH!
BLOCK
BLOCK
TAIL!
SWAT!
OW!
RRRR.

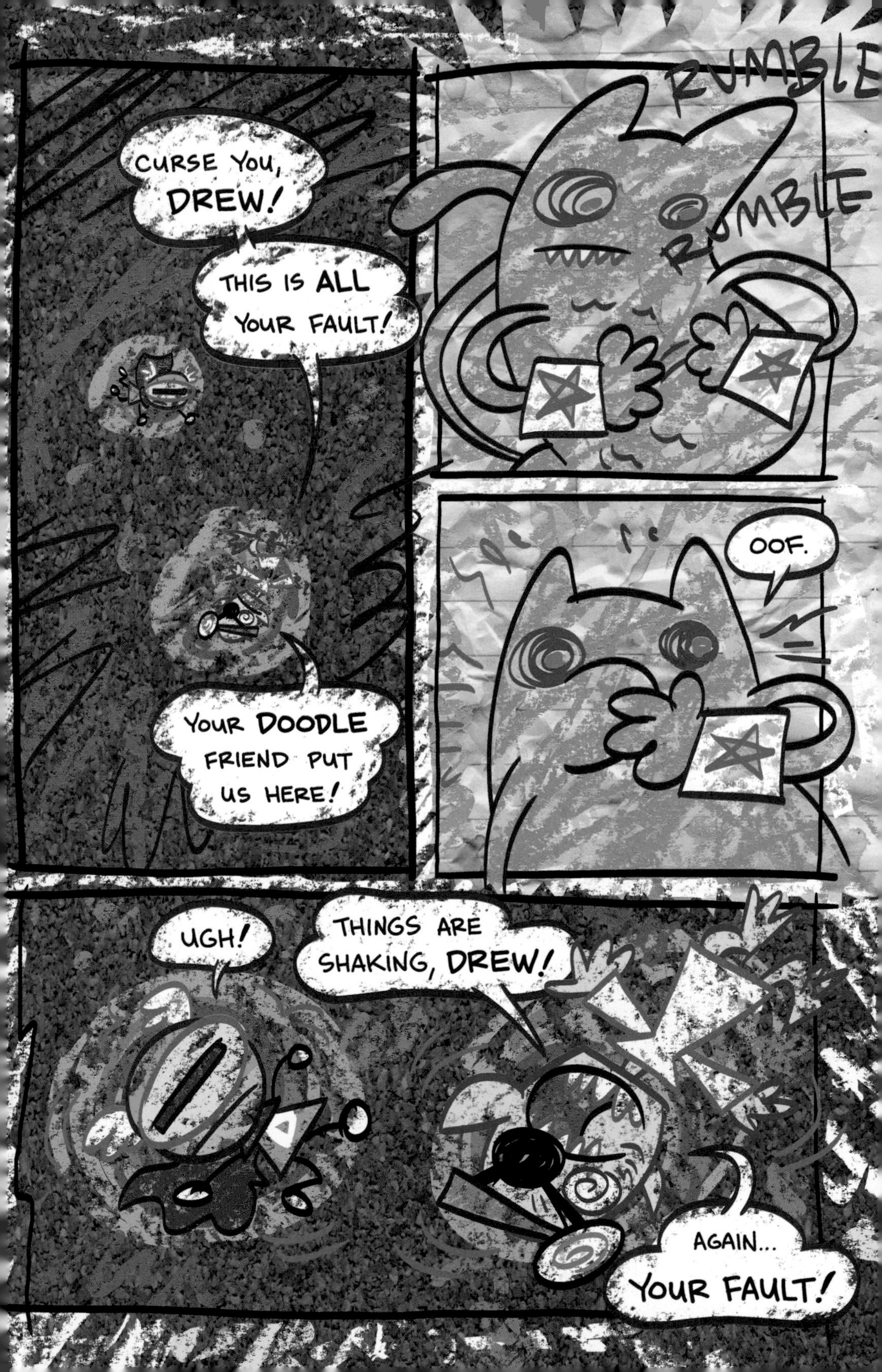
CURSE YOU, DREW!
THIS IS ALL YOUR FAULT!
YOUR DOODLE FRIEND PUT US HERE!
RUMBLE
RUMBLE
OOF.
UGH!
THINGS ARE SHAKING, DREW!
AGAIN... YOUR FAULT!

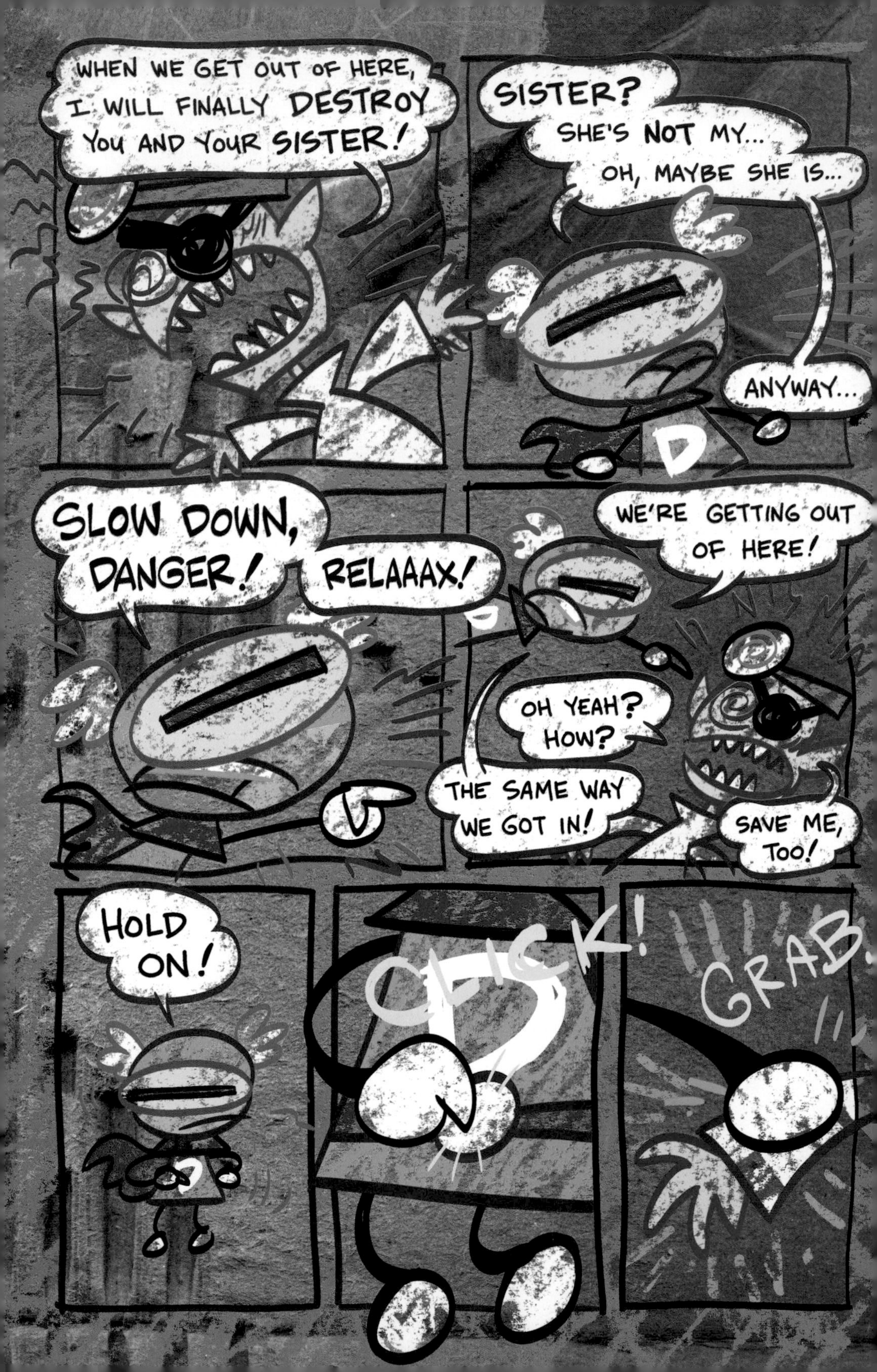
WHEN WE GET OUT OF HERE, I WILL FINALLY DESTROY YOU AND YOUR SISTER!
SISTER?
SHE'S NOT MY...
OH, MAYBE SHE IS...
ANYWAY...
SLOW DOWN, DANGER!
RELAAAX!
WE'RE GETTING OUT OF HERE!
OH YEAH? HOW?
THE SAME WAY WE GOT IN!
SAVE ME, TOO!
HOLD ON!
CLICK!
GRAB!

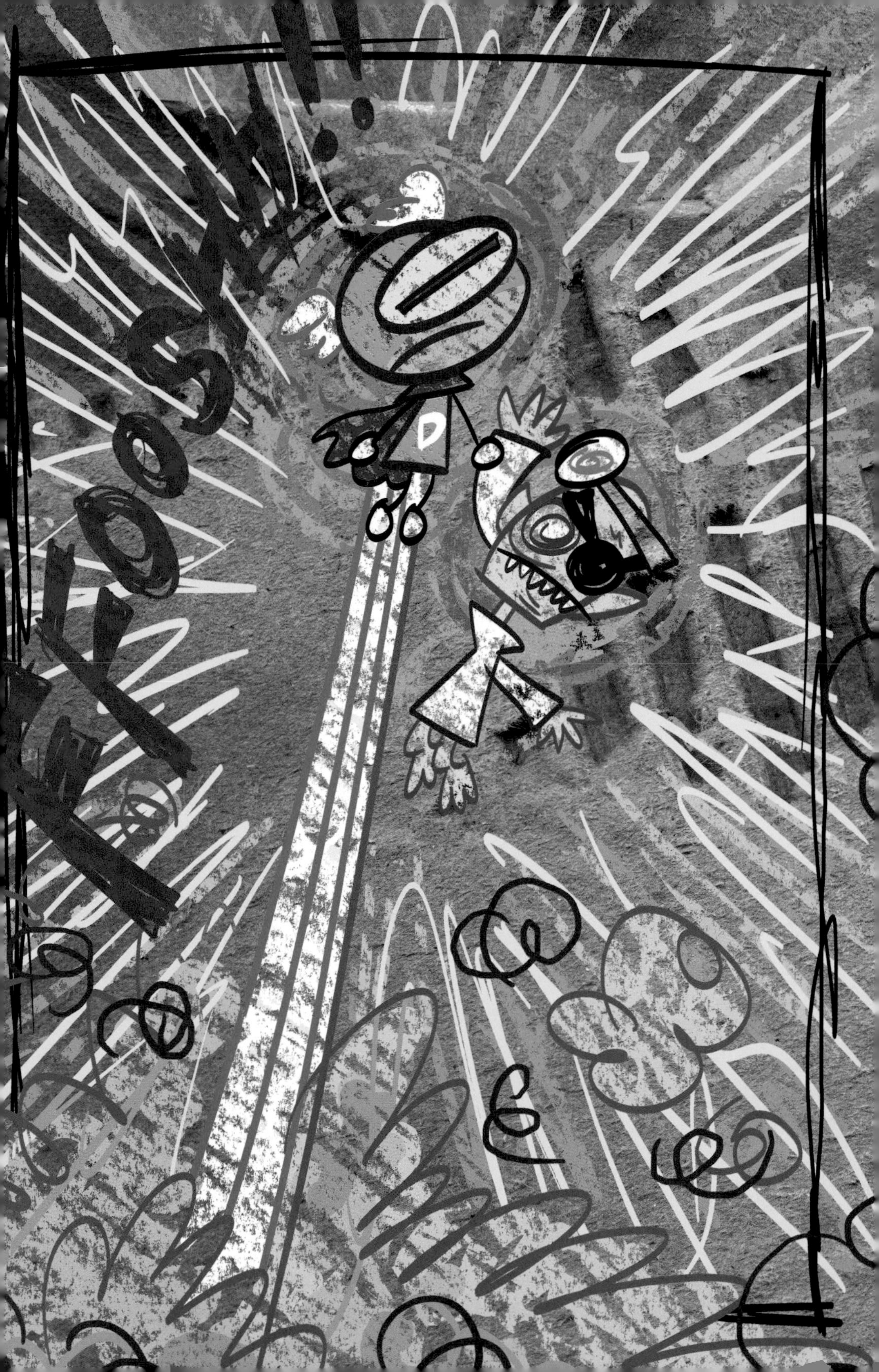
WHOOSH!!

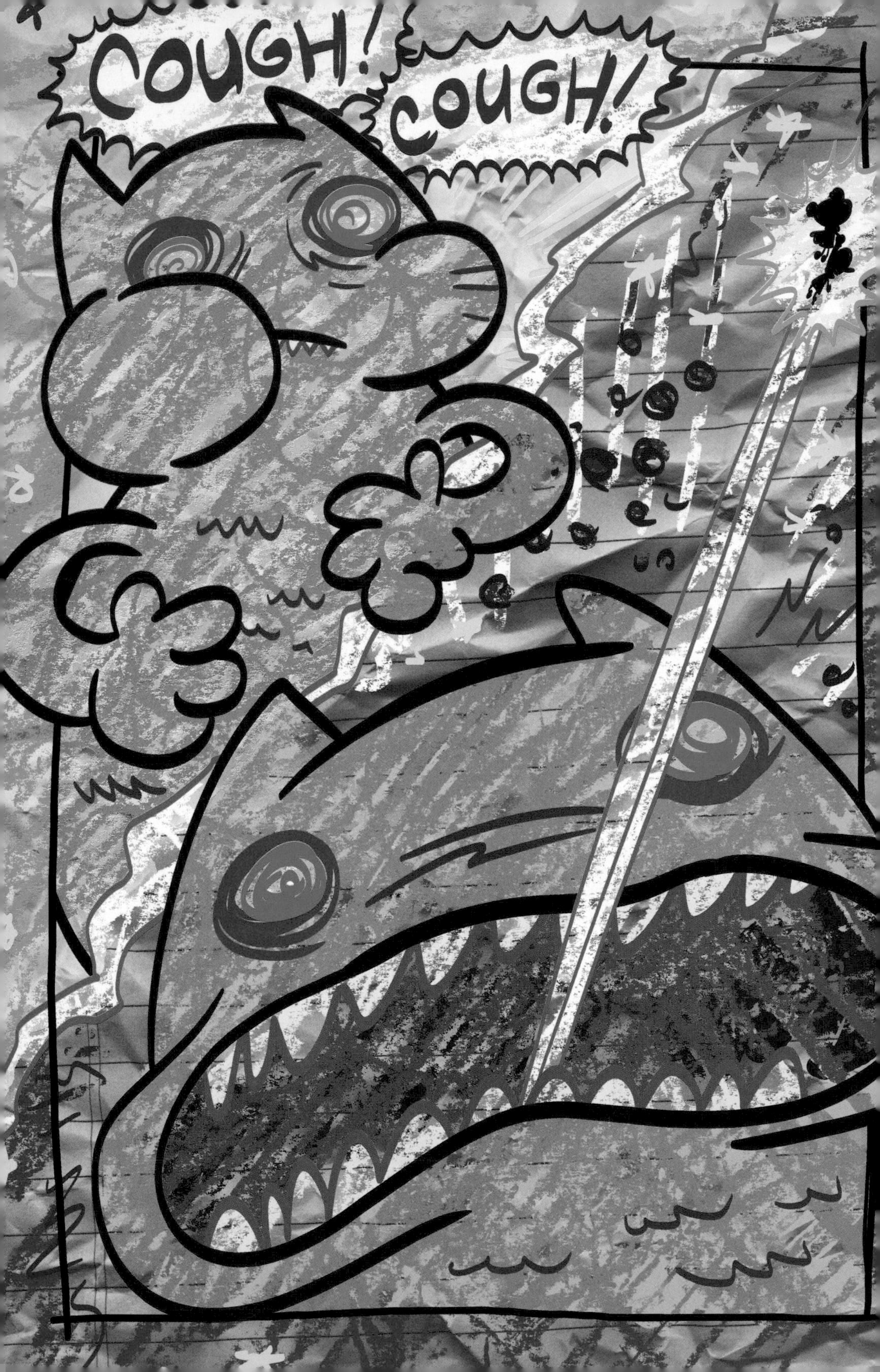
COUGH! & COUGH!

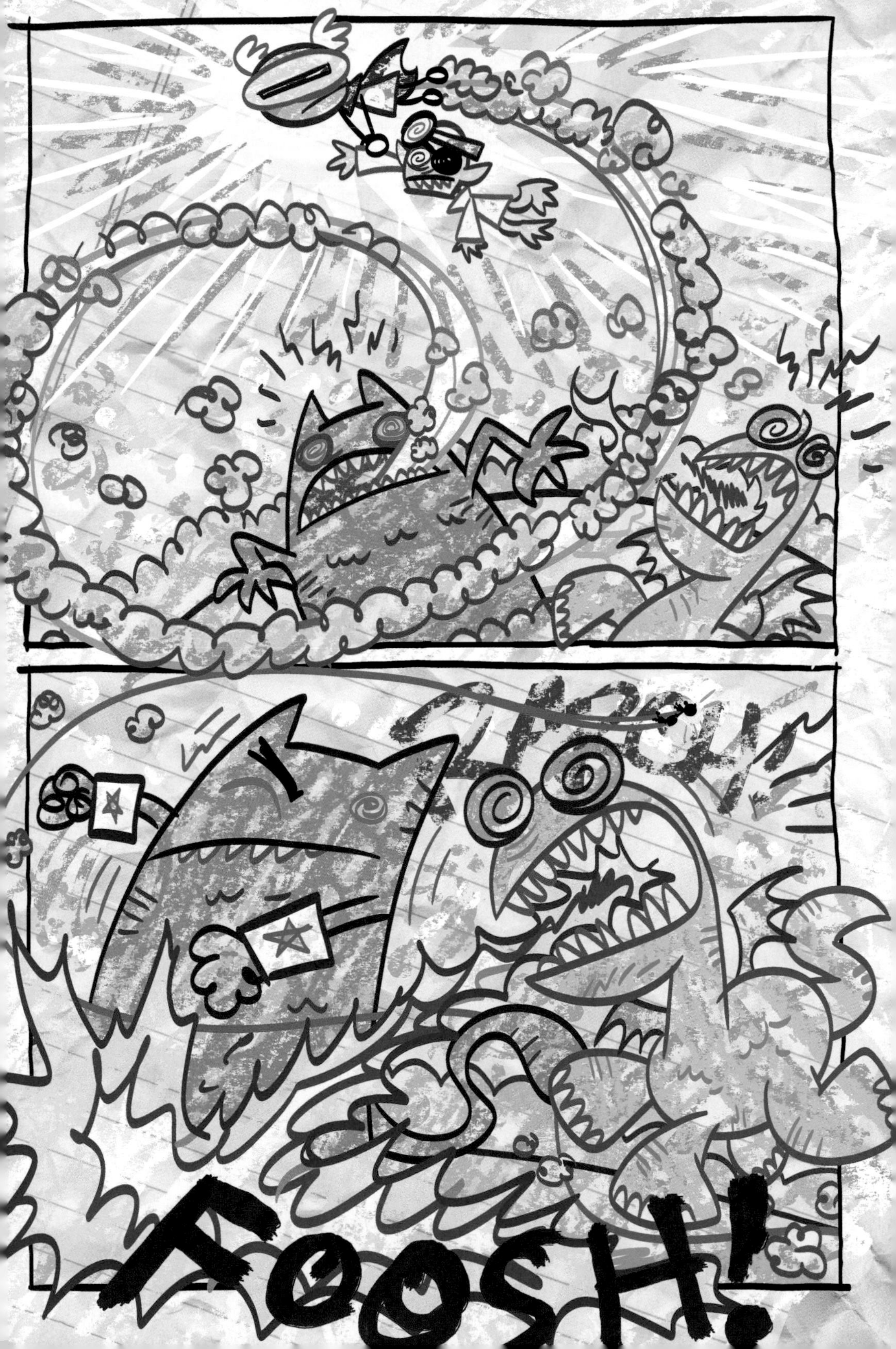
FOOSH!

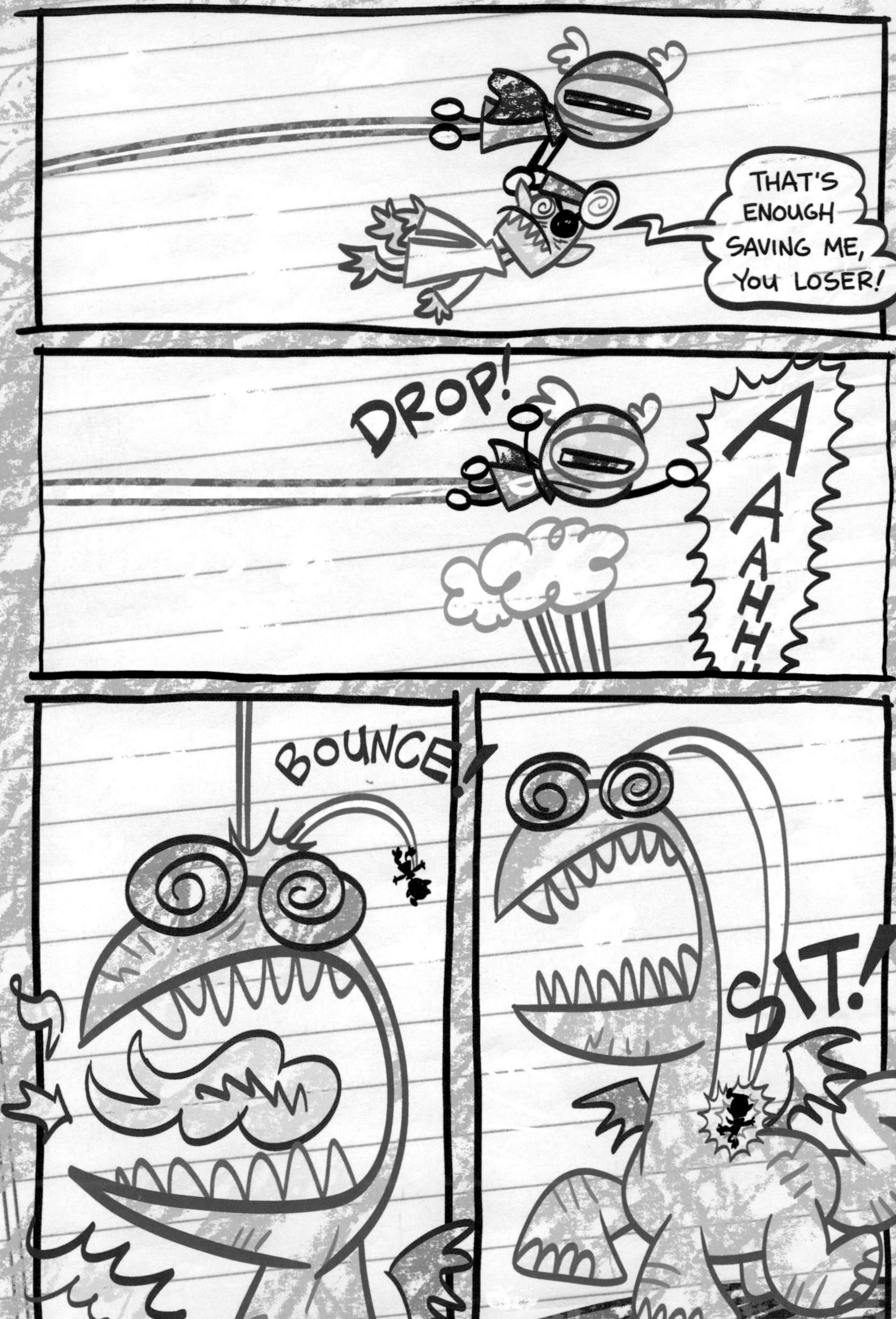
THAT'S ENOUGH SAVING ME, YOU LOSER!
DROP!
AAAHH!
BOUNCE!
SIT!

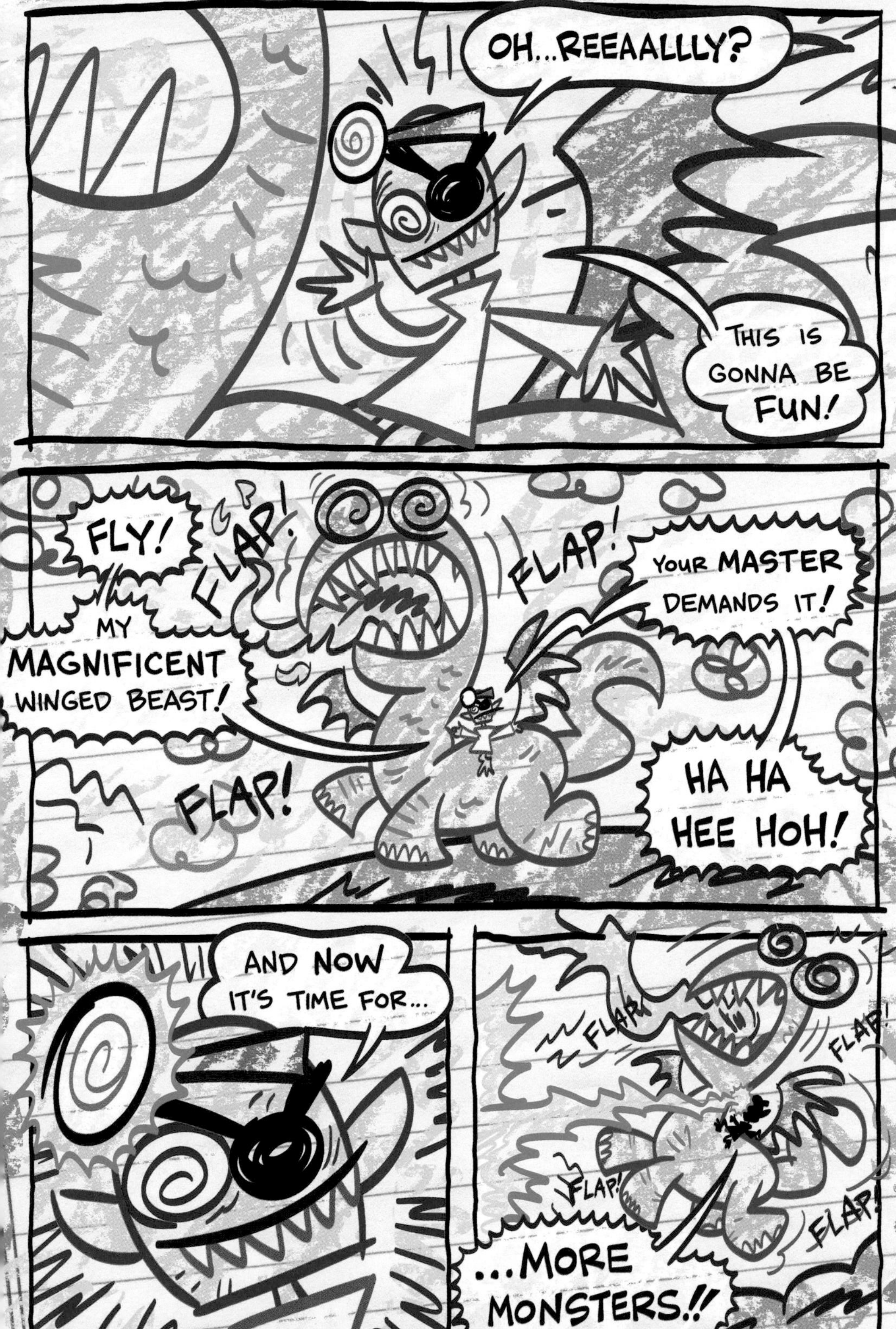

OH...REEAALLLY?
THIS IS GONNA BE FUN!
FLY!
MY MAGNIFICENT WINGED BEAST!
FLAP!
FLAP!
YOUR MASTER DEMANDS IT!
FLAP!
HA HA HEE HOH!
AND NOW IT'S TIME FOR...
FLAP!
FLAP!
FLAP!
FLAP!
...MORE MONSTERS!!

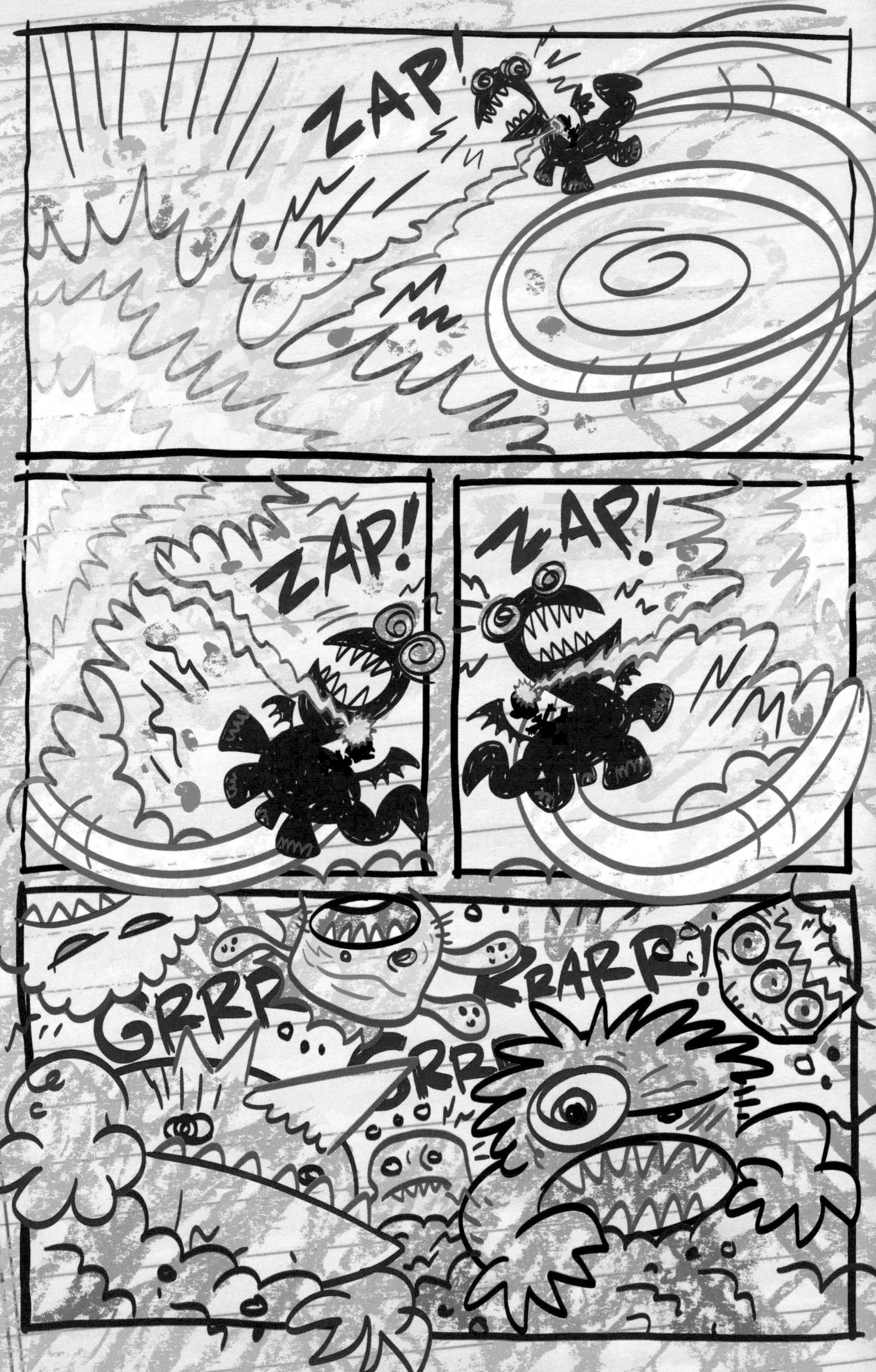
ZAP!
ZAP!
ZAP!
GRRR
RRARR!
GRR

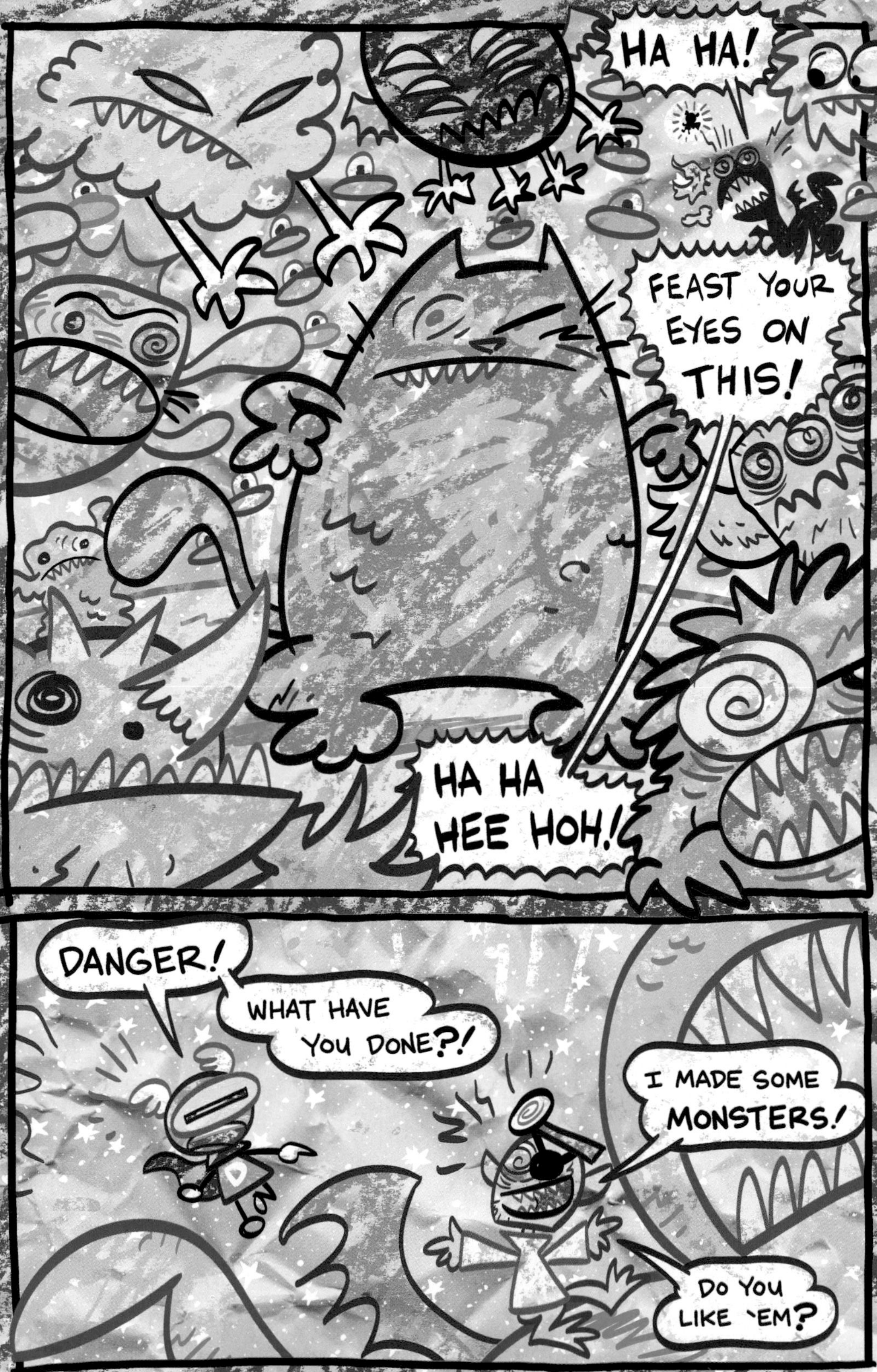
HA HA!
FEAST YOUR EYES ON THIS!
HA HA HEE HOH!
DANGER!
WHAT HAVE YOU DONE?!
I MADE SOME MONSTERS!
DO YOU LIKE `EM?

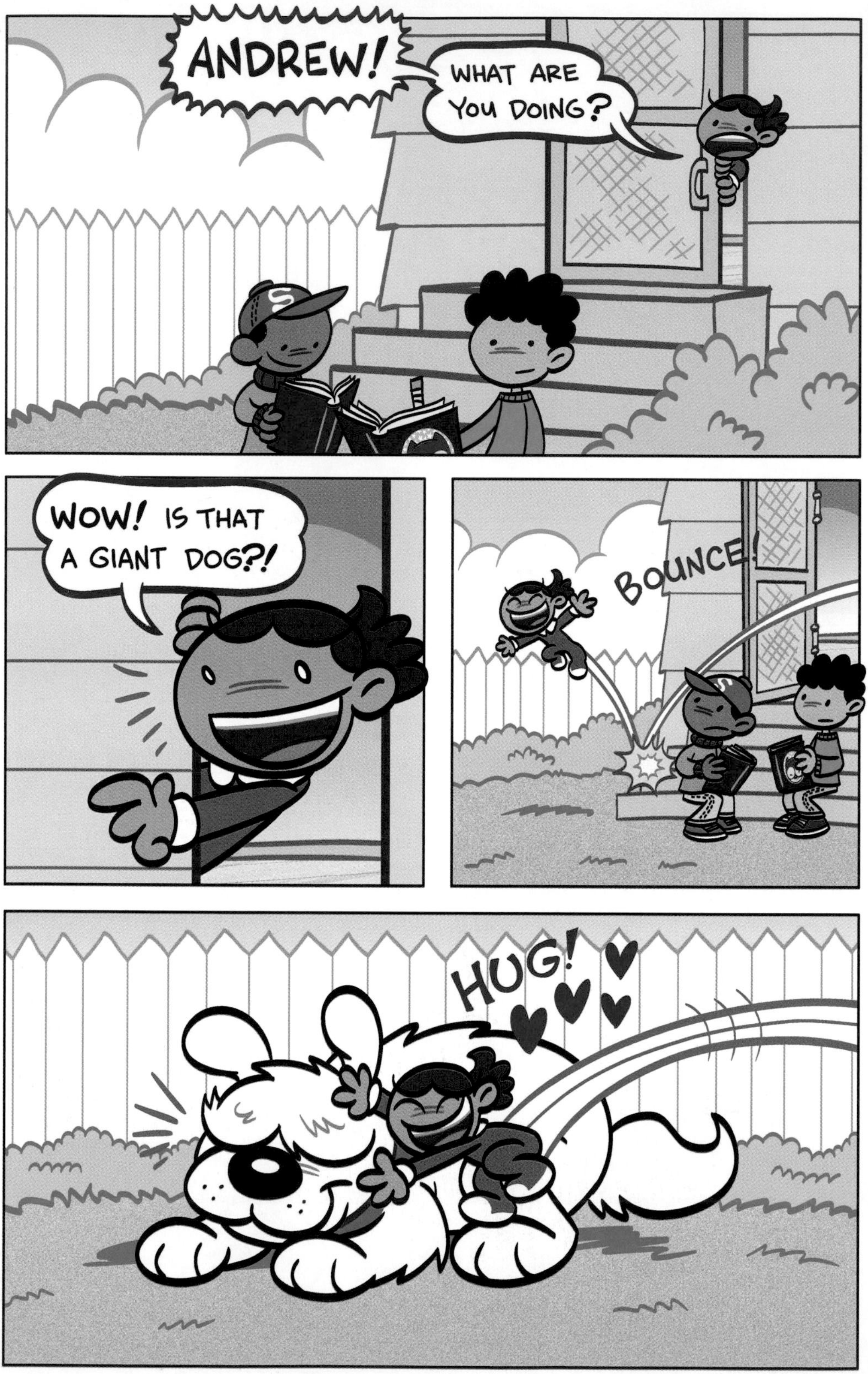

ANDREW!
WHAT ARE YOU DOING?
WOW! IS THAT A GIANT DOG?!
BOUNCE!
HUG!

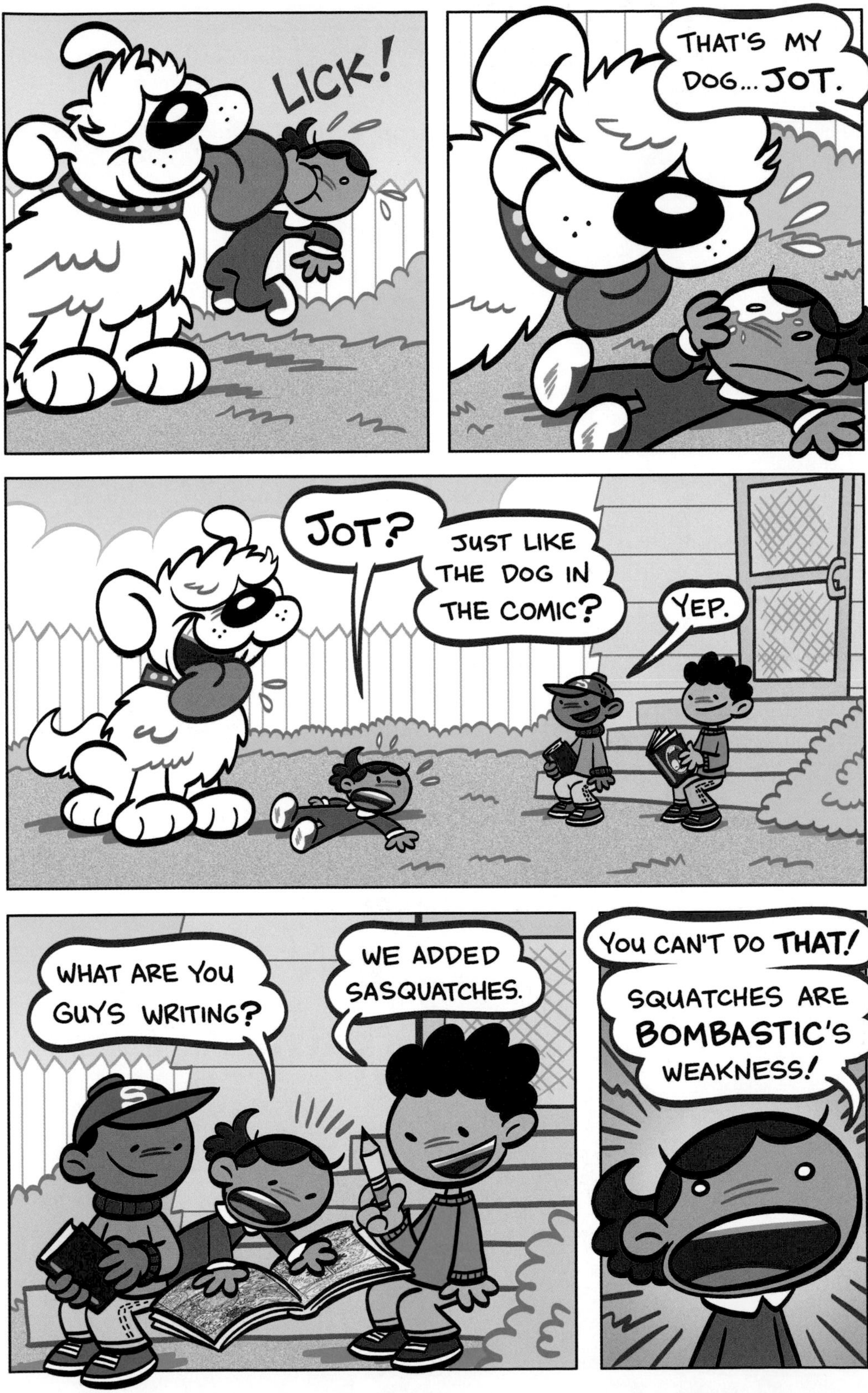
LICK!
THAT'S MY DOG... JOT.
JOT?
JUST LIKE THE DOG IN THE COMIC?
YEP.
WHAT ARE YOU GUYS WRITING?
WE ADDED SASQUATCHES.
YOU CAN'T DO THAT!
SQUATCHES ARE BOMBASTIC'S WEAKNESS!

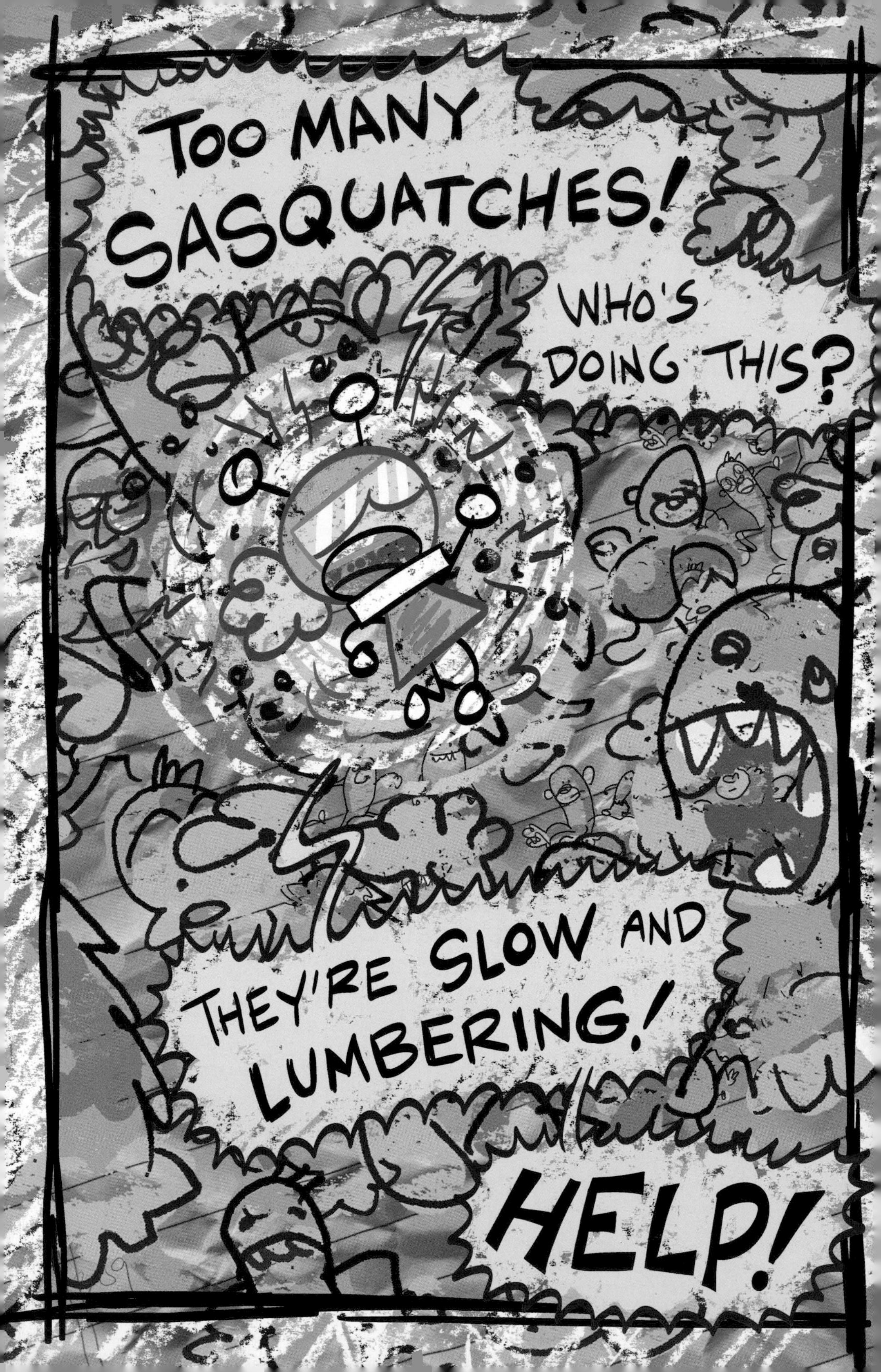
TOO MANY SASQUATCHES!
WHO'S DOING THIS?
THEY'RE SLOW AND LUMBERING!
HELP!

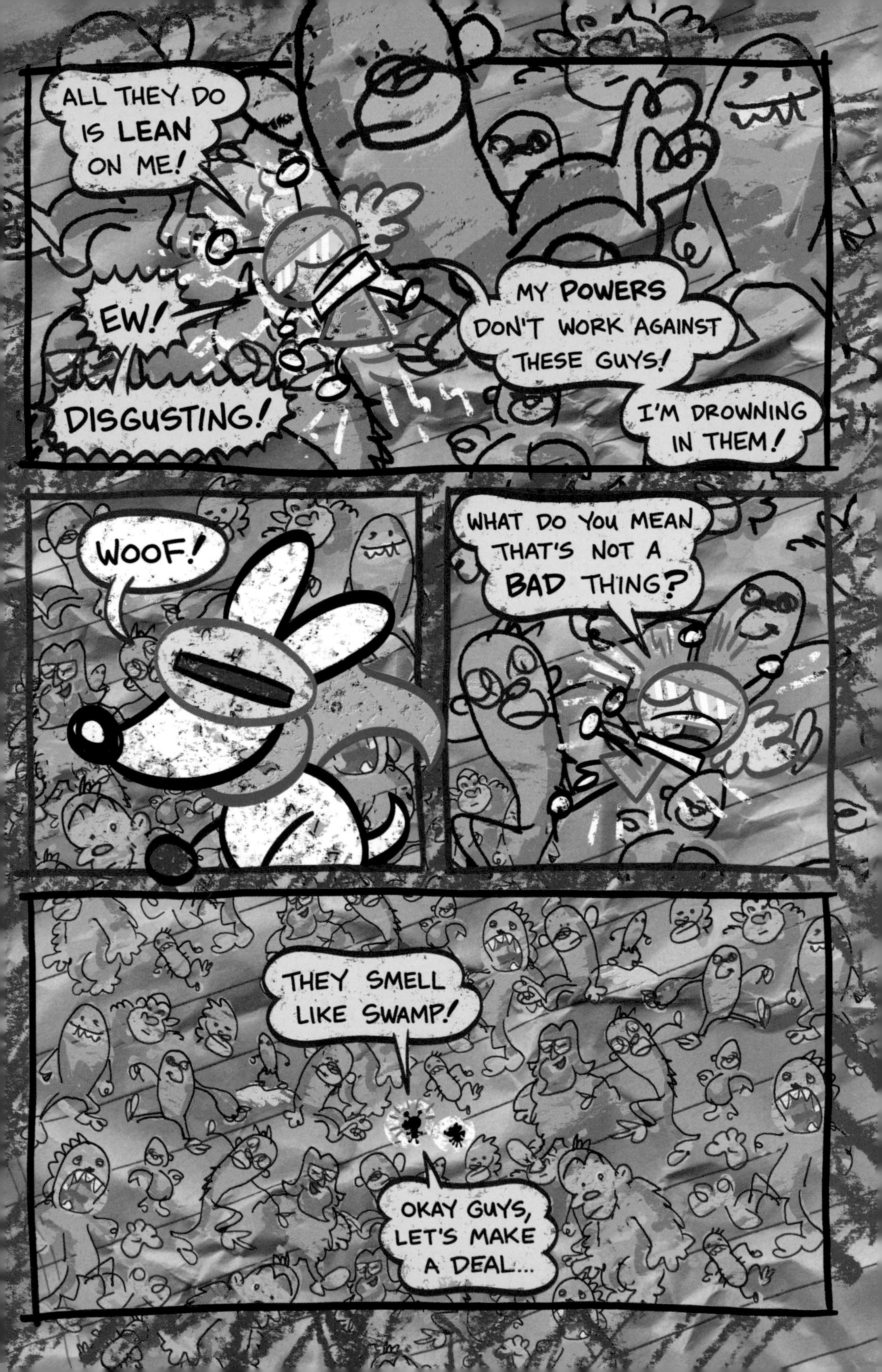
ALL THEY DO IS LEAN ON ME!
EW!
DISGUSTING!
MY POWERS DON'T WORK AGAINST THESE GUYS!
I'M DROWNING IN THEM!
WOOF!
WHAT DO YOU MEAN THAT'S NOT A BAD THING?
THEY SMELL LIKE SWAMP!
OKAY GUYS, LET'S MAKE A DEAL...

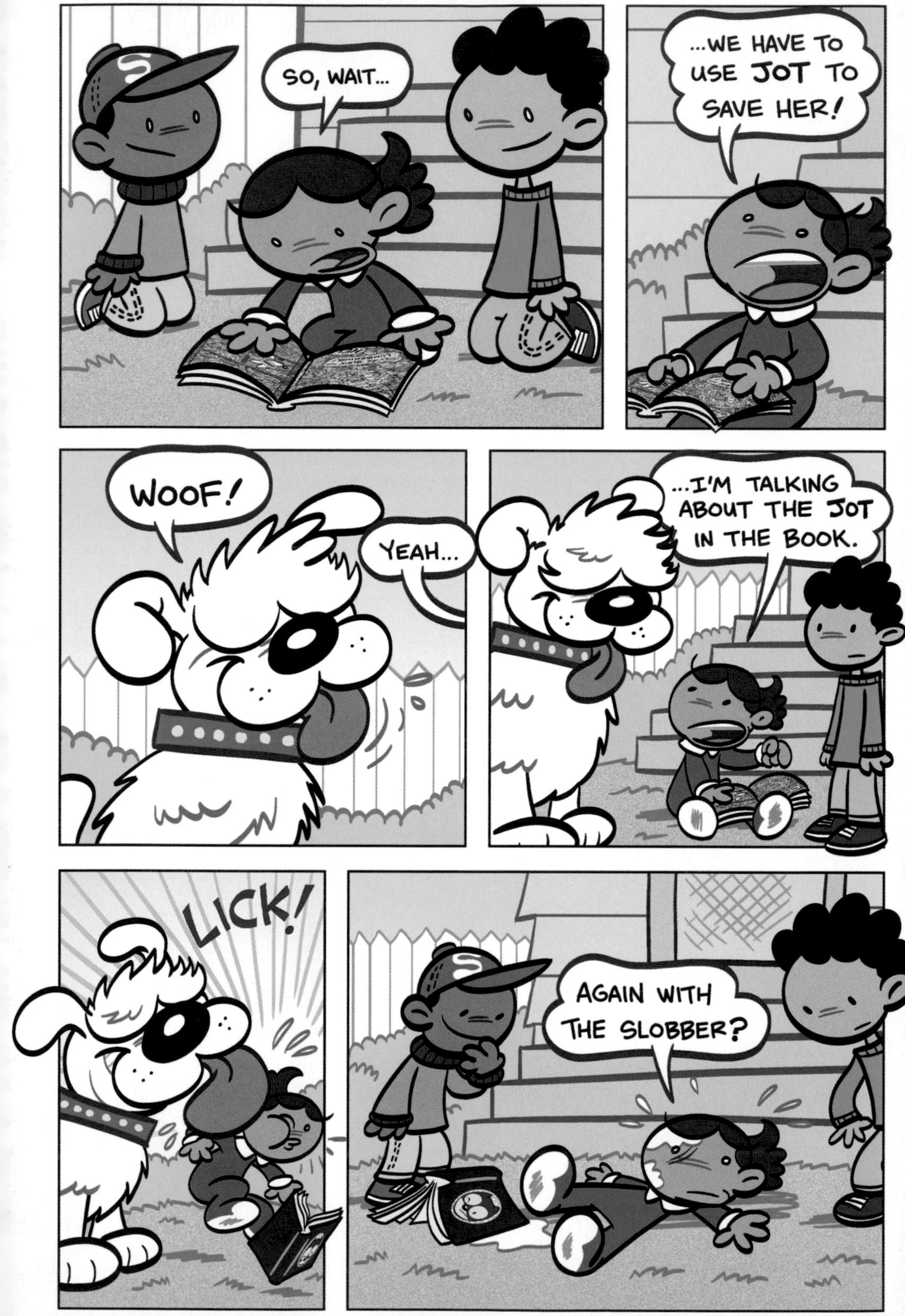

SO, WAIT...
...WE HAVE TO USE JOT TO SAVE HER!
WOOF!
YEAH...
...I'M TALKING ABOUT THE JOT IN THE BOOK.
LICK!
AGAIN WITH THE SLOBBER?

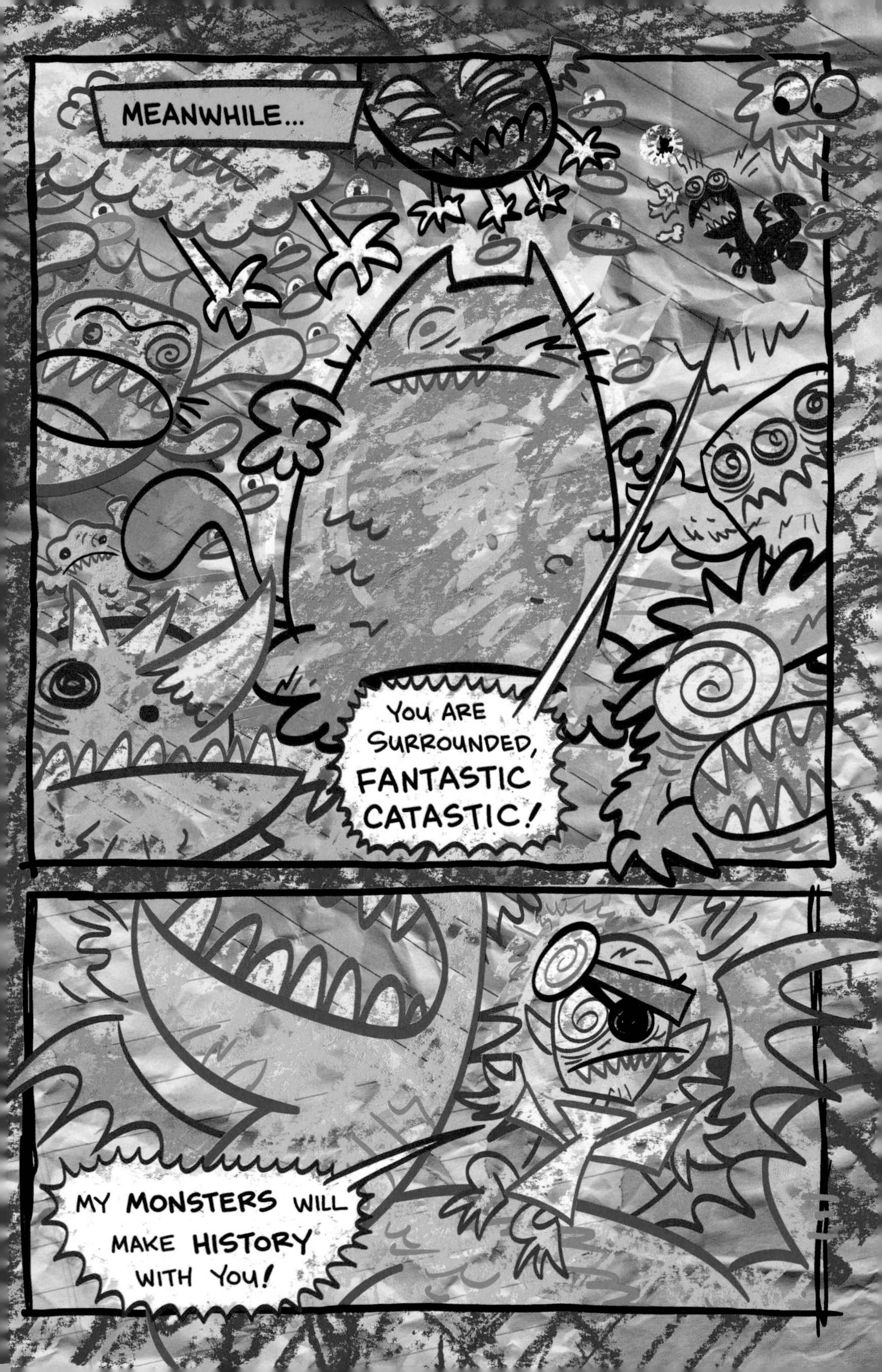
MEANWHILE...
YOU ARE SURROUNDED, FANTASTIC CATASTIC!
MY MONSTERS WILL MAKE HISTORY WITH YOU!

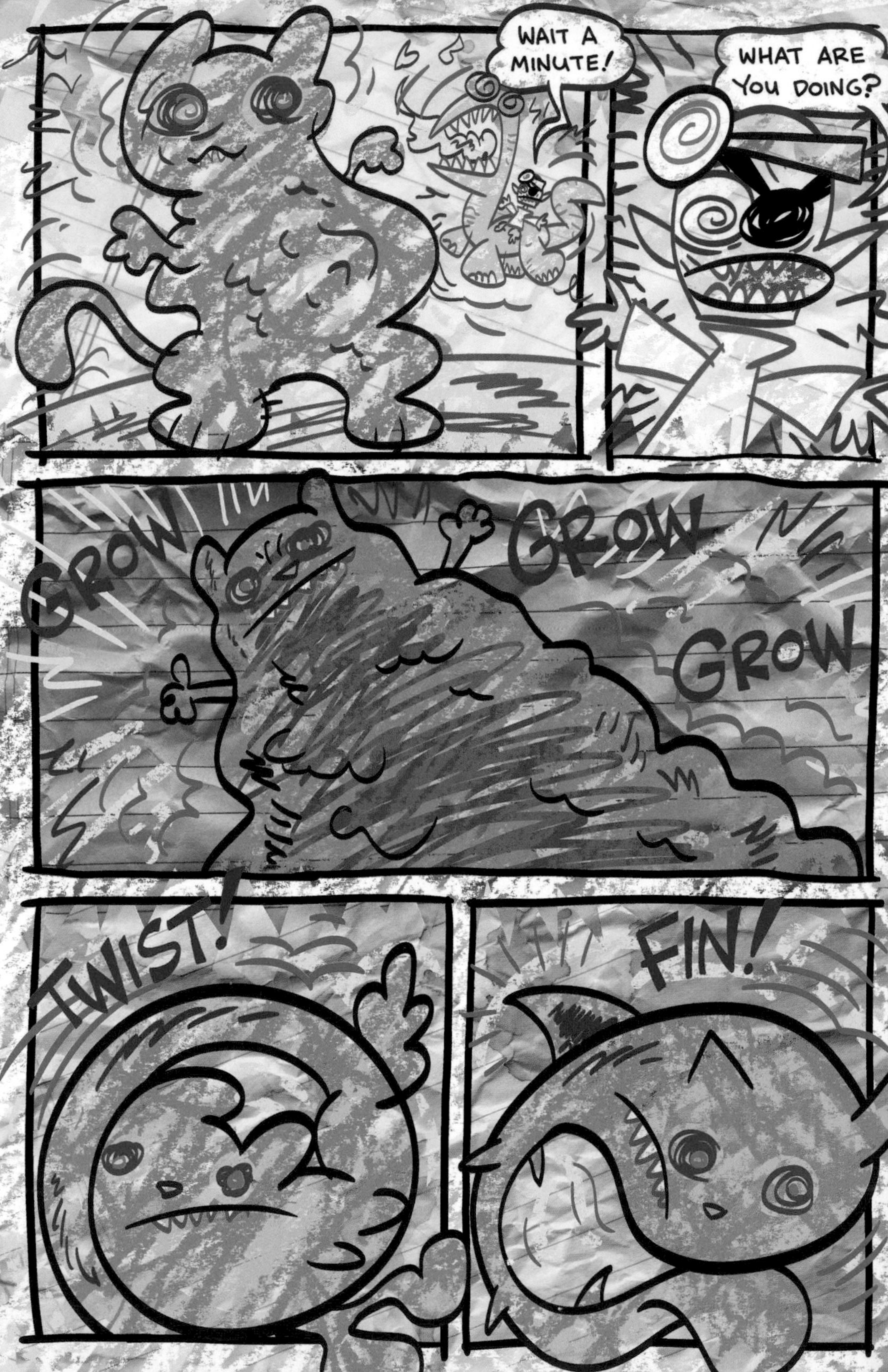
WAIT A MINUTE!
WHAT ARE YOU DOING?
GROW
GROW
GROW
TWIST!
FIN!

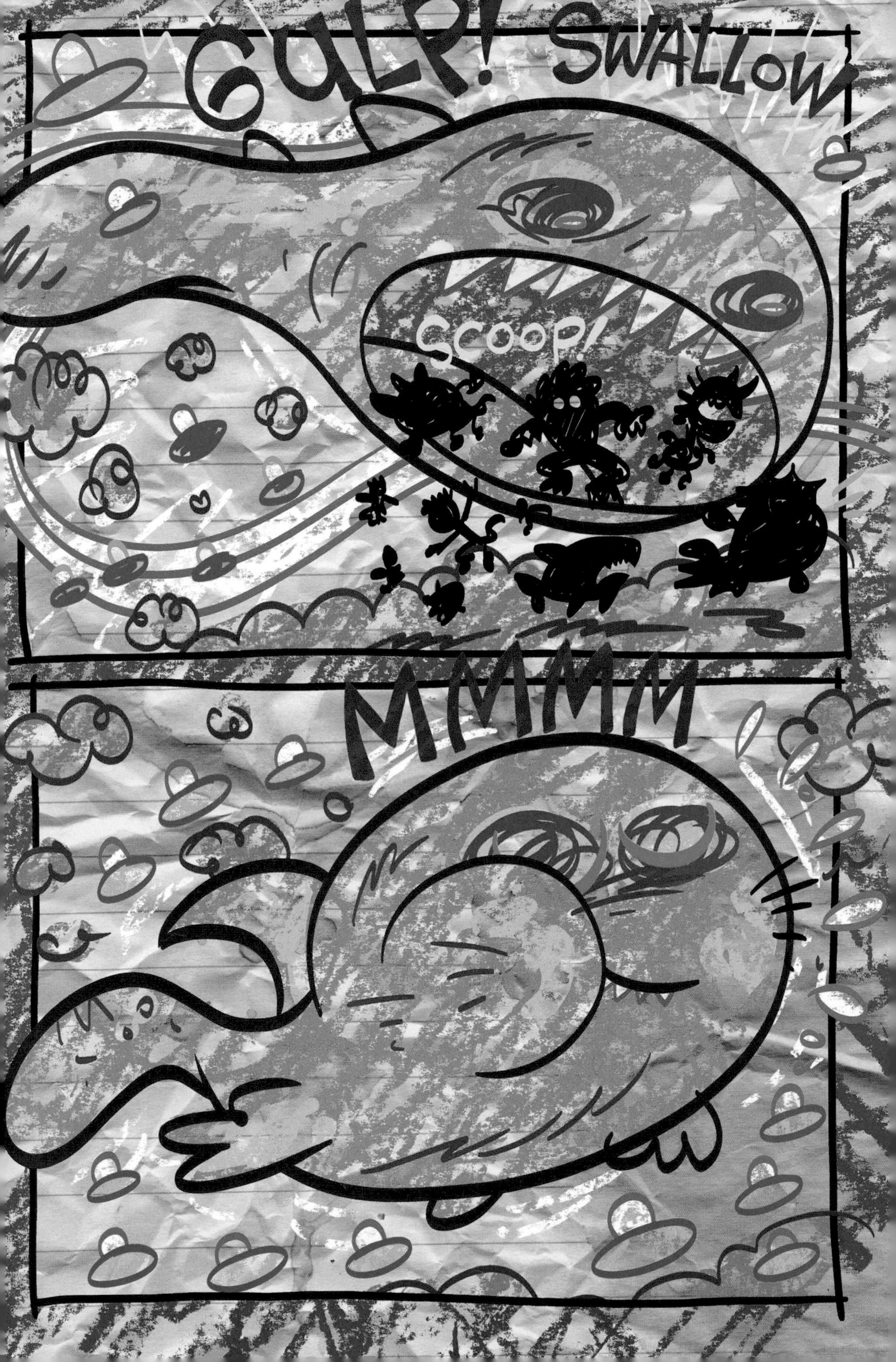
GULP!
SWALLOW
SCOOP!
MMMMM

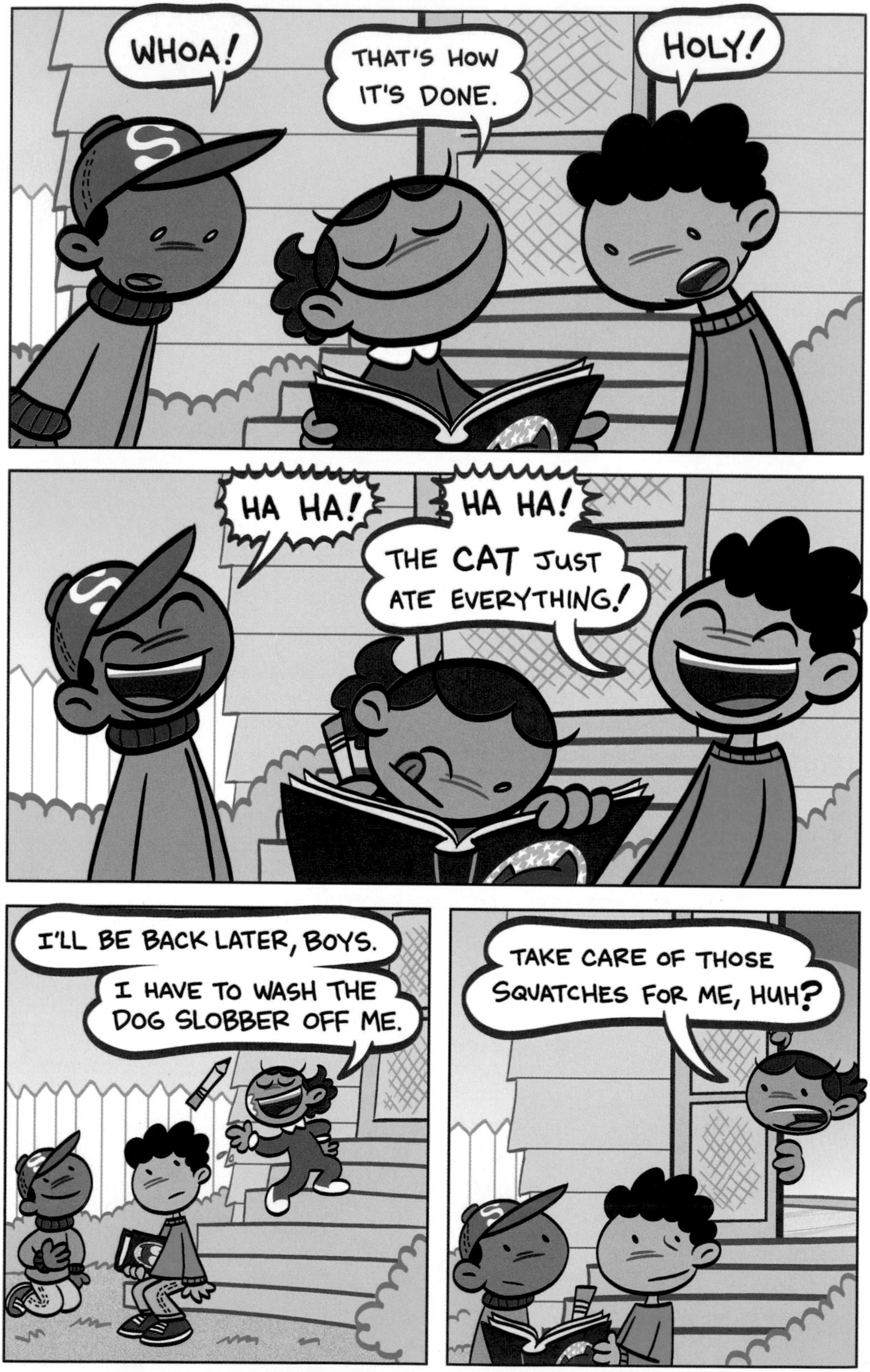
WHOA!
THAT'S HOW IT'S DONE.
HOLY!
HA HA!
HA HA!
THE CAT JUST ATE EVERYTHING!
I'LL BE BACK LATER, BOYS.
I HAVE TO WASH THE DOG SLOBBER OFF ME.
TAKE CARE OF THOSE SQUATCHES FOR ME, HUH?

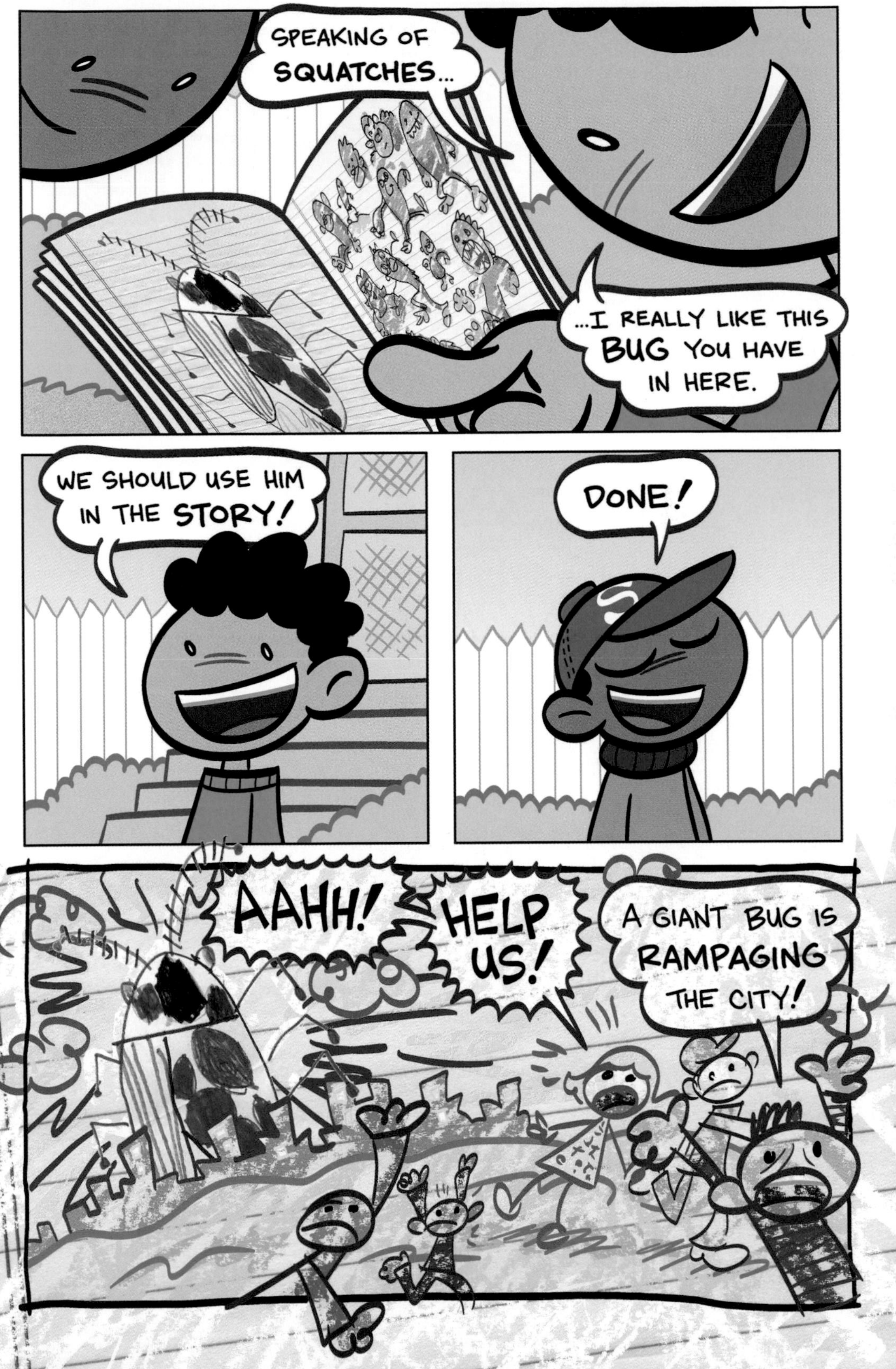
SPEAKING OF SQUATCHES...
...I REALLY LIKE THIS BUG YOU HAVE IN HERE.
WE SHOULD USE HIM IN THE STORY!
DONE!
AAHH!
HELP US!
A GIANT BUG IS RAMPAGING THE CITY!

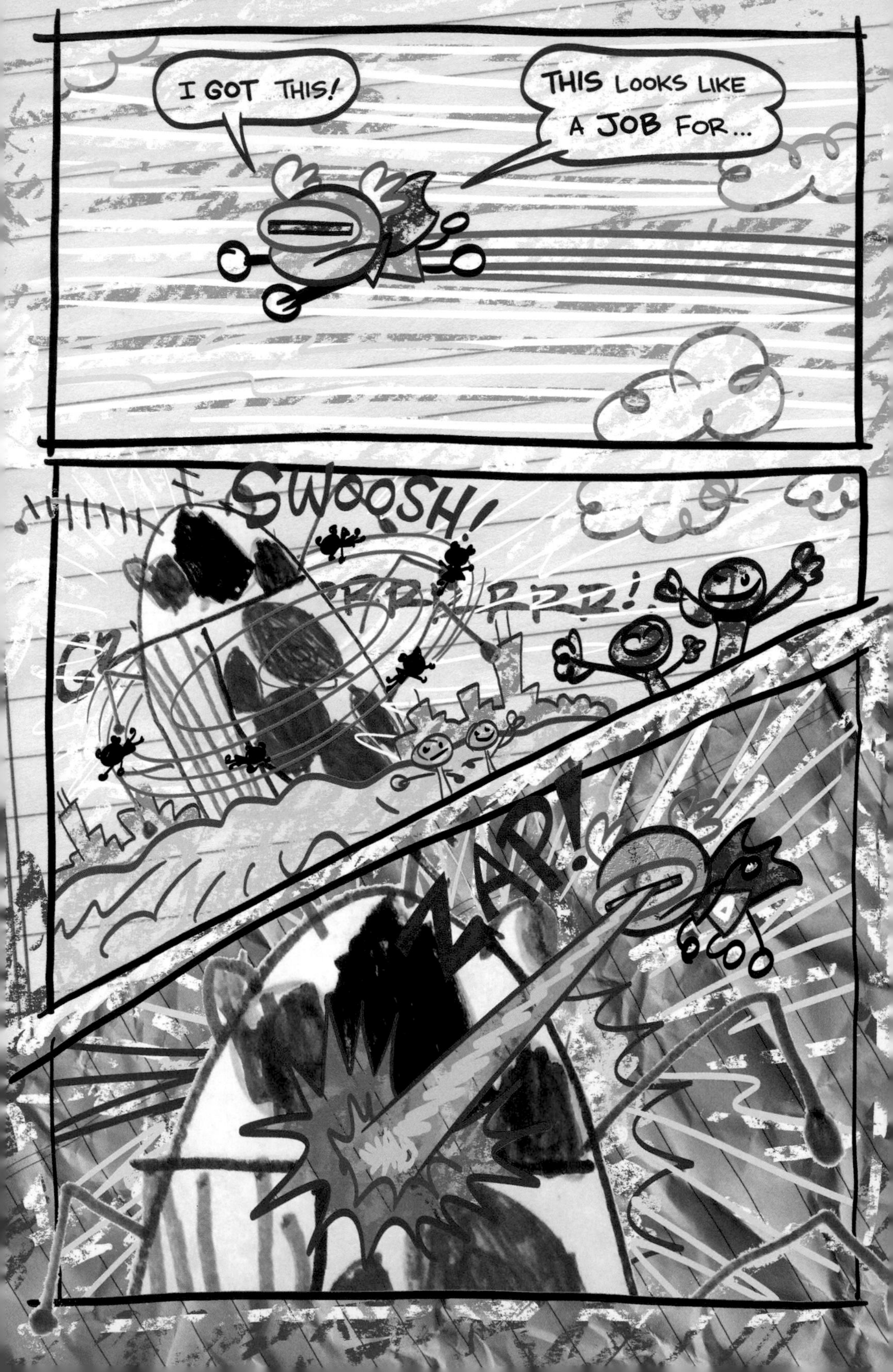
I GOT THIS!
THIS LOOKS LIKE A JOB FOR...
SWOOSH!
ZAP!

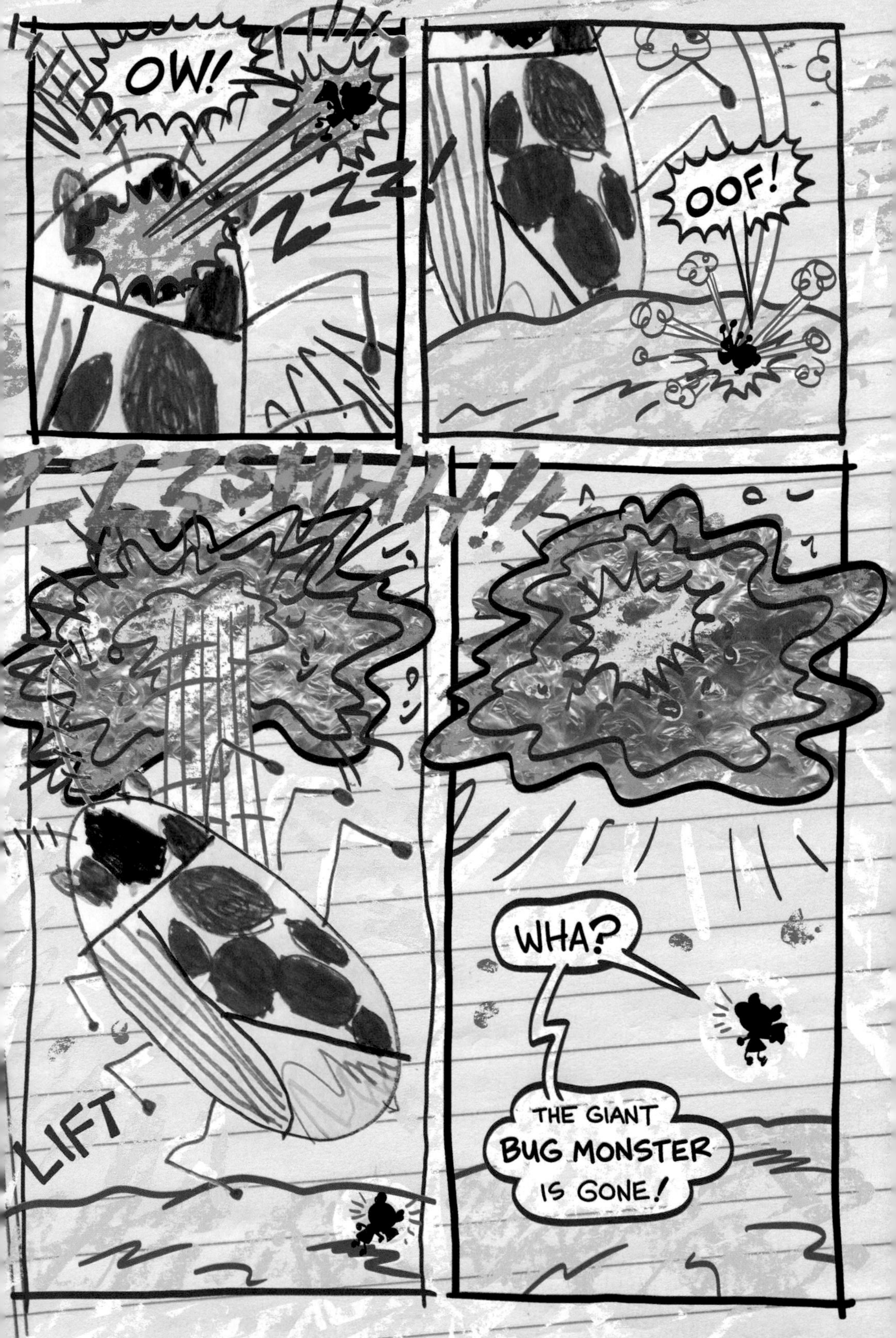
OW!
ZZZ!
OOF!
ZZZSHHH!!
LIFT
WHA?
THE GIANT BUG MONSTER IS GONE!

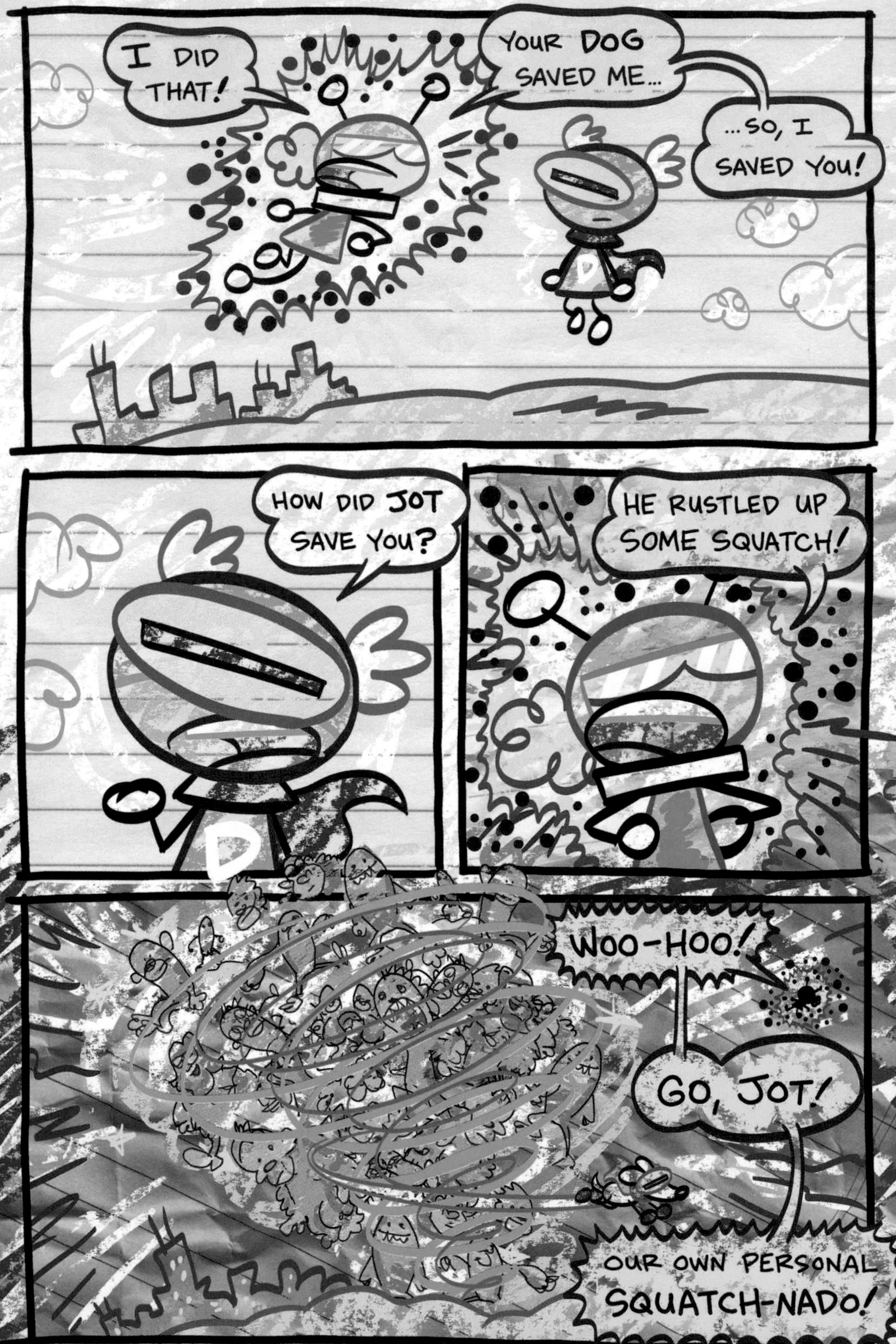
I DID THAT!
YOUR DOG SAVED ME...
...SO, I SAVED YOU!
HOW DID JOT SAVE YOU?
HE RUSTLED UP SOME SQUATCH!
WOO-HOO!
GO, JOT!
OUR OWN PERSONAL SQUATCH-NADO!

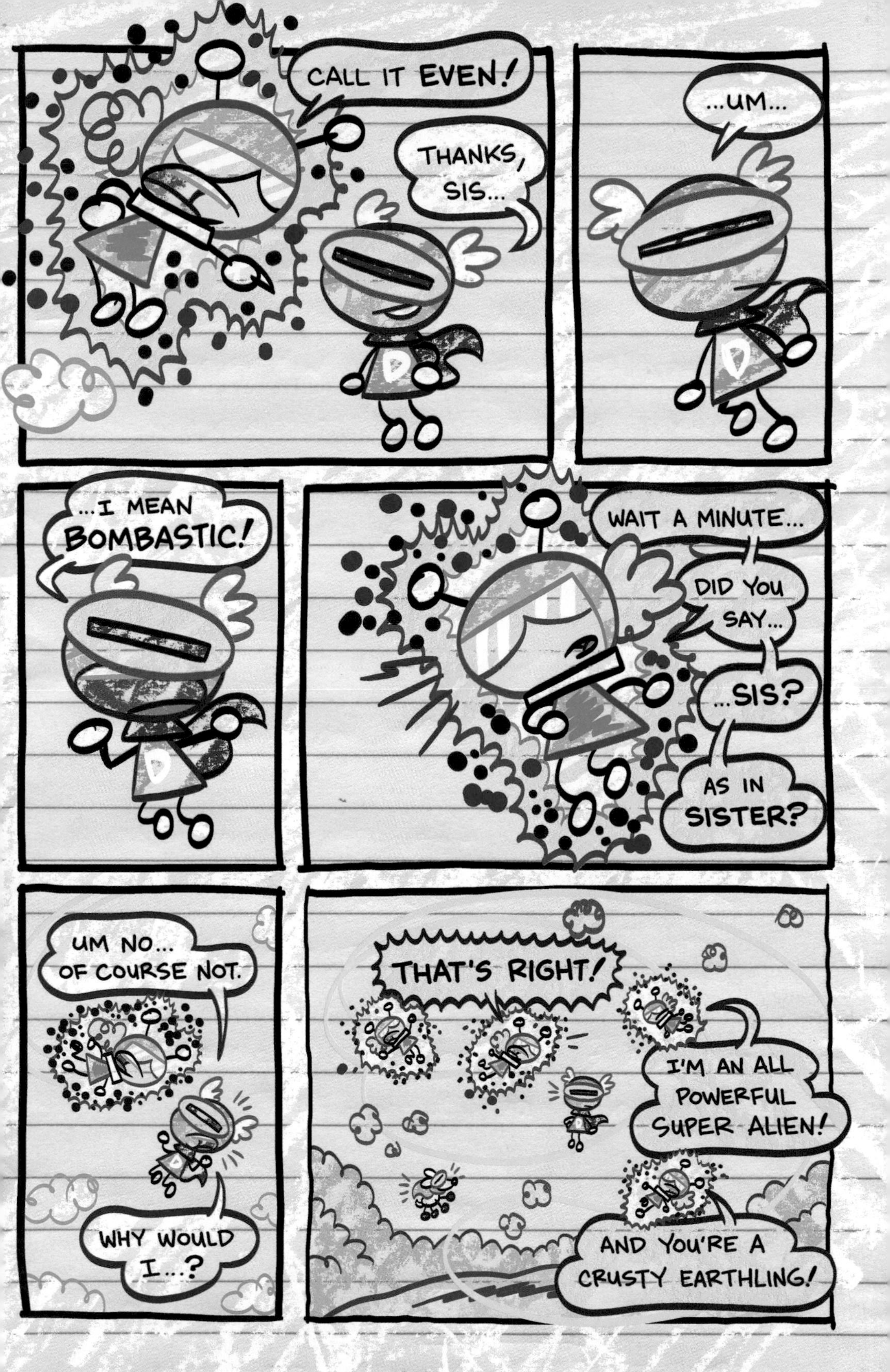
CALL IT EVEN!
THANKS, SIS...
...UM...
...I MEAN BOMBASTIC!
WAIT A MINUTE...
DID YOU SAY...
...SIS?
AS IN SISTER?
UM NO... OF COURSE NOT.
WHY WOULD I...?
THAT'S RIGHT!
I'M AN ALL POWERFUL SUPER ALIEN!
AND YOU'RE A CRUSTY EARTHLING!

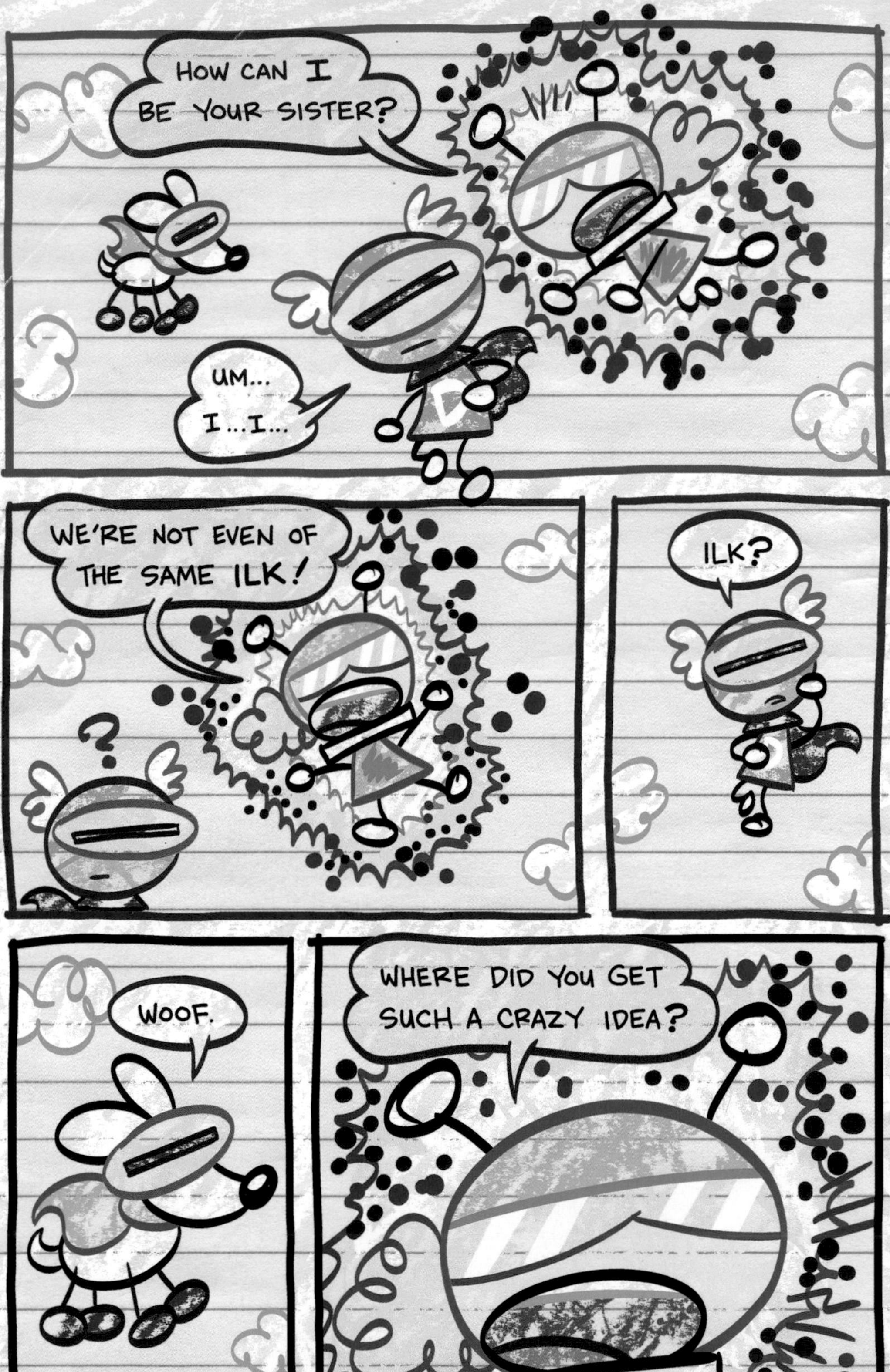
HOW CAN I BE YOUR SISTER?
UM... I...I...
WE'RE NOT EVEN OF THE SAME ILK!
ILK?
WOOF.
WHERE DID YOU GET SUCH A CRAZY IDEA?

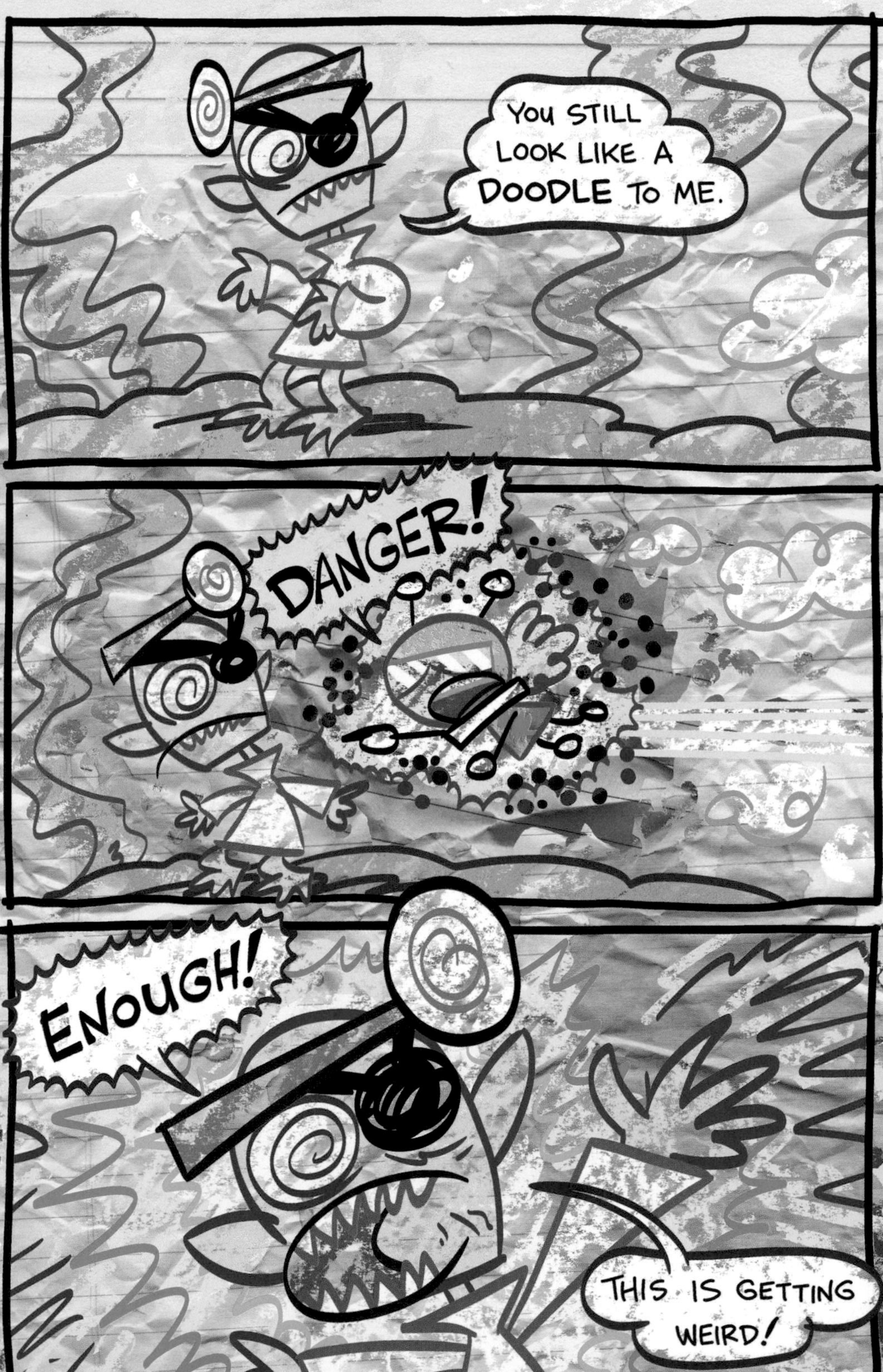
YOU STILL LOOK LIKE A DOODLE TO ME.
DANGER!
ENOUGH!
THIS IS GETTING WEIRD!

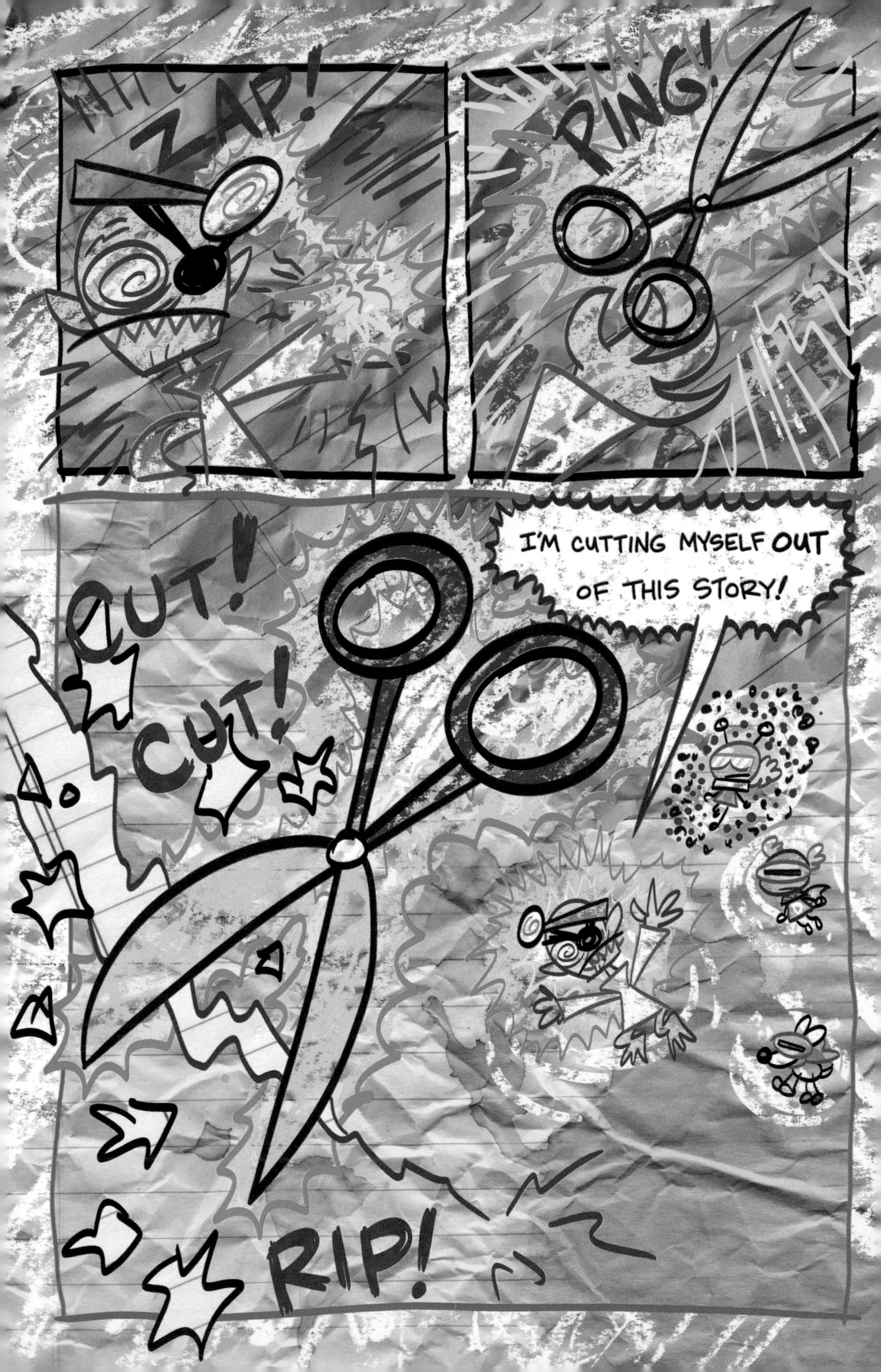
ZAP!
PING!
CUT!
CUT!
I'M CUTTING MYSELF OUT OF THIS STORY!
RIP!

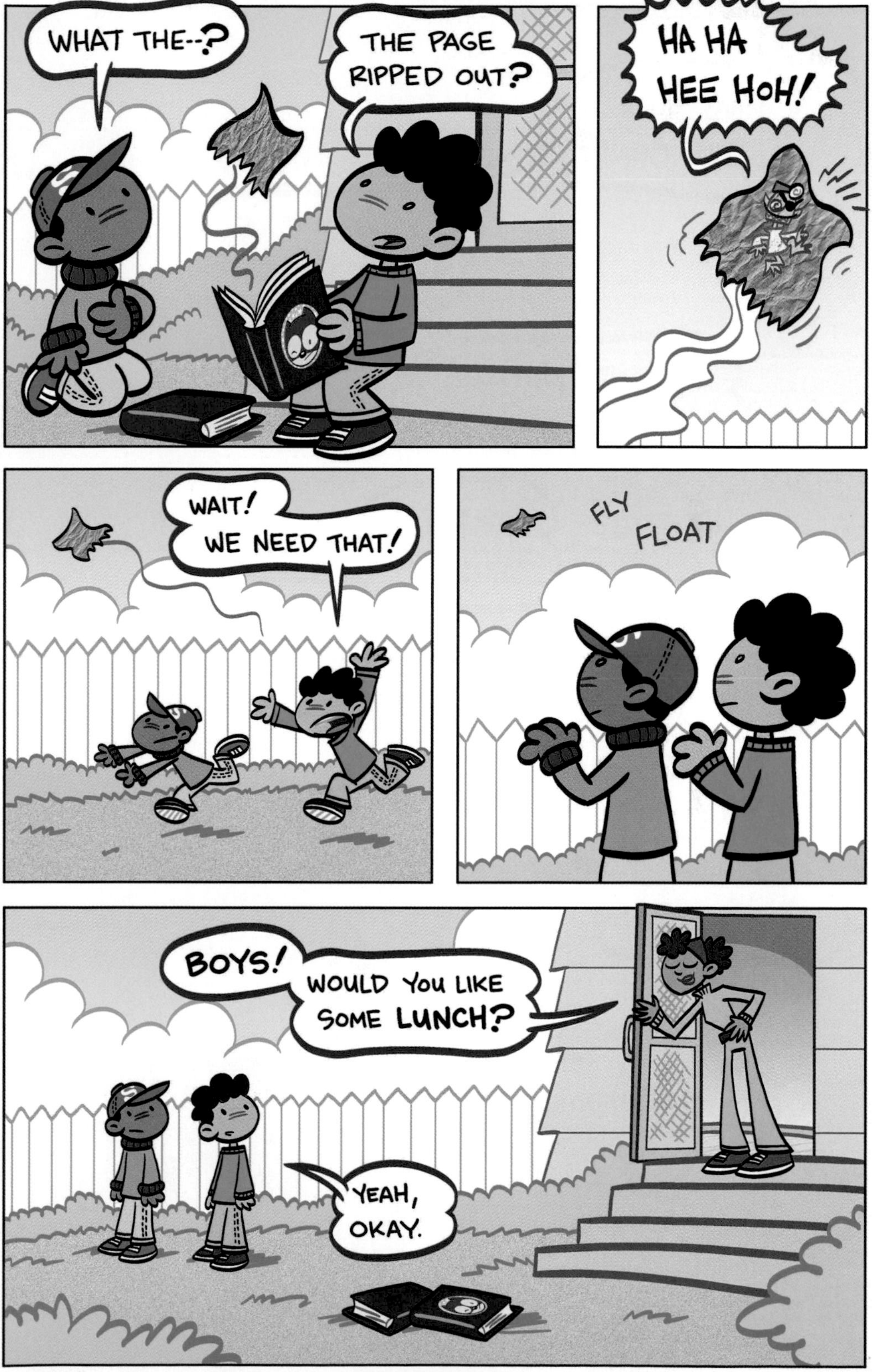
WHAT THE--?
THE PAGE RIPPED OUT?
HA HA HEE HOH!
WAIT! WE NEED THAT!
FLY
FLOAT
BOYS!
WOULD YOU LIKE SOME LUNCH?
YEAH, OKAY.

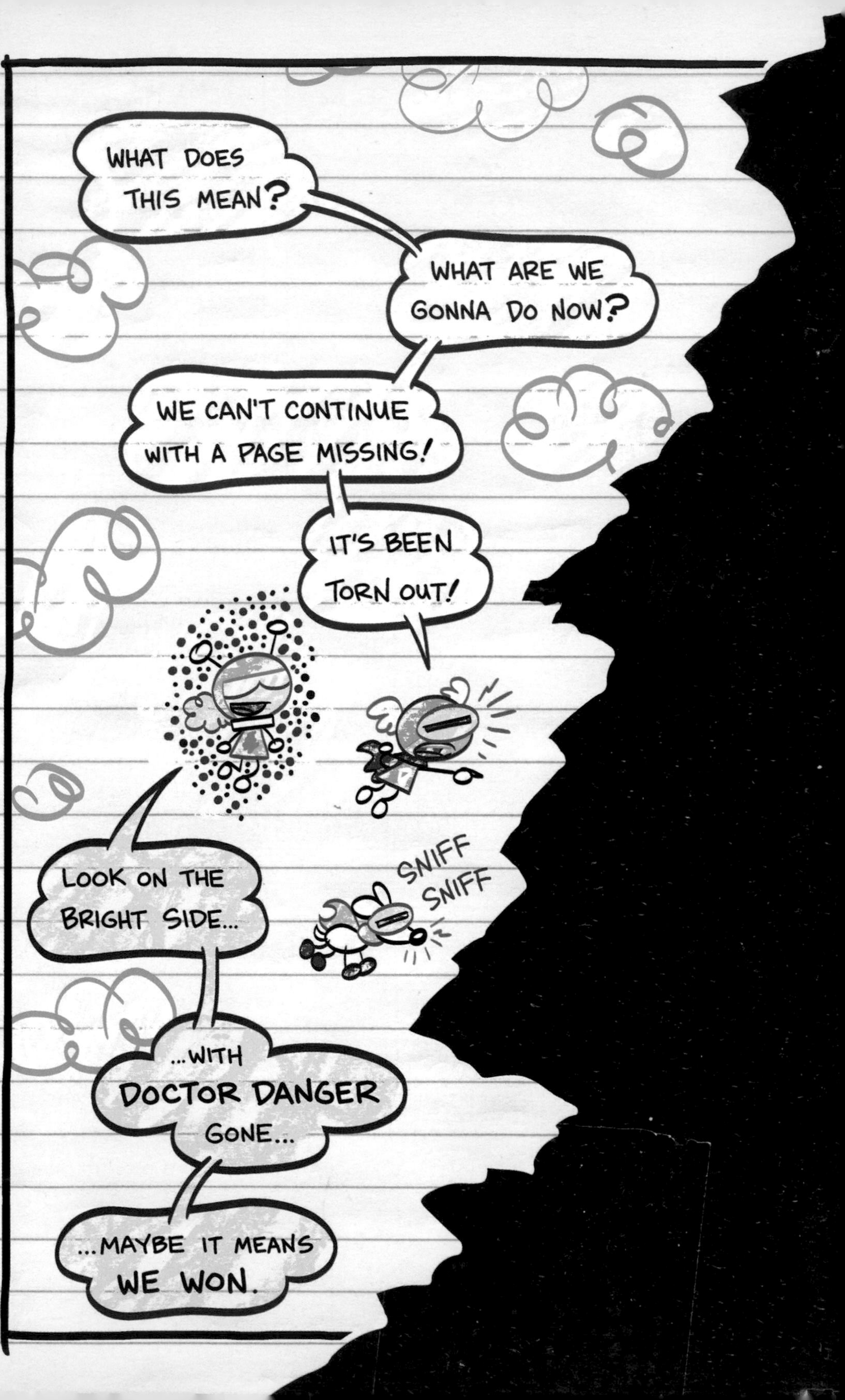
WHAT DOES THIS MEAN?
WHAT ARE WE GONNA DO NOW?
WE CAN'T CONTINUE WITH A PAGE MISSING!
IT'S BEEN TORN OUT!
LOOK ON THE BRIGHT SIDE...
SNIFF SNIFF
...WITH DOCTOR DANGER GONE...
...MAYBE IT MEANS WE WON.

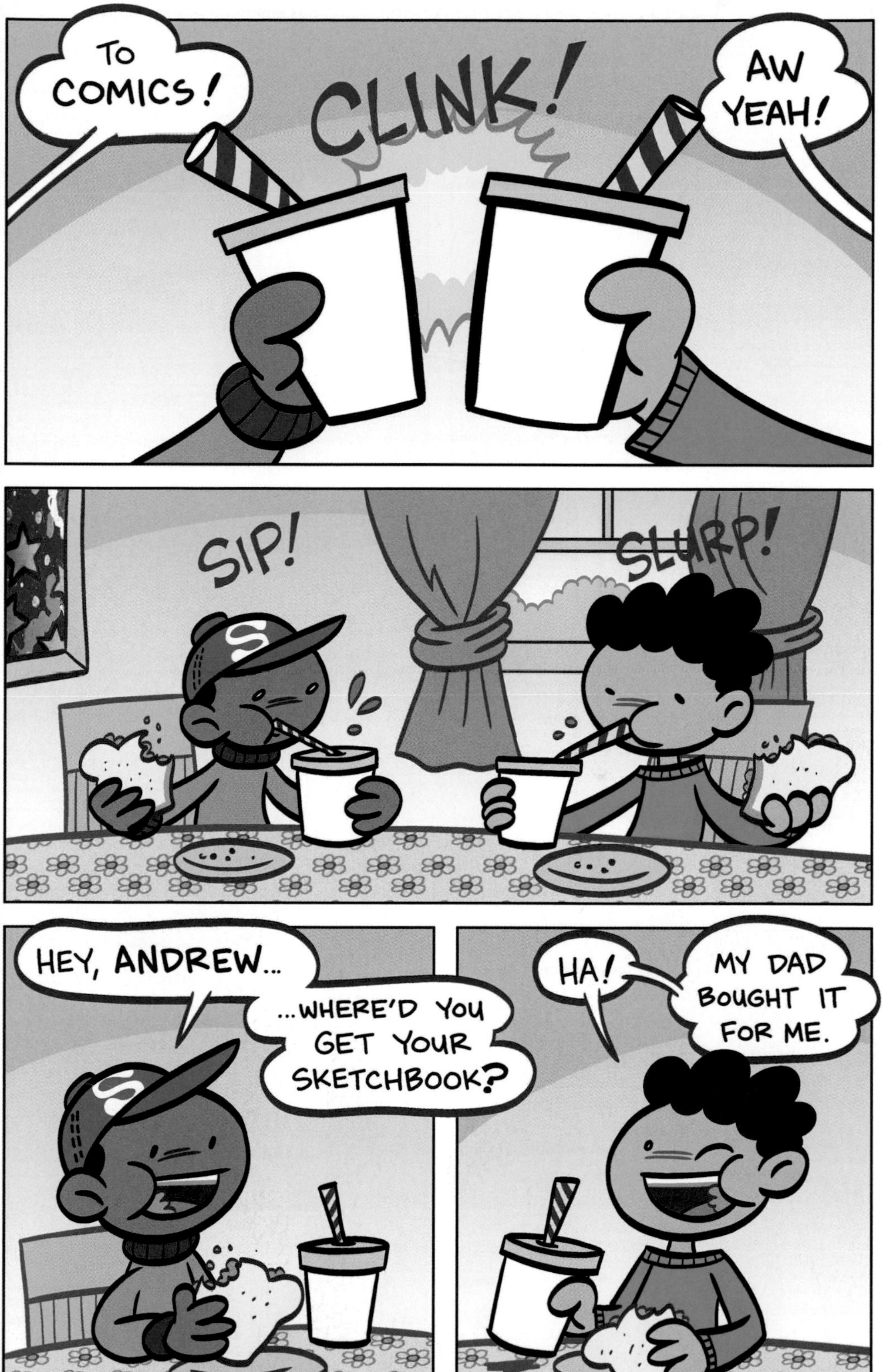
TO COMICS!
CLINK!
AW YEAH!
SIP!
SLURP!
HEY, ANDREW...
...WHERE'D YOU GET YOUR SKETCHBOOK?
HA!
MY DAD BOUGHT IT FOR ME.

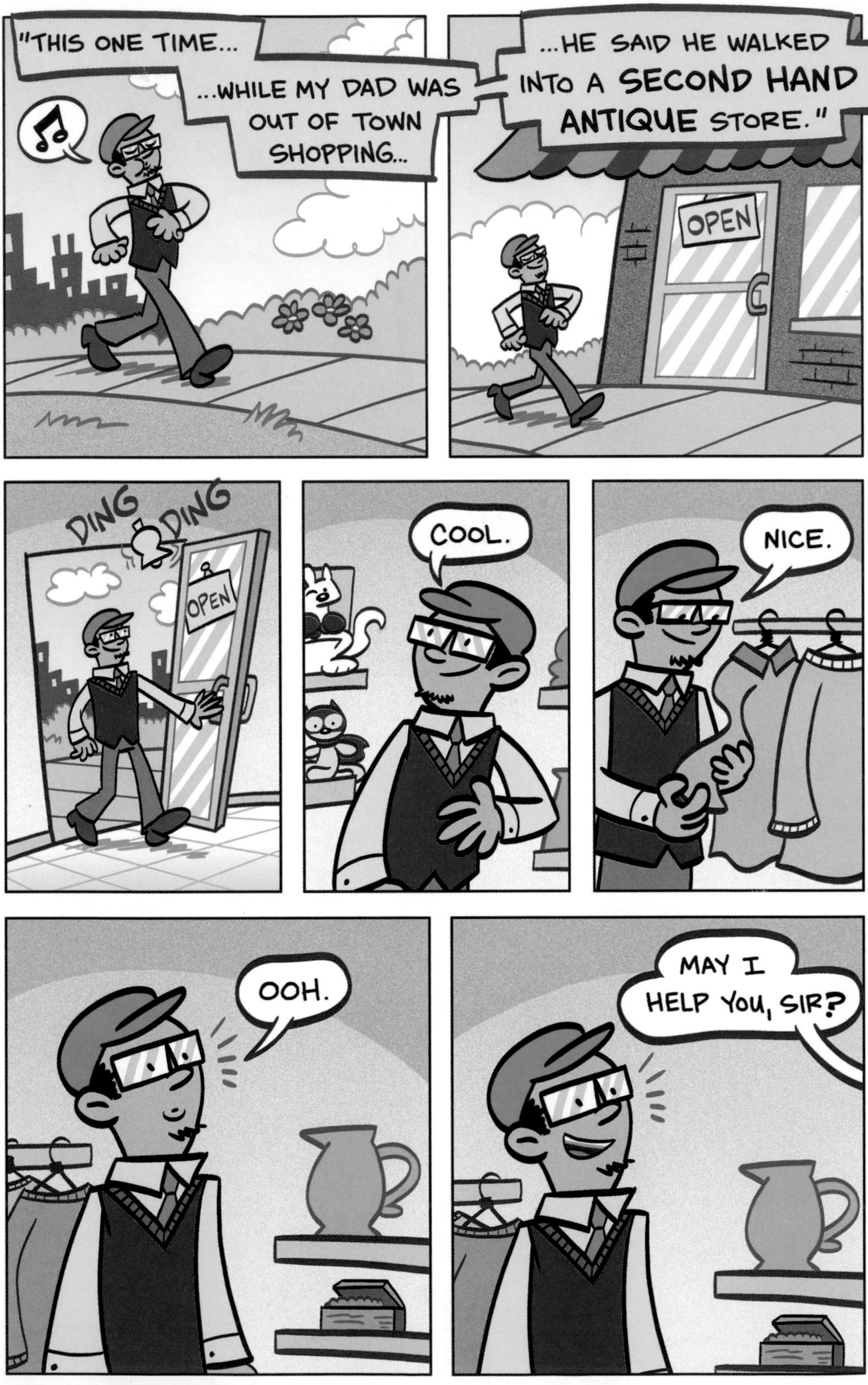
"THIS ONE TIME...
...WHILE MY DAD WAS OUT OF TOWN SHOPPING...
...HE SAID HE WALKED INTO A SECOND HAND ANTIQUE STORE."
OPEN
DING DING
OPEN
COOL.
NICE.
OOH.
MAY I HELP YOU, SIR?

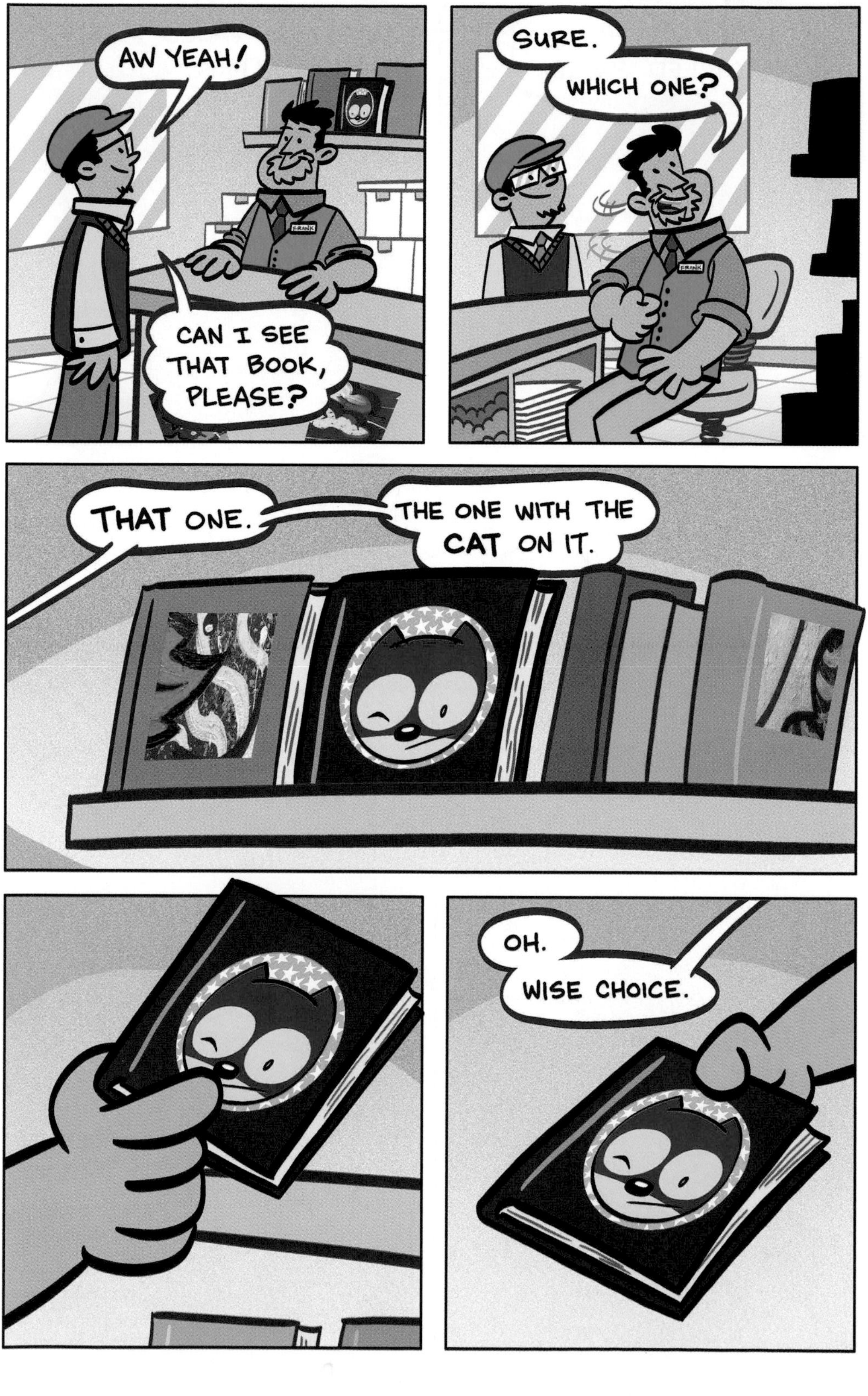
AW YEAH!
CAN I SEE THAT BOOK, PLEASE?
FRANK
SURE.
WHICH ONE?
FRANK
THAT ONE.
THE ONE WITH THE CAT ON IT.
OH.
WISE CHOICE.

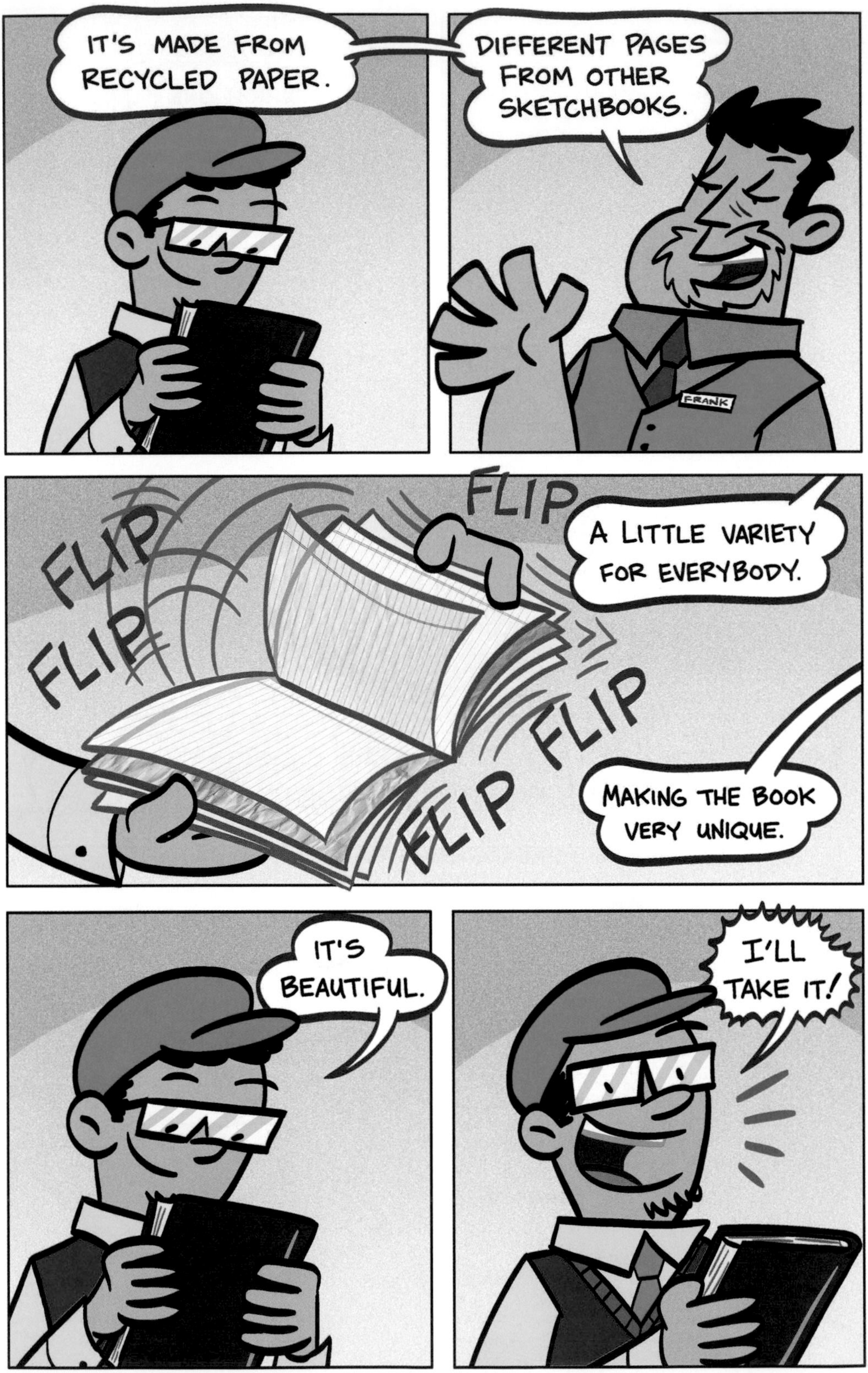
IT'S MADE FROM RECYCLED PAPER.
DIFFERENT PAGES FROM OTHER SKETCHBOOKS.
FRANK
FLIP
FLIP
FLIP
A LITTLE VARIETY FOR EVERYBODY.
FLIP
FLIP
MAKING THE BOOK VERY UNIQUE.
IT'S BEAUTIFUL.
I'LL TAKE IT!

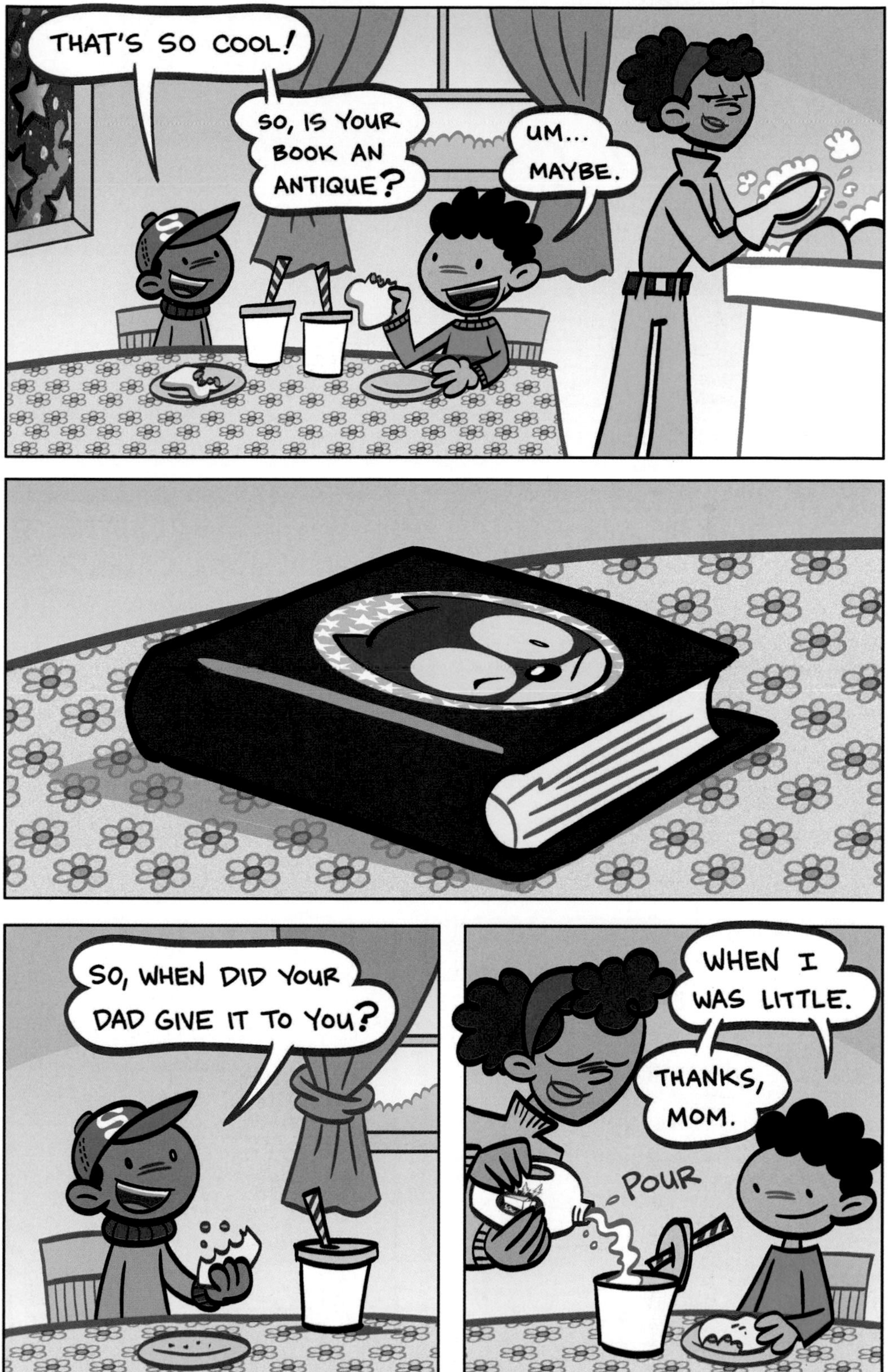
THAT'S SO COOL!
SO, IS YOUR BOOK AN ANTIQUE?
UM... MAYBE.
SO, WHEN DID YOUR DAD GIVE IT TO YOU?
WHEN I WAS LITTLE.
THANKS, MOM.
POUR

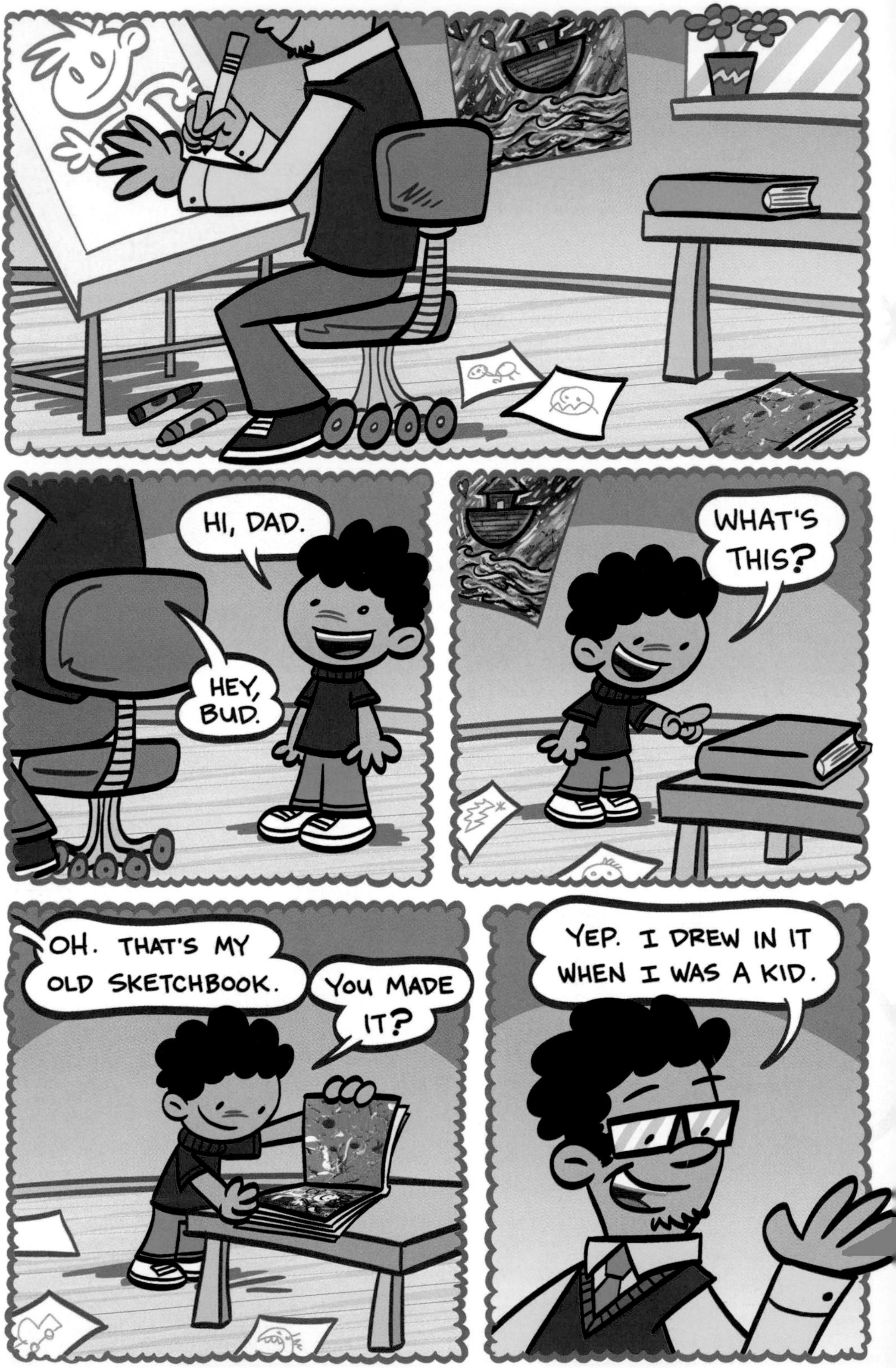
HI, DAD.
HEY, BUD.
WHAT'S THIS?
OH. THAT'S MY OLD SKETCHBOOK.
YOU MADE IT?
YEP. I DREW IN IT WHEN I WAS A KID.

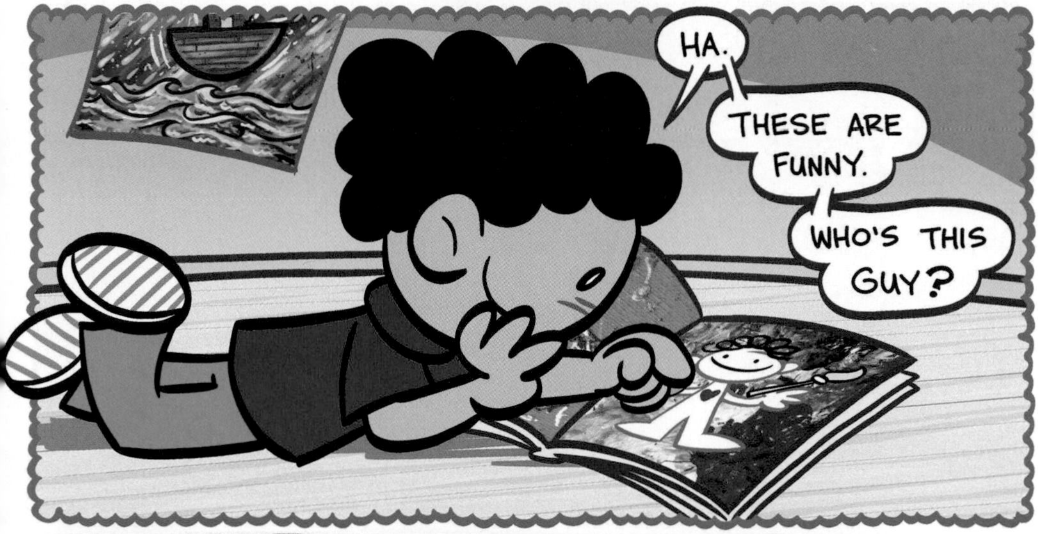
HA.
THESE ARE FUNNY.
WHO'S THIS GUY?

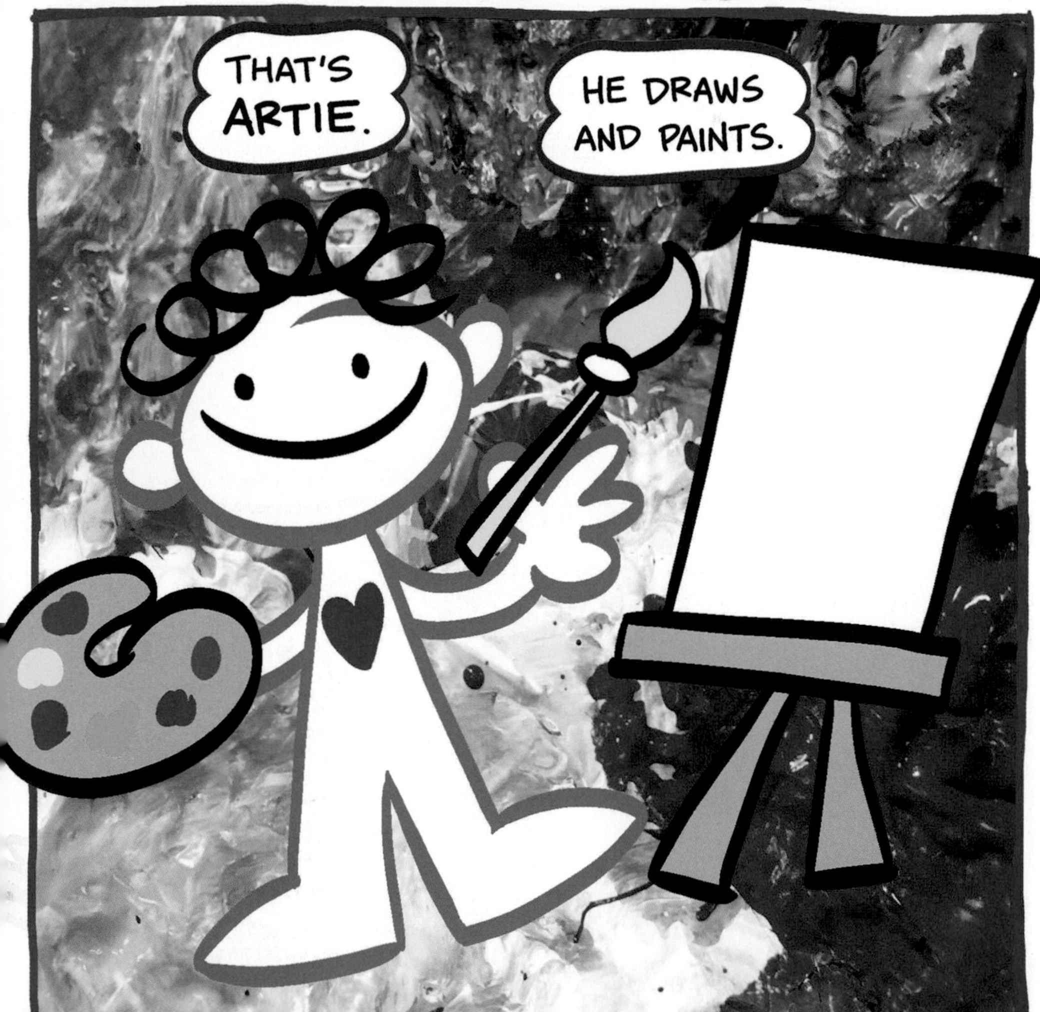
THAT'S ARTIE.
HE DRAWS AND PAINTS.

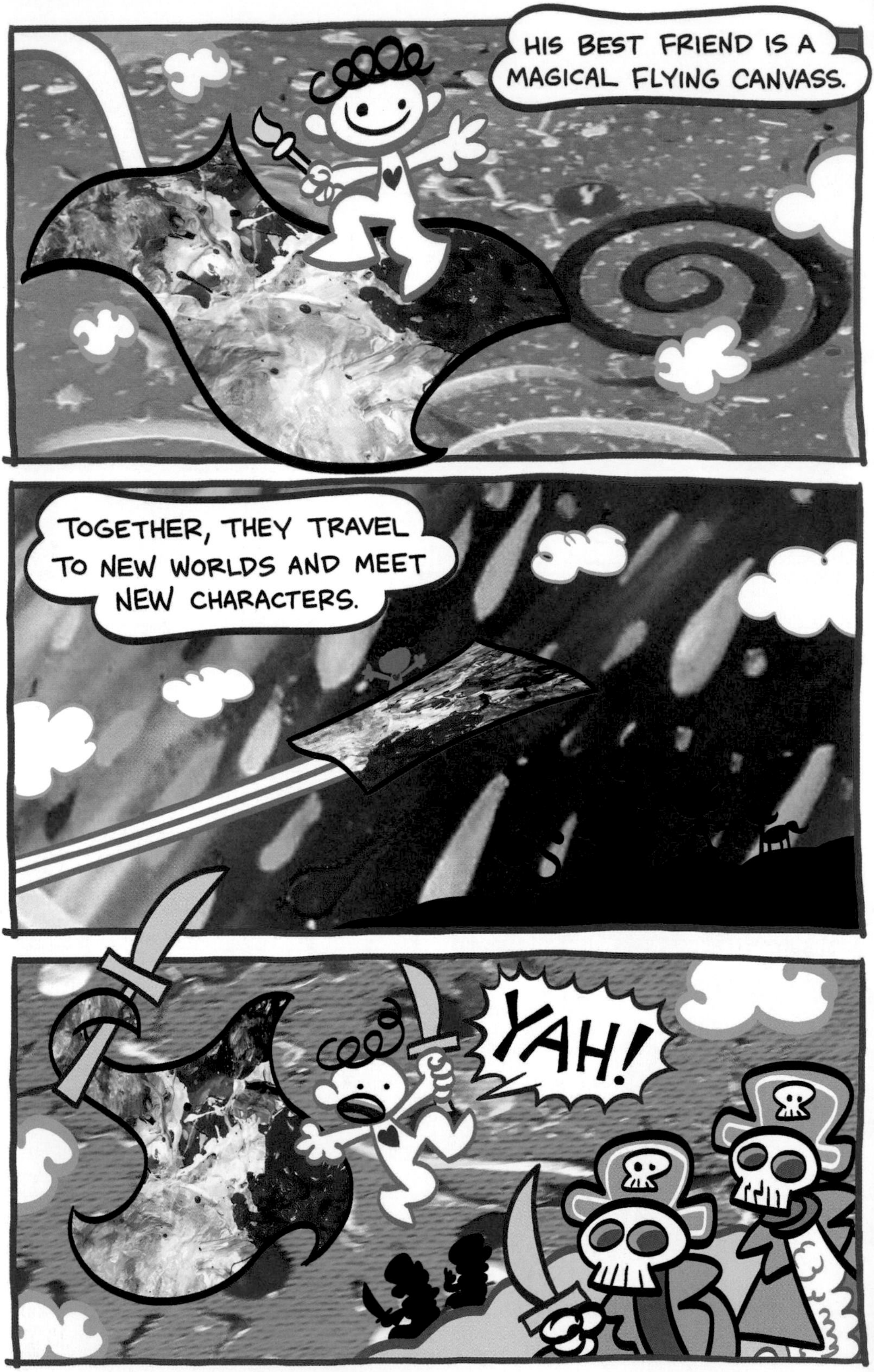
HIS BEST FRIEND IS A MAGICAL FLYING CANVASS.
TOGETHER, THEY TRAVEL TO NEW WORLDS AND MEET NEW CHARACTERS.
YAH!

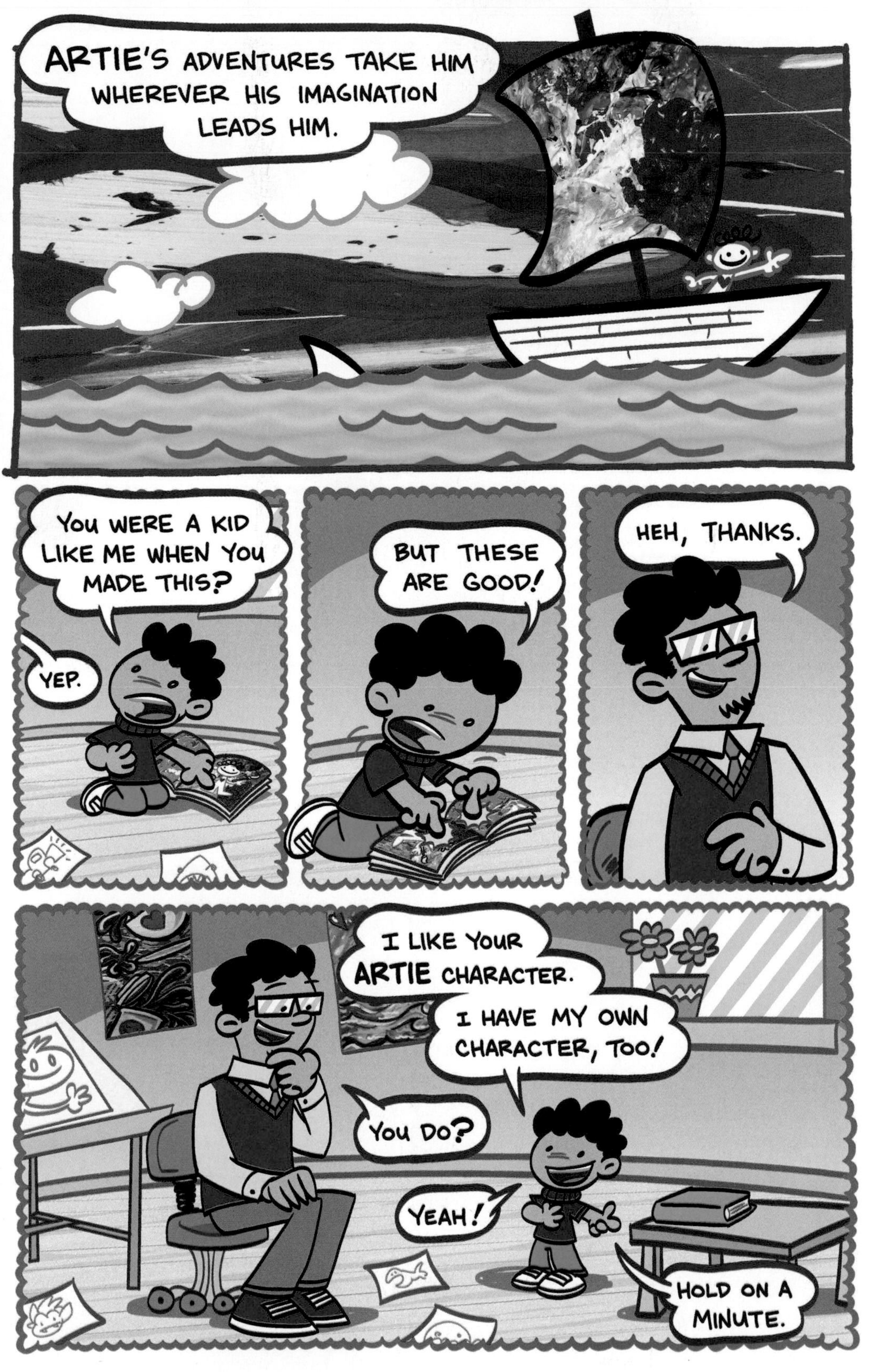
ARTIE'S ADVENTURES TAKE HIM WHEREVER HIS IMAGINATION LEADS HIM.
YOU WERE A KID LIKE ME WHEN YOU MADE THIS?
YEP.
BUT THESE ARE GOOD!
HEH, THANKS.
I LIKE YOUR ARTIE CHARACTER.
I HAVE MY OWN CHARACTER, TOO!
YOU DO?
YEAH!
HOLD ON A MINUTE.

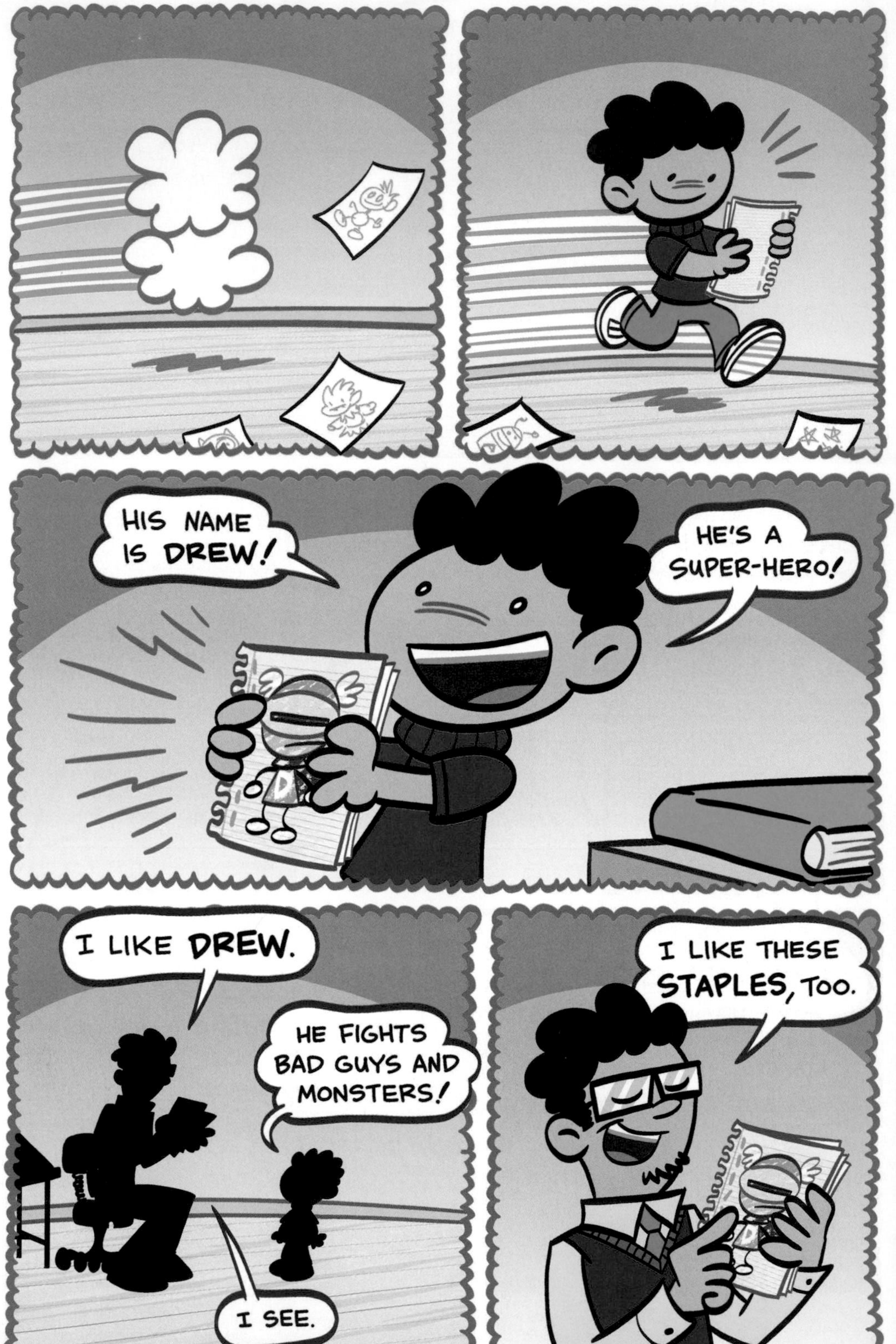
HIS NAME IS DREW!
HE'S A SUPER-HERO!
I LIKE DREW.
HE FIGHTS BAD GUYS AND MONSTERS!
I SEE.
I LIKE THESE STAPLES, TOO.

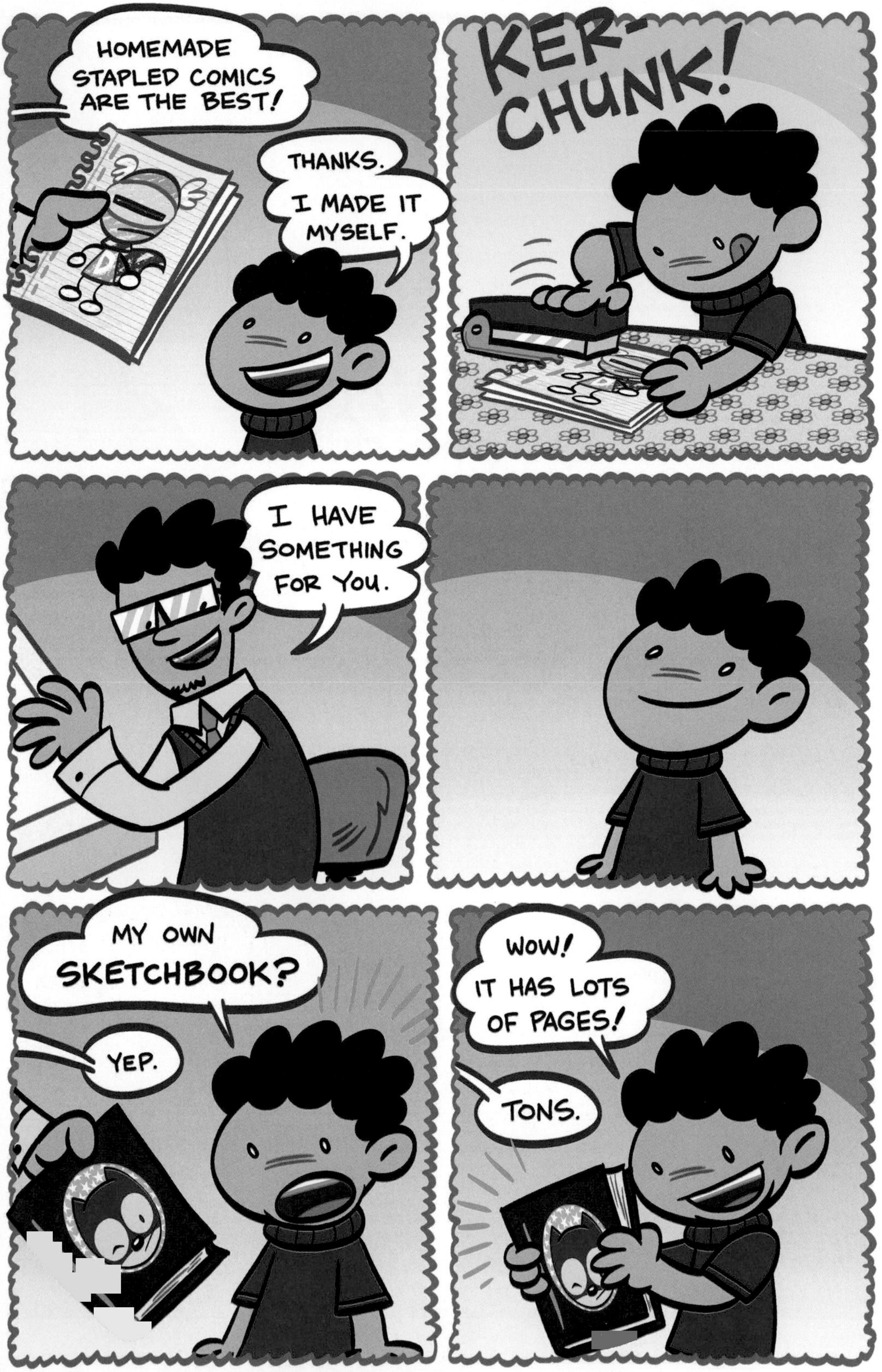

HOMEMADE STAPLED COMICS ARE THE BEST!
THANKS.
I MADE IT MYSELF.
KER-CHUNK!
I HAVE SOMETHING FOR YOU.
MY OWN SKETCHBOOK?
YEP.
WOW!
IT HAS LOTS OF PAGES!
TONS.

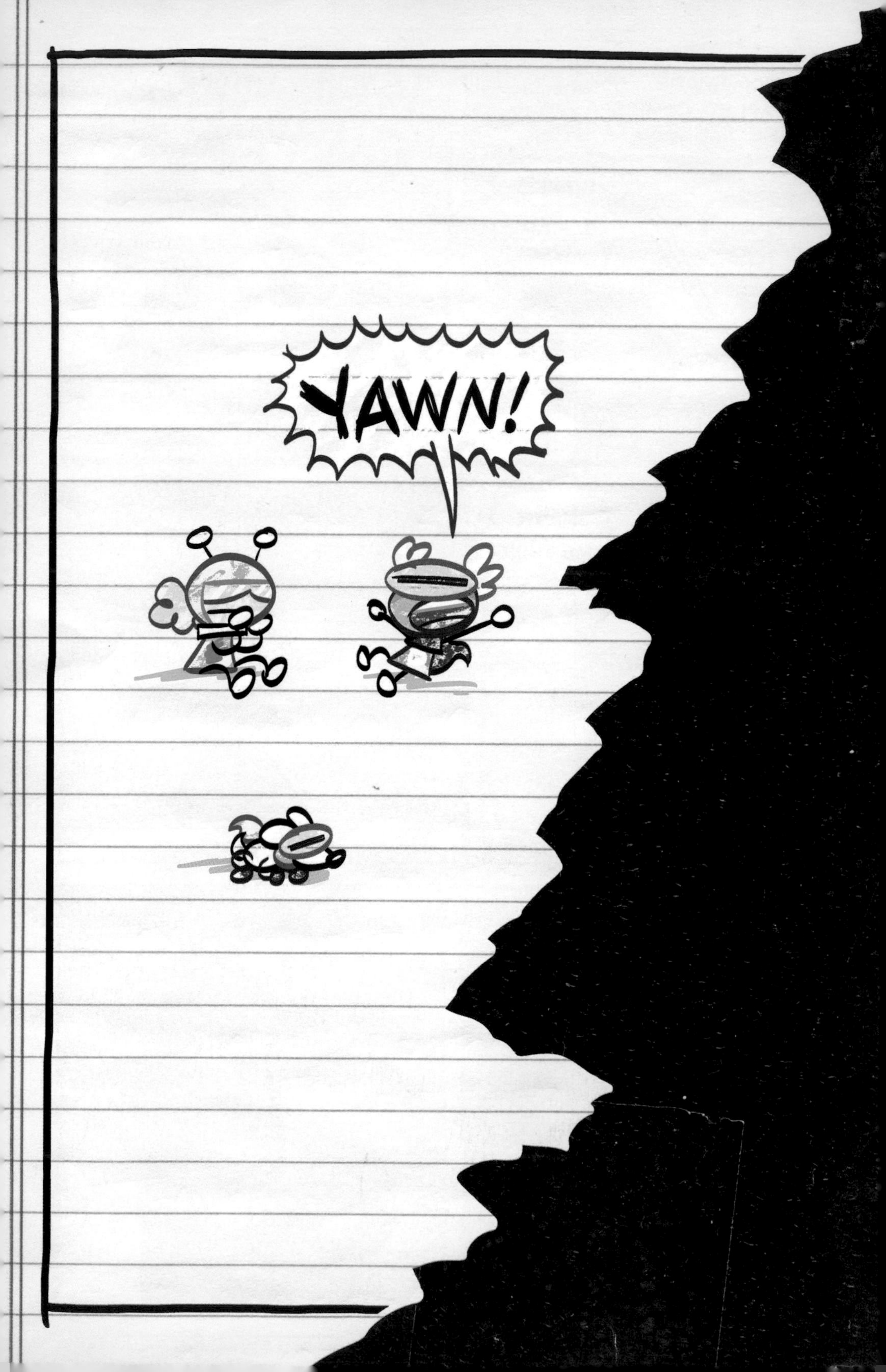
YAWN!

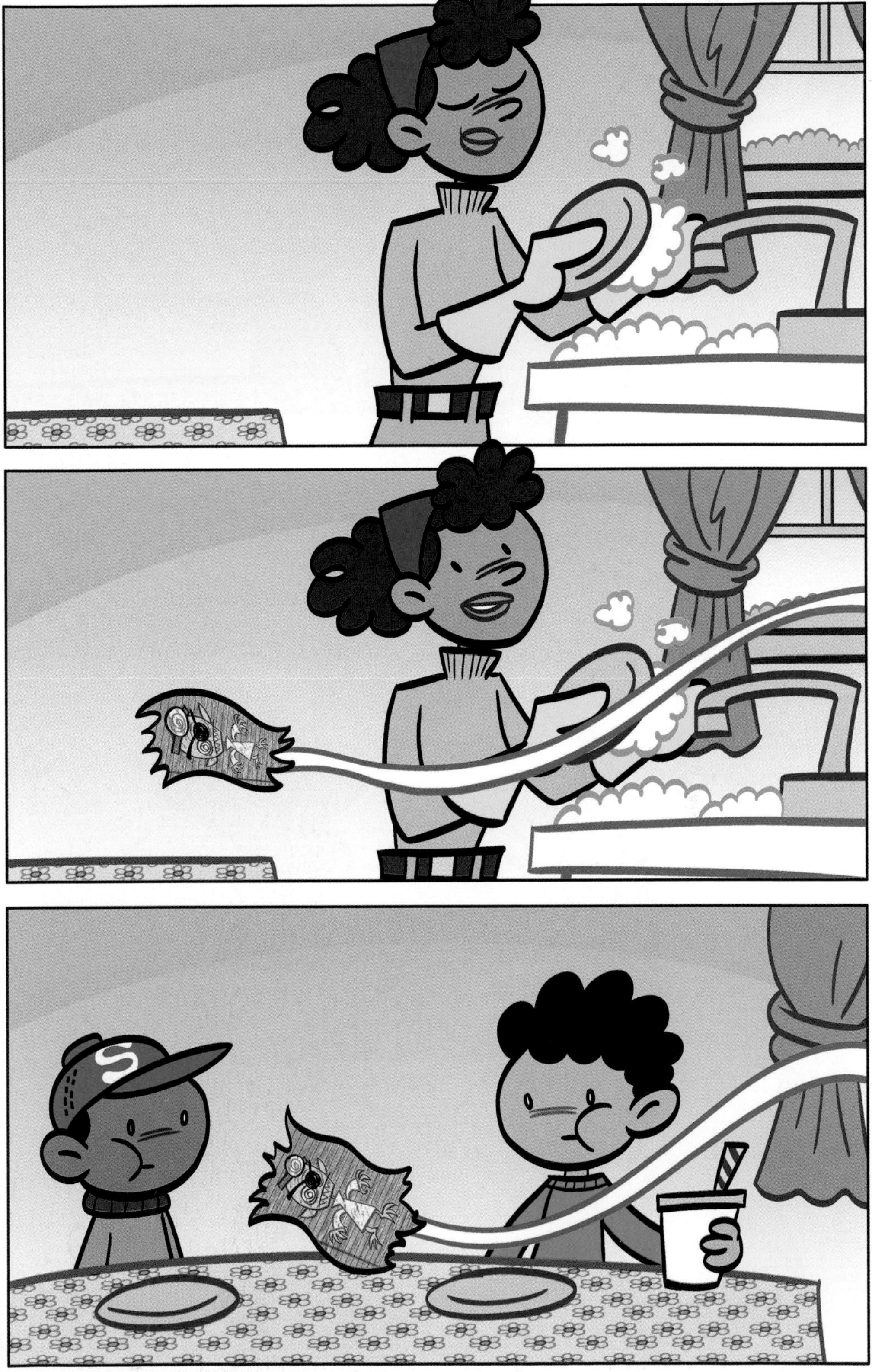

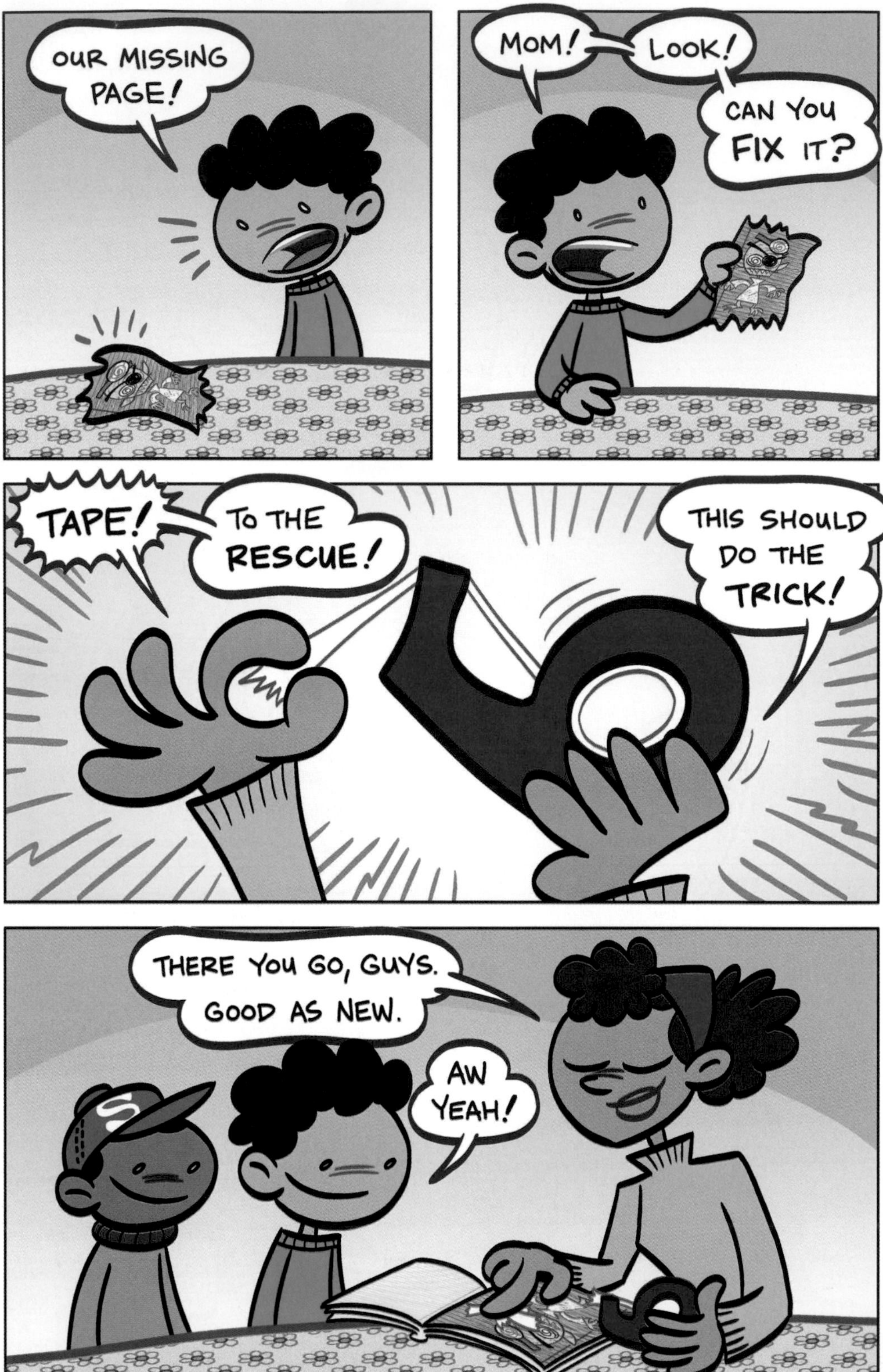
OUR MISSING PAGE!
MOM!
LOOK!
CAN YOU FIX IT?
TAPE!
TO THE RESCUE!
THIS SHOULD DO THE TRICK!
THERE YOU GO, GUYS. GOOD AS NEW.
AW YEAH!

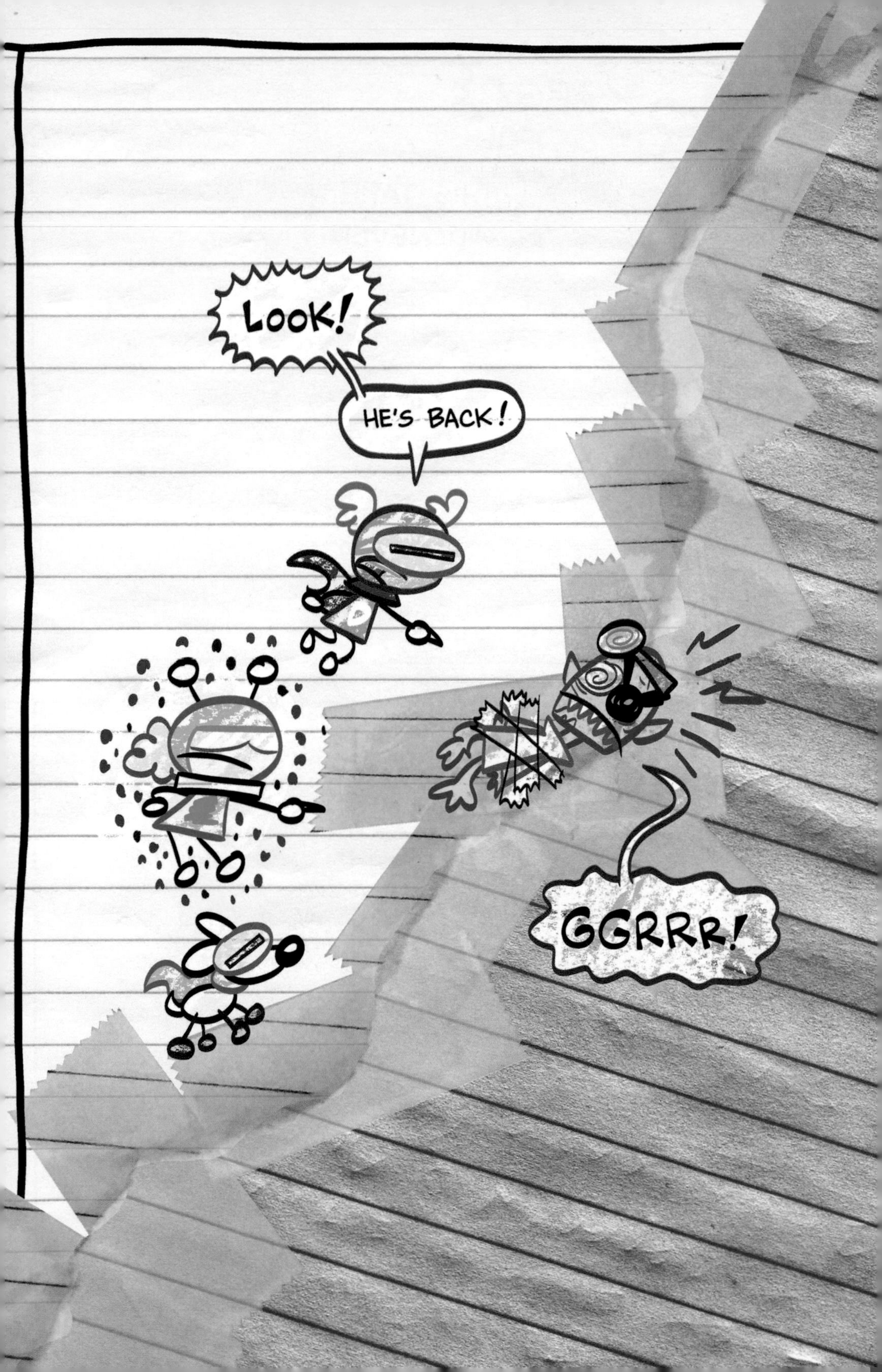
LOOK!
HE'S BACK!
GGRRR!

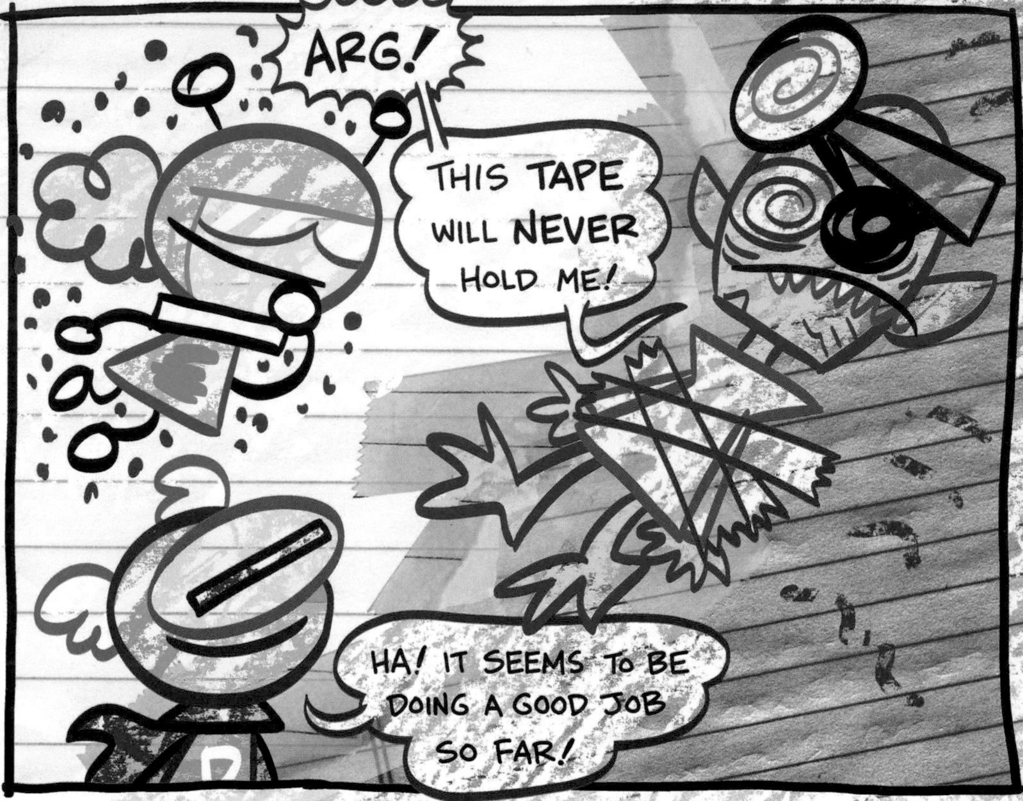
ARG!
THIS TAPE WILL NEVER HOLD ME!
HA! IT SEEMS TO BE DOING A GOOD JOB SO FAR!

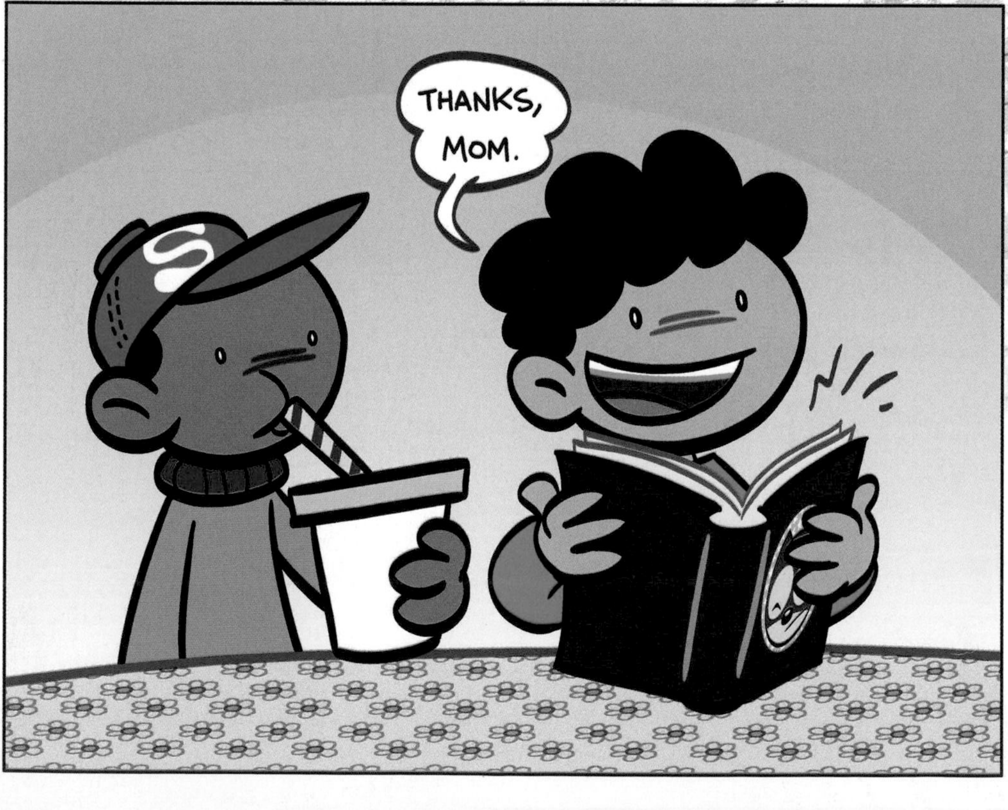
THANKS, MOM.

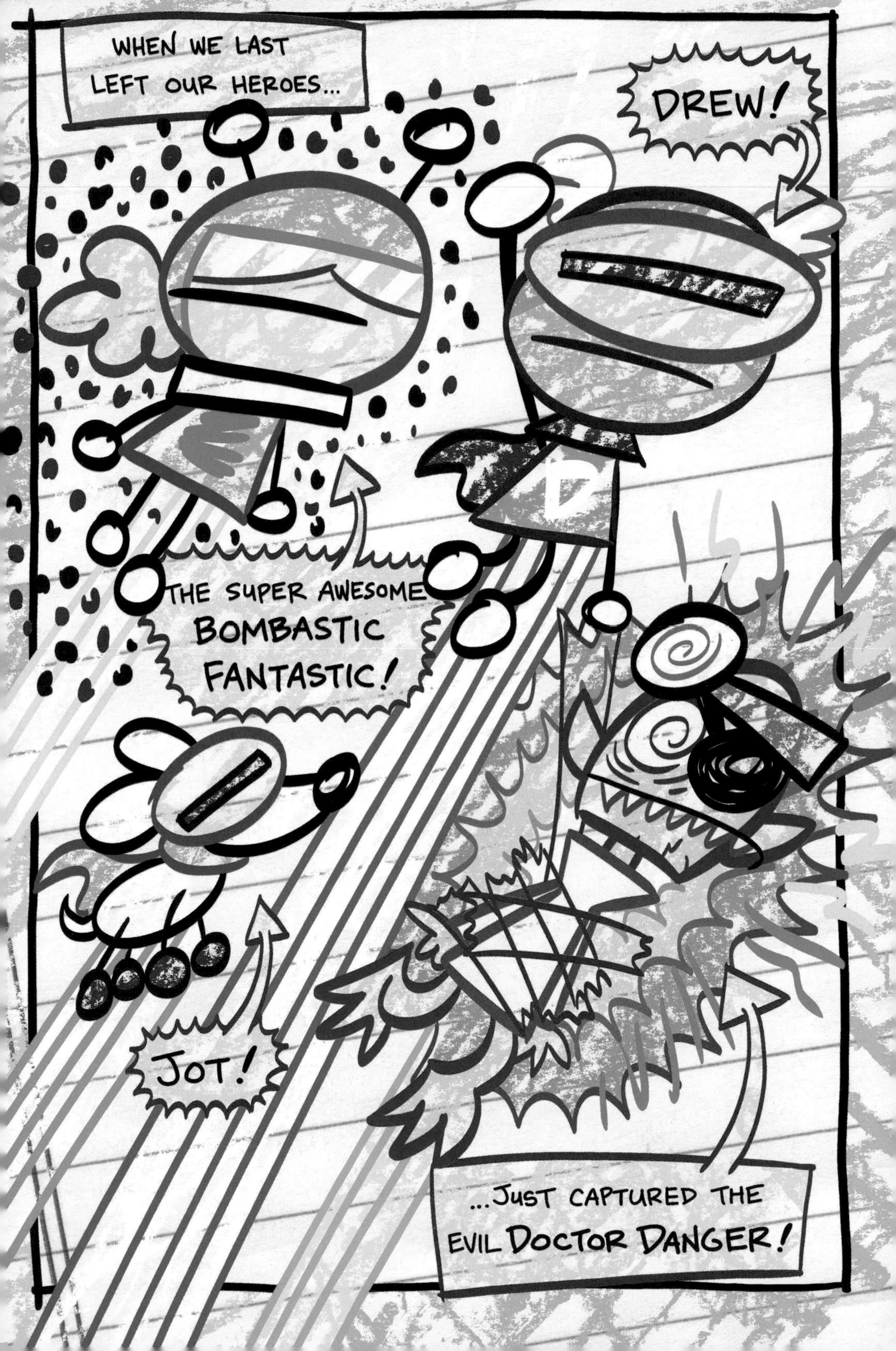
WHEN WE LAST LEFT OUR HEROES...
DREW!
THE SUPER AWESOME BOMBASTIC FANTASTIC!
JOT!
...JUST CAPTURED THE EVIL DOCTOR DANGER!

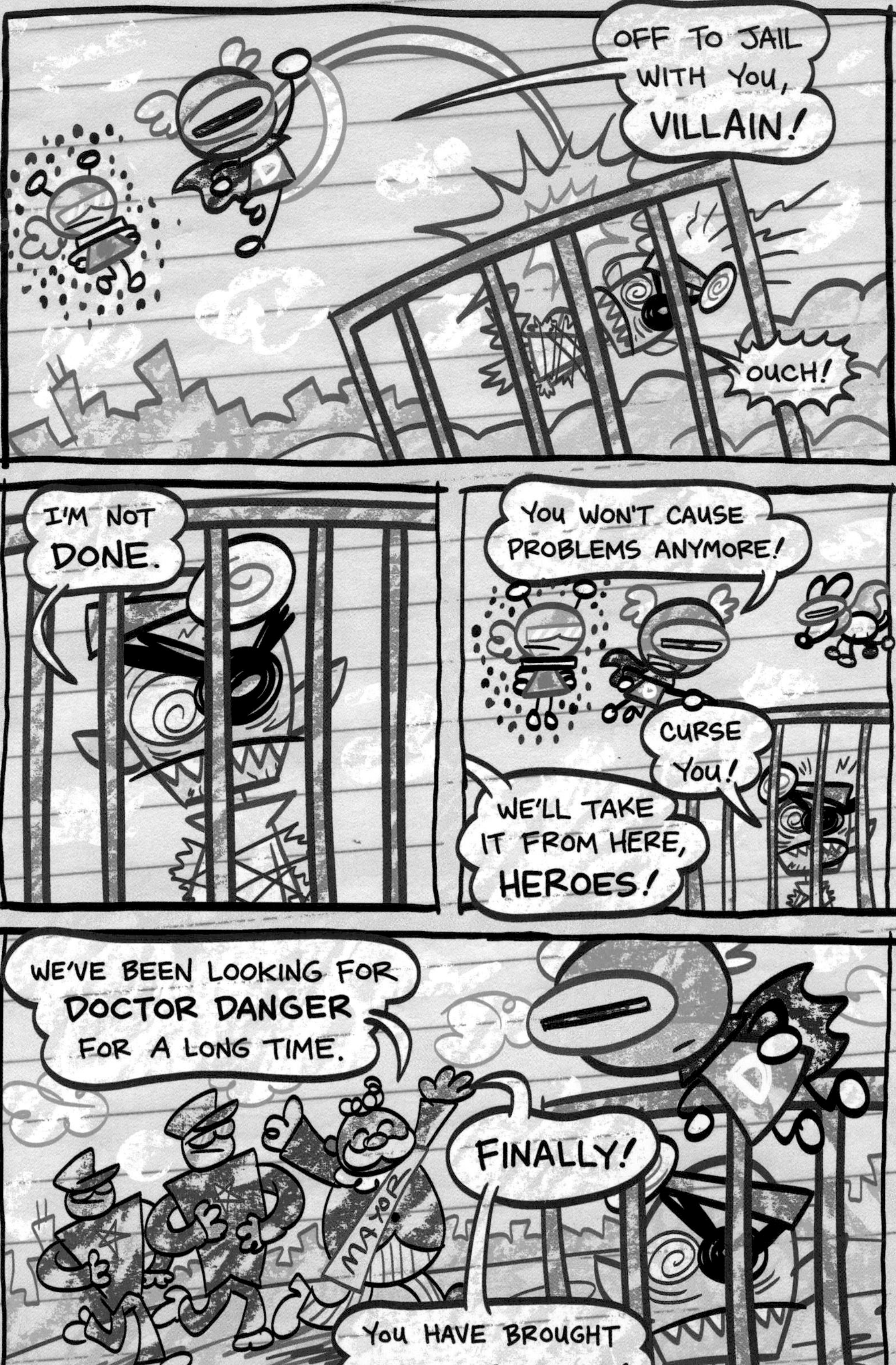
OFF TO JAIL WITH YOU, VILLAIN!
OUCH!
I'M NOT DONE.
YOU WON'T CAUSE PROBLEMS ANYMORE!
CURSE YOU!
WE'LL TAKE IT FROM HERE, HEROES!
WE'VE BEEN LOOKING FOR DOCTOR DANGER FOR A LONG TIME.
FINALLY!
MAYOR
YOU HAVE BROUGHT HIM TO JUSTICE!

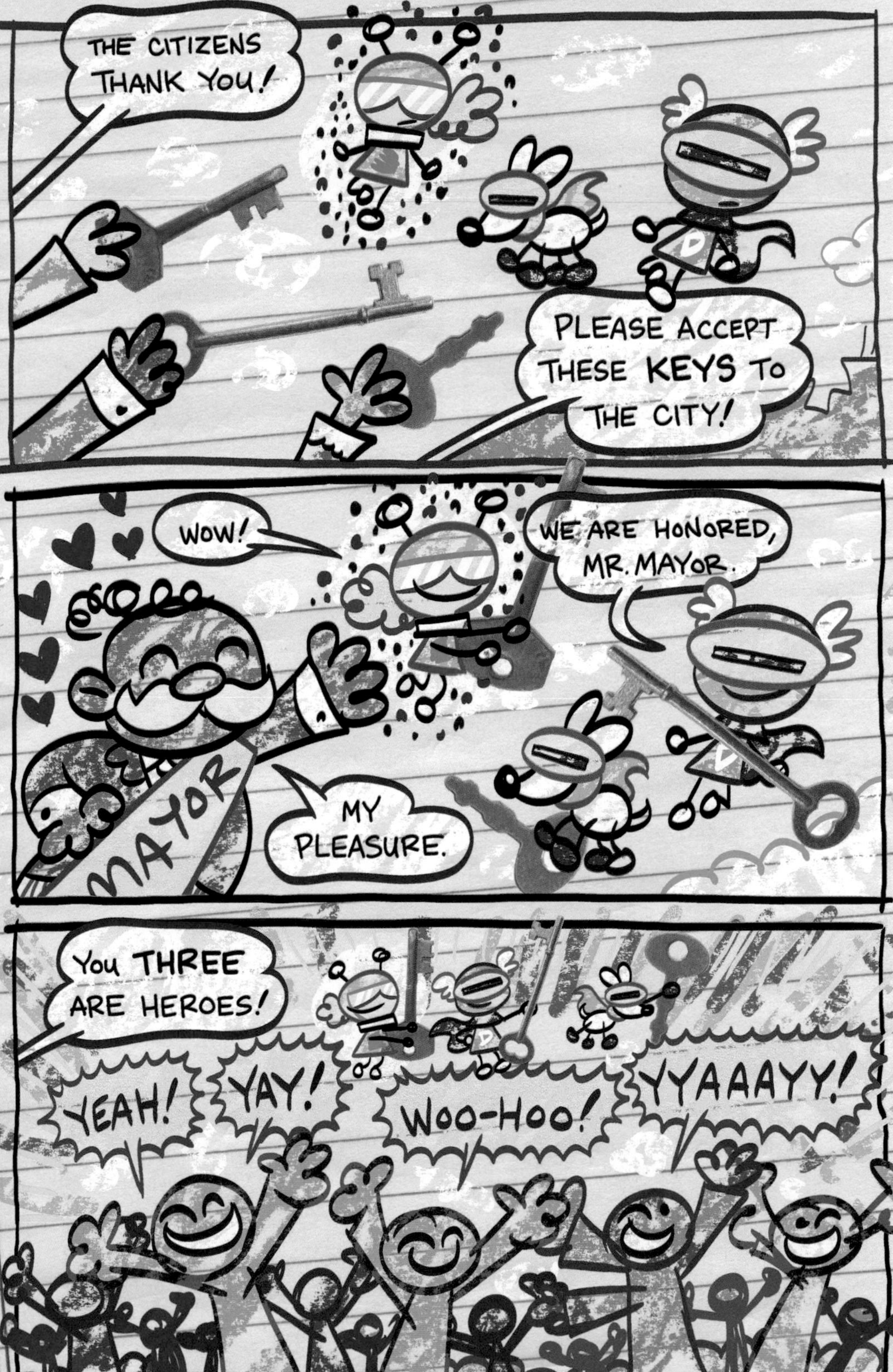
THE CITIZENS THANK YOU!
PLEASE ACCEPT THESE KEYS TO THE CITY!
WOW!
WE ARE HONORED, MR. MAYOR.
MAYOR
MY PLEASURE.
You THREE ARE HEROES!
YEAH!
YAY!
WOO-HOO!
YYAAAYY!

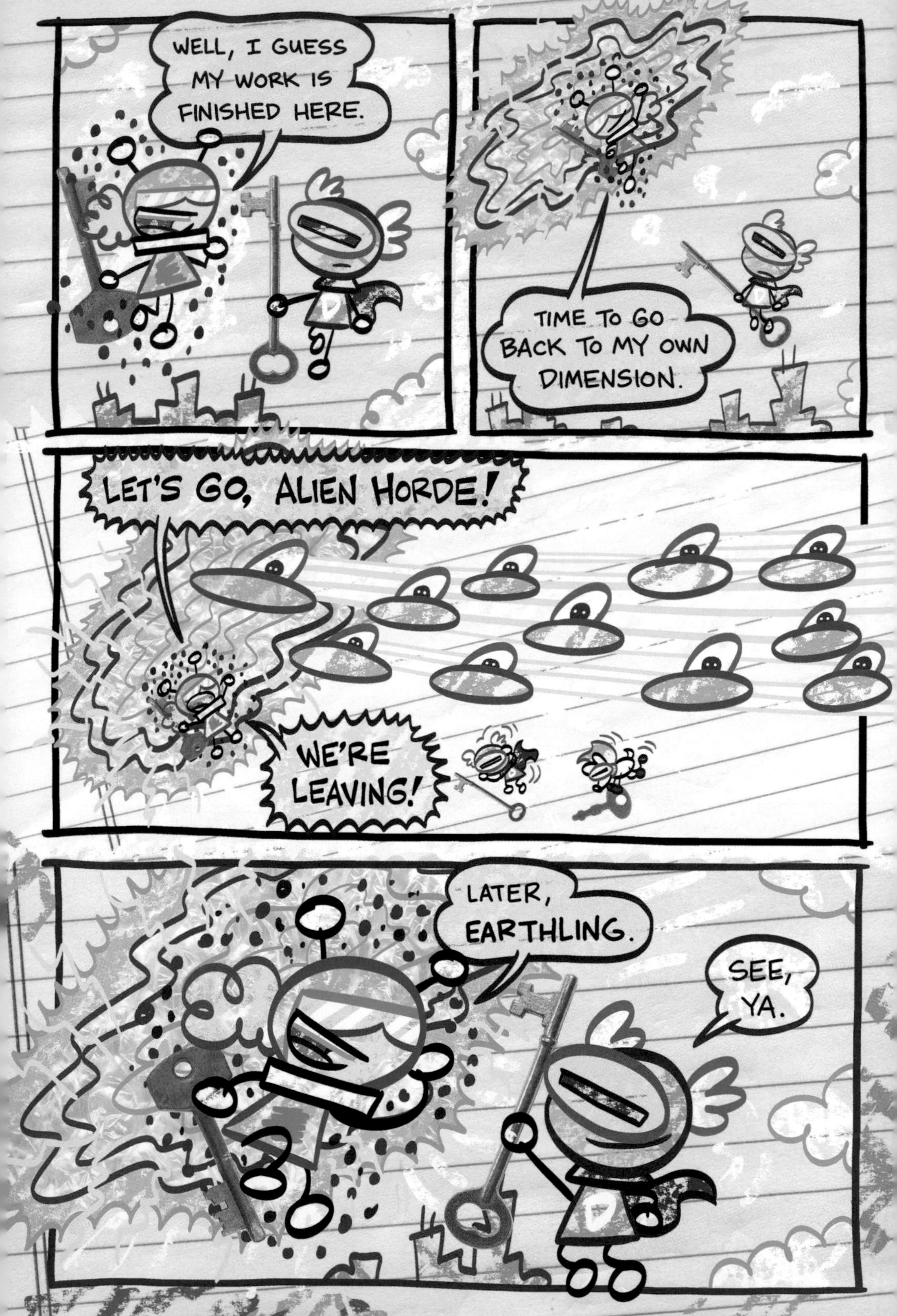
WELL, I GUESS MY WORK IS FINISHED HERE.
TIME TO GO BACK TO MY OWN DIMENSION.
LET'S GO, ALIEN HORDE!
WE'RE LEAVING!
LATER, EARTHLING.
SEE, YA.

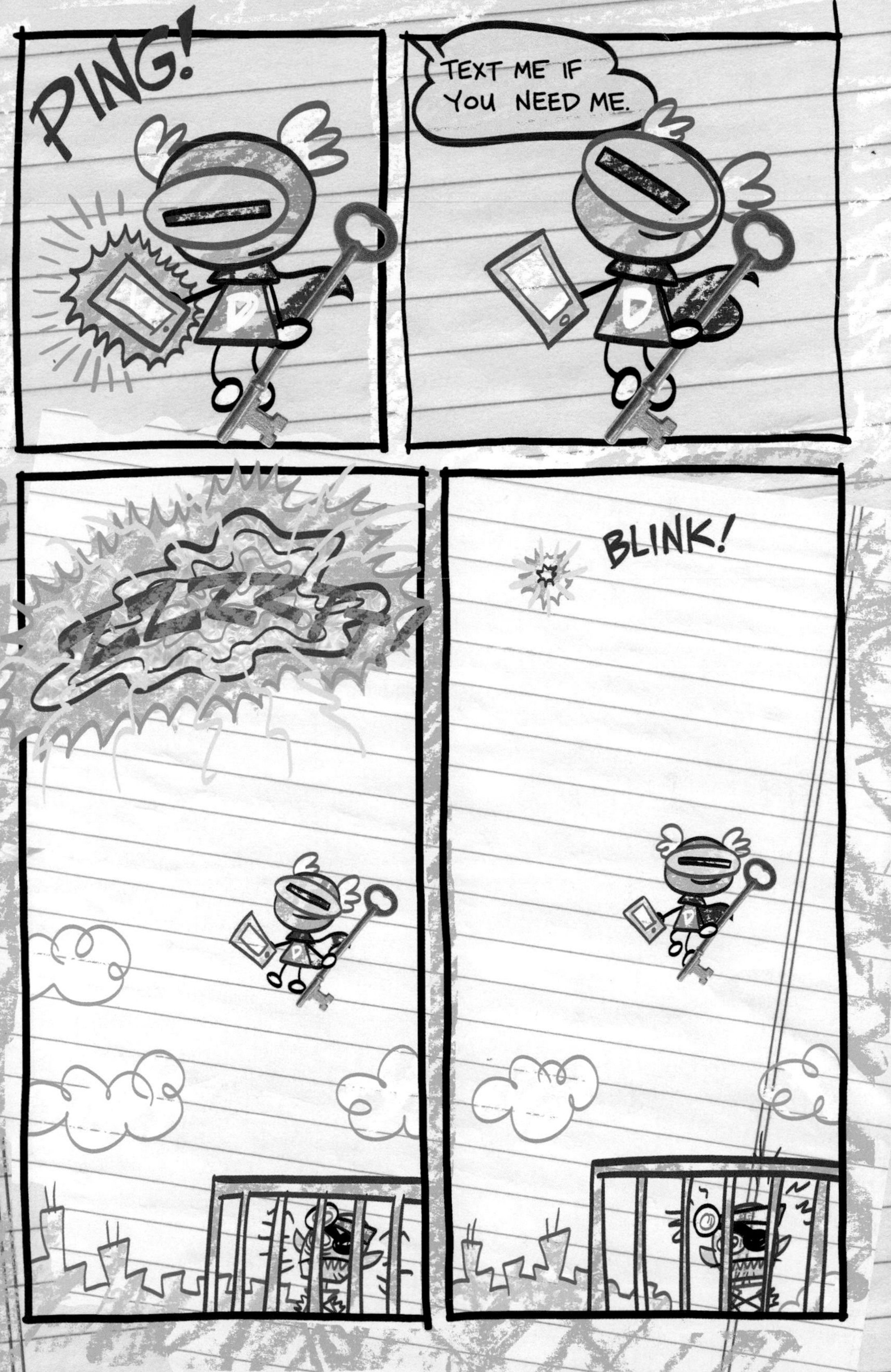
PING!
TEXT ME IF YOU NEED ME.
ZZZZT!
BLINK!

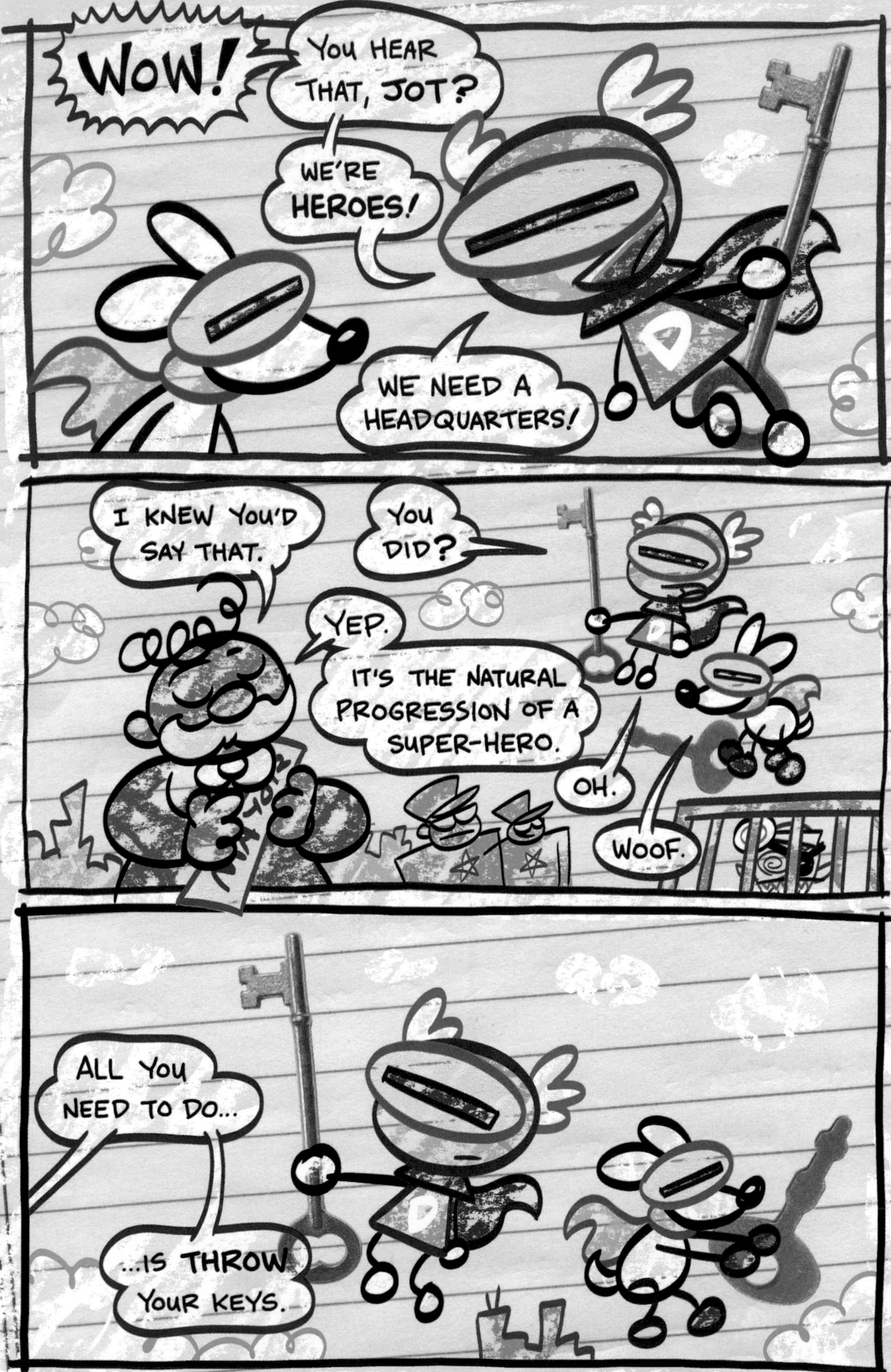
WOW!
YOU HEAR THAT, JOT?
WE'RE HEROES!
WE NEED A HEADQUARTERS!
I KNEW YOU'D SAY THAT.
YOU DID?
YEP.
IT'S THE NATURAL PROGRESSION OF A SUPER-HERO.
OH.
WOOF.
ALL YOU NEED TO DO...
...IS THROW YOUR KEYS.

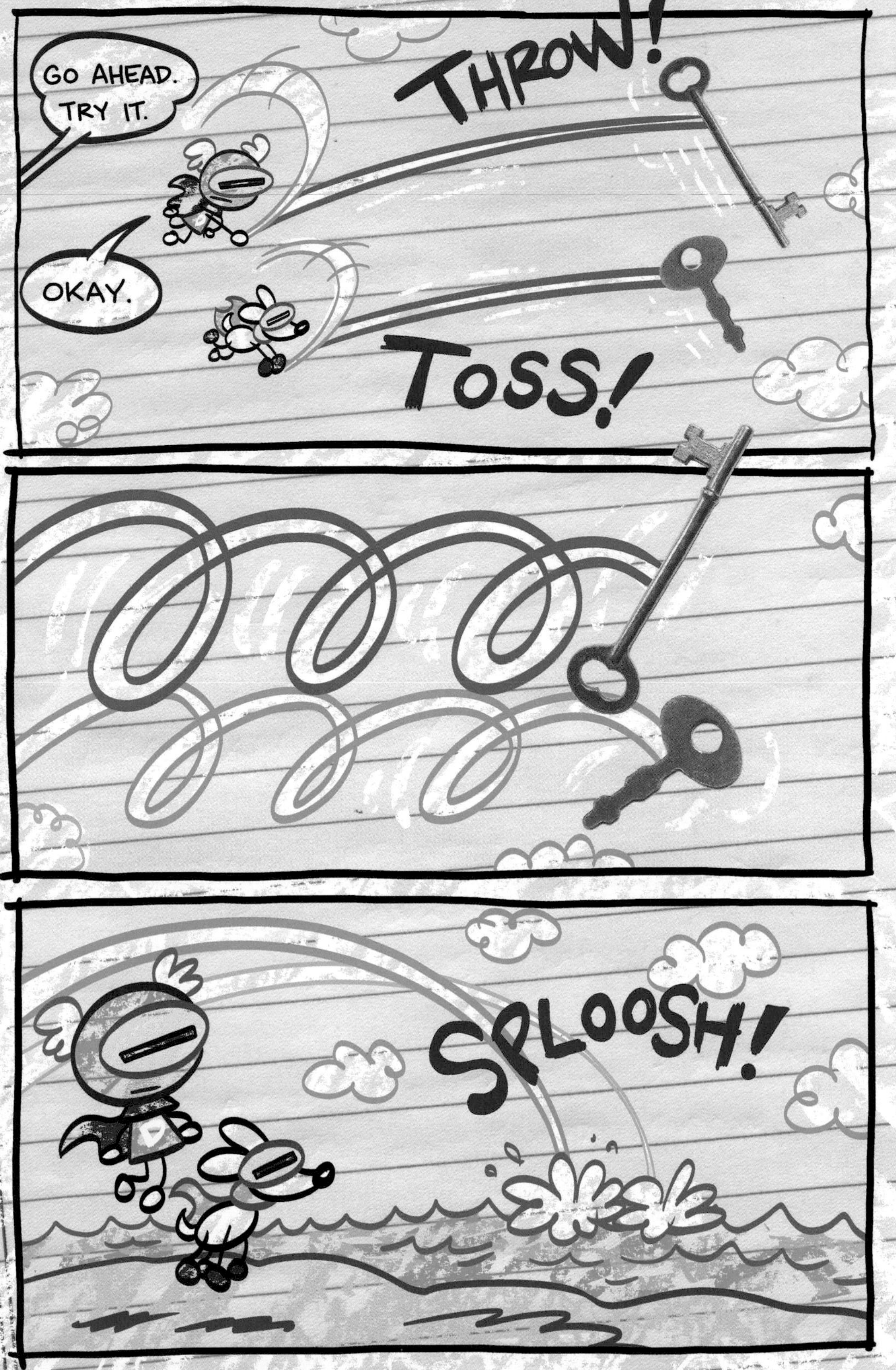
GO AHEAD. TRY IT.
THROW!
OKAY.
TOSS!
SPLOOSH!

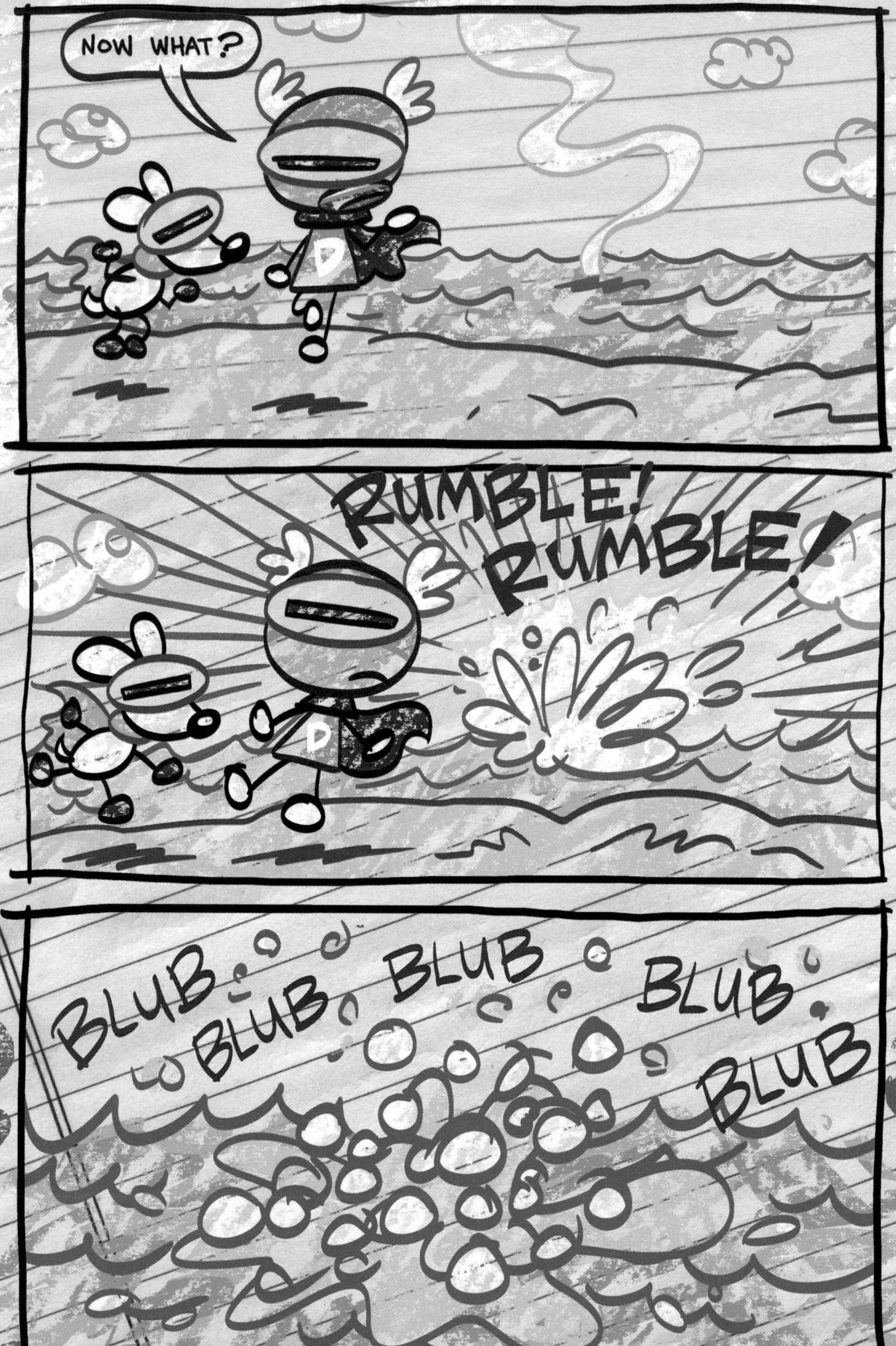

NOW WHAT?
RUMBLE!
RUMBLE!
BLUB
BLUB
BLUB
BLUB
BLUB

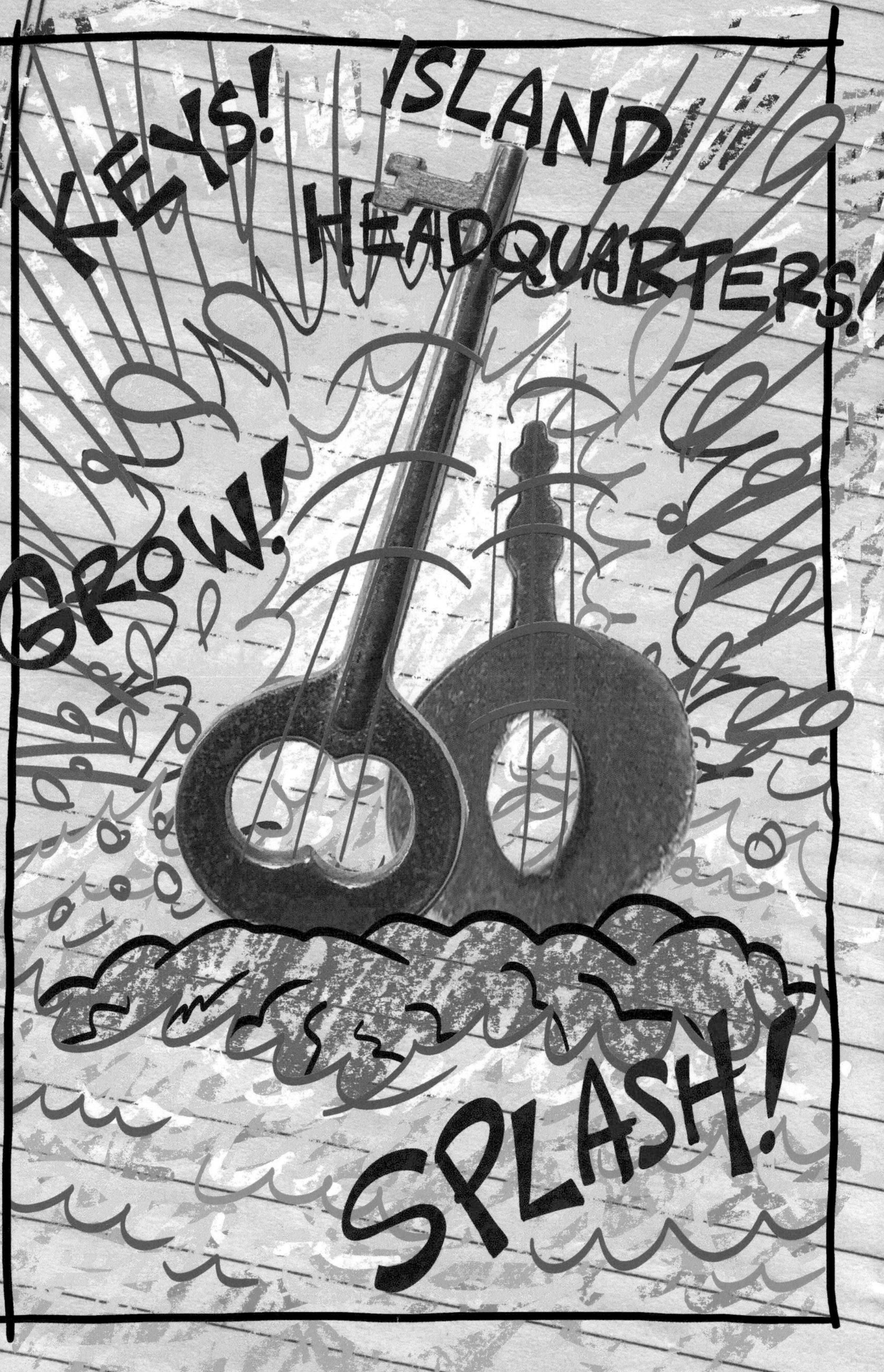
KEYS!
ISLAND
HEADQUARTERS!
GROW!
SPLASH!

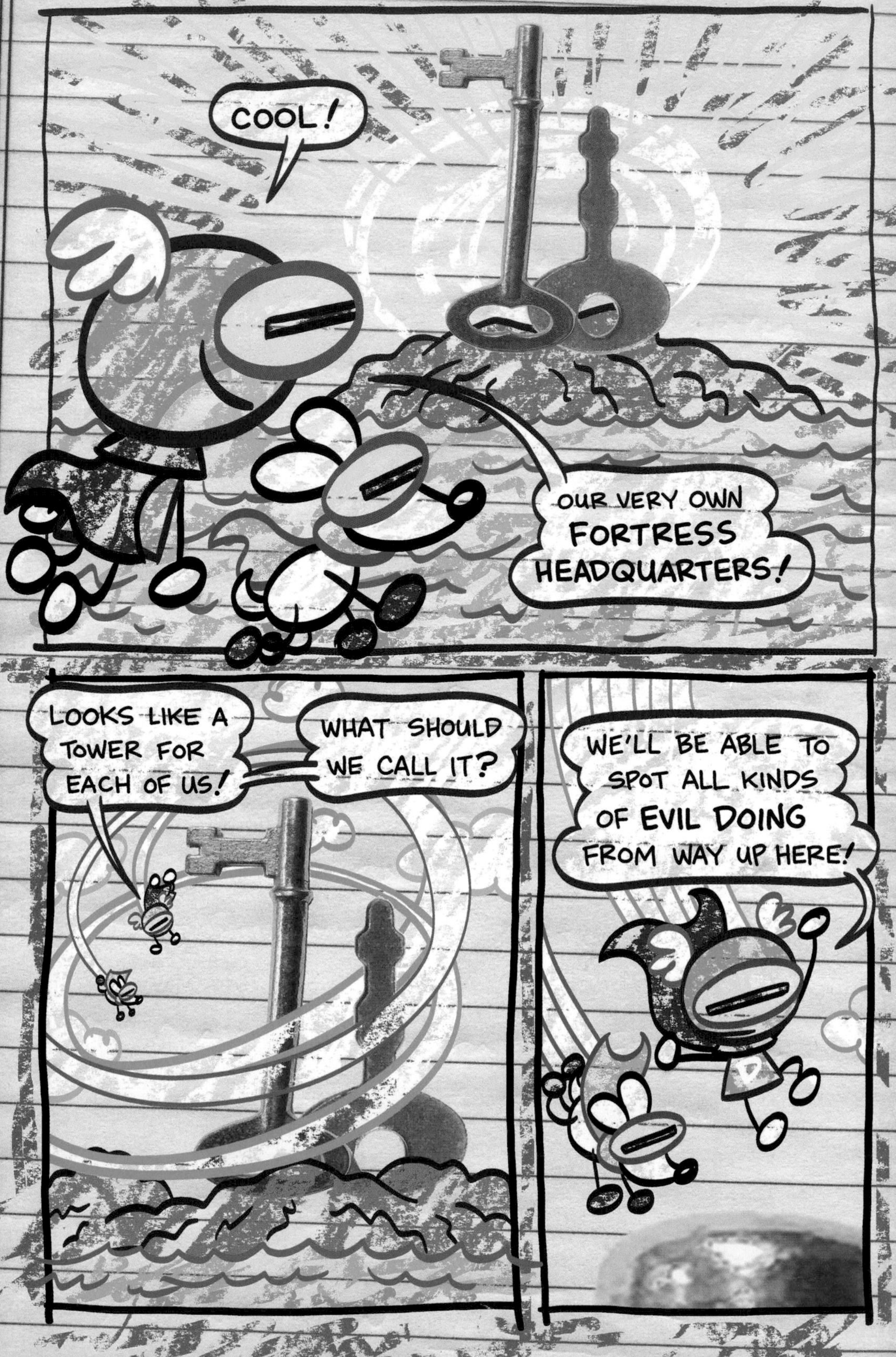
COOL!
OUR VERY OWN FORTRESS HEADQUARTERS!
LOOKS LIKE A TOWER FOR EACH OF US!
WHAT SHOULD WE CALL IT?
WE'LL BE ABLE TO SPOT ALL KINDS OF EVIL DOING FROM WAY UP HERE!

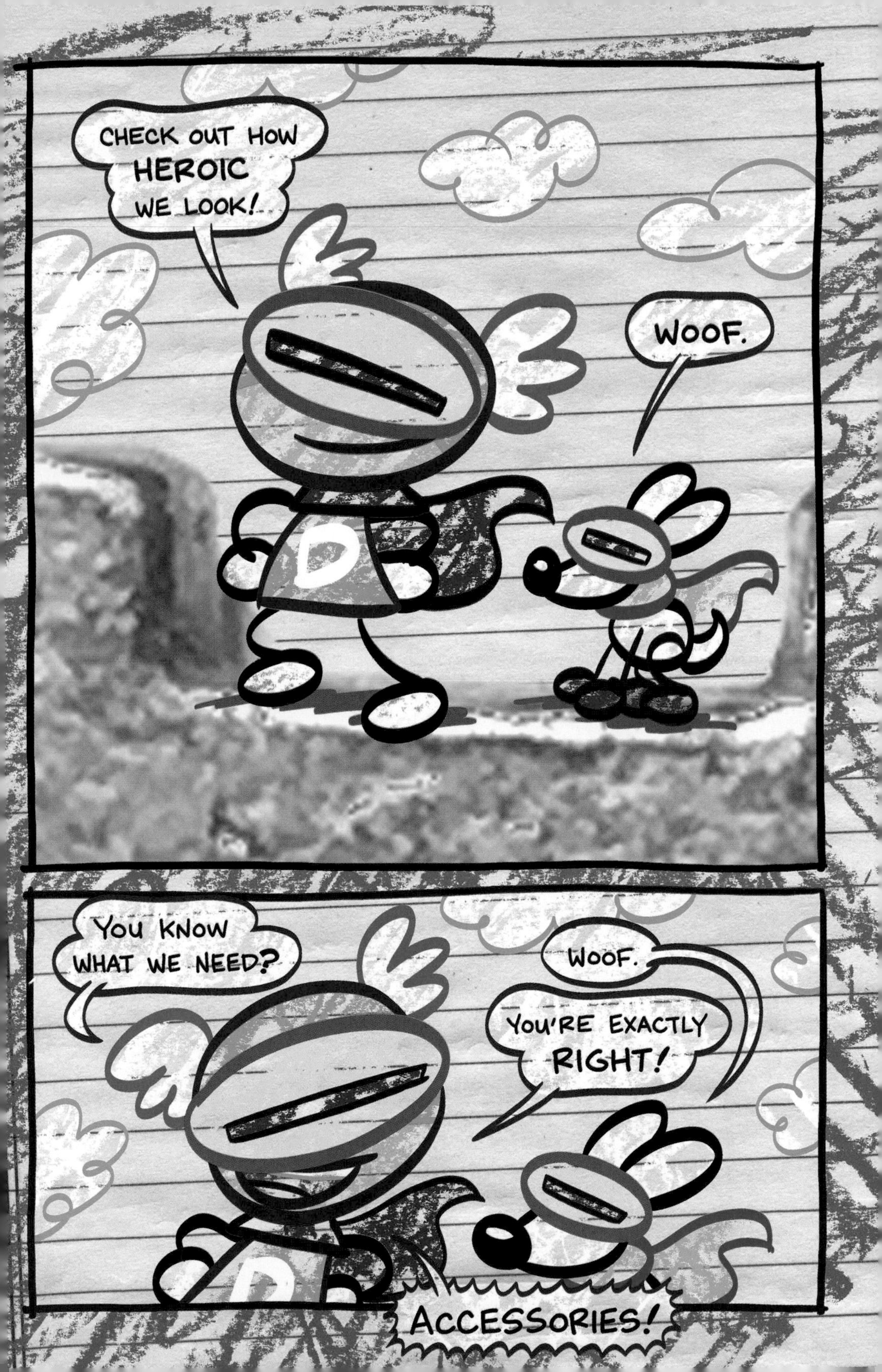
CHECK OUT HOW HEROIC WE LOOK!
WOOF.
YOU KNOW WHAT WE NEED?
WOOF.
YOU'RE EXACTLY RIGHT!
ACCESSORIES!

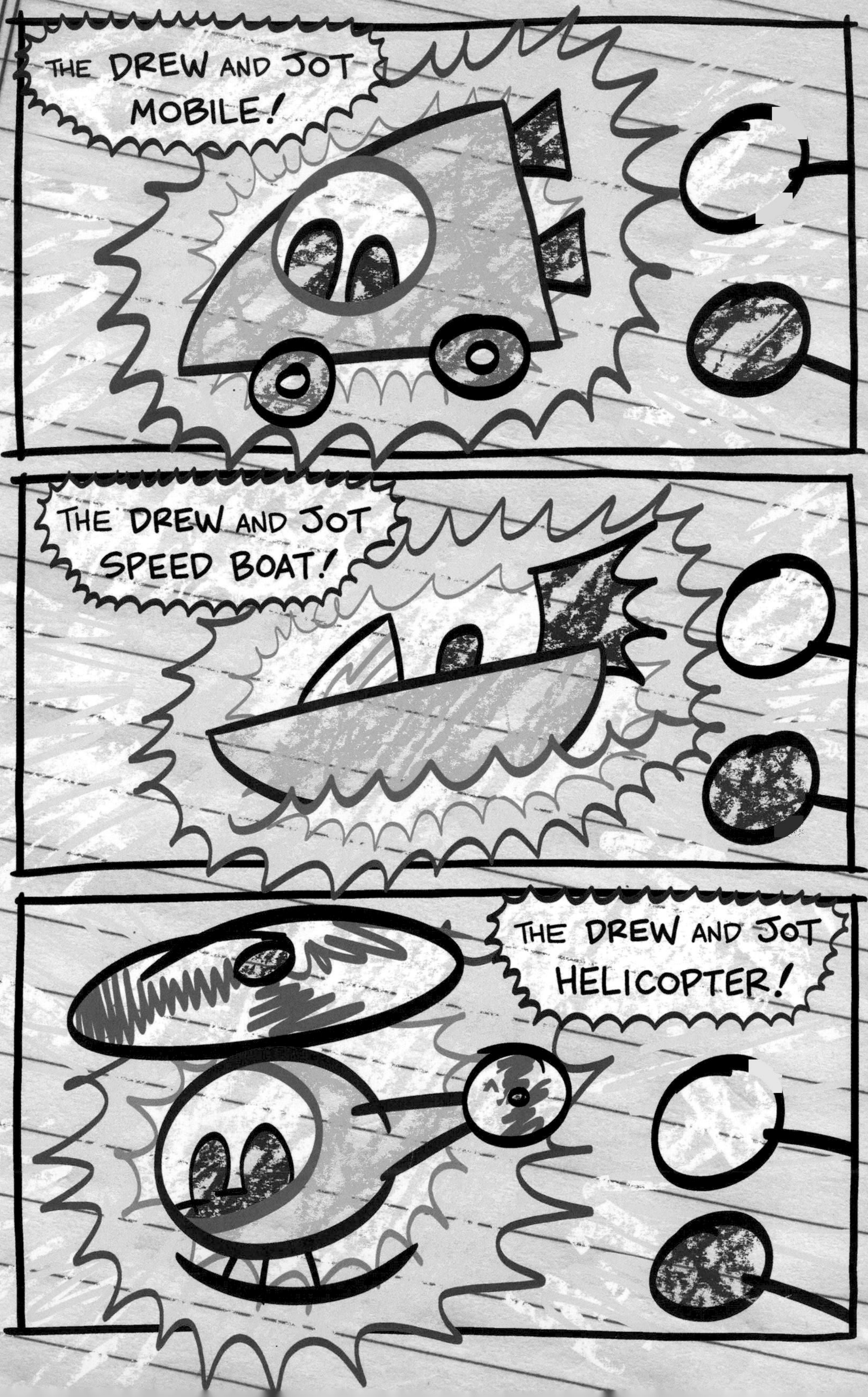
THE DREW AND JOT MOBILE!
THE DREW AND JOT SPEED BOAT!
THE DREW AND JOT HELICOPTER!

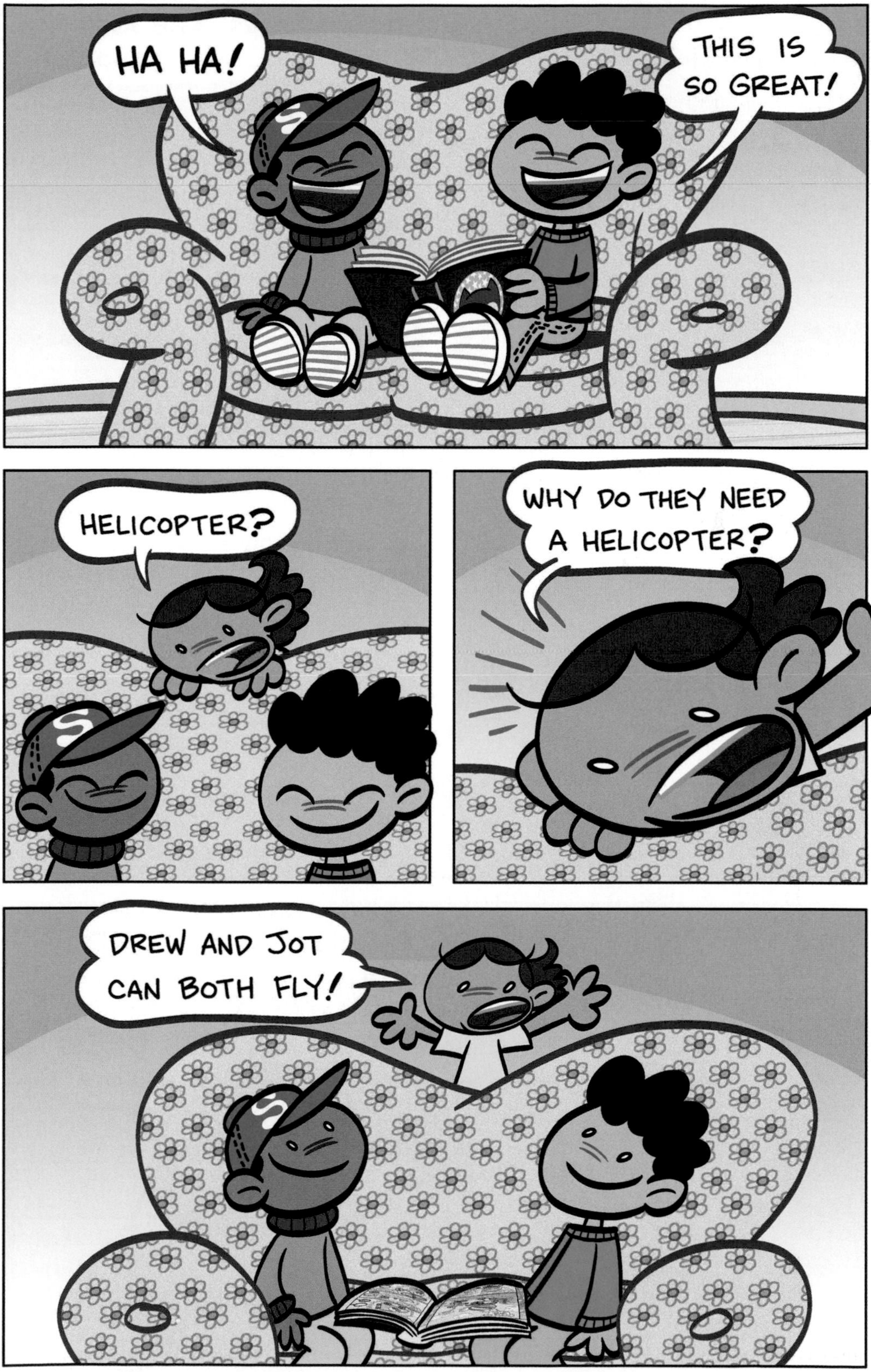
HA HA!
THIS IS SO GREAT!
HELICOPTER?
WHY DO THEY NEED A HELICOPTER?
DREW AND JOT CAN BOTH FLY!

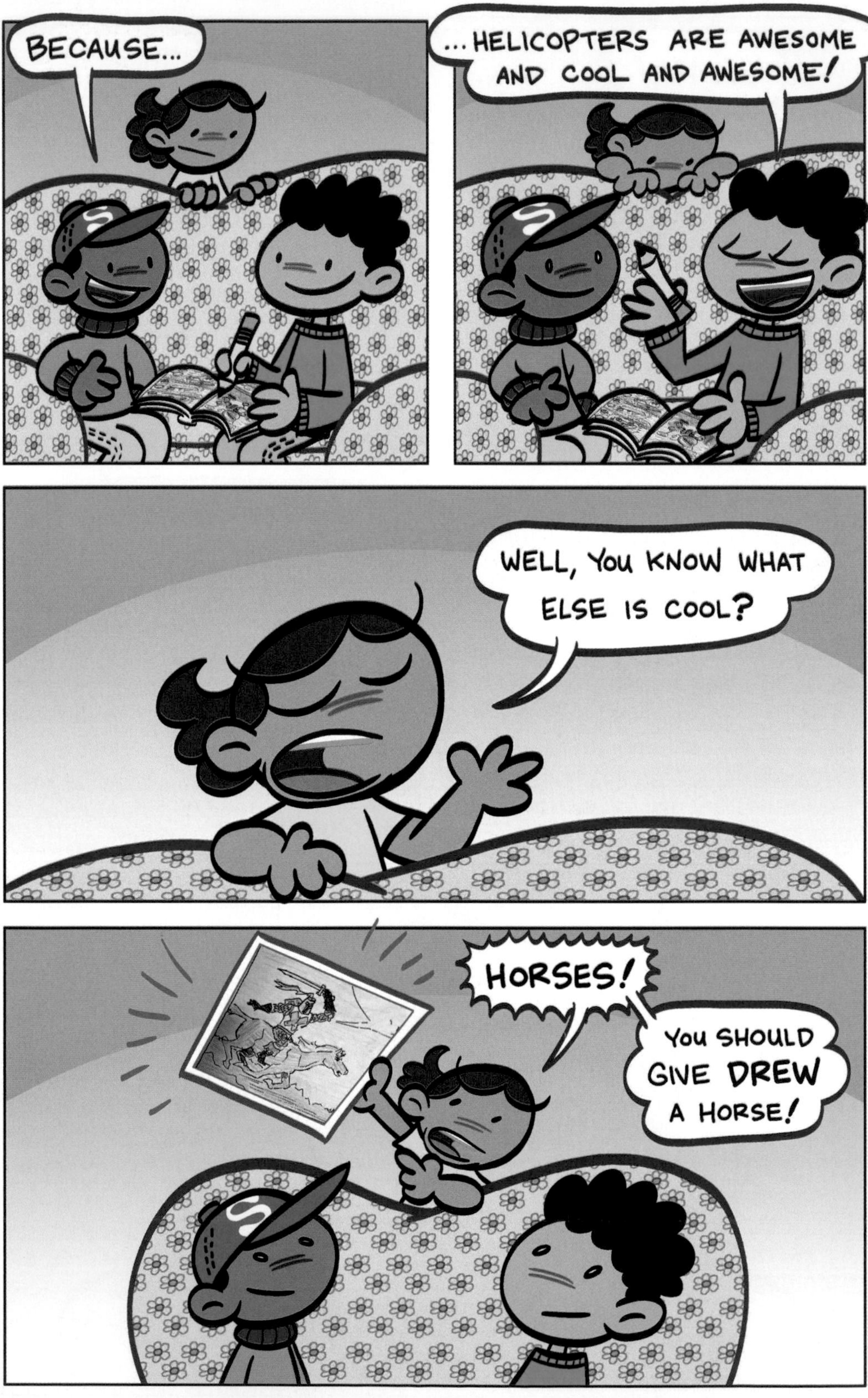
BECAUSE...
...HELICOPTERS ARE AWESOME AND COOL AND AWESOME!
WELL, YOU KNOW WHAT ELSE IS COOL?
HORSES!
YOU SHOULD GIVE DREW A HORSE!

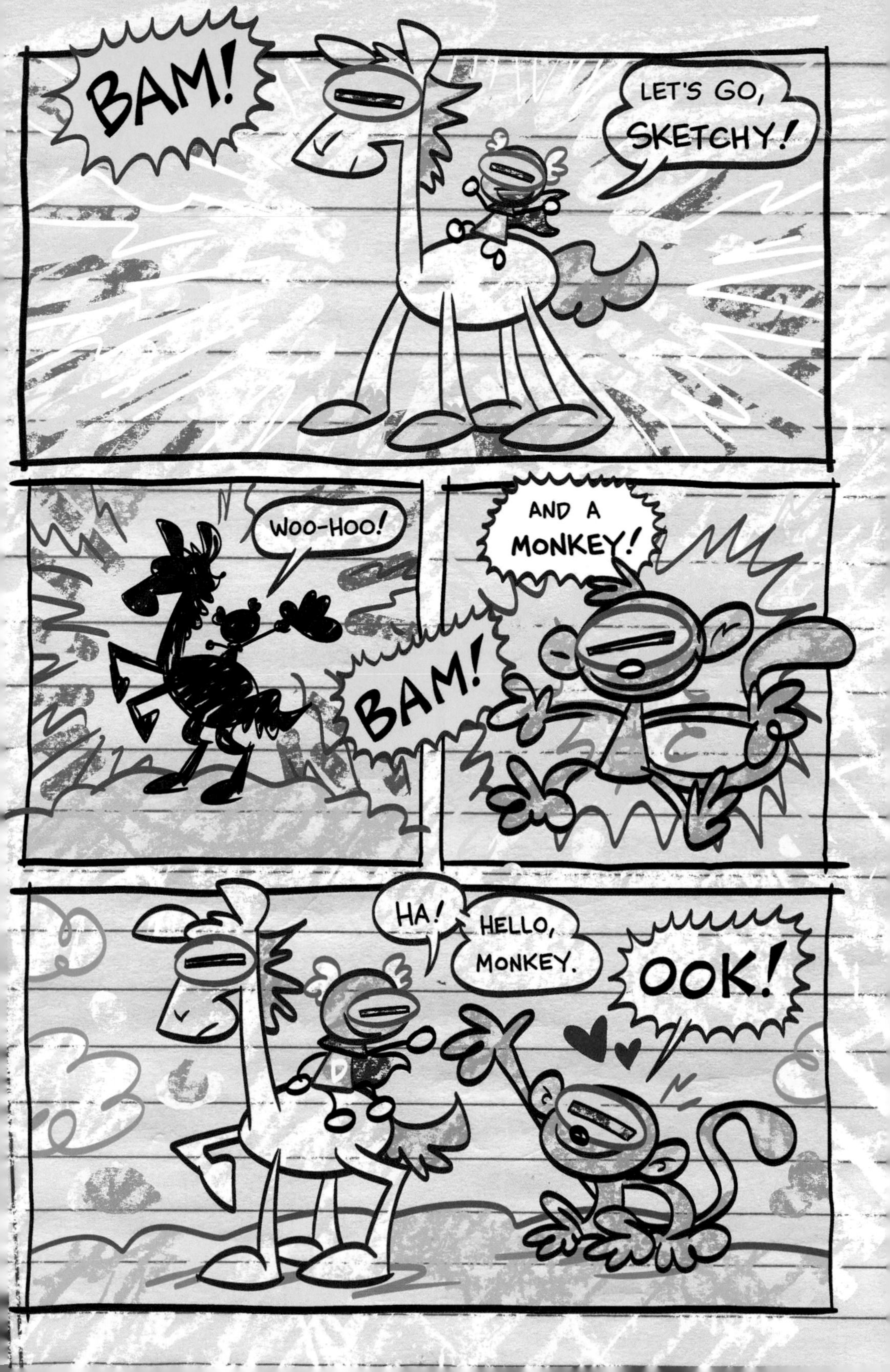
BAM!
LET'S GO, SKETCHY!
WOO-HOO!
BAM!
AND A MONKEY!
HA!
HELLO, MONKEY.
OOK!

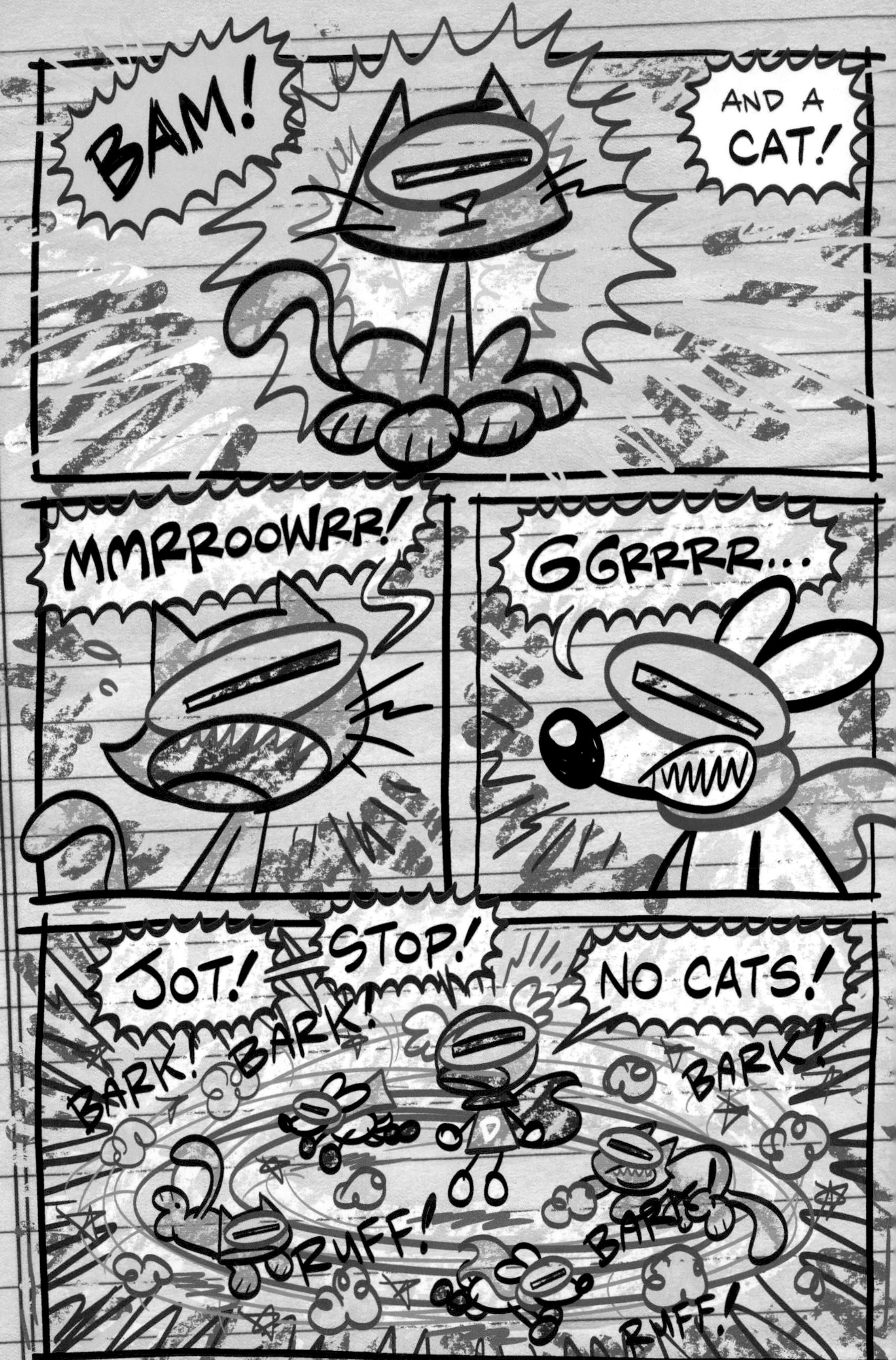
BAM!
AND A CAT!
MMRROOWRR!
GGRRRR...
JOT! STOP!
NO CATS!
BARK!
BARK!
BARK!
RUFF!
BARK!
RUFF!

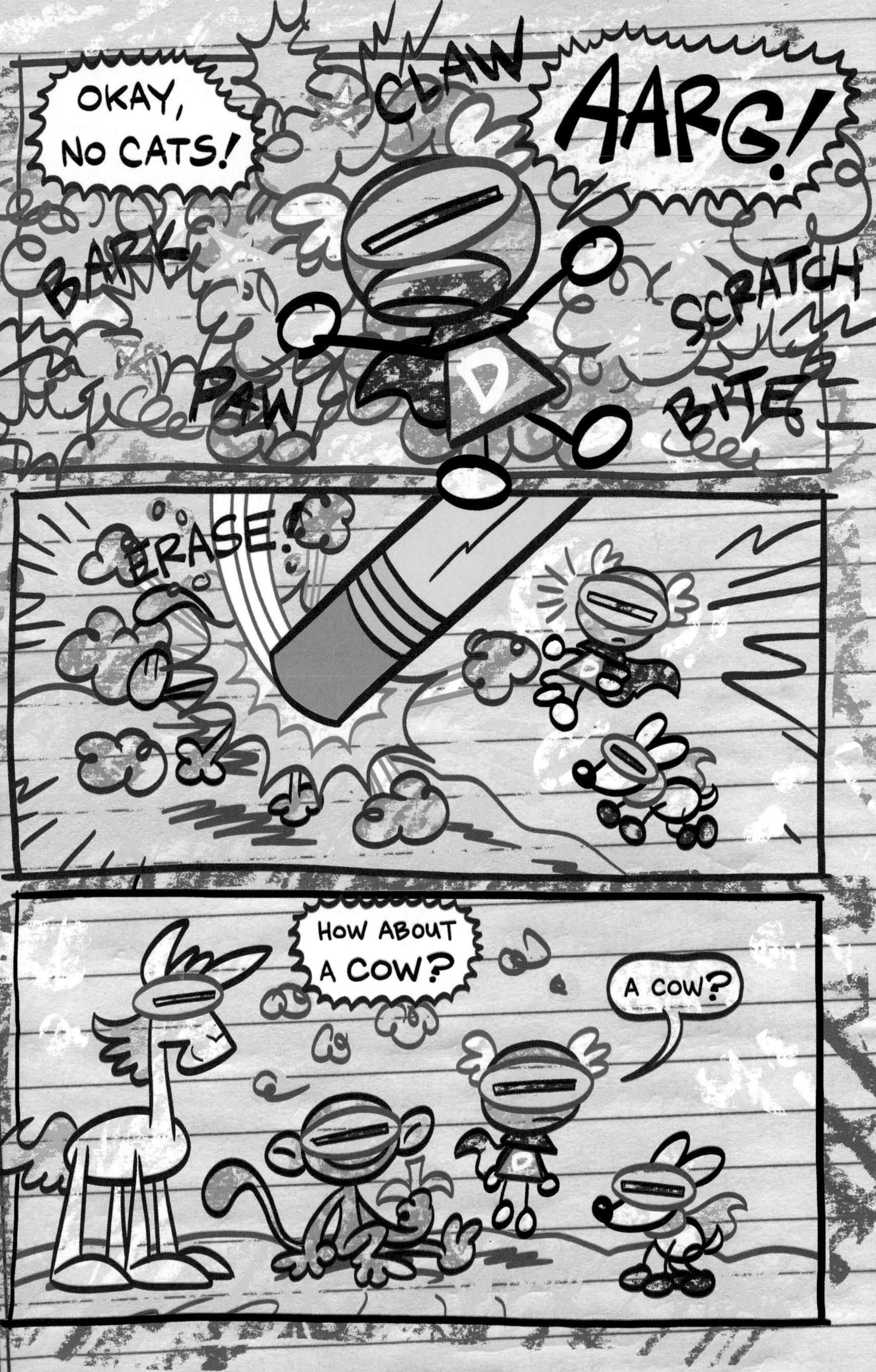
OKAY, NO CATS!
CLAW
AARG!
BARK
SCRATCH
PAW
BITE
ERASE!
HOW ABOUT A COW?
A COW?

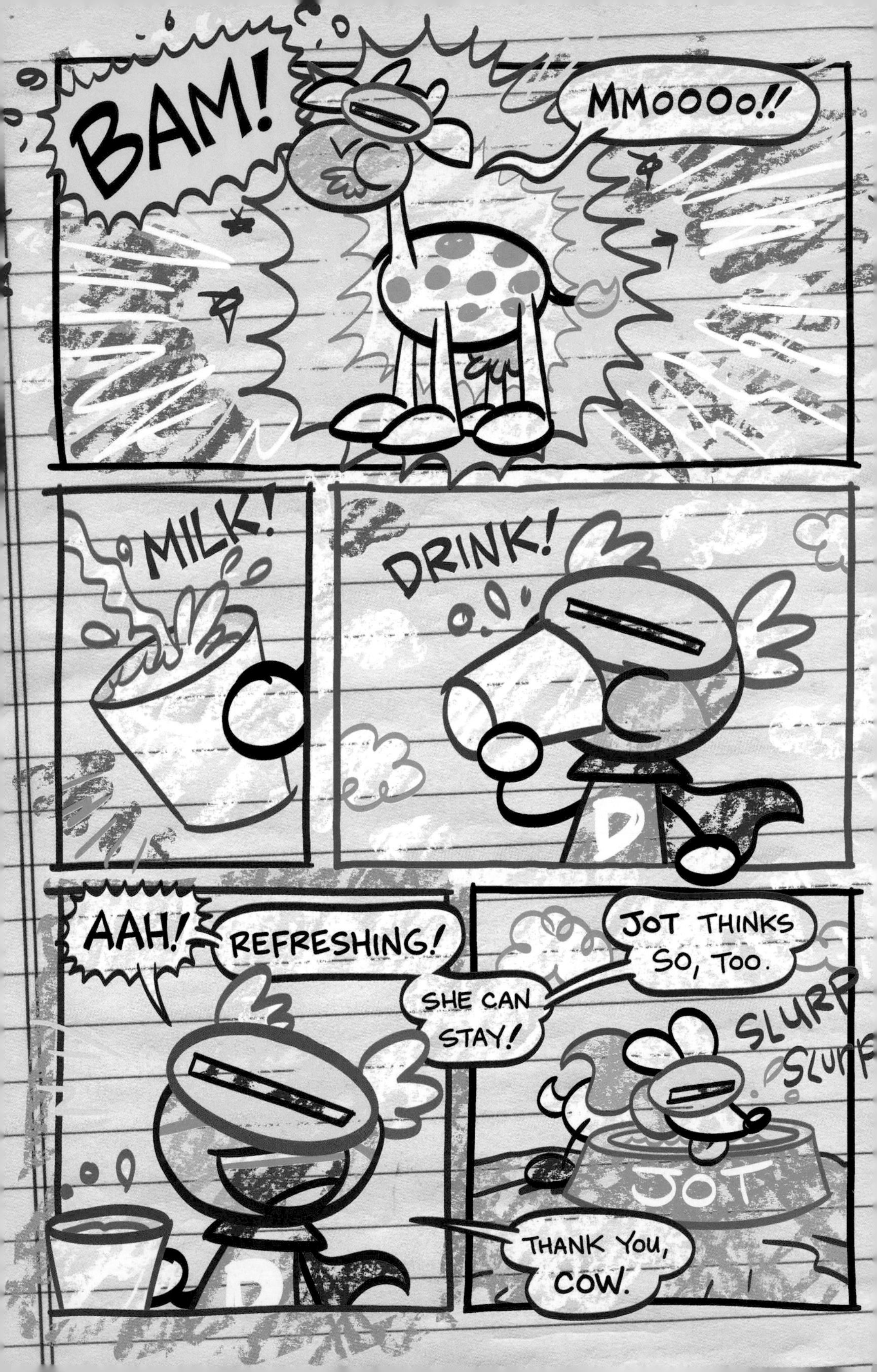
BAM!
MMOOOo!!
MILK!
DRINK!
AAH!
REFRESHING!
SHE CAN STAY!
JOT THINKS SO, TOO.
SLURP
JOT
THANK YOU, COW.

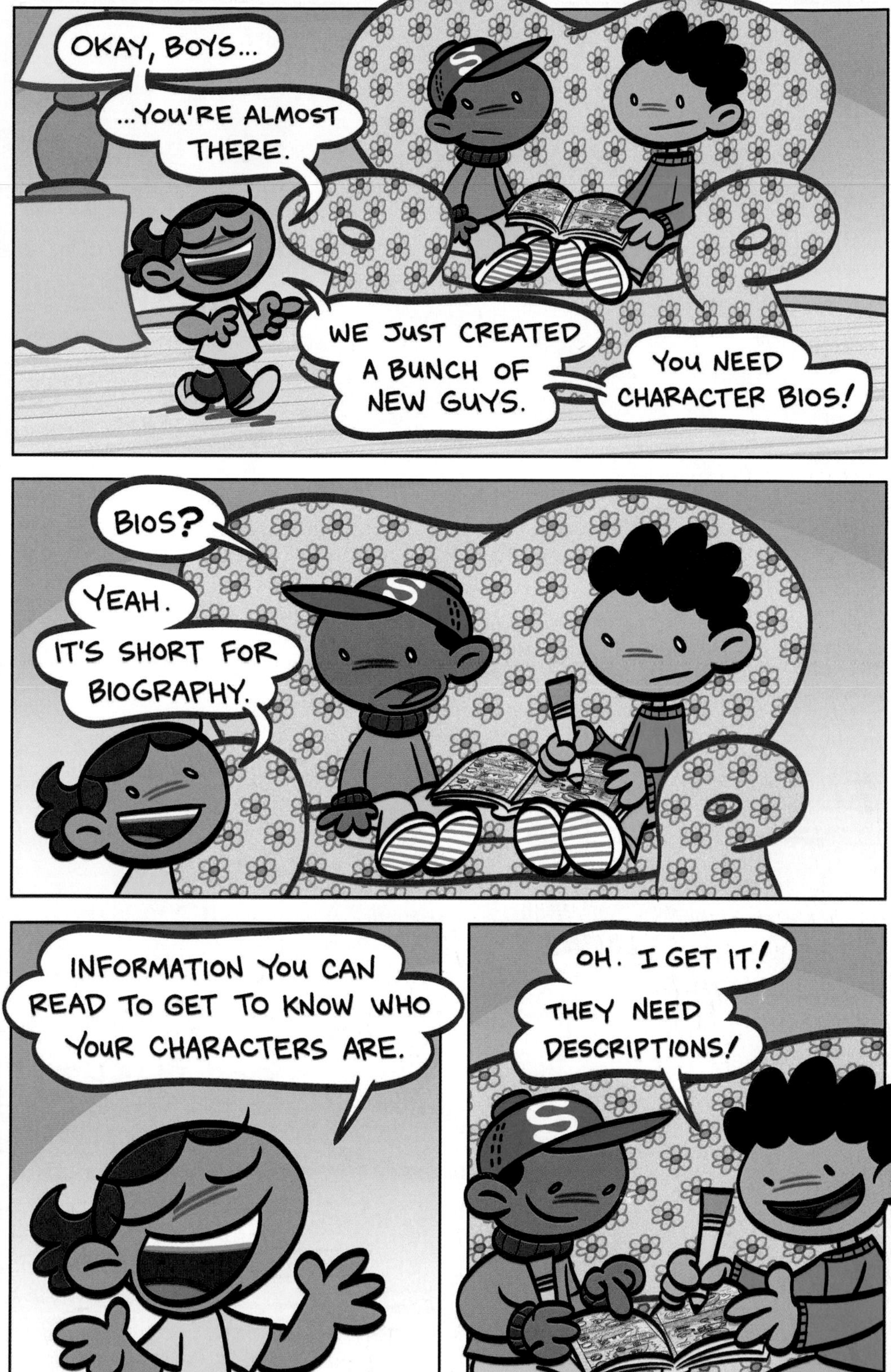
OKAY, BOYS...
...YOU'RE ALMOST THERE.
WE JUST CREATED A BUNCH OF NEW GUYS.
YOU NEED CHARACTER BIOS!
BIOS?
YEAH.
IT'S SHORT FOR BIOGRAPHY.
INFORMATION YOU CAN READ TO GET TO KNOW WHO YOUR CHARACTERS ARE.
OH. I GET IT!
THEY NEED DESCRIPTIONS!

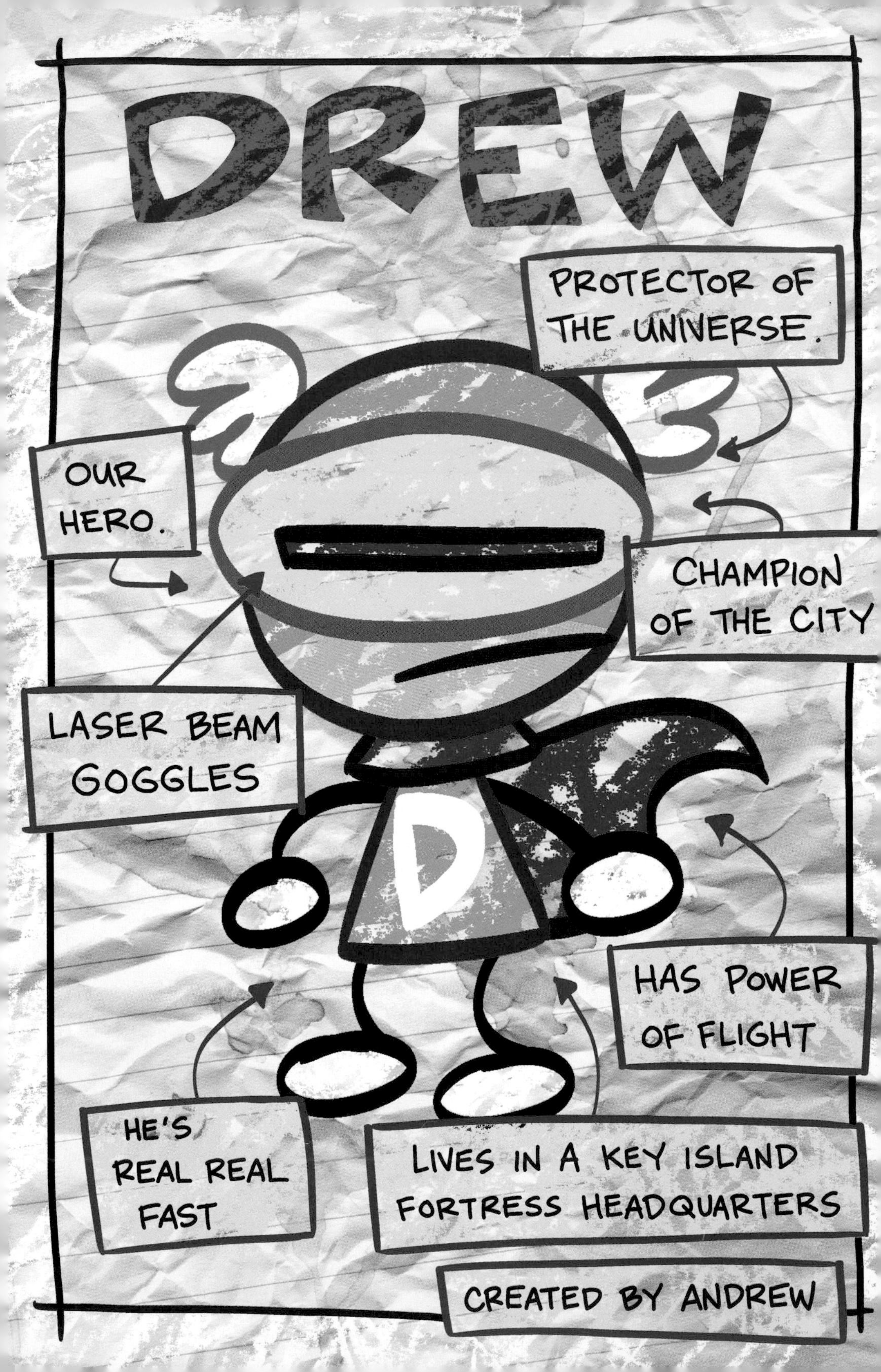
DREW
PROTECTOR OF THE UNIVERSE.
OUR HERO.
CHAMPION OF THE CITY
LASER BEAM GOGGLES
HAS POWER OF FLIGHT
HE'S REAL REAL FAST
LIVES IN A KEY ISLAND FORTRESS HEADQUARTERS
CREATED BY ANDREW

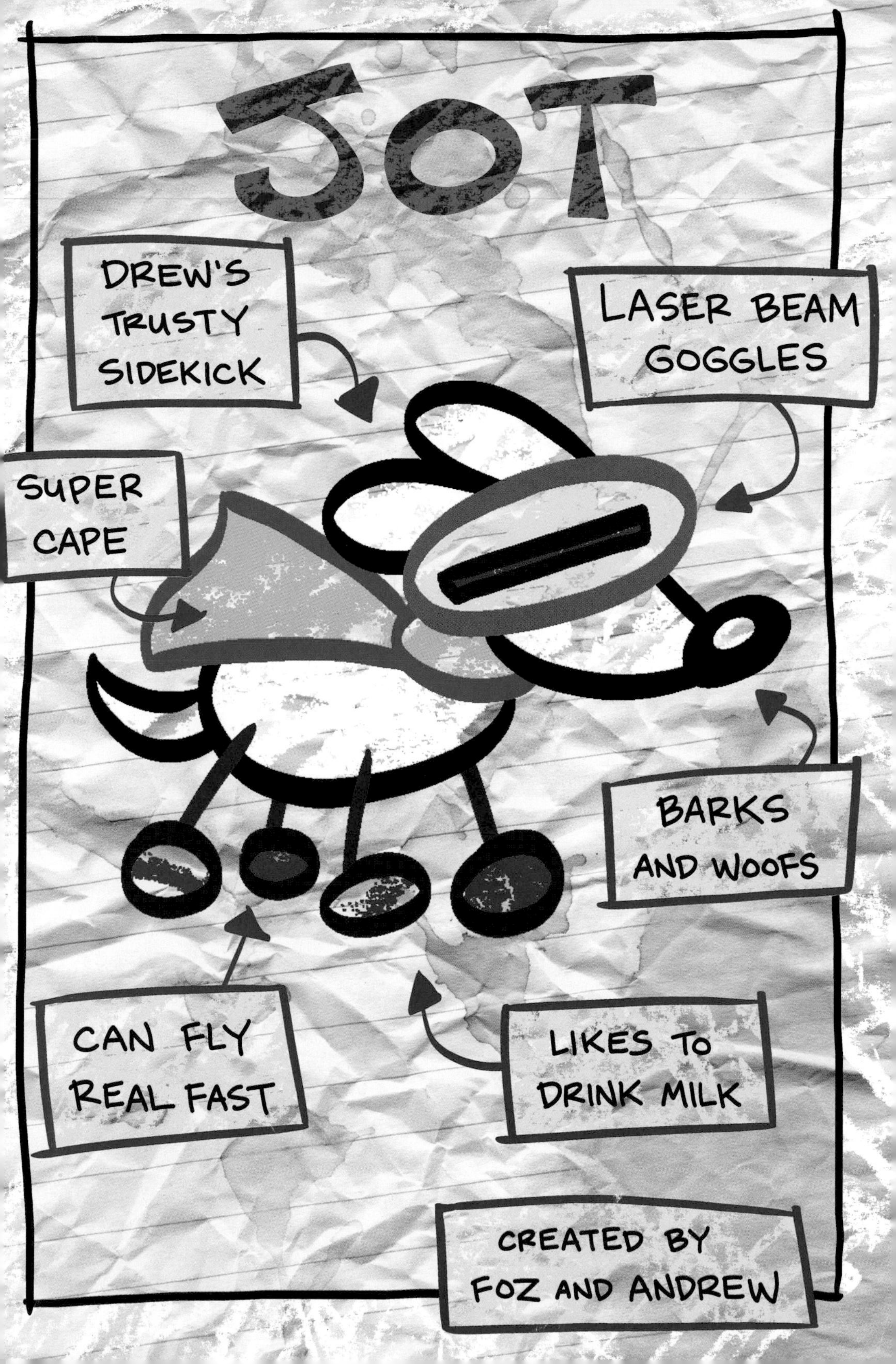
JOT
DREW'S TRUSTY SIDEKICK
LASER BEAM GOGGLES
SUPER CAPE
BARKS AND WOOFS
CAN FLY REAL FAST
LIKES TO DRINK MILK
CREATED BY FOZ AND ANDREW

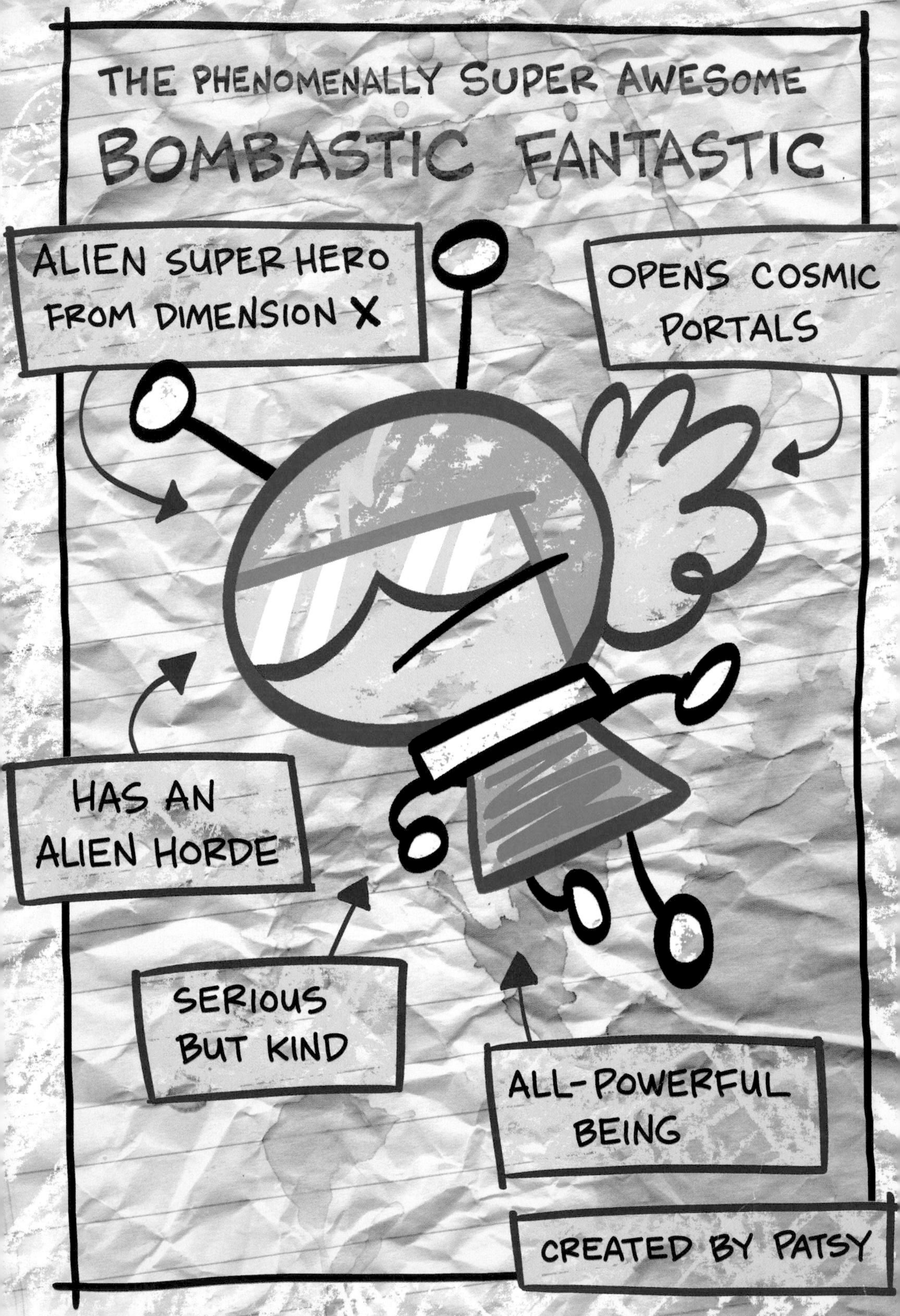
THE PHENOMENALLY SUPER AWESOME
BOMBASTIC FANTASTIC
ALIEN SUPER HERO FROM DIMENSION X
OPENS COSMIC PORTALS
HAS AN ALIEN HORDE
SERIOUS BUT KIND
ALL-POWERFUL BEING
CREATED BY PATSY

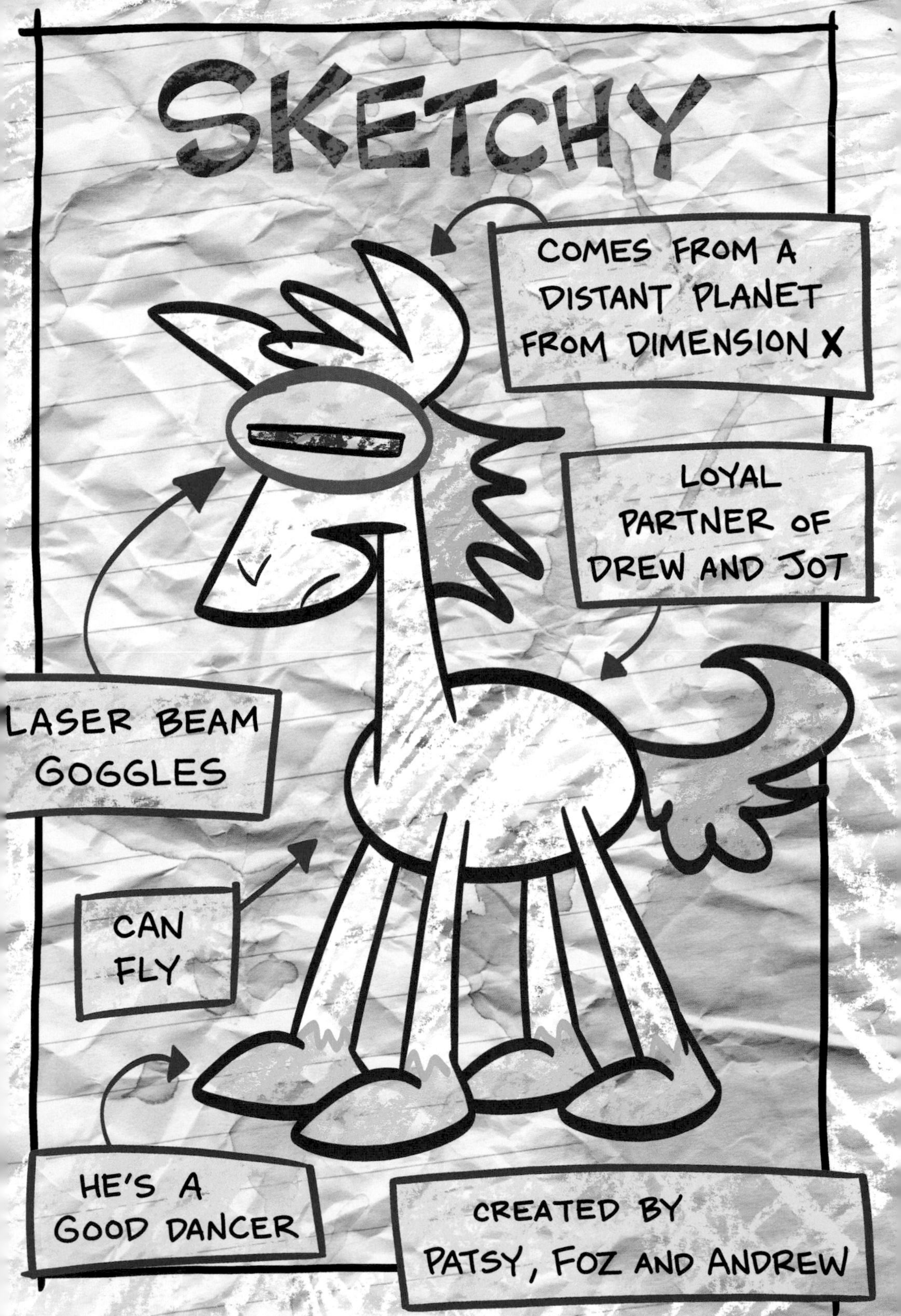
SKETCHY
COMES FROM A DISTANT PLANET FROM DIMENSION X
LOYAL PARTNER OF DREW AND JOT
LASER BEAM GOGGLES
CAN FLY
HE'S A GOOD DANCER
CREATED BY PATSY, FOZ AND ANDREW

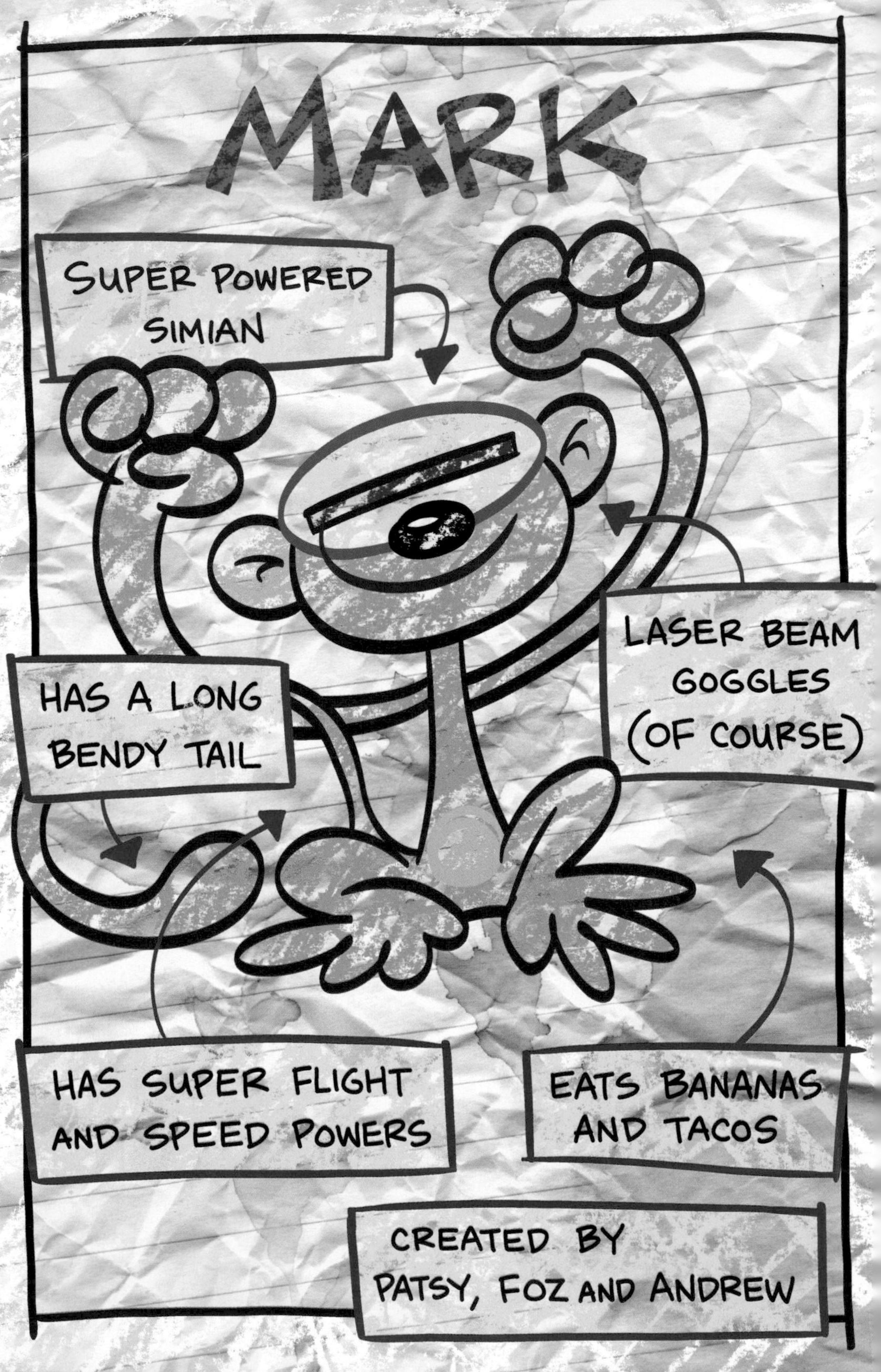
MARK
SUPER POWERED SIMIAN
LASER BEAM GOGGLES (OF COURSE)
HAS A LONG BENDY TAIL
HAS SUPER FLIGHT AND SPEED POWERS
EATS BANANAS AND TACOS
CREATED BY PATSY, FOZ AND ANDREW

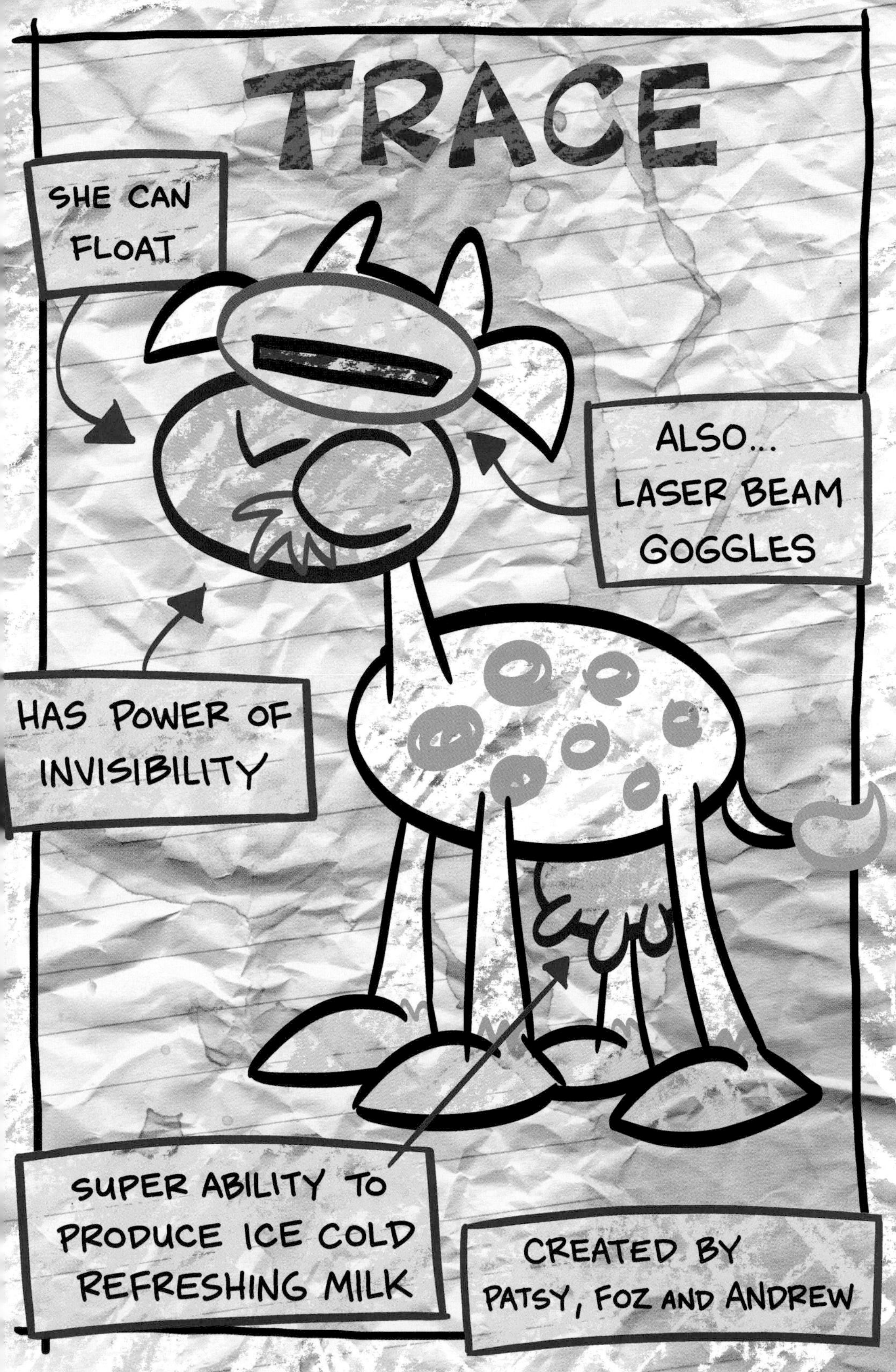
TRACE
SHE CAN FLOAT
ALSO... LASER BEAM GOGGLES
HAS POWER OF INVISIBILITY
SUPER ABILITY TO PRODUCE ICE COLD REFRESHING MILK
CREATED BY PATSY, FOZ AND ANDREW

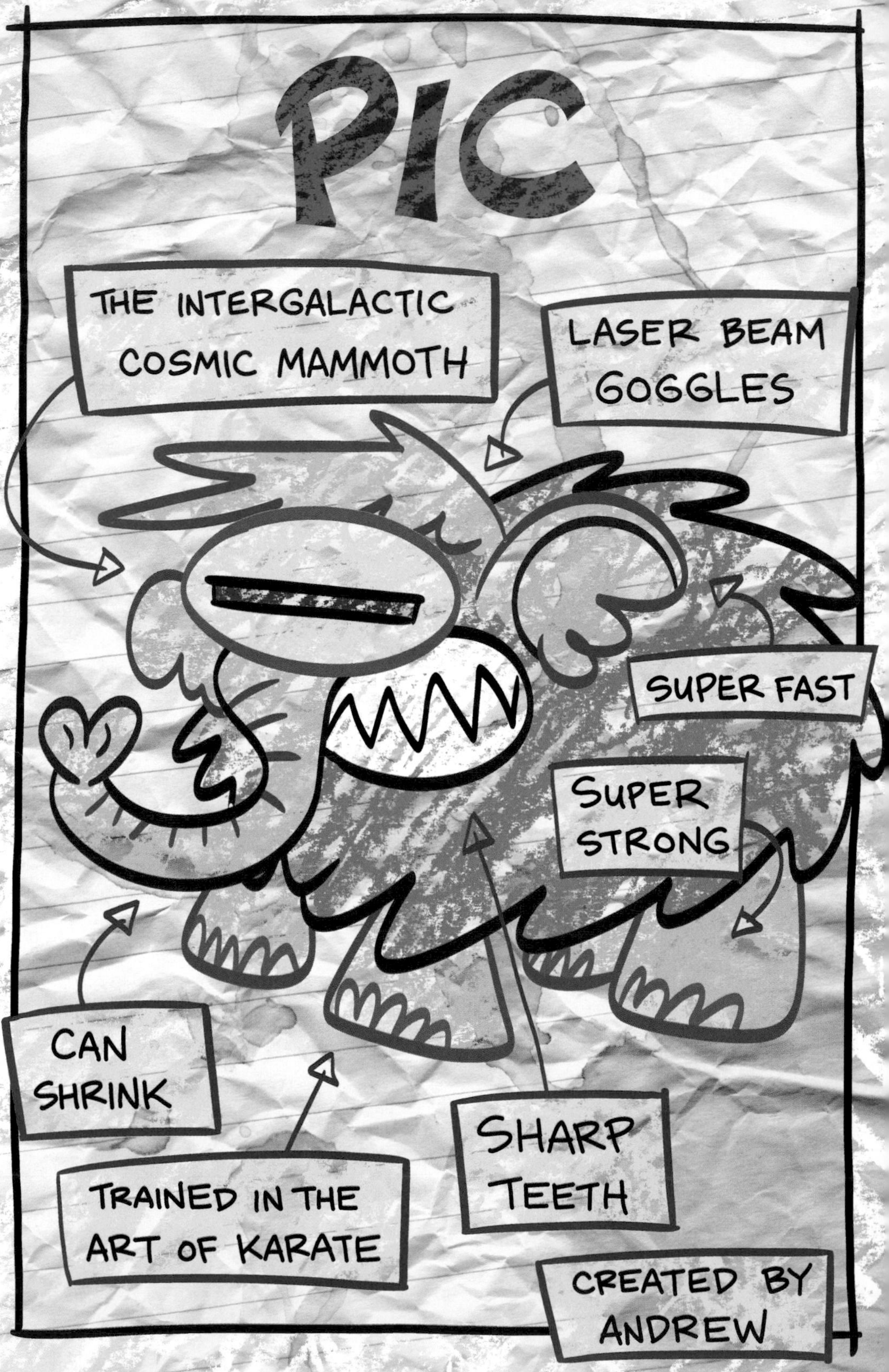
PIC
THE INTERGALACTIC COSMIC MAMMOTH
LASER BEAM GOGGLES
SUPER FAST
SUPER STRONG
CAN SHRINK
SHARP TEETH
TRAINED IN THE ART OF KARATE
CREATED BY ANDREW

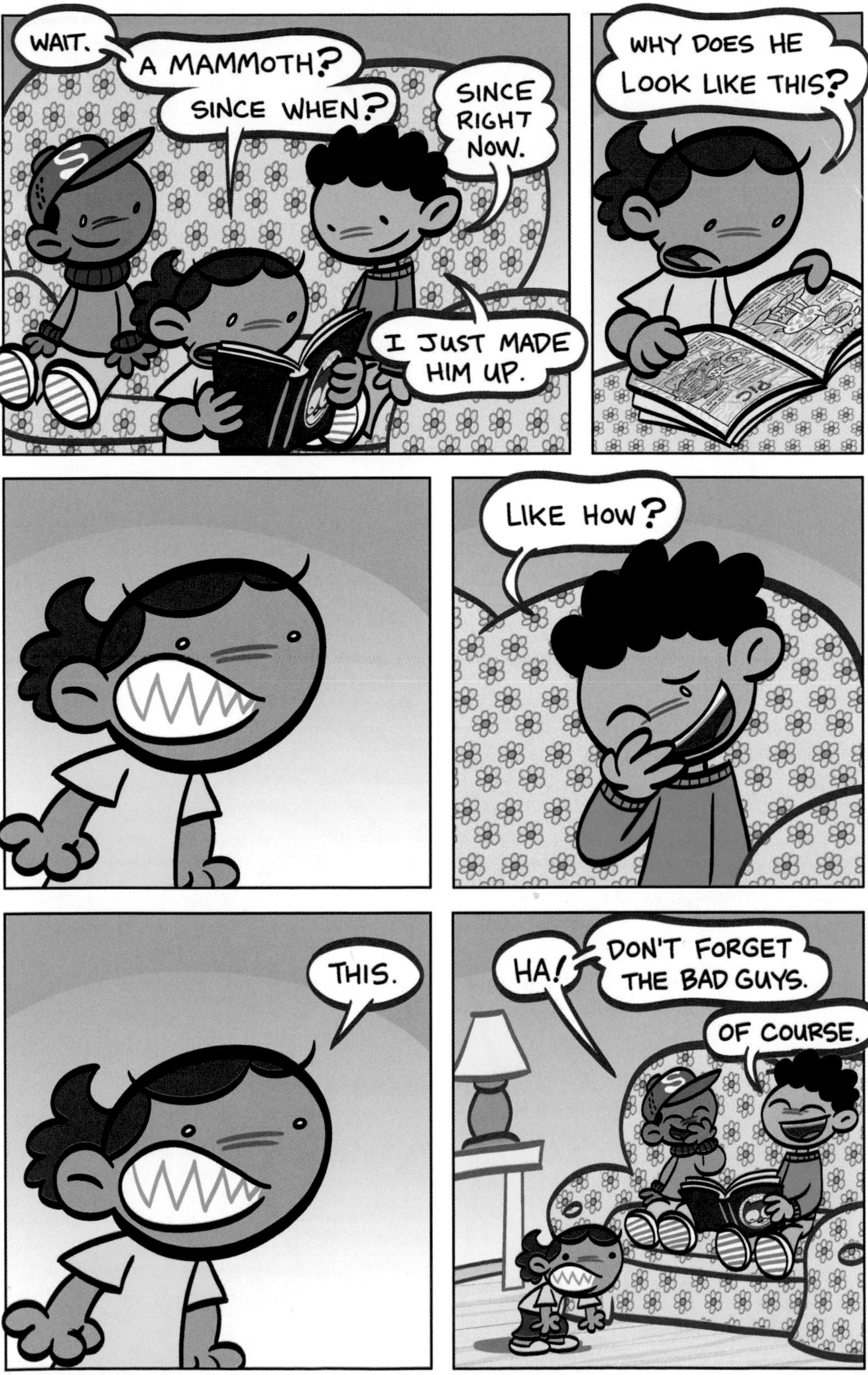
WAIT.
A MAMMOTH?
SINCE WHEN?
SINCE RIGHT NOW.
I JUST MADE HIM UP.
WHY DOES HE LOOK LIKE THIS?
LIKE HOW?
THIS.
HA!
DON'T FORGET THE BAD GUYS.
OF COURSE.

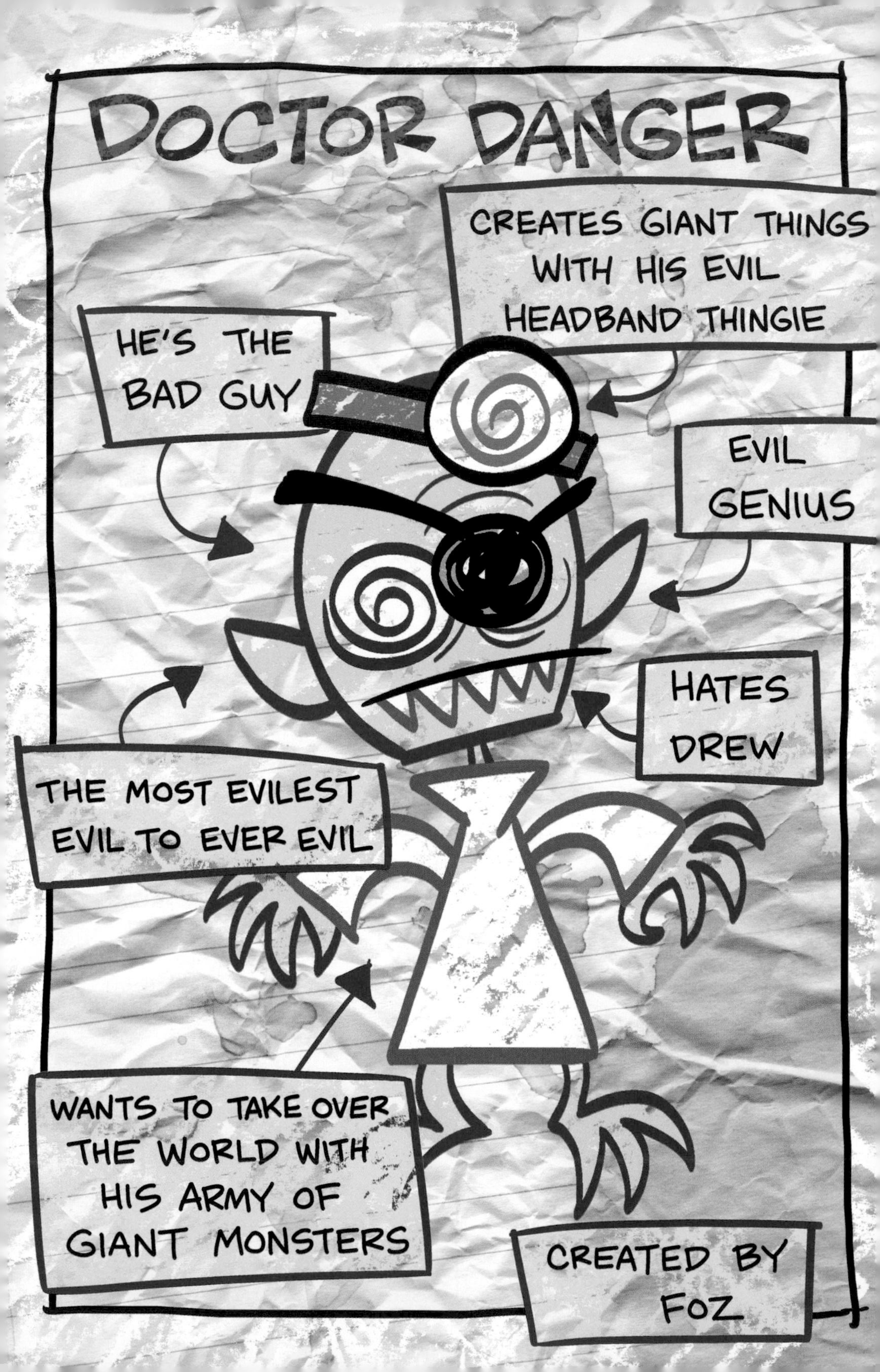
DOCTOR DANGER
CREATES GIANT THINGS WITH HIS EVIL HEADBAND THINGIE
HE'S THE BAD GUY
EVIL GENIUS
HATES DREW
THE MOST EVILEST EVIL TO EVER EVIL
WANTS TO TAKE OVER THE WORLD WITH HIS ARMY OF GIANT MONSTERS
CREATED BY FOZ

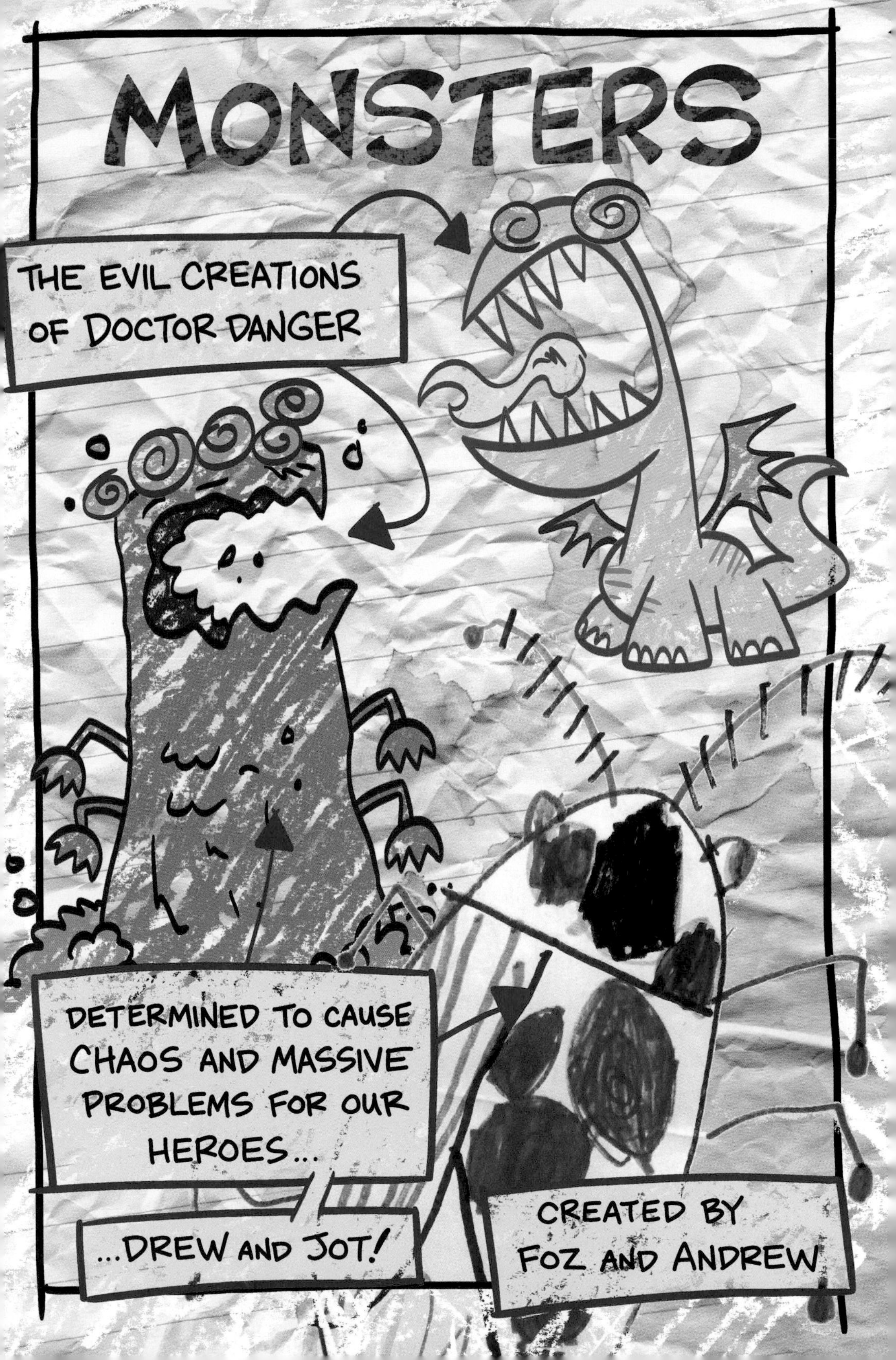
MONSTERS
THE EVIL CREATIONS OF DOCTOR DANGER
DETERMINED TO CAUSE CHAOS AND MASSIVE PROBLEMS FOR OUR HEROES...
...DREW AND JOT!
CREATED BY FOZ AND ANDREW

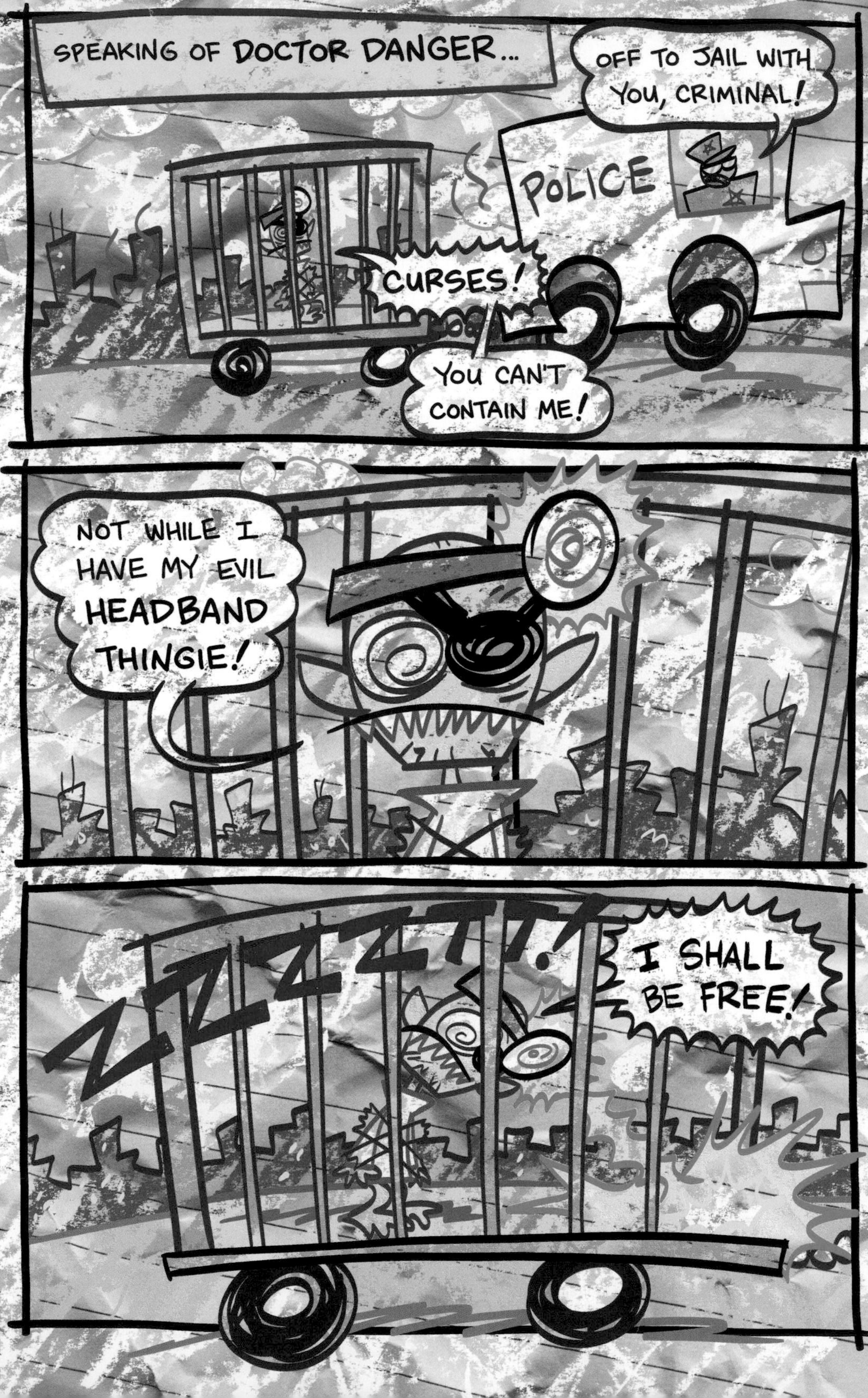
SPEAKING OF DOCTOR DANGER...
OFF TO JAIL WITH YOU, CRIMINAL!
POLICE
CURSES!
YOU CAN'T CONTAIN ME!
NOT WHILE I HAVE MY EVIL HEADBAND THINGIE!
ZZZZTT!
I SHALL BE FREE!

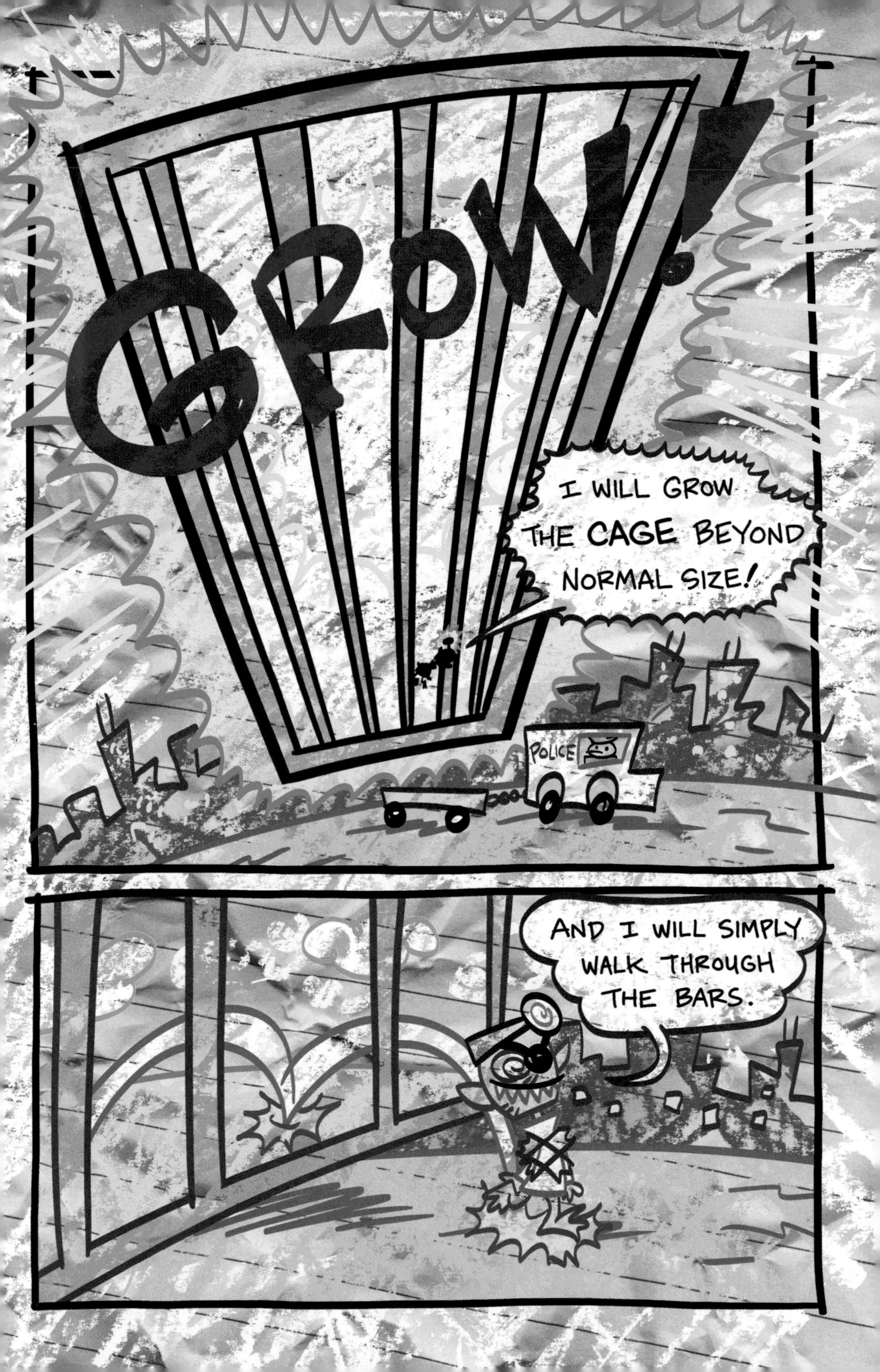
GROW!
I WILL GROW THE CAGE BEYOND NORMAL SIZE!
POLICE
AND I WILL SIMPLY WALK THROUGH THE BARS.

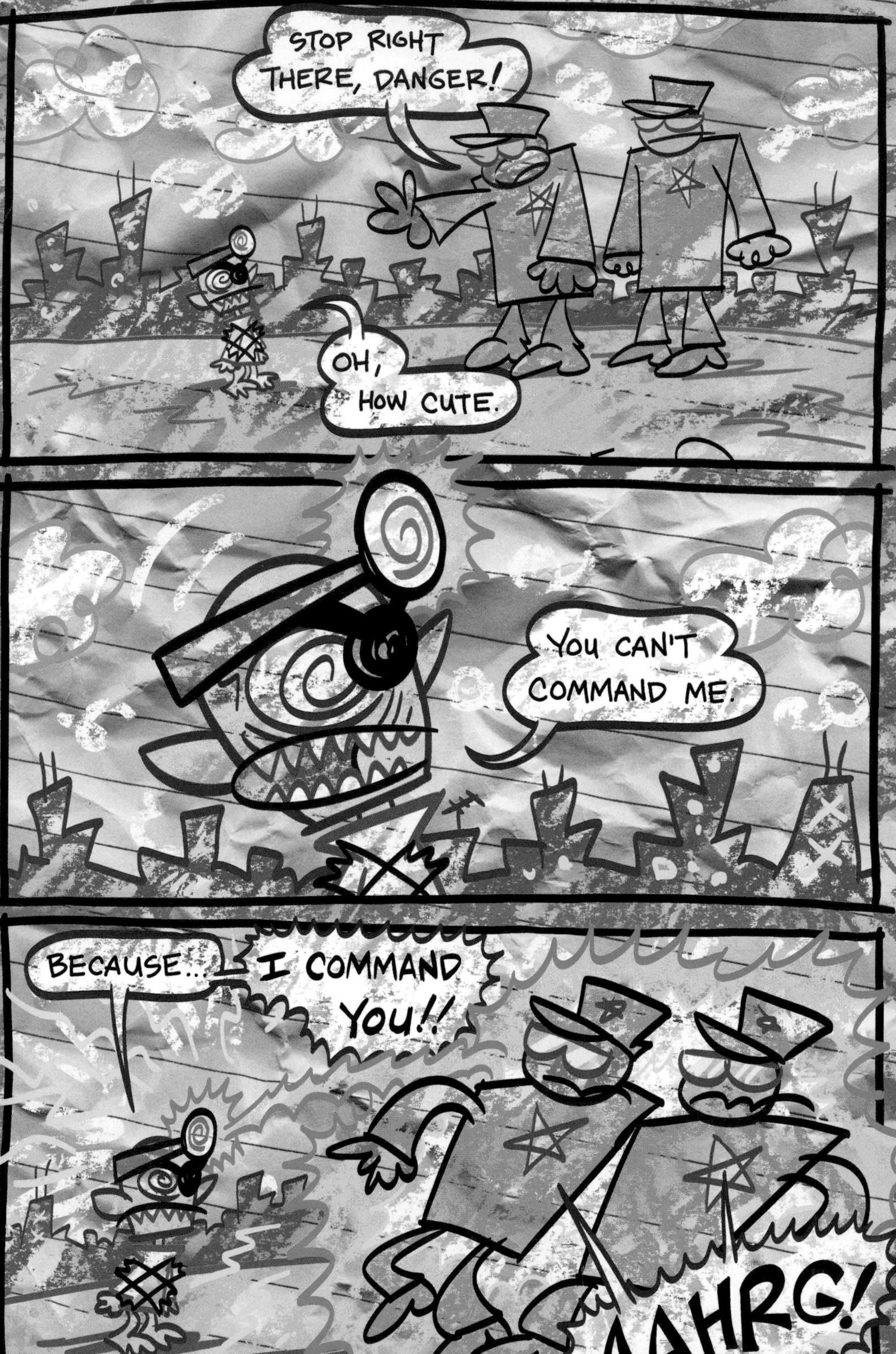
STOP RIGHT THERE, DANGER!
OH, HOW CUTE.
YOU CAN'T COMMAND ME.
BECAUSE...
I COMMAND YOU!!
AAHRG!

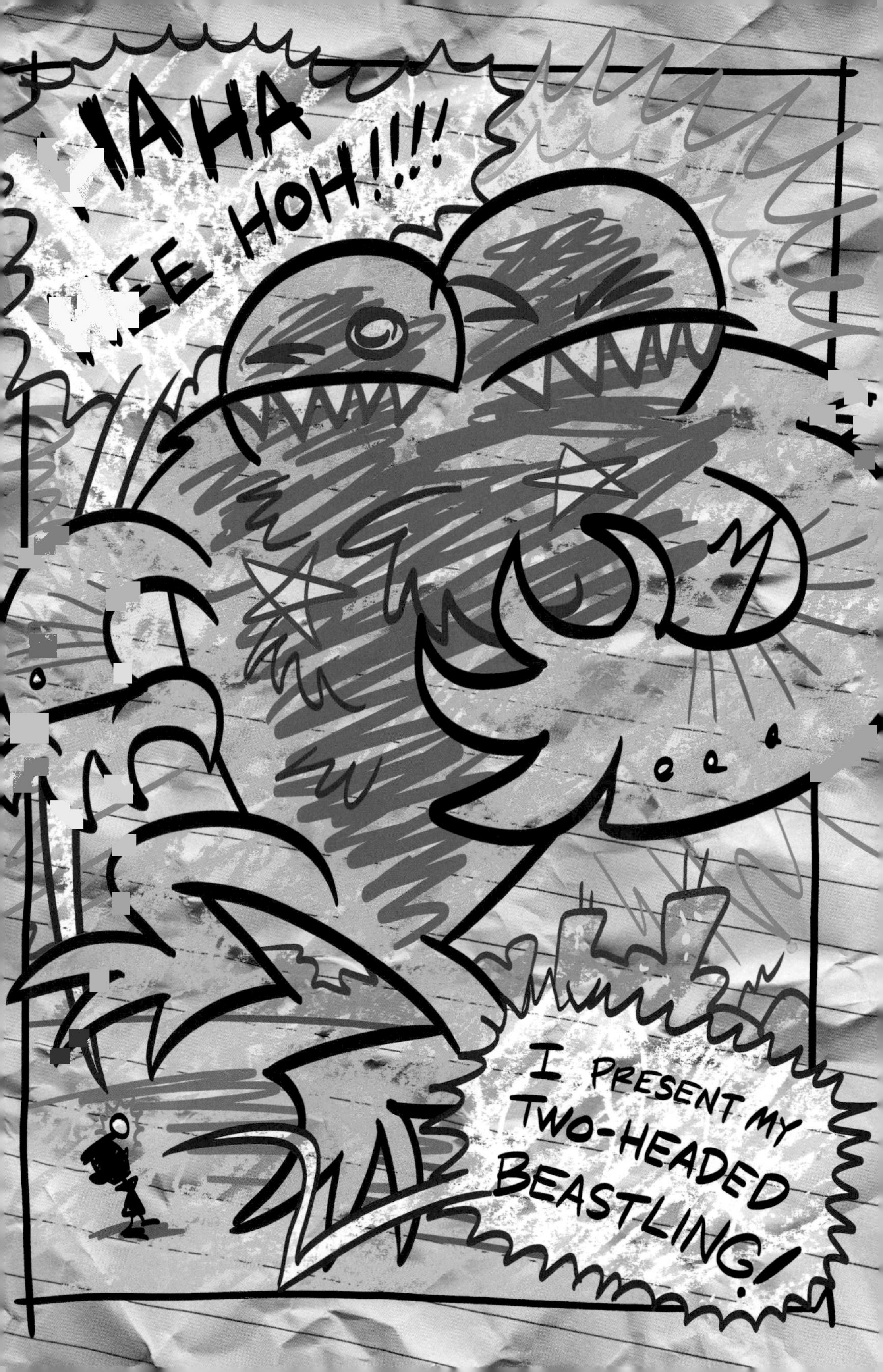
HAHA HEE HOH!!!!
I PRESENT MY TWO-HEADED BEASTLING!

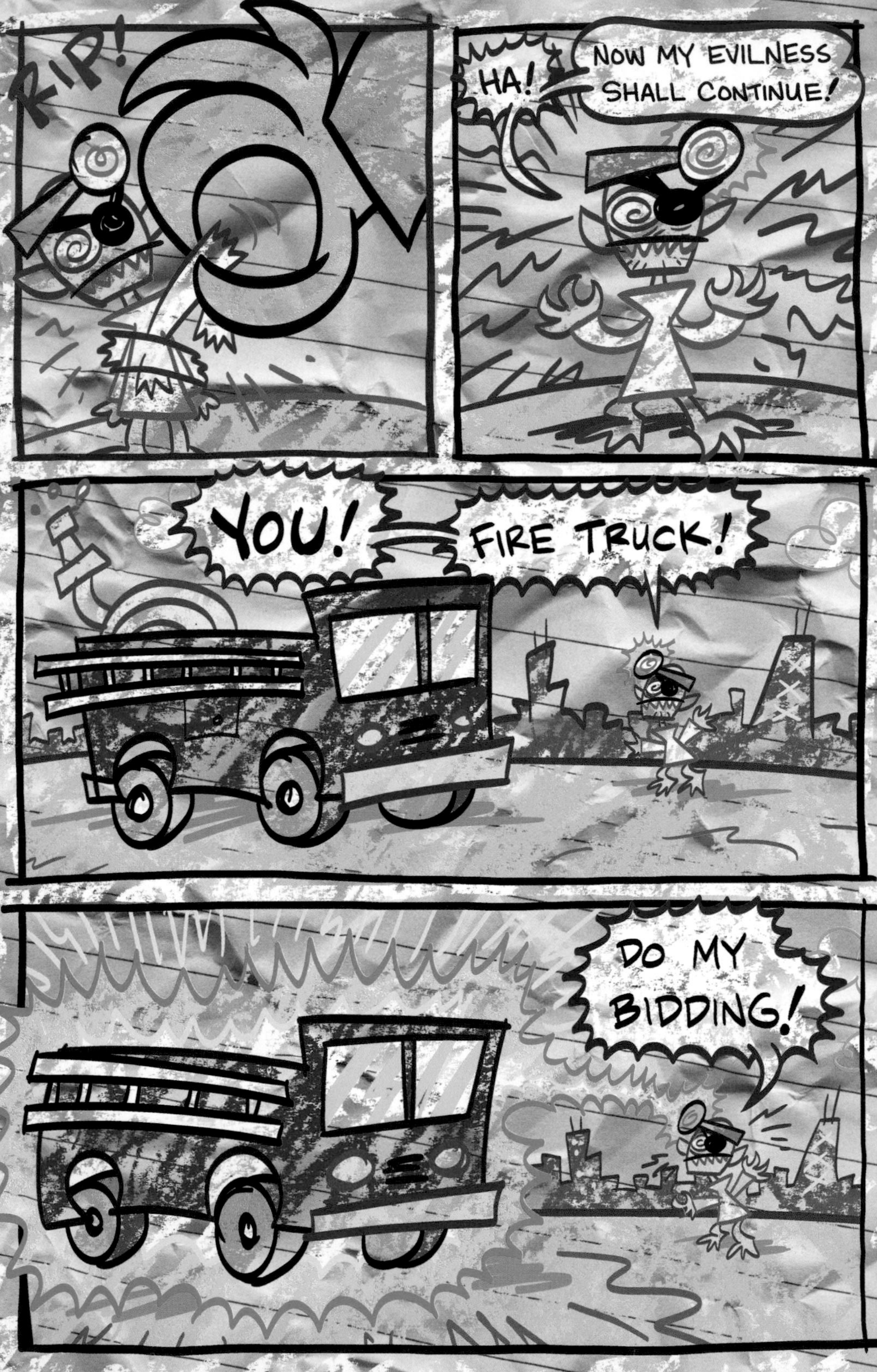
RIP!
HA!
NOW MY EVILNESS SHALL CONTINUE!
YOU!
FIRE TRUCK!
DO MY BIDDING!

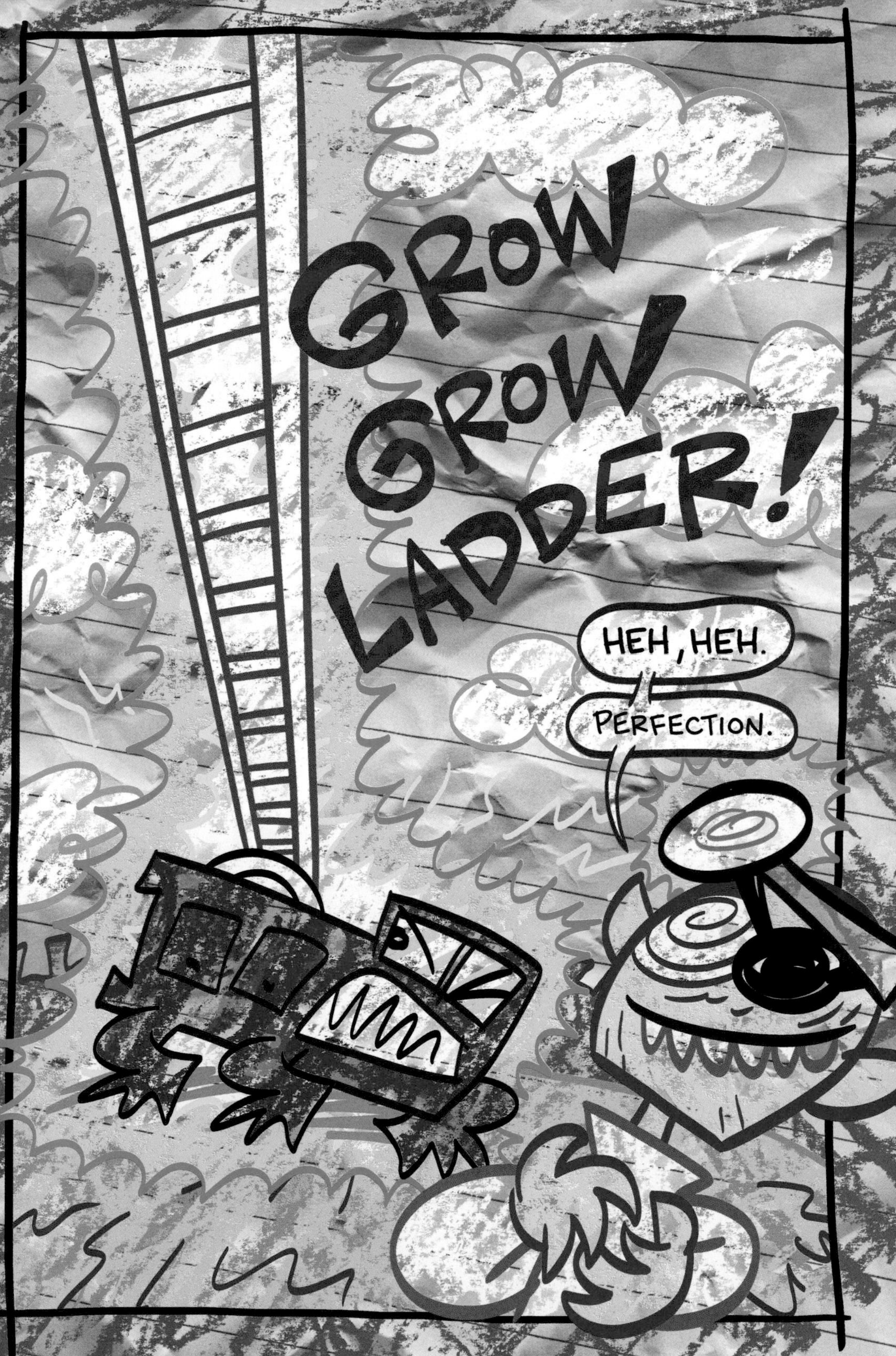
GROW GROW LADDER!
HEH, HEH.
PERFECTION.

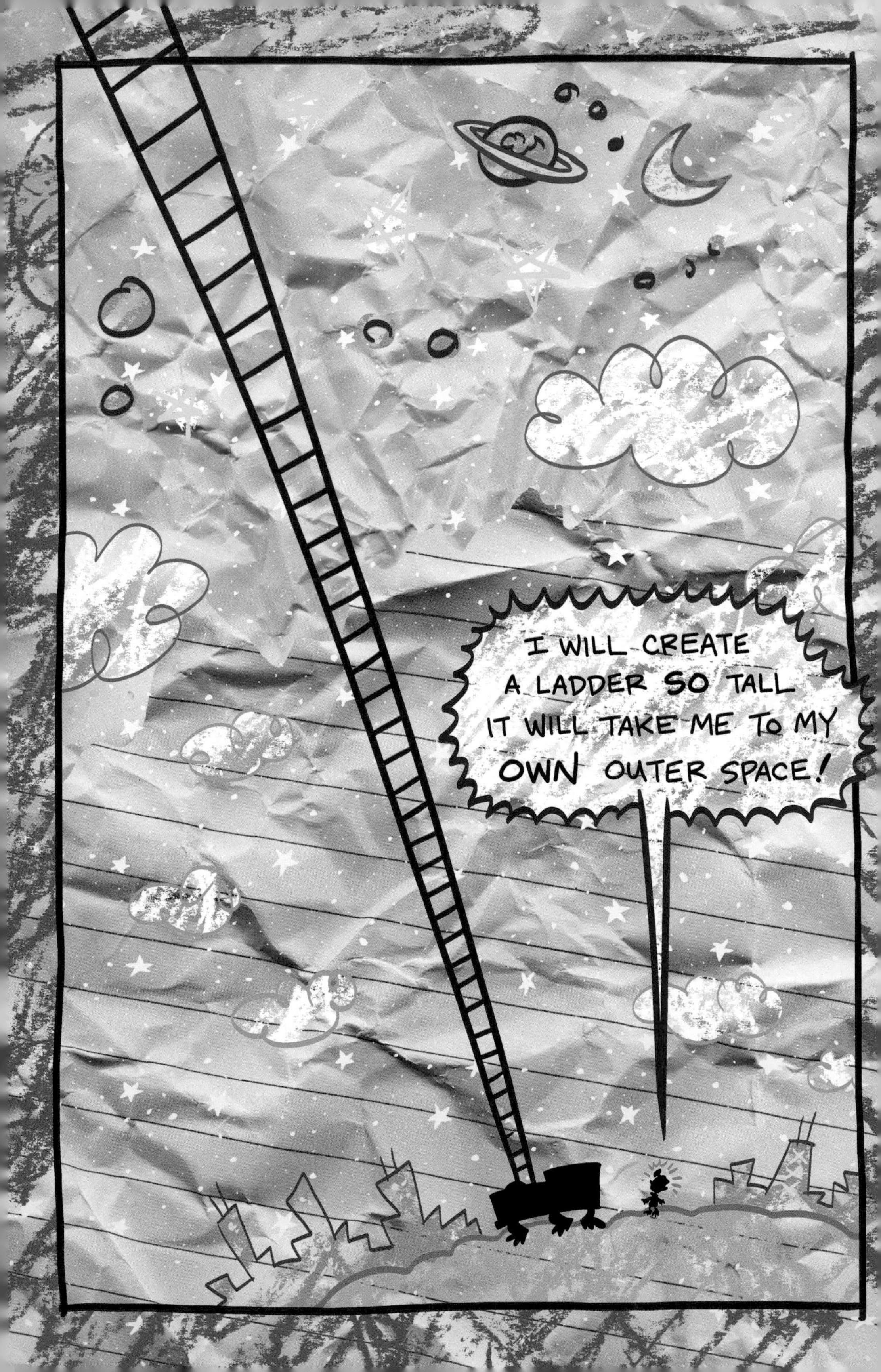
I WILL CREATE A LADDER SO TALL IT WILL TAKE ME TO MY OWN OUTER SPACE!

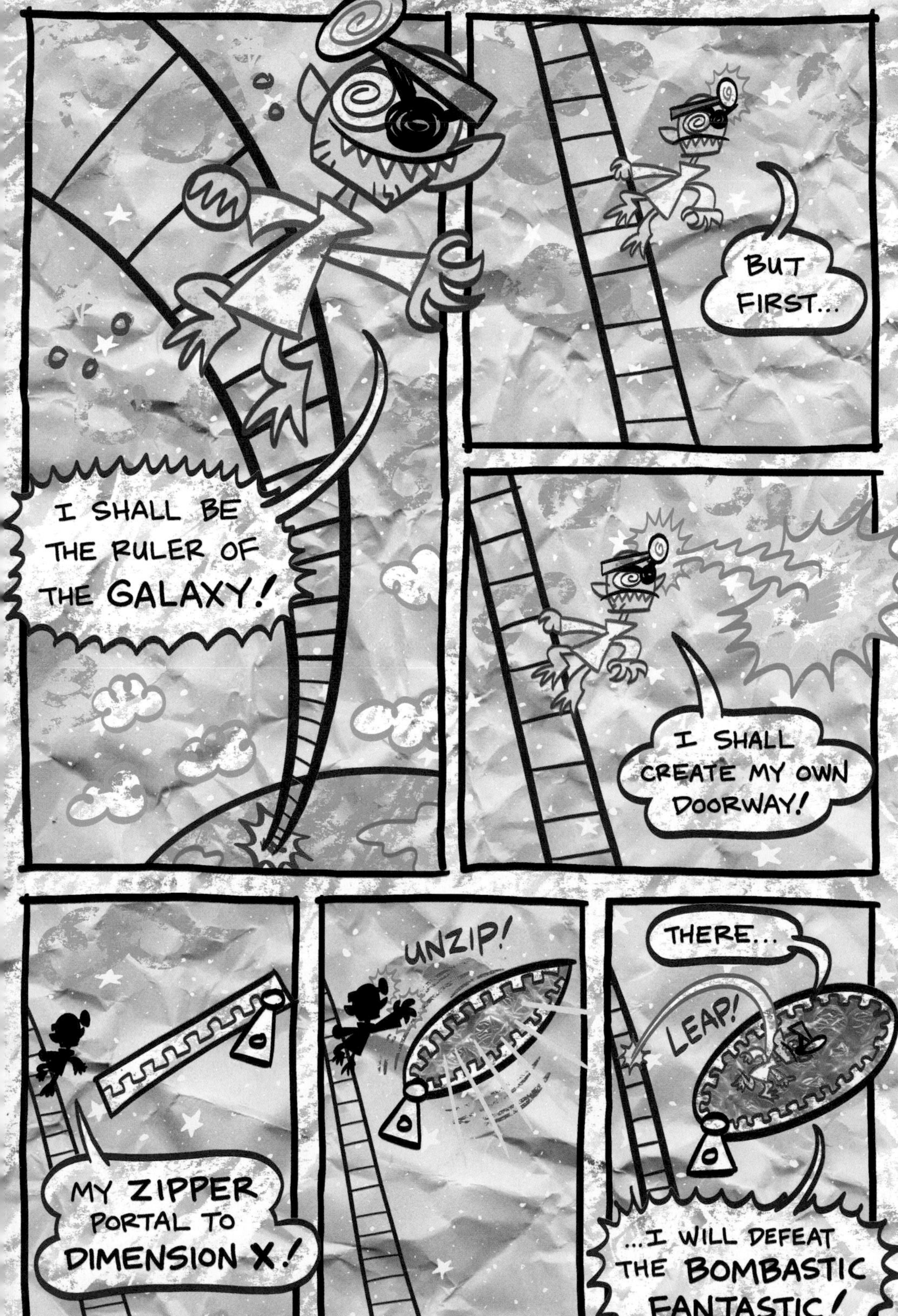
I SHALL BE THE RULER OF THE GALAXY!
BUT FIRST...
I SHALL CREATE MY OWN DOORWAY!
MY ZIPPER PORTAL TO DIMENSION X!
UNZIP!
THERE...
LEAP!
...I WILL DEFEAT THE BOMBASTIC FANTASTIC!

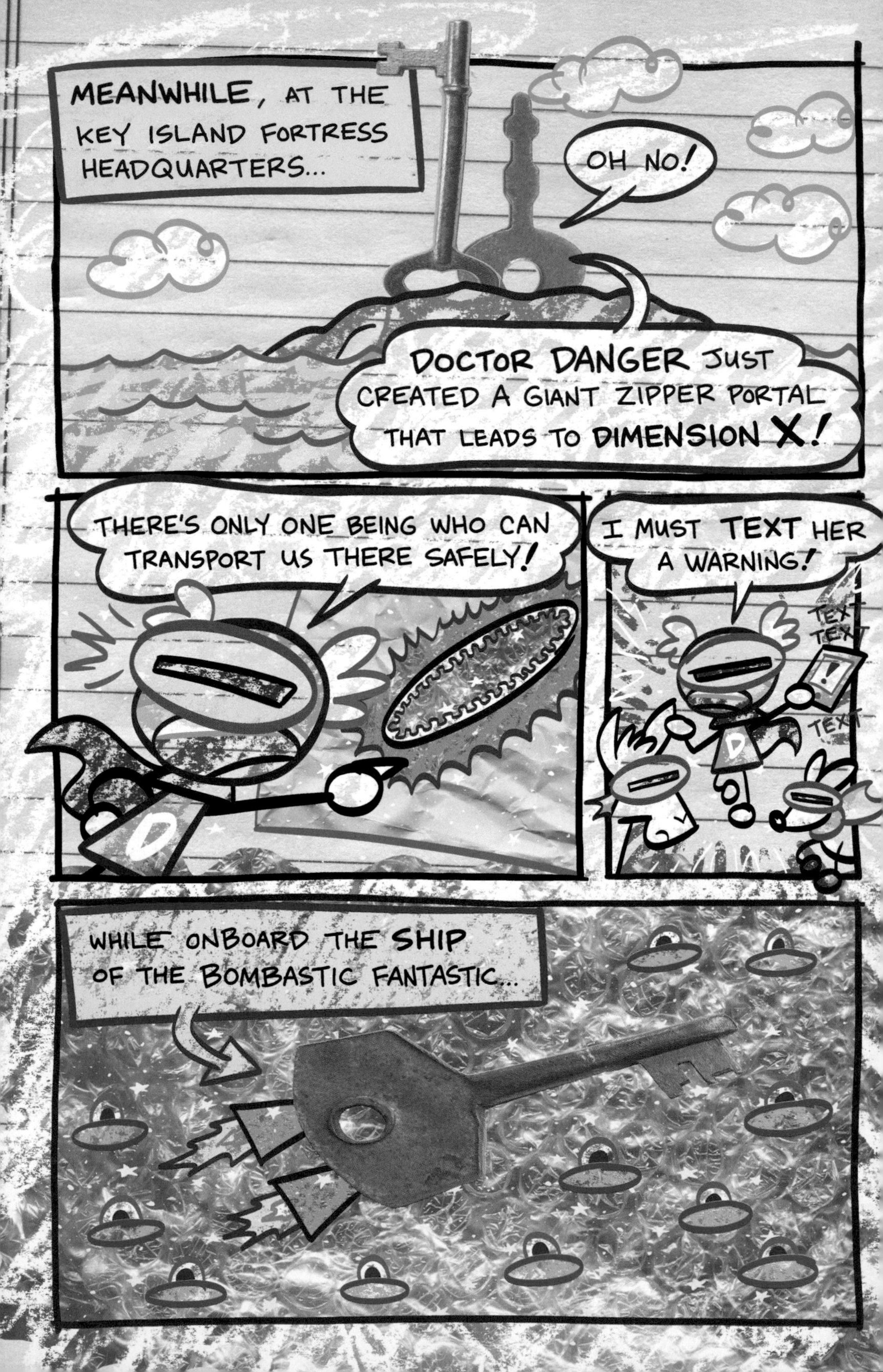
MEANWHILE, AT THE KEY ISLAND FORTRESS HEADQUARTERS...
OH NO!
DOCTOR DANGER JUST CREATED A GIANT ZIPPER PORTAL THAT LEADS TO DIMENSION X!
THERE'S ONLY ONE BEING WHO CAN TRANSPORT US THERE SAFELY!
I MUST TEXT HER A WARNING!
TEXT
TEXT
TEXT
WHILE ONBOARD THE SHIP OF THE BOMBASTIC FANTASTIC...

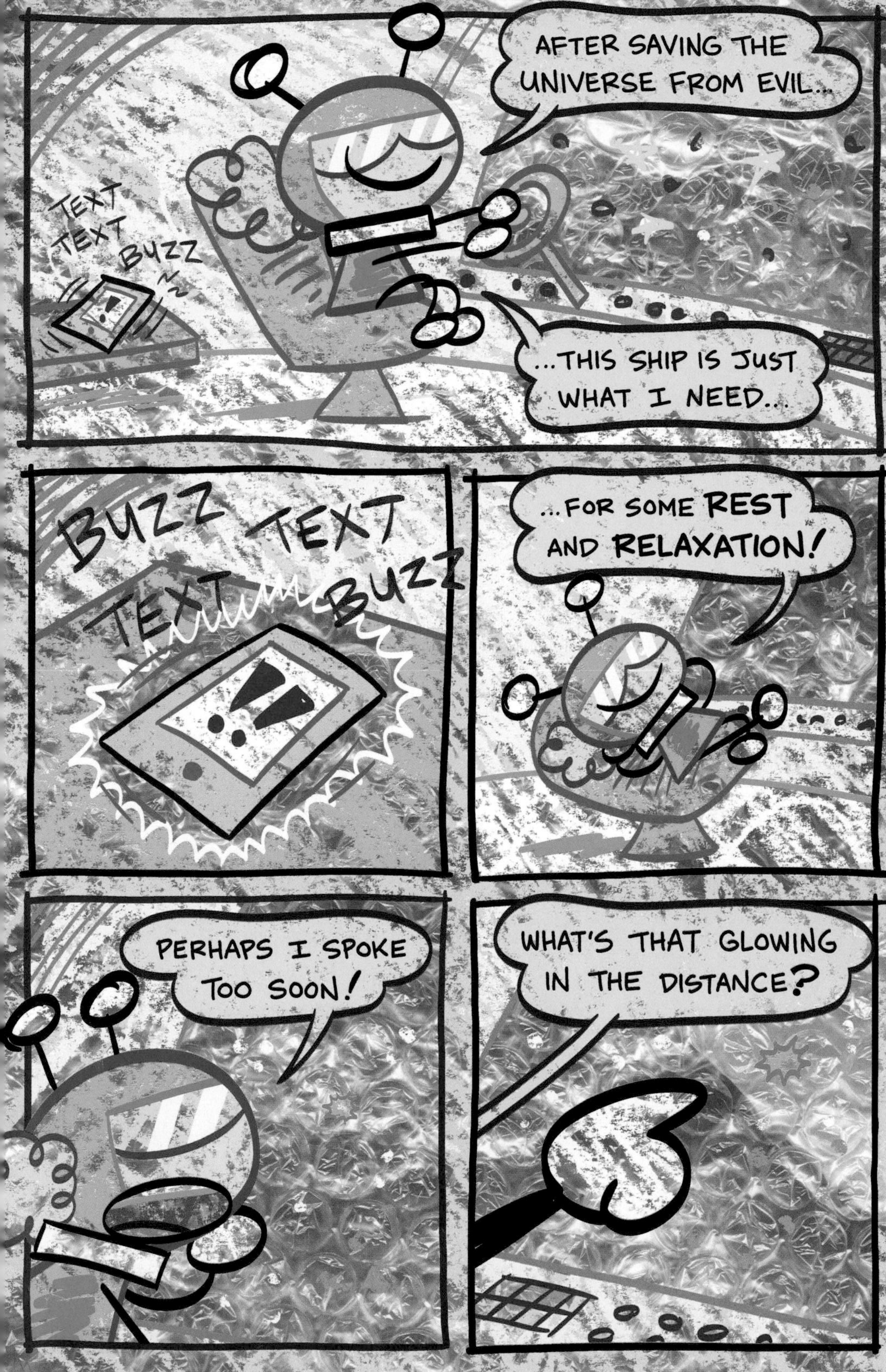
AFTER SAVING THE UNIVERSE FROM EVIL...
TEXT TEXT BUZZ
...THIS SHIP IS JUST WHAT I NEED...
BUZZ TEXT TEXT BUZZ
...FOR SOME REST AND RELAXATION!
PERHAPS I SPOKE TOO SOON!
WHAT'S THAT GLOWING IN THE DISTANCE?

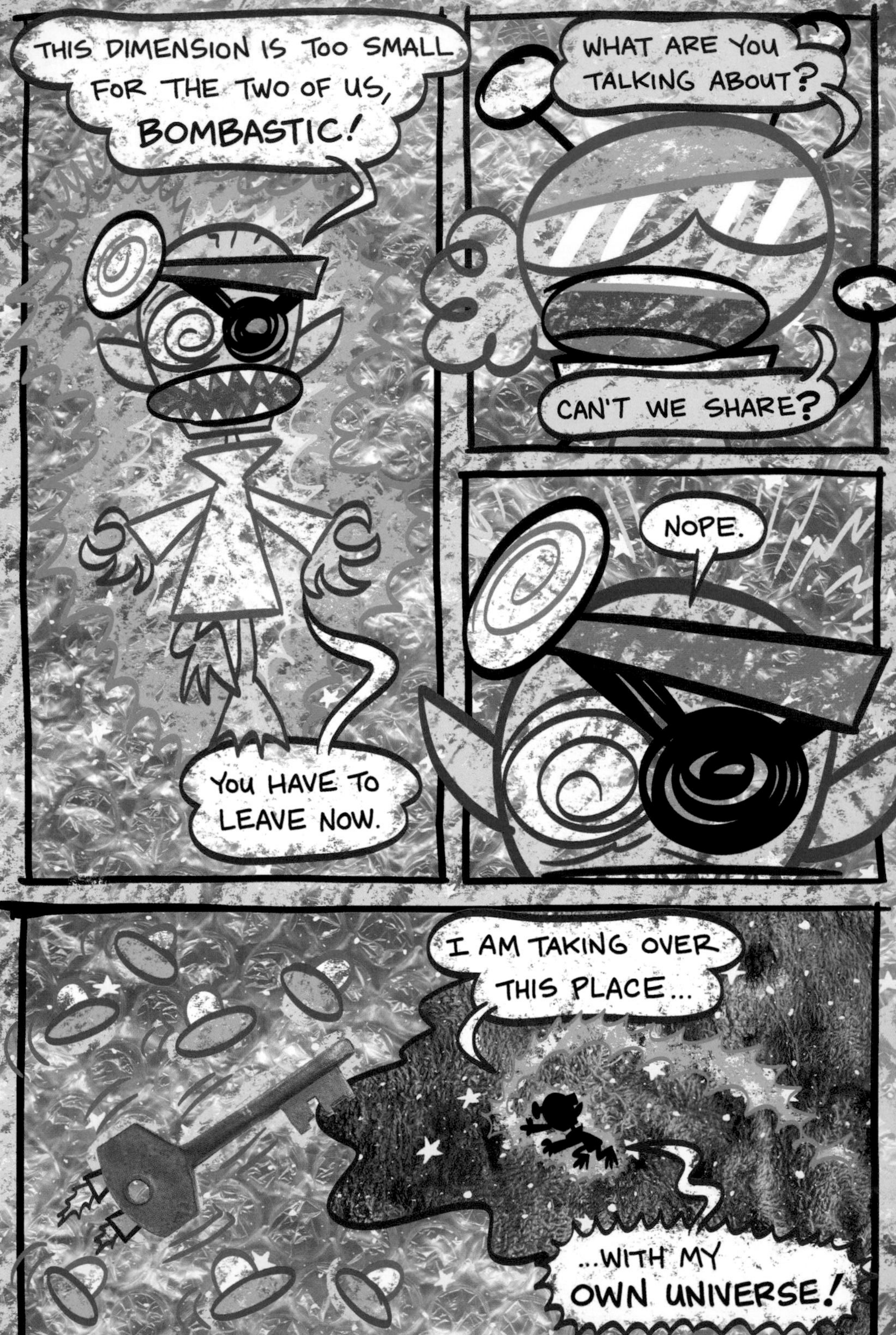
THIS DIMENSION IS TOO SMALL FOR THE TWO OF US, BOMBASTIC!
YOU HAVE TO LEAVE NOW.
WHAT ARE YOU TALKING ABOUT?
CAN'T WE SHARE?
NOPE.
I AM TAKING OVER THIS PLACE...
...WITH MY OWN UNIVERSE!

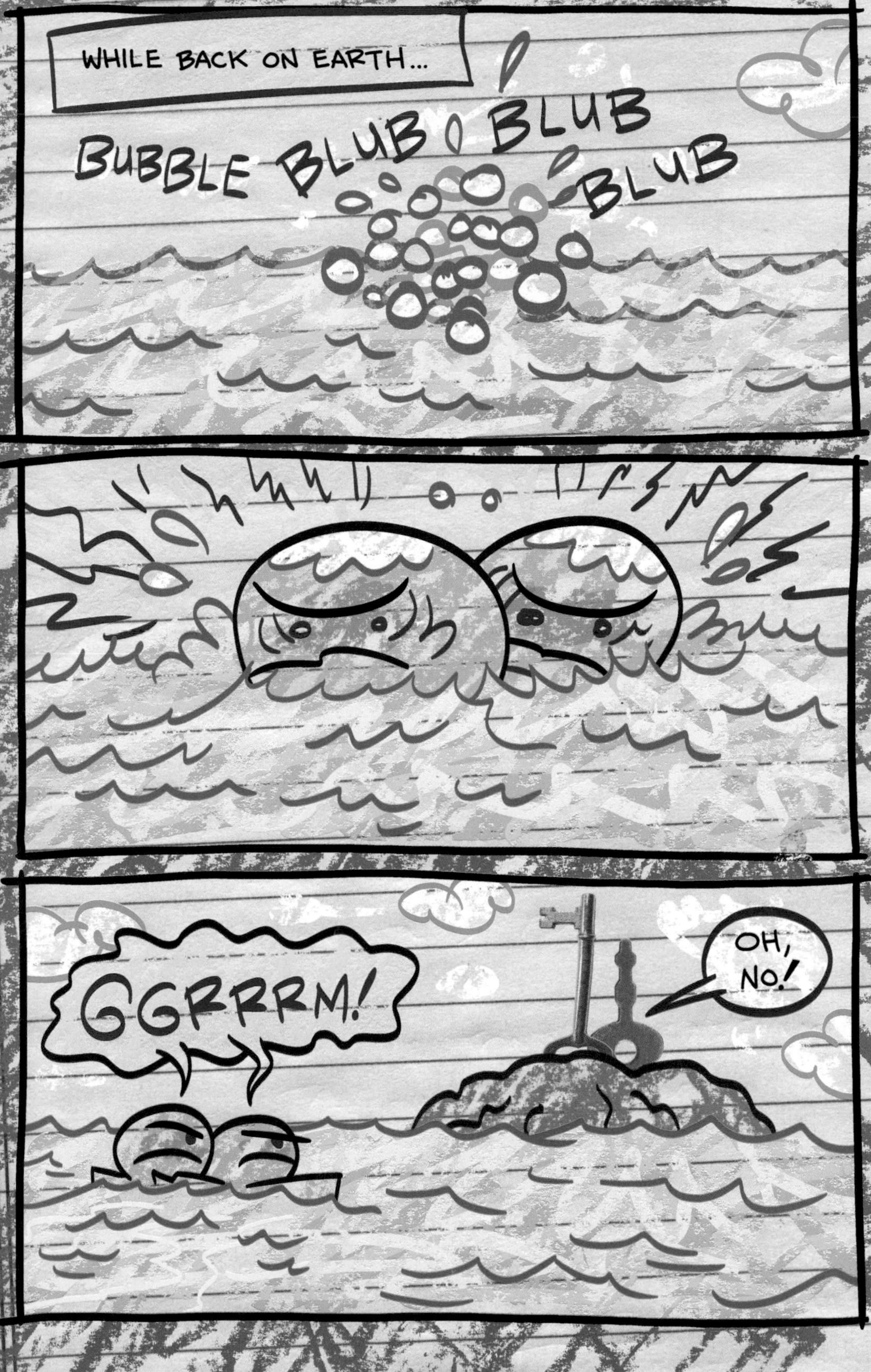
WHILE BACK ON EARTH...
BUBBLE BLUB BLUB BLUB
GGRRRM!
OH, NO!

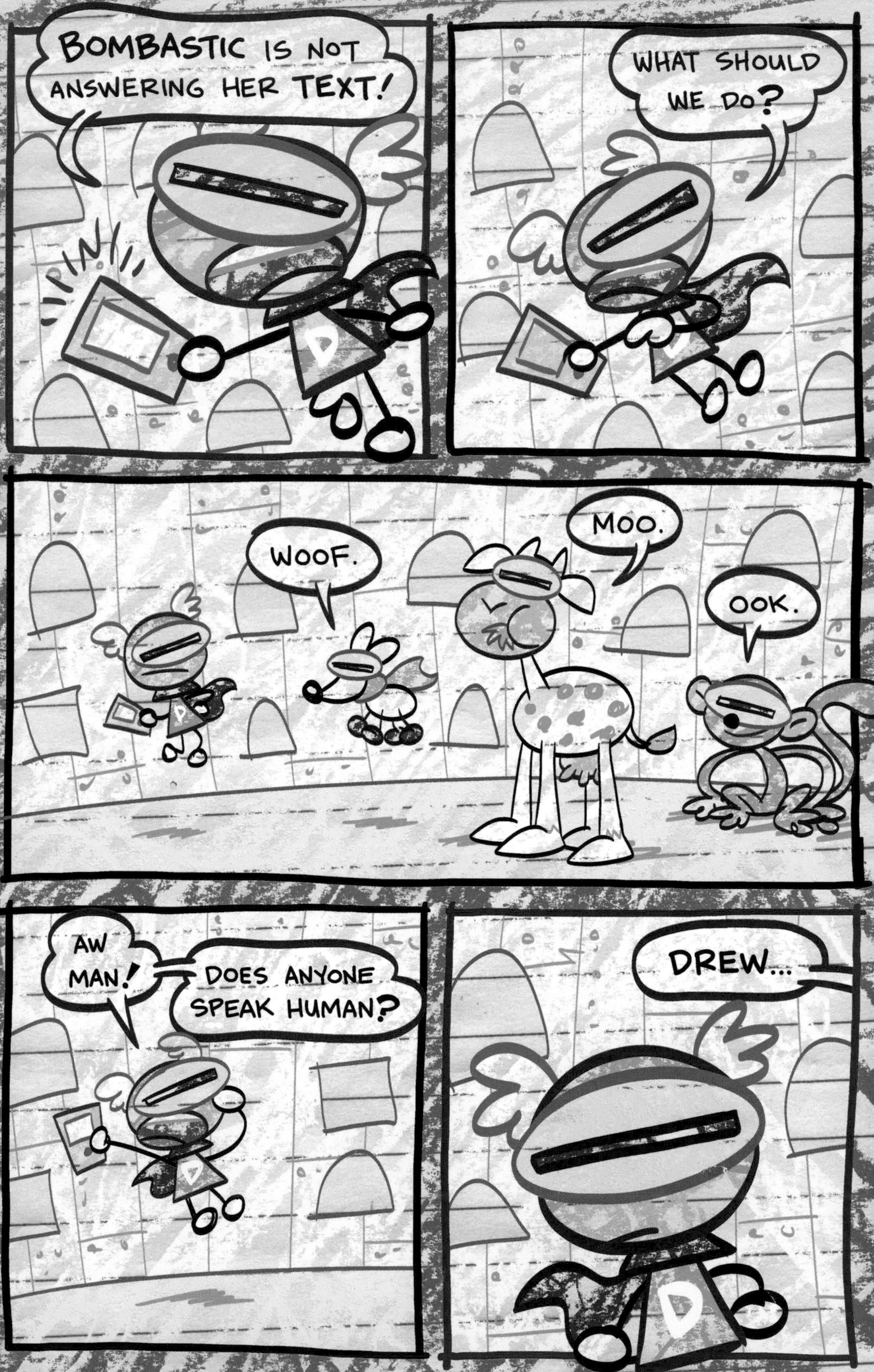
BOMBASTIC IS NOT ANSWERING HER TEXT!
PING
WHAT SHOULD WE DO?
WOOF.
MOO.
OOK.
AW MAN!
DOES ANYONE SPEAK HUMAN?
DREW...

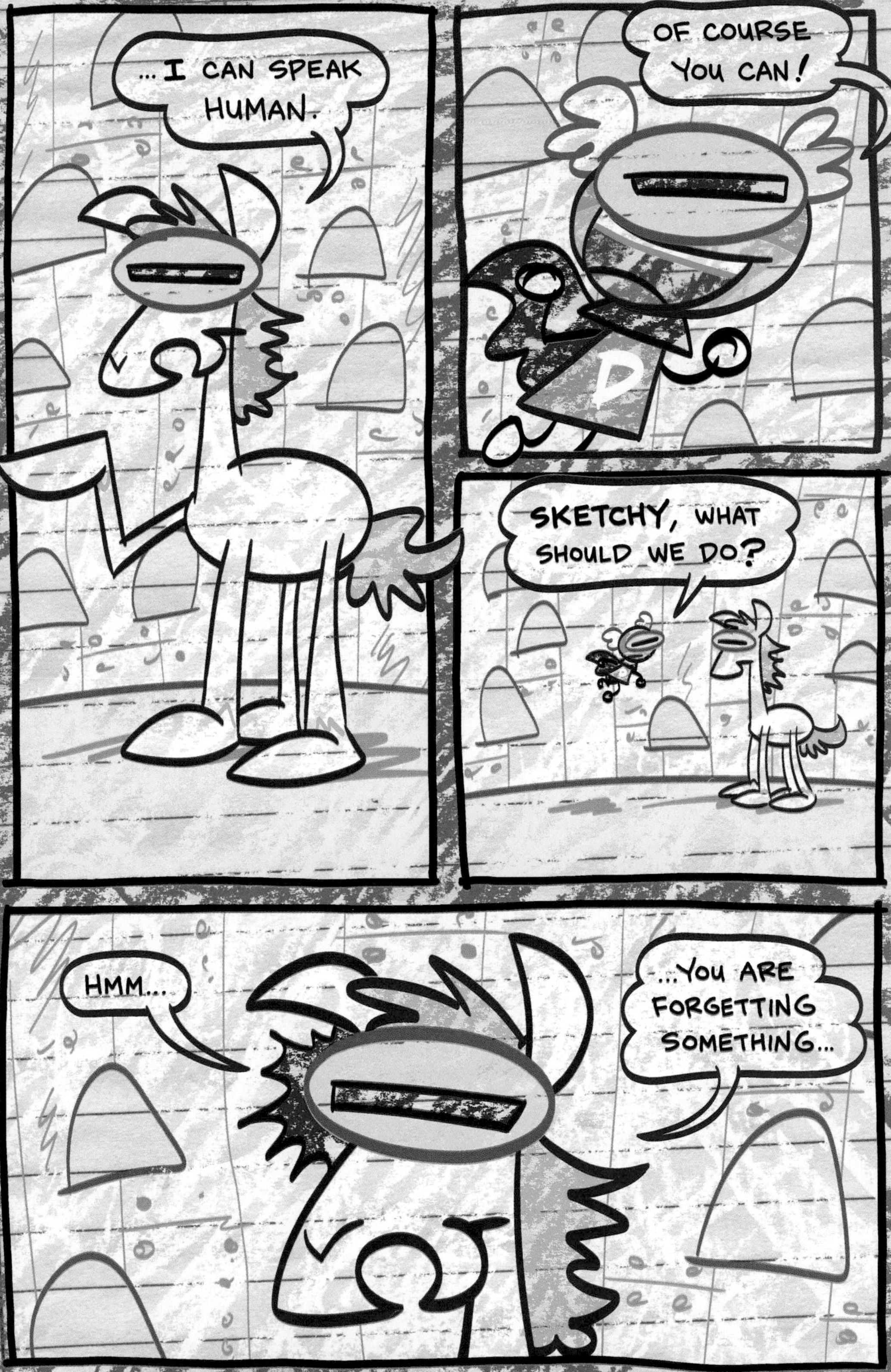
...I CAN SPEAK HUMAN.
OF COURSE YOU CAN!
SKETCHY, WHAT SHOULD WE DO?
HMM...
...YOU ARE FORGETTING SOMETHING...

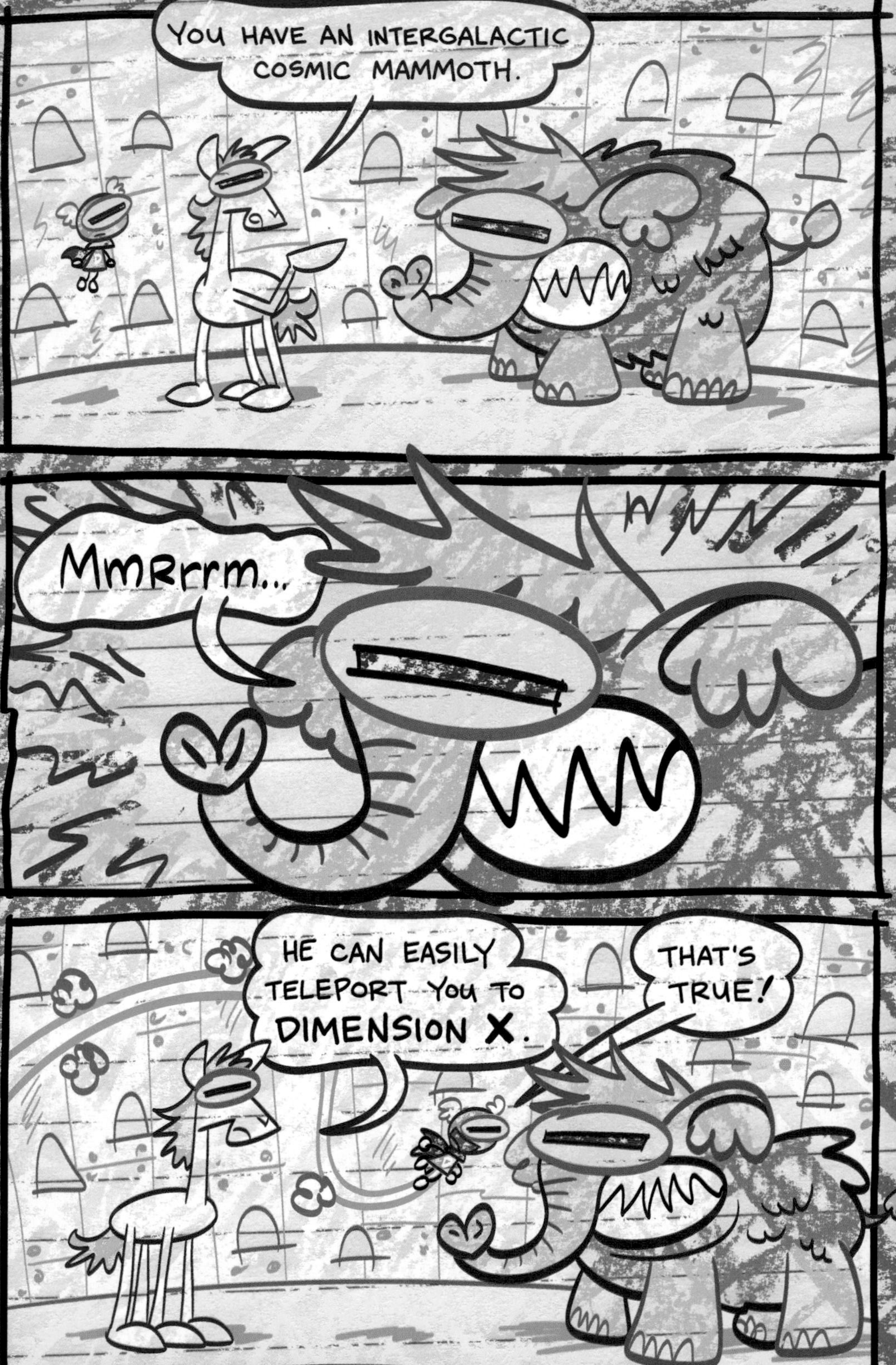
YOU HAVE AN INTERGALACTIC COSMIC MAMMOTH.
MMRrrm...
HE CAN EASILY TELEPORT YOU TO DIMENSION X.
THAT'S TRUE!

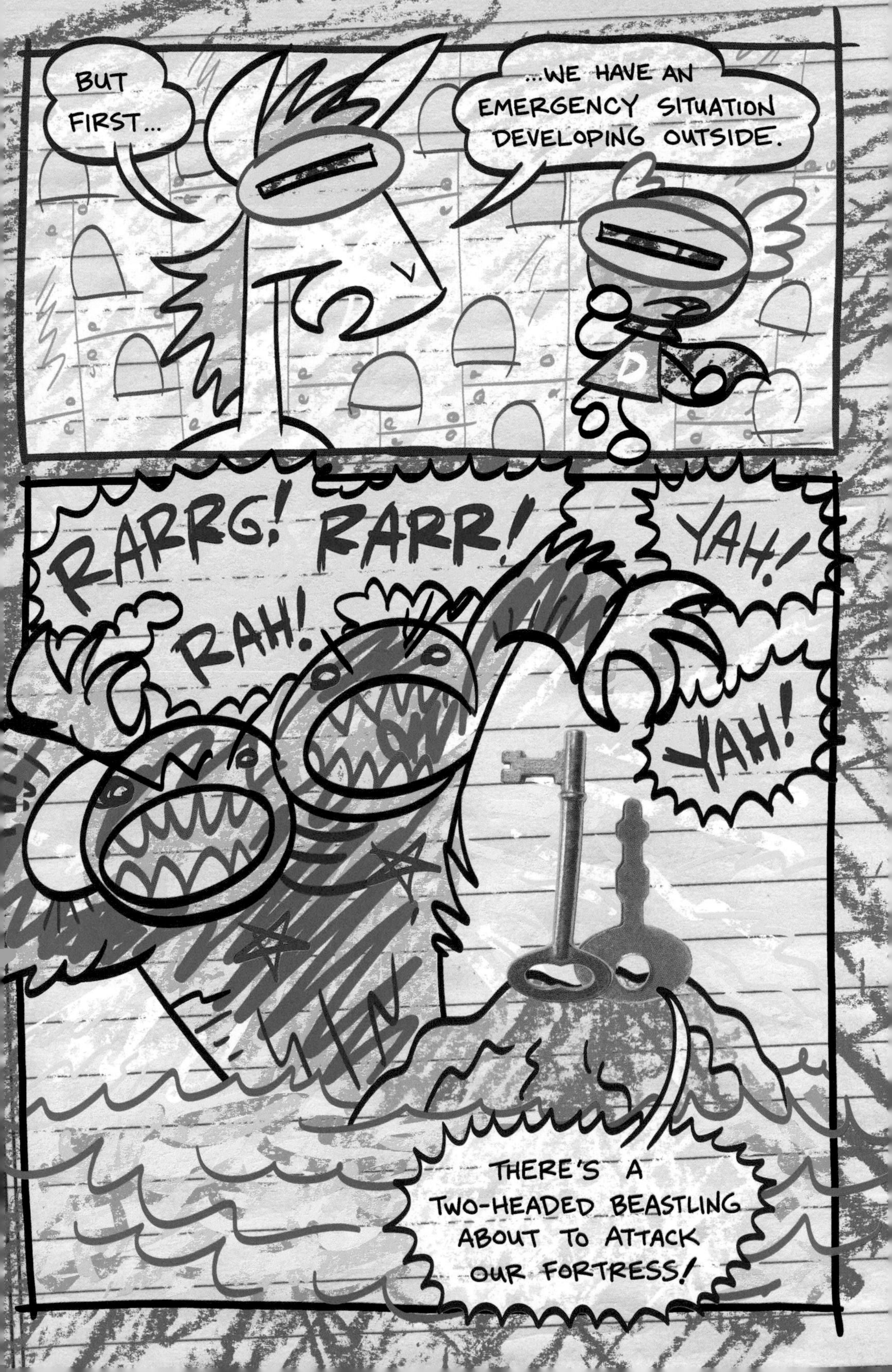
BUT FIRST...
...WE HAVE AN EMERGENCY SITUATION DEVELOPING OUTSIDE.
RARRG! RARR!
YAH!
RAH!
YAH!
THERE'S A TWO-HEADED BEASTLING ABOUT TO ATTACK OUR FORTRESS!

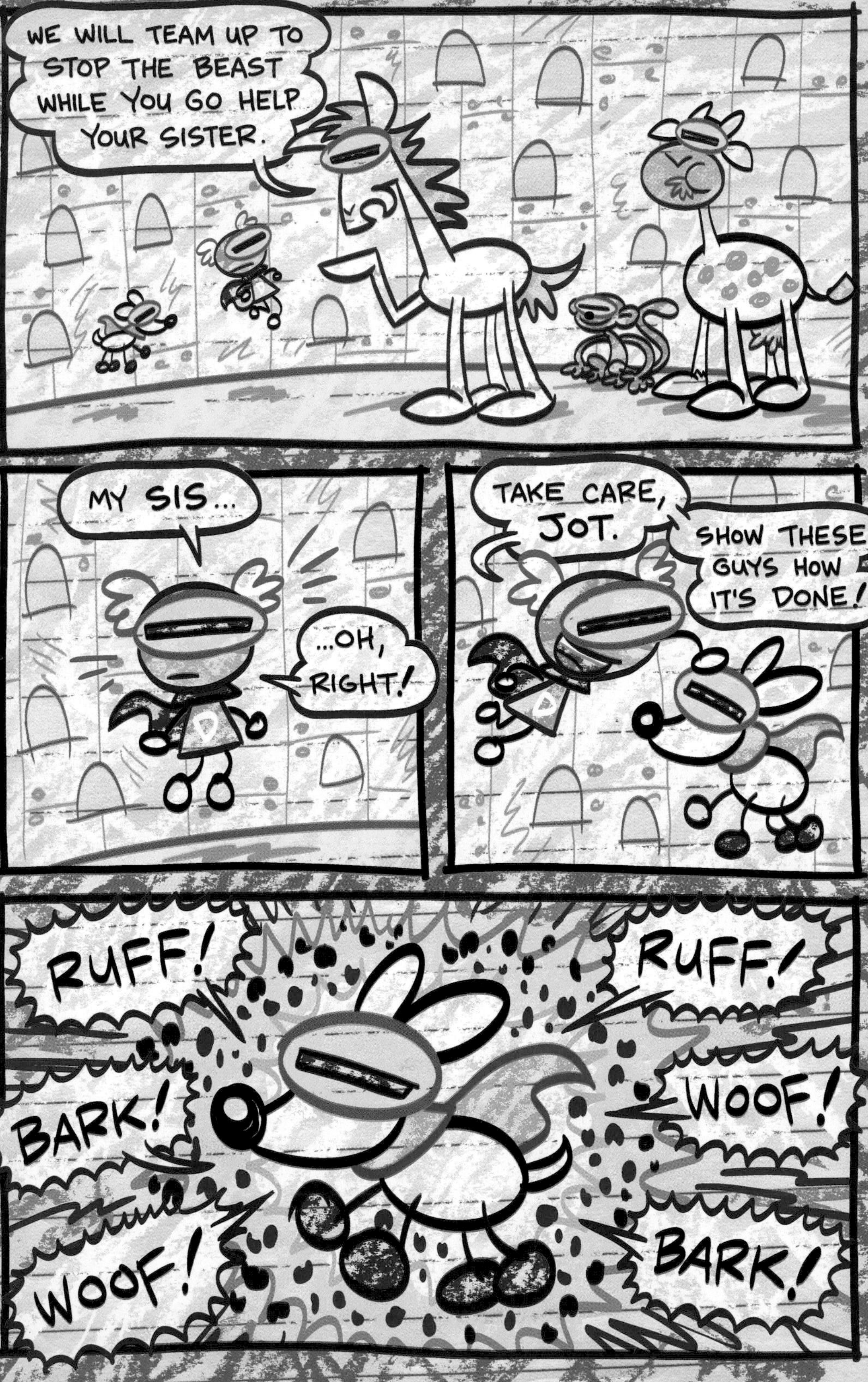
WE WILL TEAM UP TO STOP THE BEAST WHILE YOU GO HELP YOUR SISTER.
MY SIS...
...OH, RIGHT!
TAKE CARE, JOT.
SHOW THESE GUYS HOW IT'S DONE!
RUFF!
RUFF!
BARK!
WOOF!
WOOF!
BARK!

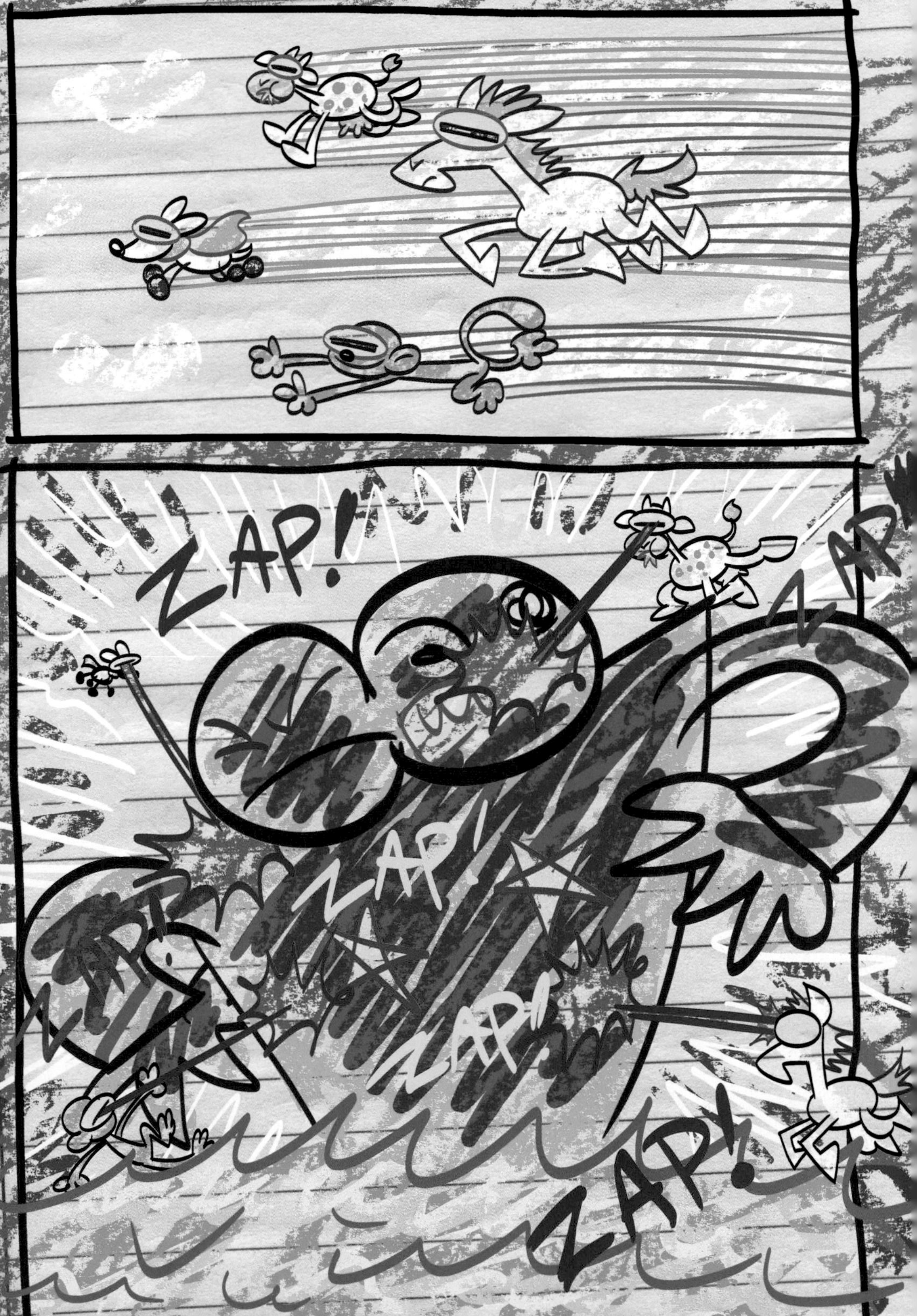

ZAP!
ZAP!
ZAP!
ZAP!
ZAP!

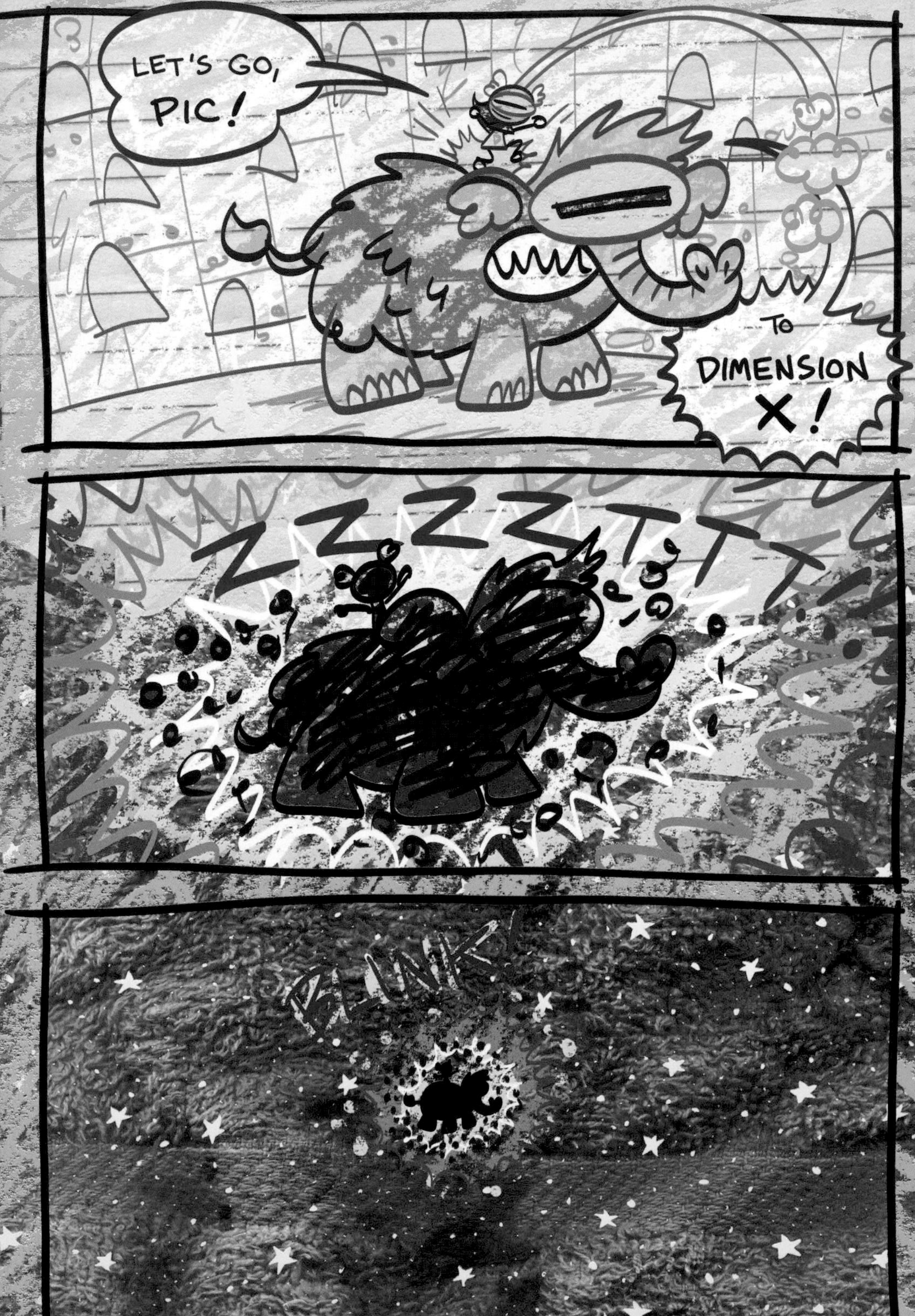
LET'S GO, PIC!
TO DIMENSION X!
ZZZZZTTTT!
BLINK!

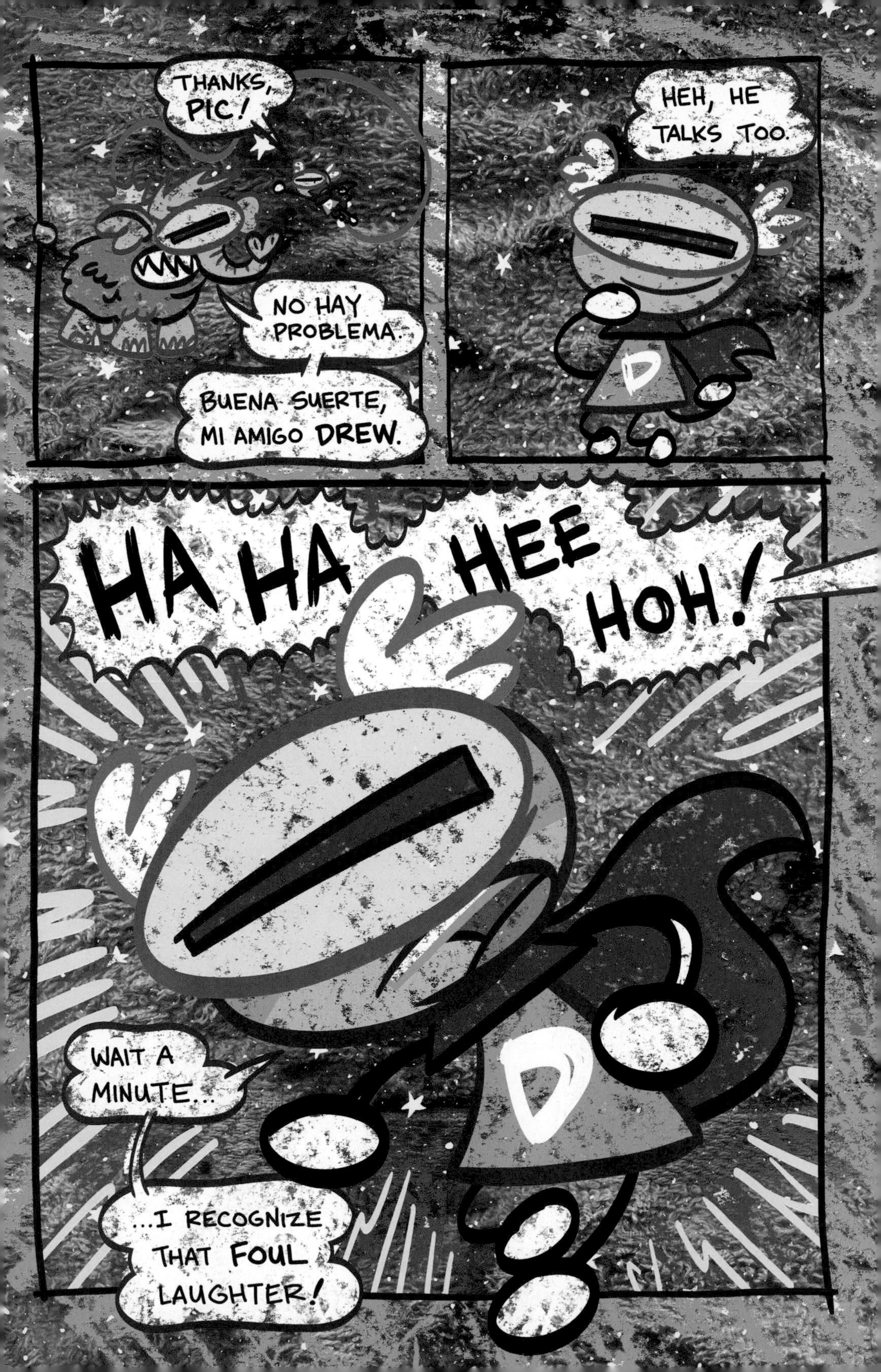
THANKS, PIC!
NO HAY PROBLEMA.
BUENA SUERTE, MI AMIGO DREW.
HEH, HE TALKS TOO.
HA HA HEE HOH!
WAIT A MINUTE...
...I RECOGNIZE THAT FOUL LAUGHTER!

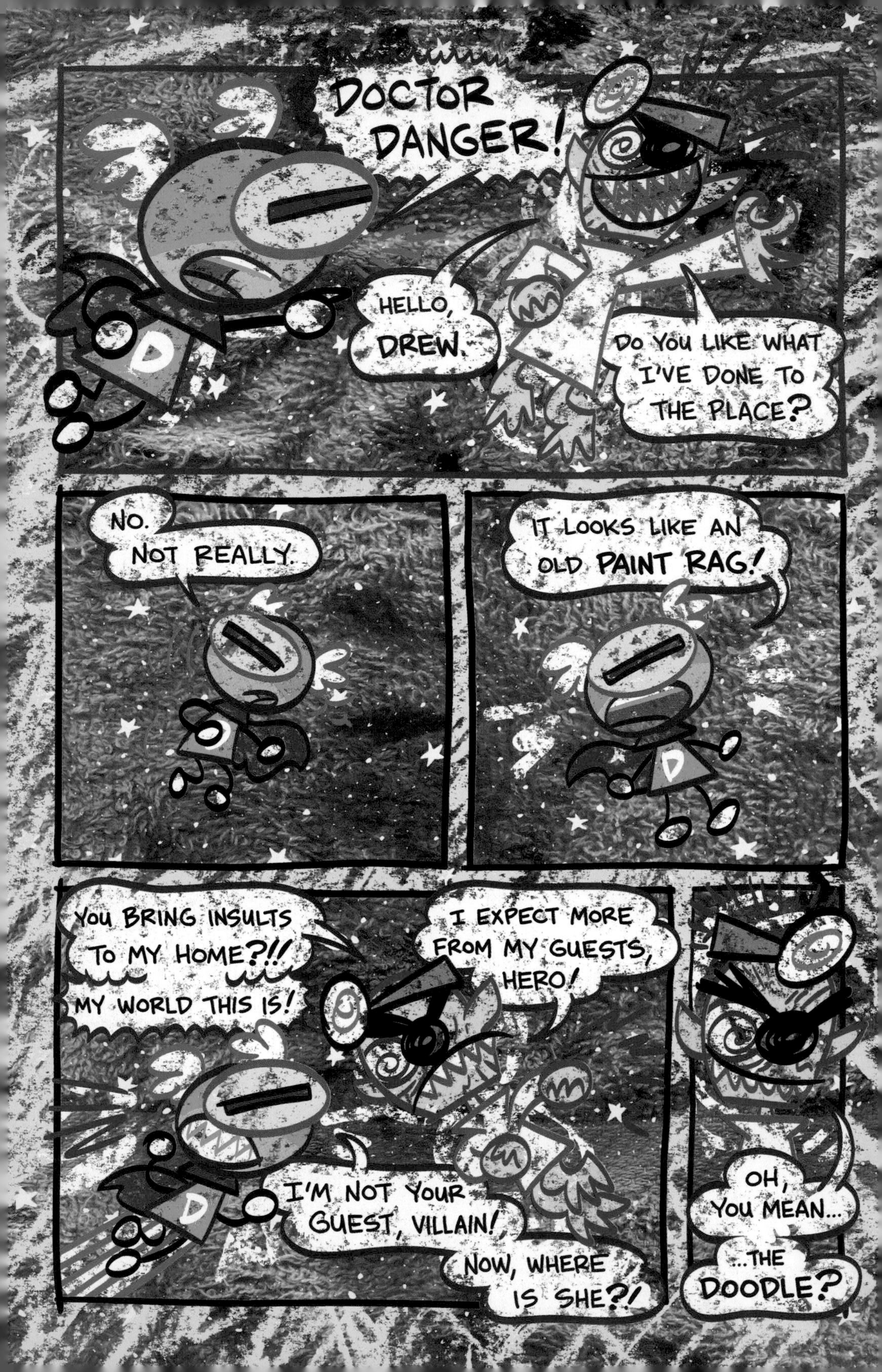
DOCTOR DANGER!
HELLO, DREW.
DO YOU LIKE WHAT I'VE DONE TO THE PLACE?
NO. NOT REALLY.
IT LOOKS LIKE AN OLD PAINT RAG!
YOU BRING INSULTS TO MY HOME?!!
MY WORLD THIS IS!
I EXPECT MORE FROM MY GUESTS, HERO!
I'M NOT YOUR GUEST, VILLAIN!
NOW, WHERE IS SHE?!
OH, YOU MEAN...
...THE DOODLE?

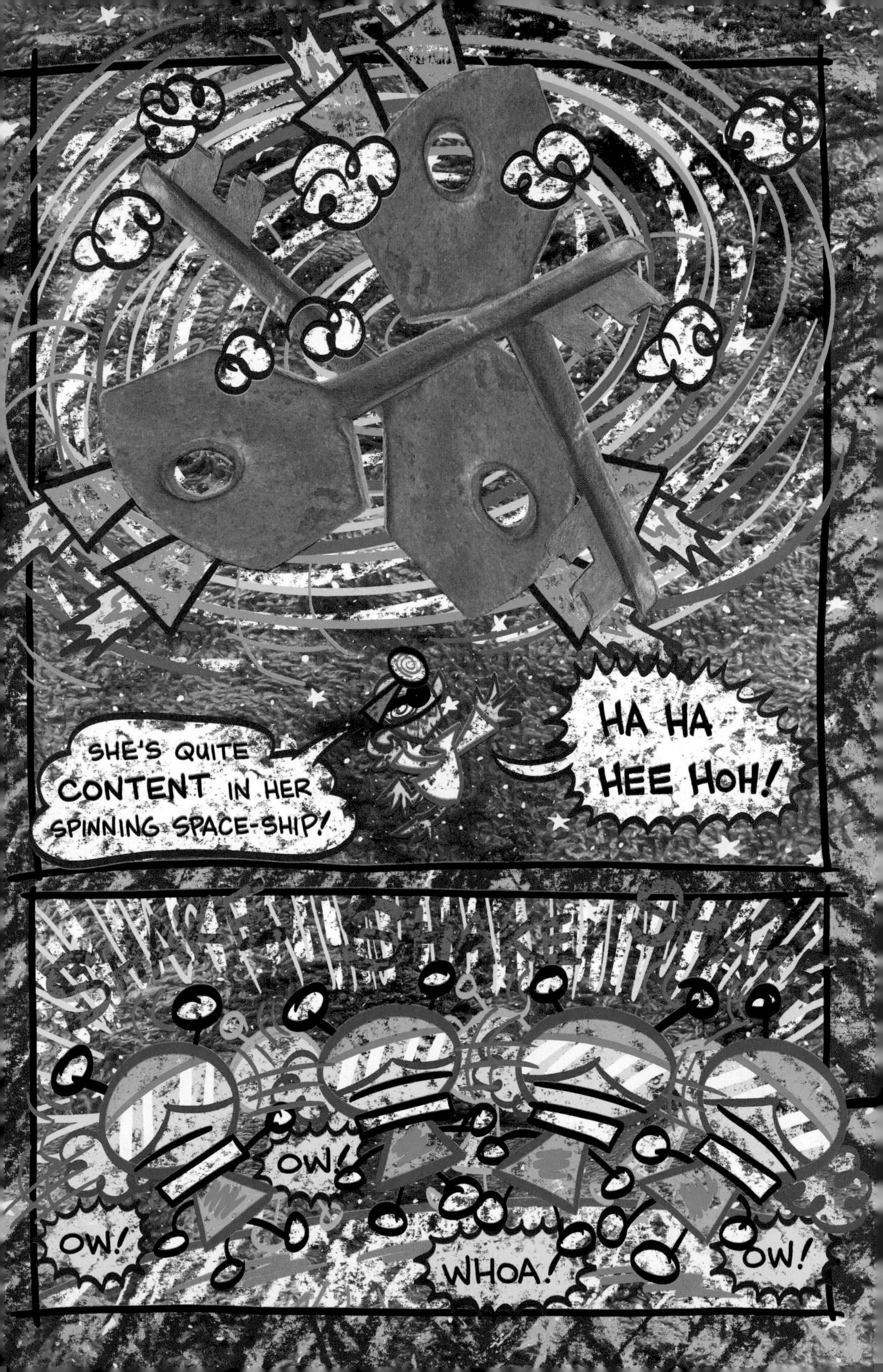
SHE'S QUITE CONTENT IN HER SPINNING SPACE-SHIP!
HA HA HEE HOH!
OW!
OW!
WHOA!
OW!

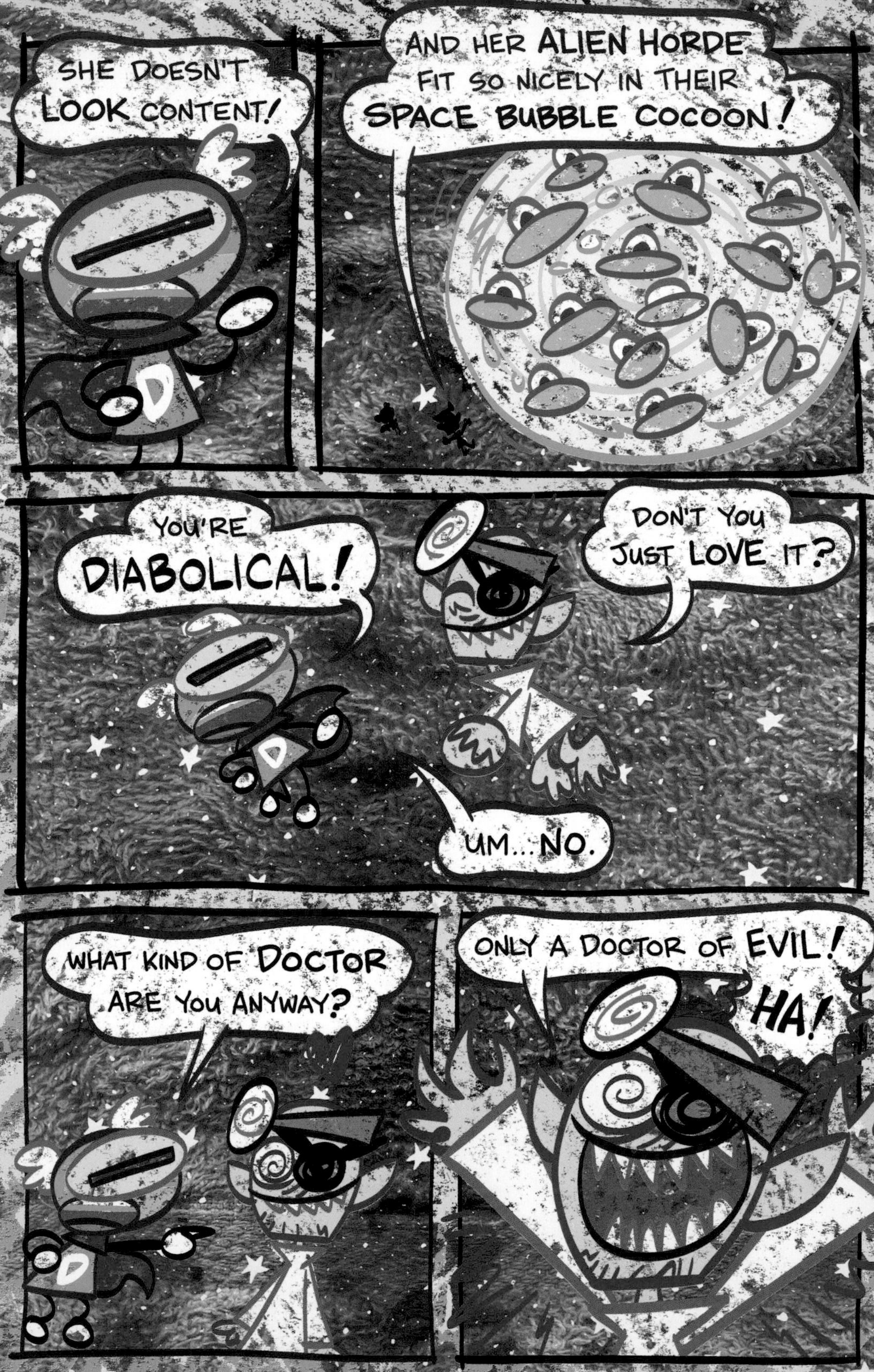
SHE DOESN'T LOOK CONTENT!
AND HER ALIEN HORDE FIT SO NICELY IN THEIR SPACE BUBBLE COCOON!
YOU'RE DIABOLICAL!
DON'T YOU JUST LOVE IT?
UM...NO.
WHAT KIND OF DOCTOR ARE YOU ANYWAY?
ONLY A DOCTOR OF EVIL!
HA!

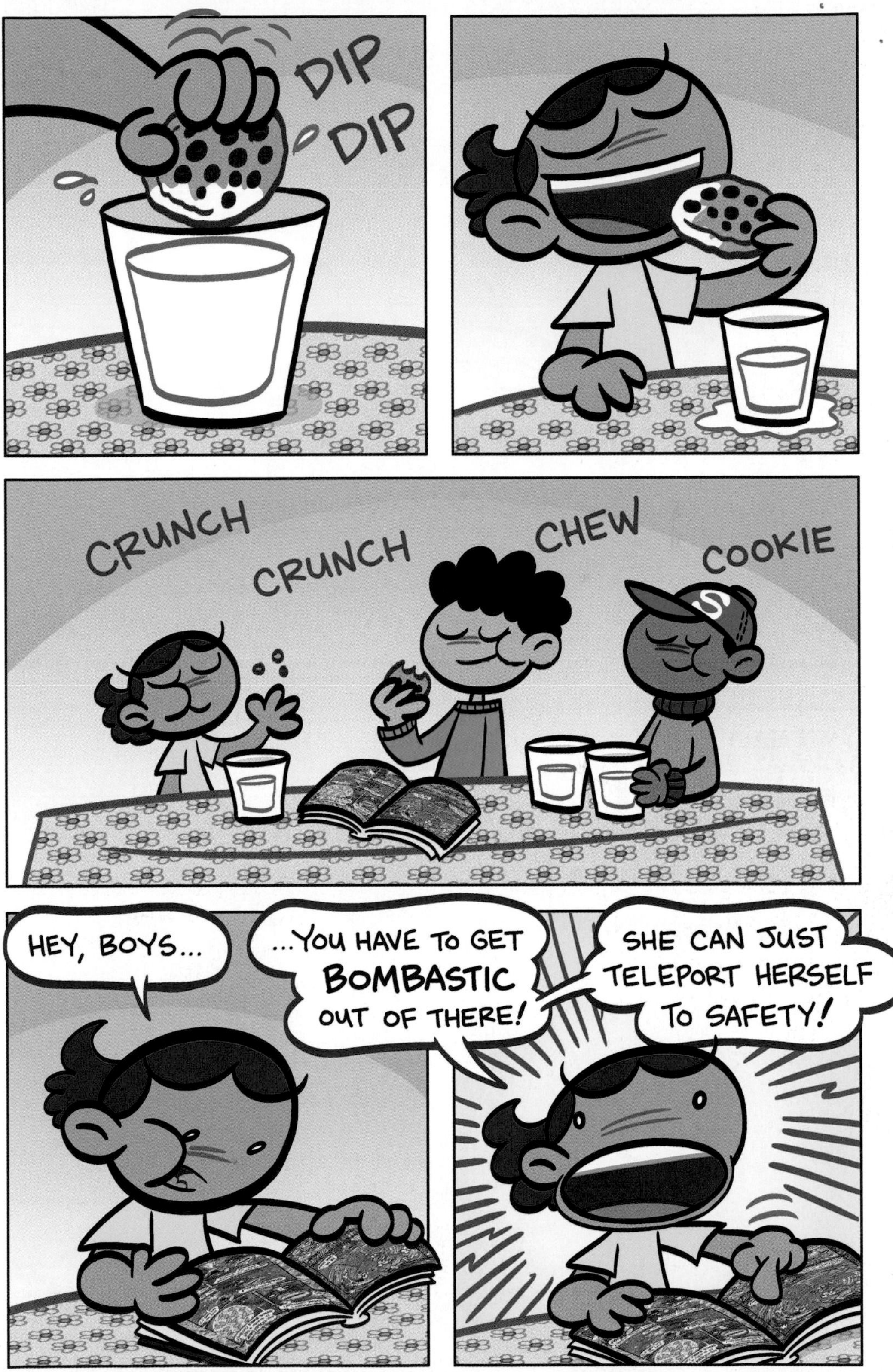
DIP
DIP
CRUNCH
CRUNCH
CHEW
COOKIE
HEY, BOYS...
...YOU HAVE TO GET BOMBASTIC OUT OF THERE!
SHE CAN JUST TELEPORT HERSELF TO SAFETY!

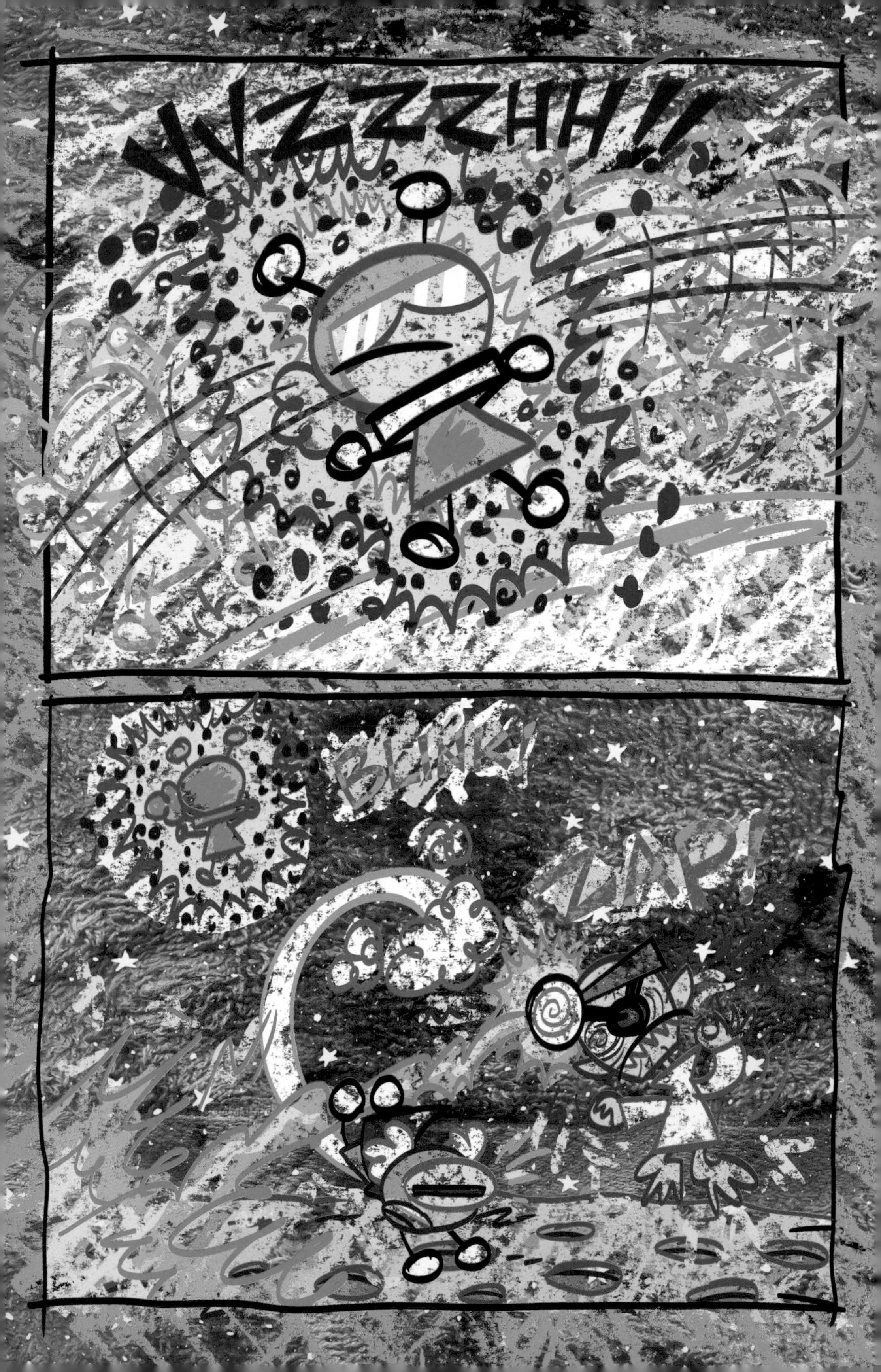
VVZZZHH!!
BLINK!
ZAP!

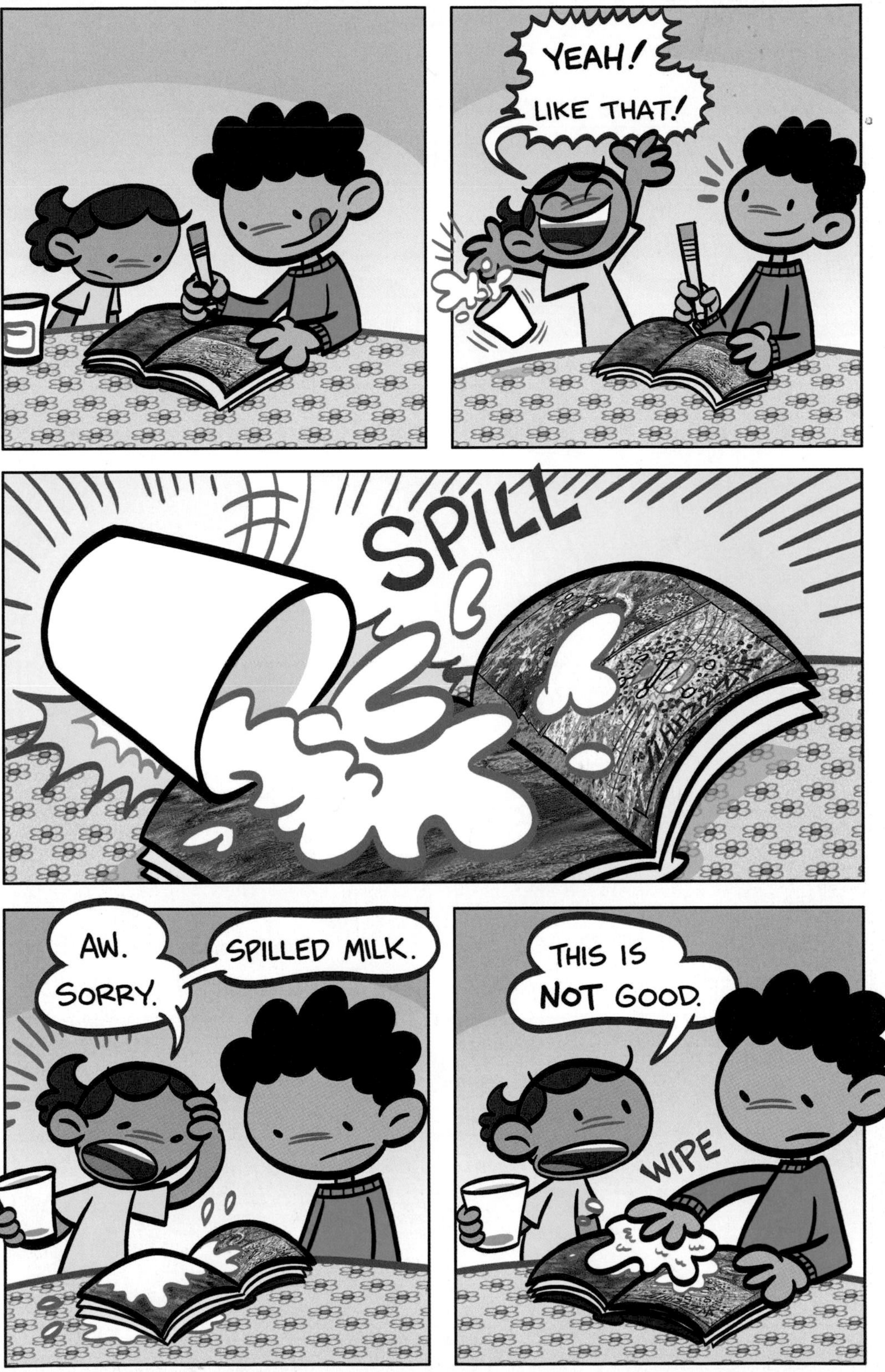
YEAH! LIKE THAT!
SPILL
AW. SORRY.
SPILLED MILK.
THIS IS NOT GOOD.
WIPE

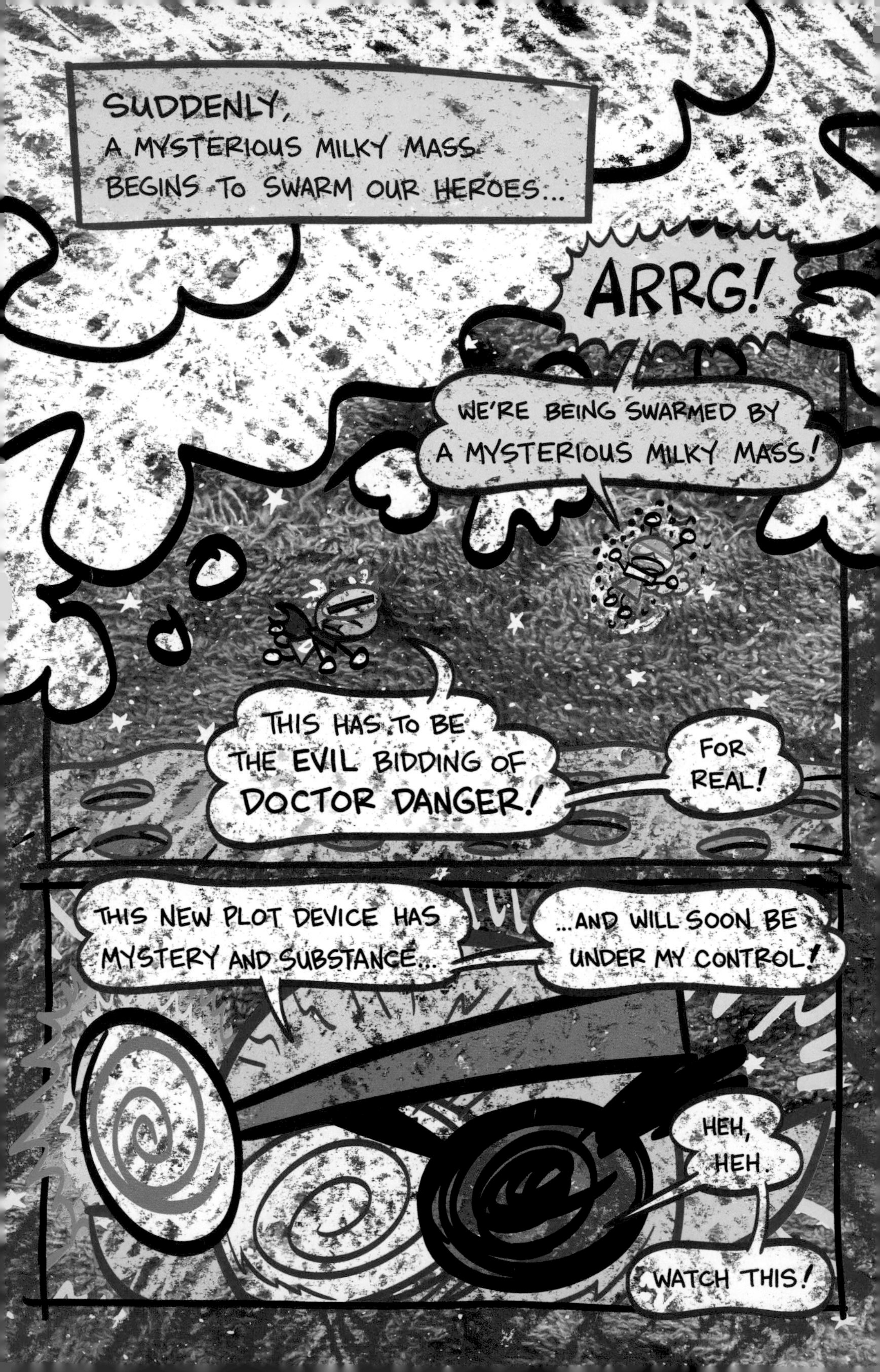
SUDDENLY, A MYSTERIOUS MILKY MASS BEGINS TO SWARM OUR HEROES...
ARRG!
WE'RE BEING SWARMED BY A MYSTERIOUS MILKY MASS!
THIS HAS TO BE THE EVIL BIDDING OF DOCTOR DANGER!
FOR REAL!
THIS NEW PLOT DEVICE HAS MYSTERY AND SUBSTANCE...
...AND WILL SOON BE UNDER MY CONTROL!
HEH, HEH.
WATCH THIS!

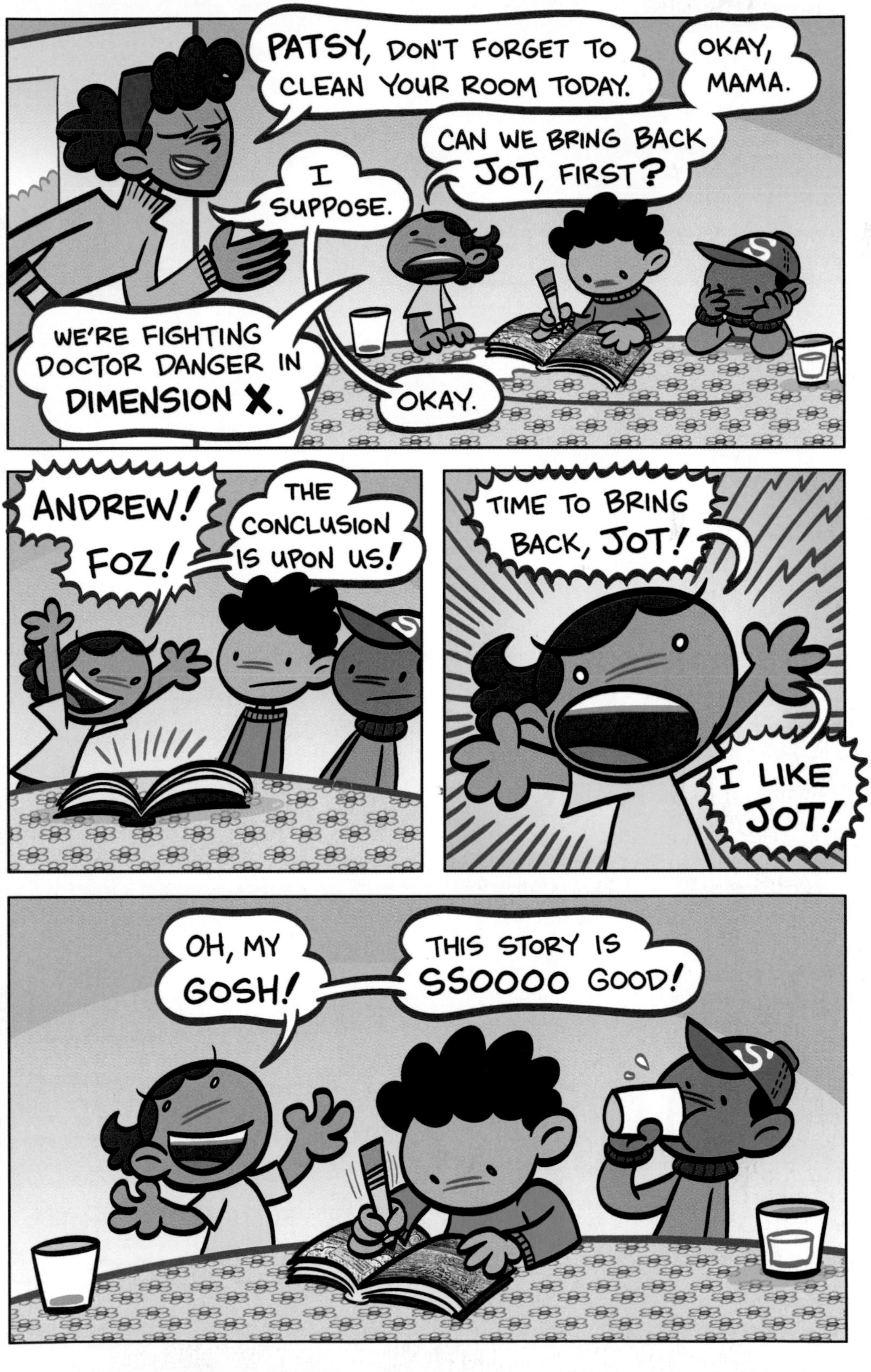
PATSY, DON'T FORGET TO CLEAN YOUR ROOM TODAY.
OKAY, MAMA.
CAN WE BRING BACK JOT, FIRST?
I SUPPOSE.
WE'RE FIGHTING DOCTOR DANGER IN DIMENSION X.
OKAY.
ANDREW! FOZ!
THE CONCLUSION IS UPON US!
TIME TO BRING BACK, JOT!
I LIKE JOT!
OH, MY GOSH!
THIS STORY IS SSOOOO GOOD!

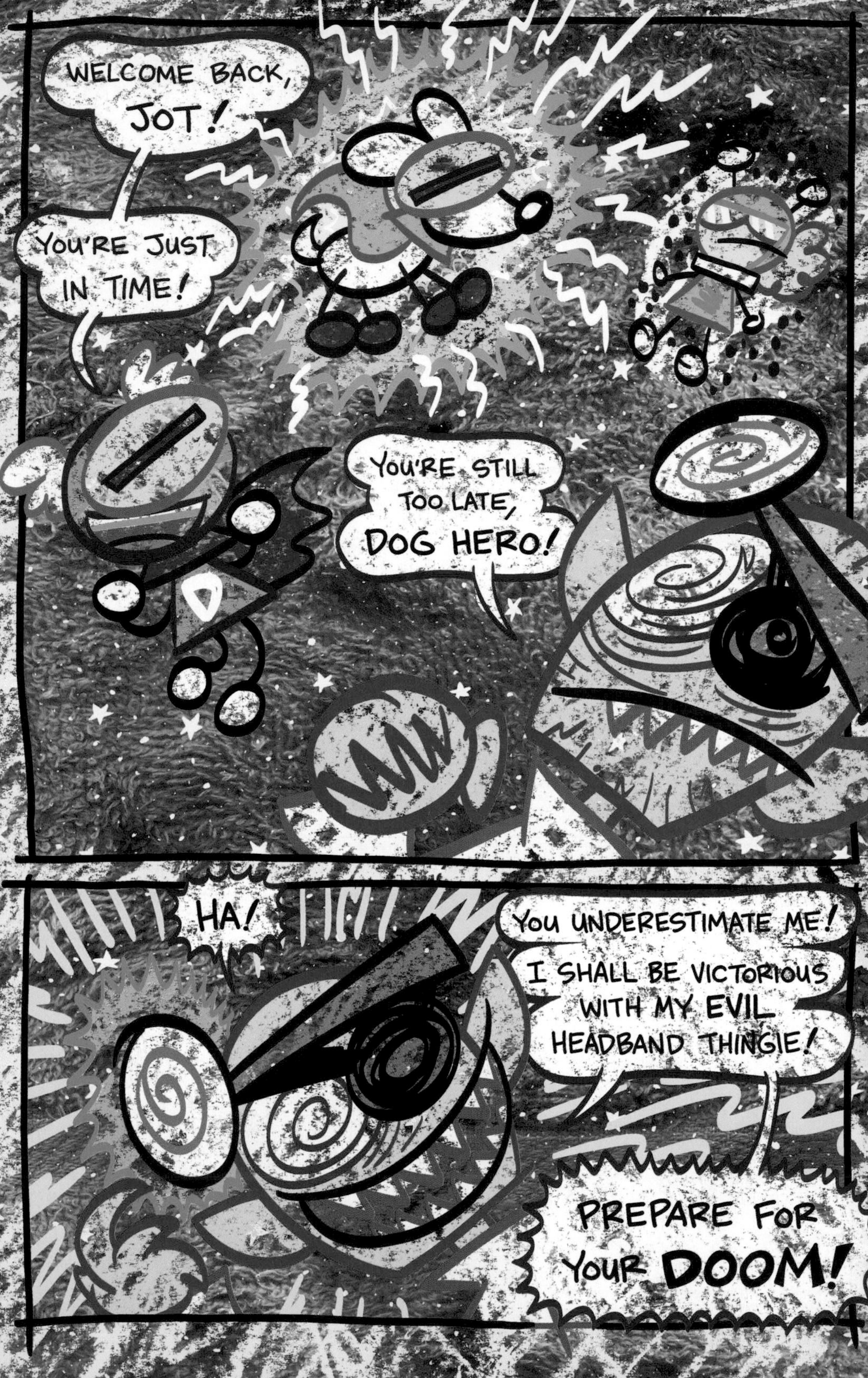
WELCOME BACK, JOT!
YOU'RE JUST IN TIME!
YOU'RE STILL TOO LATE, DOG HERO!
HA!
YOU UNDERESTIMATE ME!
I SHALL BE VICTORIOUS WITH MY EVIL HEADBAND THINGIE!
PREPARE FOR YOUR DOOM!

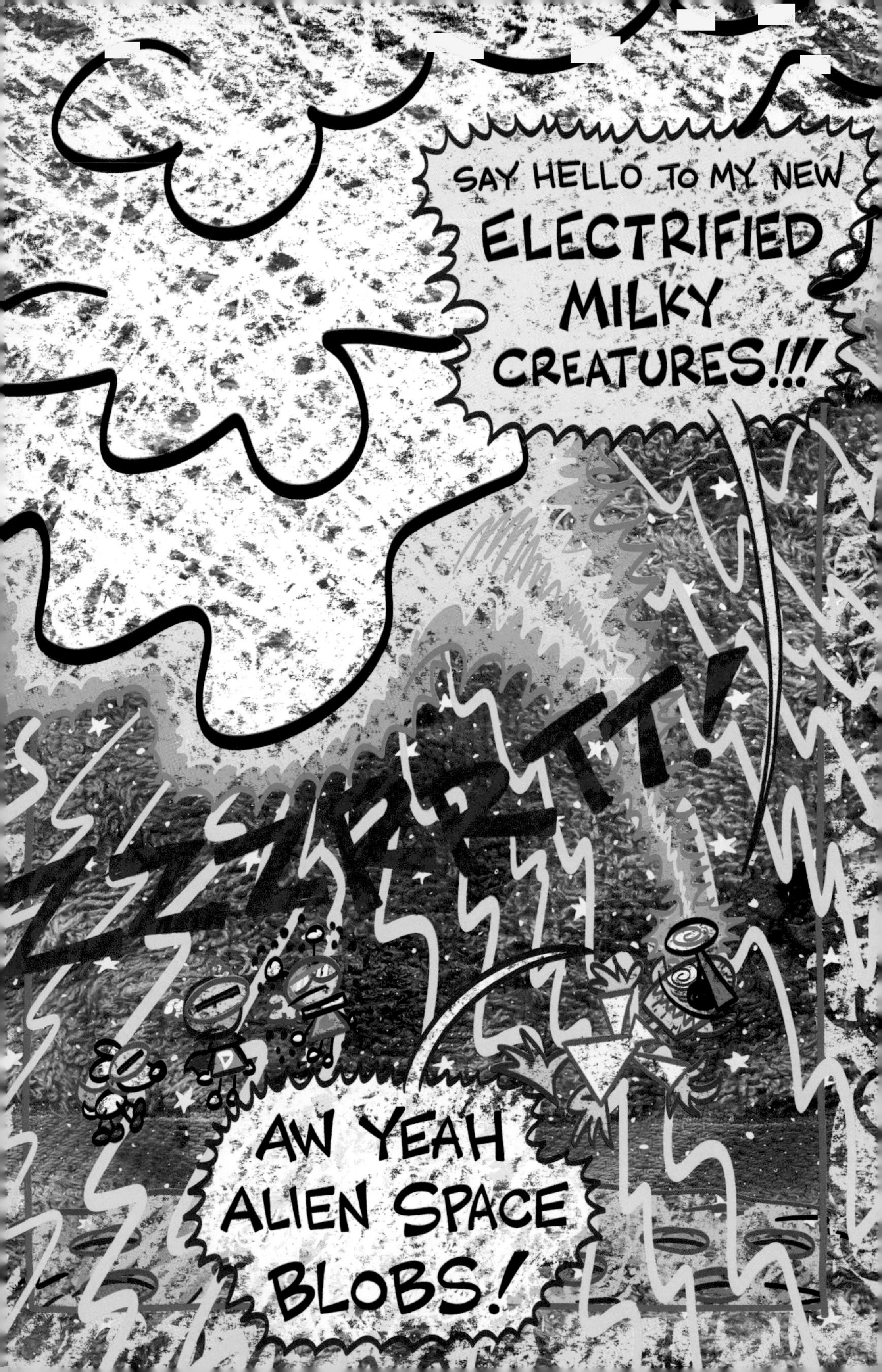
SAY HELLO TO MY NEW ELECTRIFIED MILKY CREATURES!!!
ZZZRRTT!
AW YEAH ALIEN SPACE BLOBS!

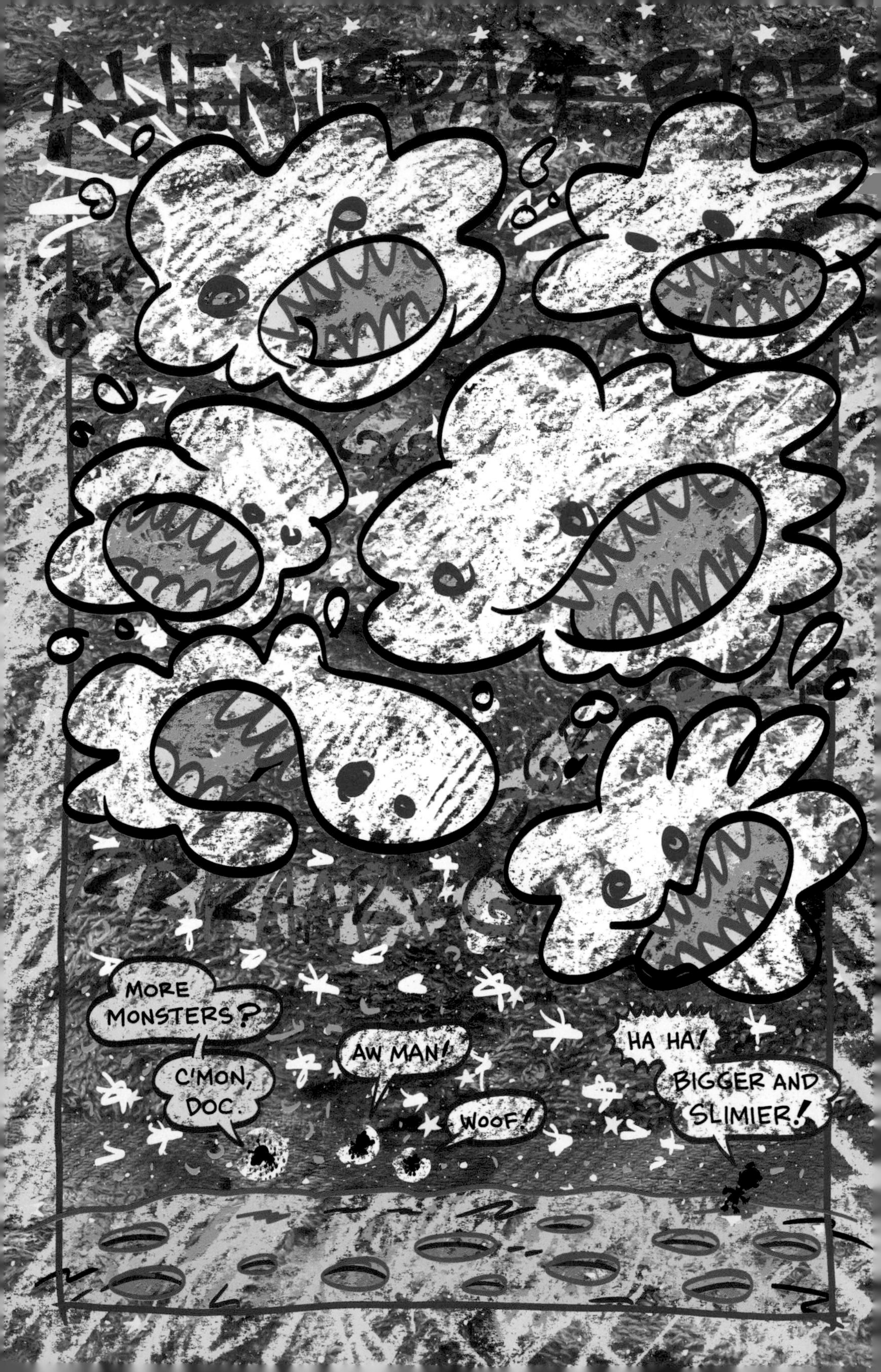
ALIEN SPACE BLOBS
MORE MONSTERS?
C'MON, DOC.
AW MAN!
WOOF!
HA HA!
BIGGER AND SLIMIER!

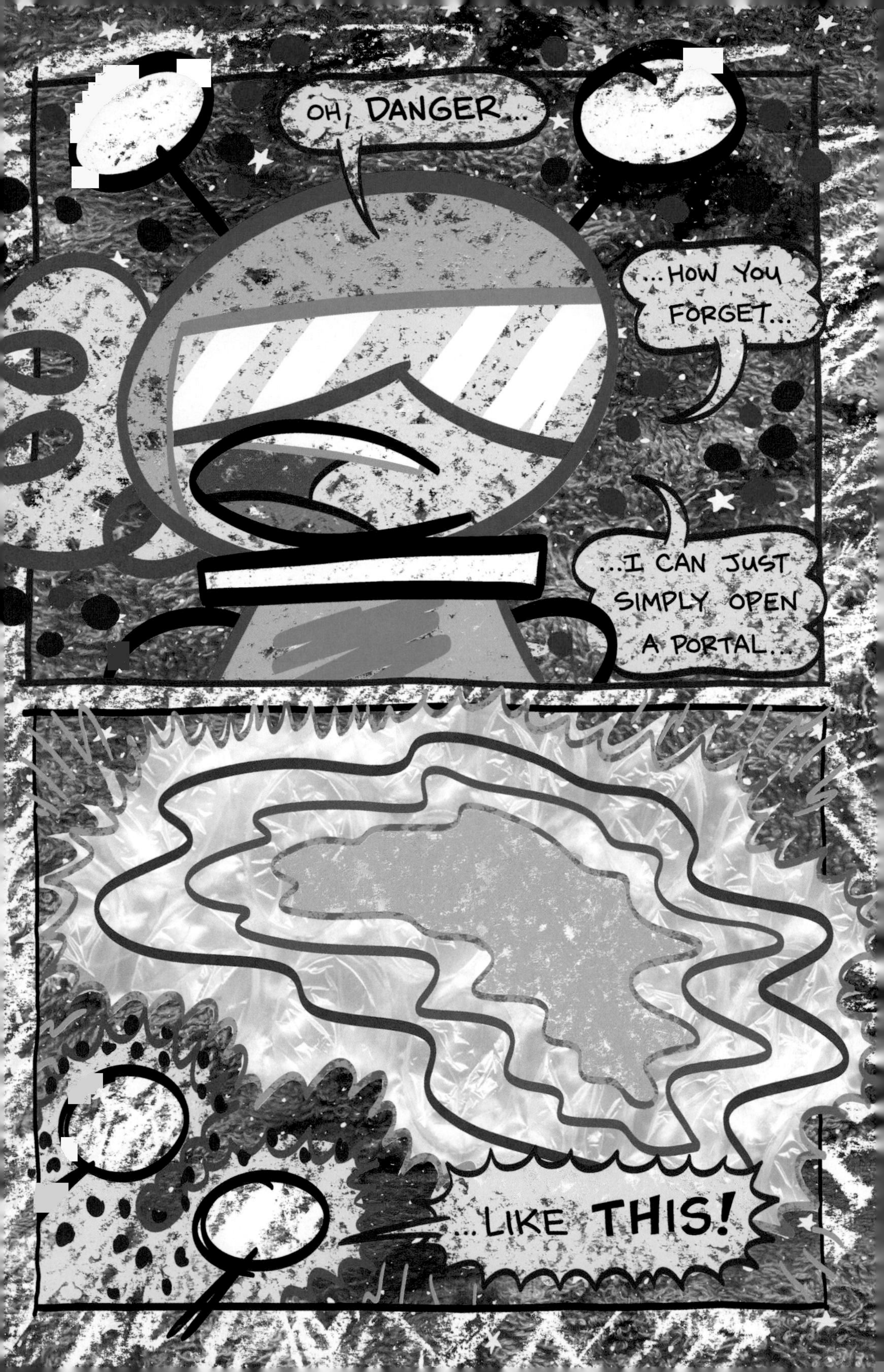
OH, DANGER...
...HOW YOU FORGET...
...I CAN JUST SIMPLY OPEN A PORTAL...
...LIKE THIS!

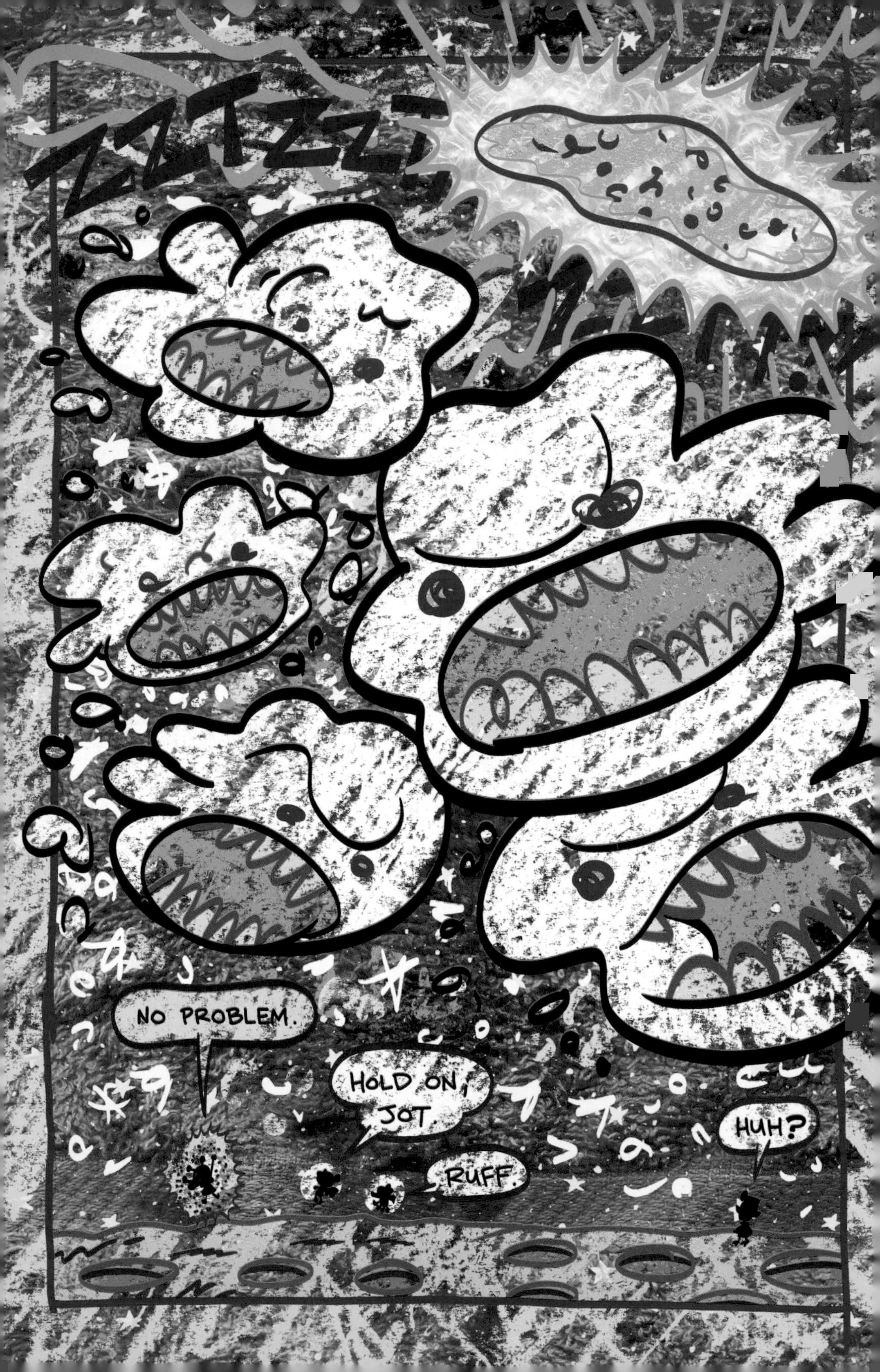

NO PROBLEM.
HOLD ON, JOT.
RUFF.
HUH?

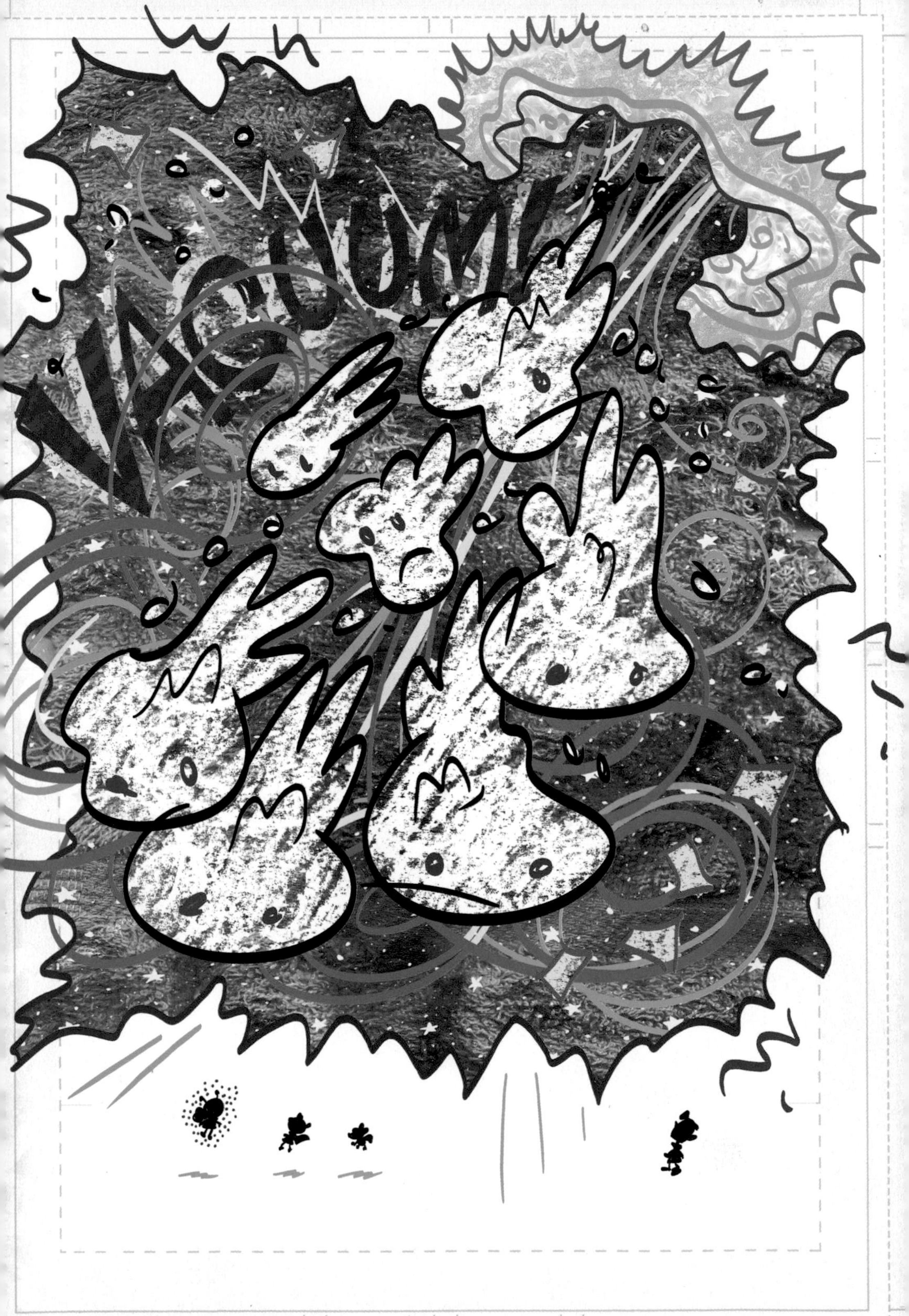

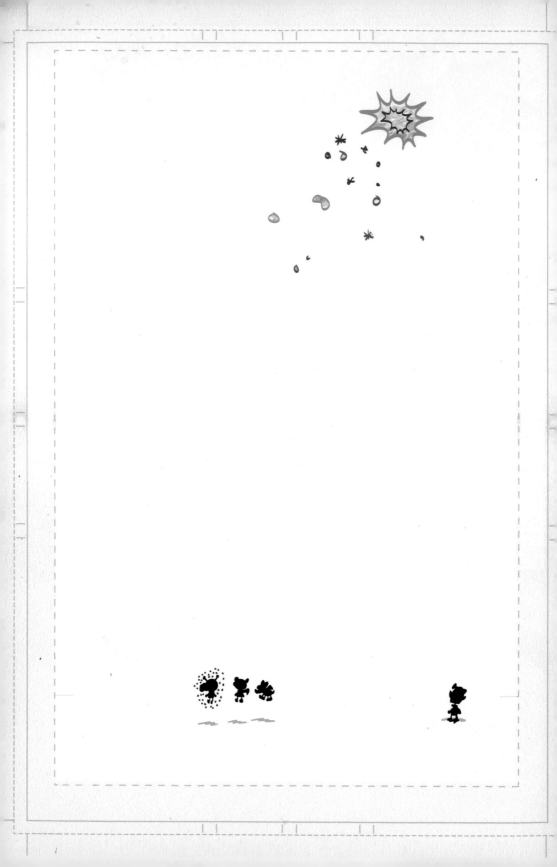

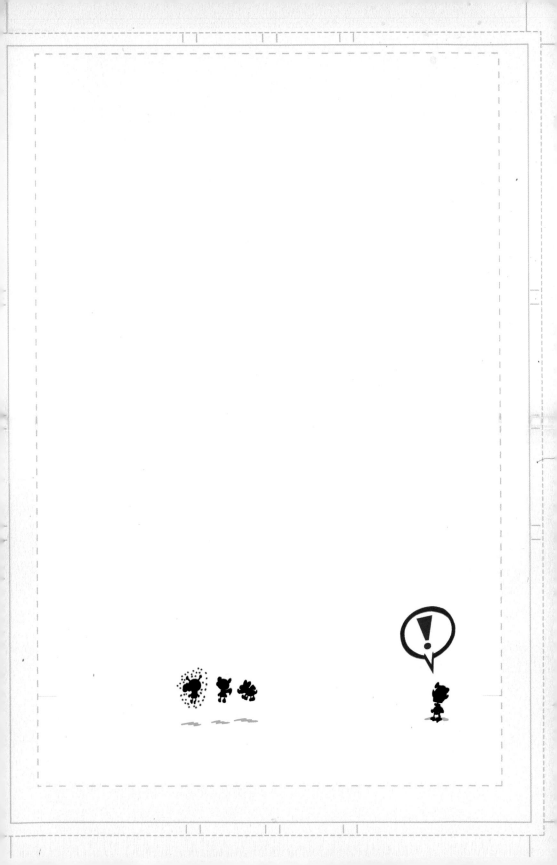

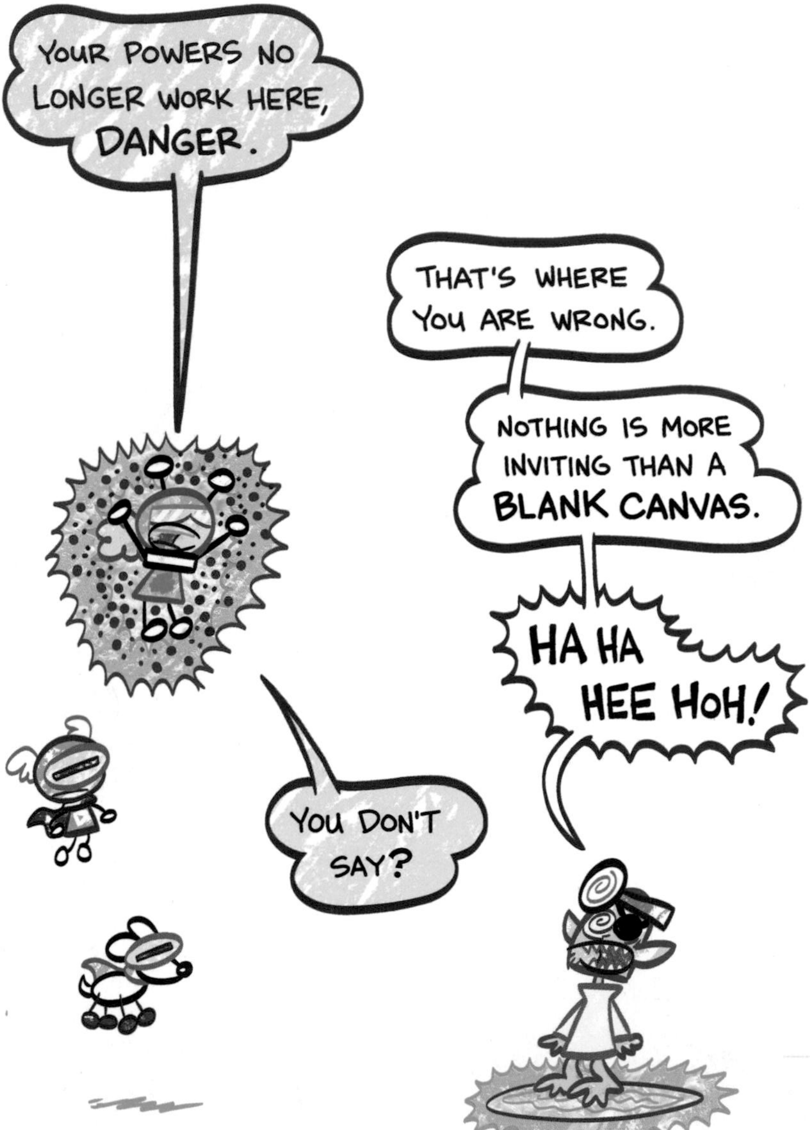
YOUR POWERS NO LONGER WORK HERE, DANGER.
THAT'S WHERE YOU ARE WRONG.
NOTHING IS MORE INVITING THAN A BLANK CANVAS.
HA HA HEE HOH!
YOU DON'T SAY?

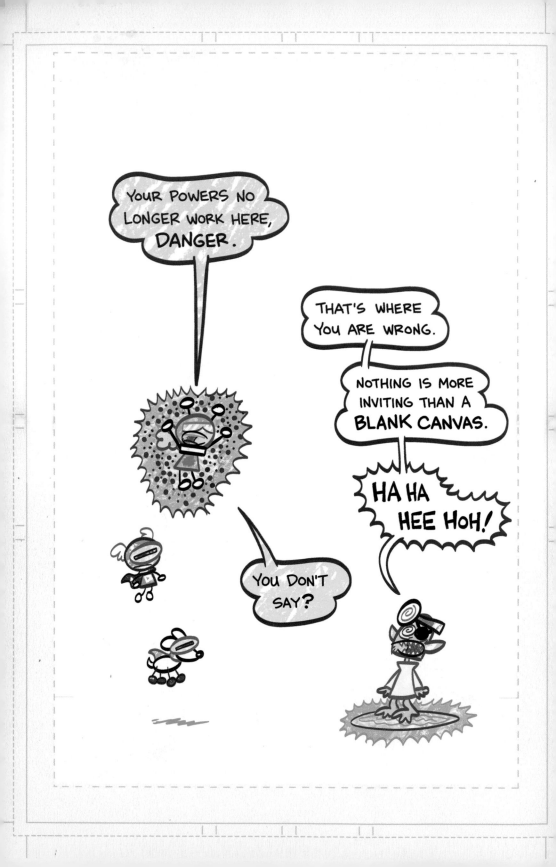

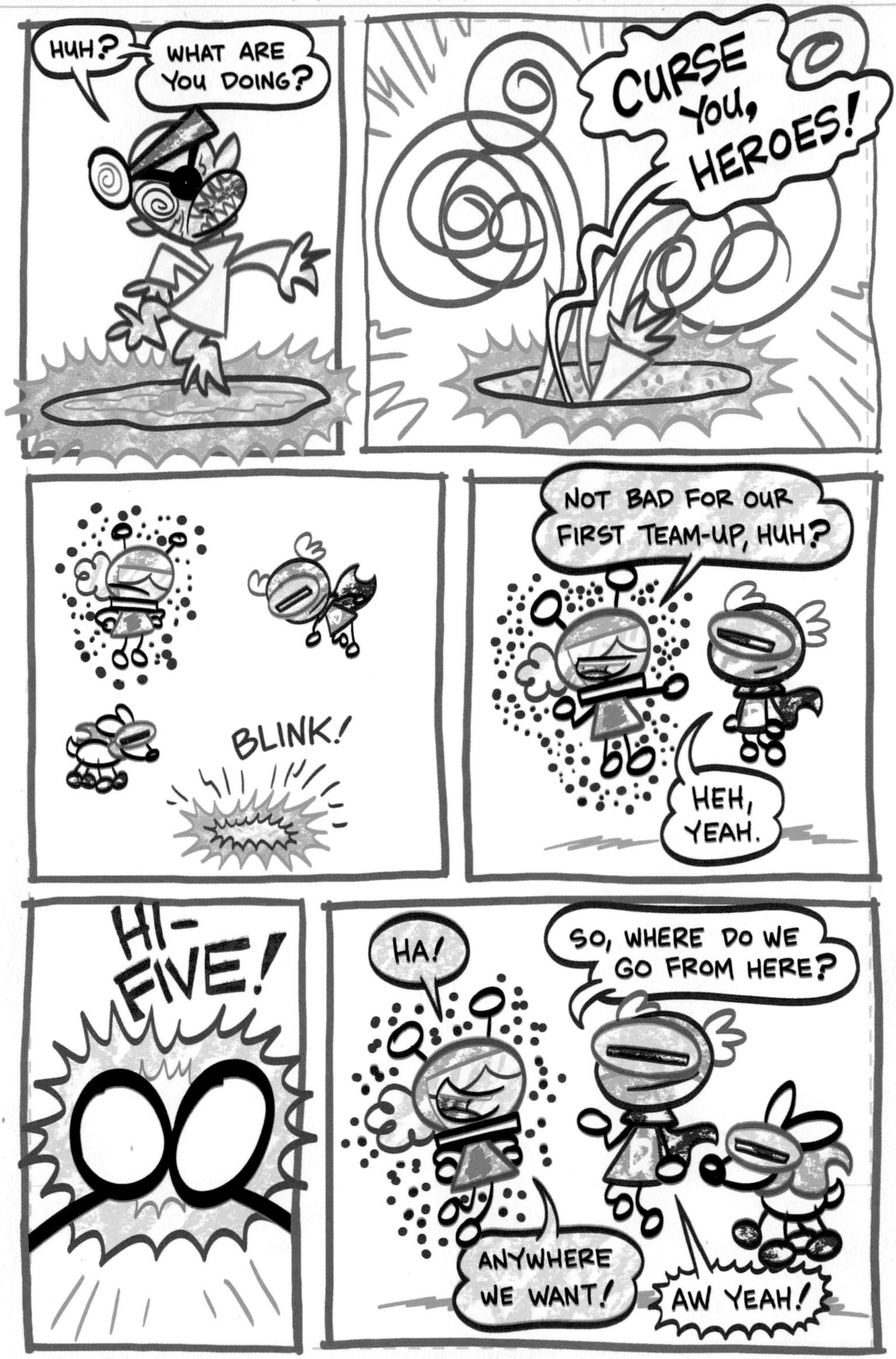
HUH?
WHAT ARE YOU DOING?
CURSE YOU, HEROES!
BLINK!
NOT BAD FOR OUR FIRST TEAM-UP, HUH?
HEH, YEAH.
HI-FIVE!
HA!
SO, WHERE DO WE GO FROM HERE?
ANYWHERE WE WANT!
AW YEAH!

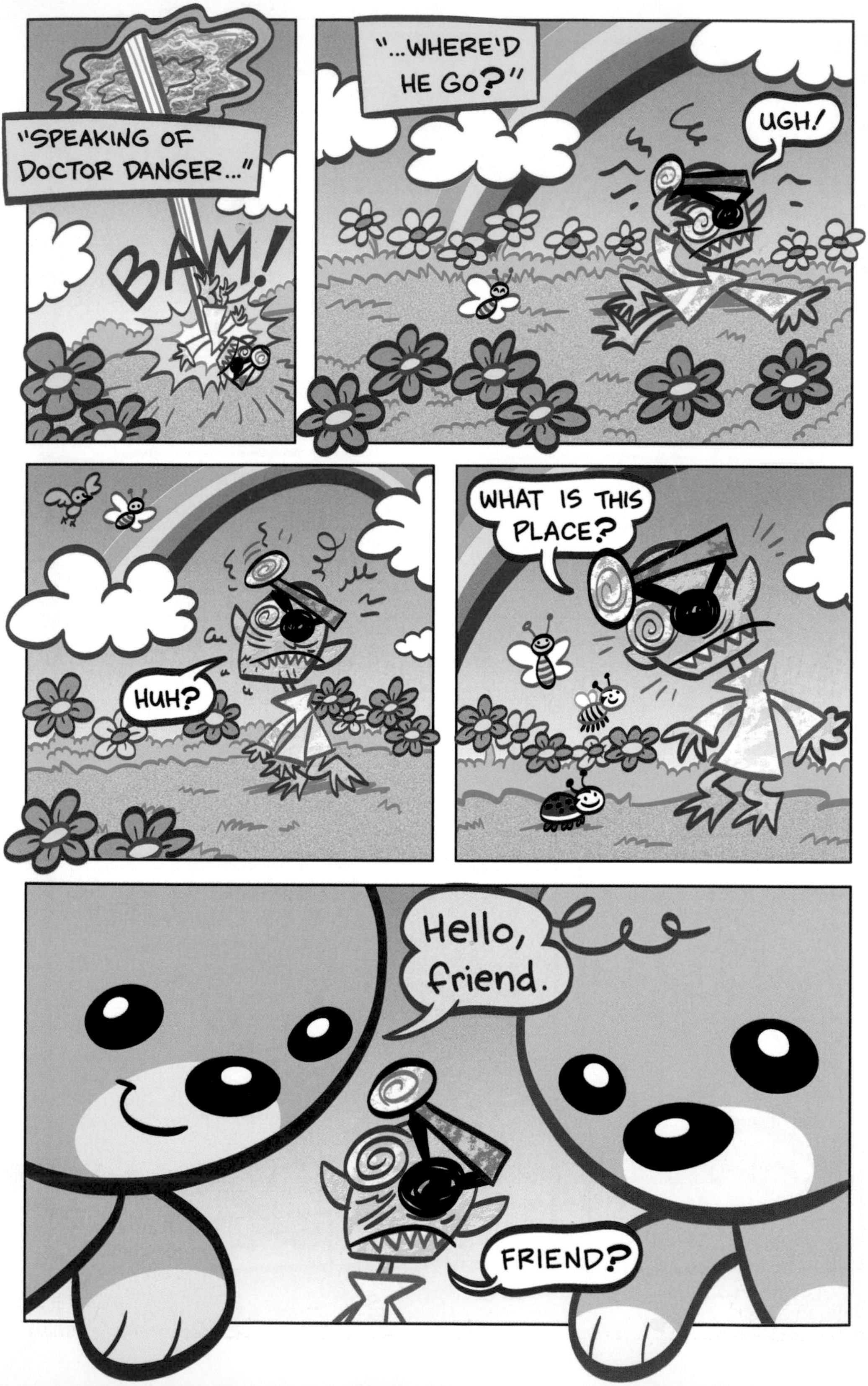
"SPEAKING OF DOCTOR DANGER..."
BAM!
"...WHERE'D HE GO?"
UGH!
HUH?
WHAT IS THIS PLACE?
Hello, friend.
FRIEND?

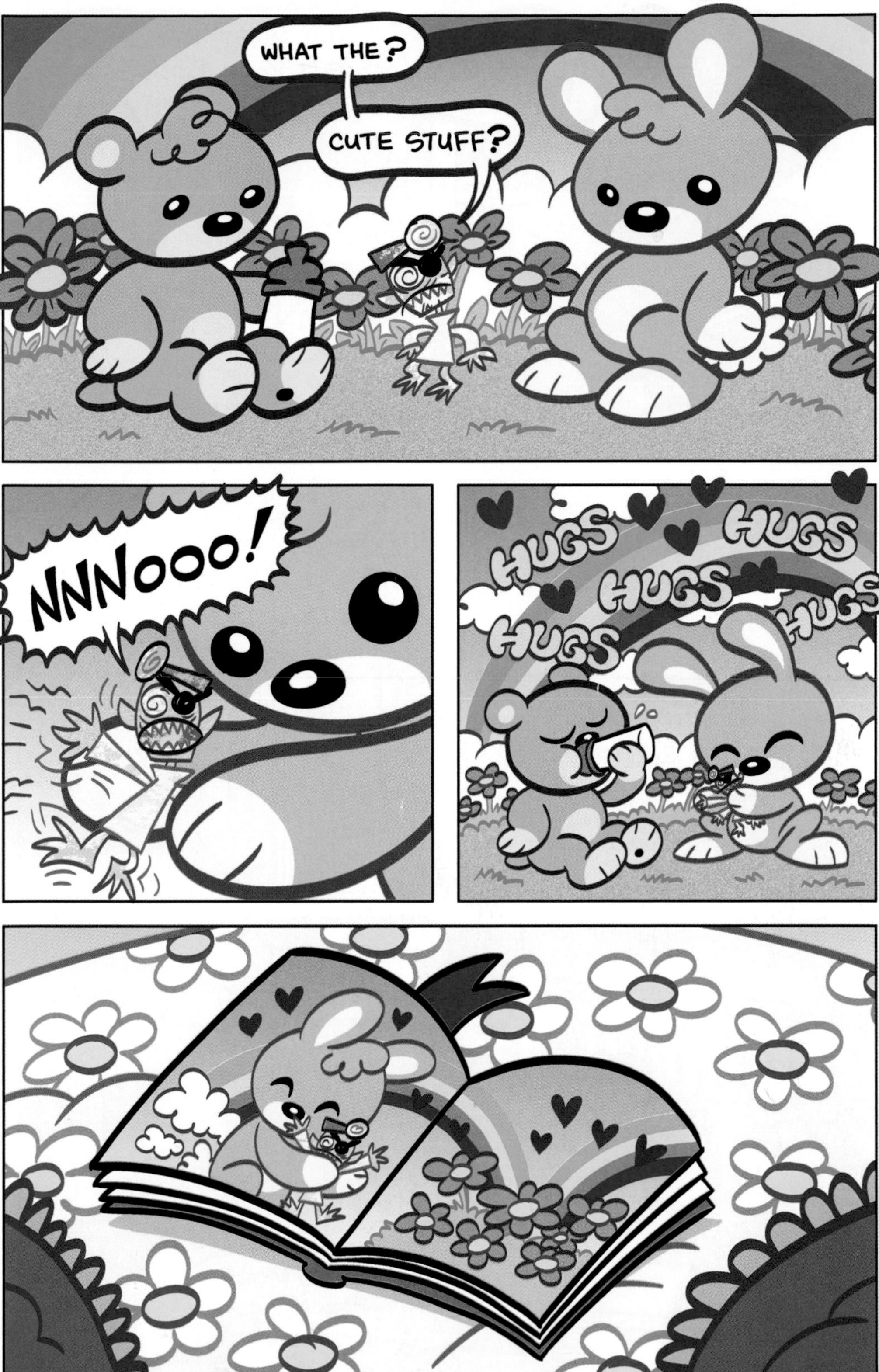
WHAT THE?
CUTE STUFF?
NNNooo!
HUGS
HUGS
HUGS
HUGS
HUGS

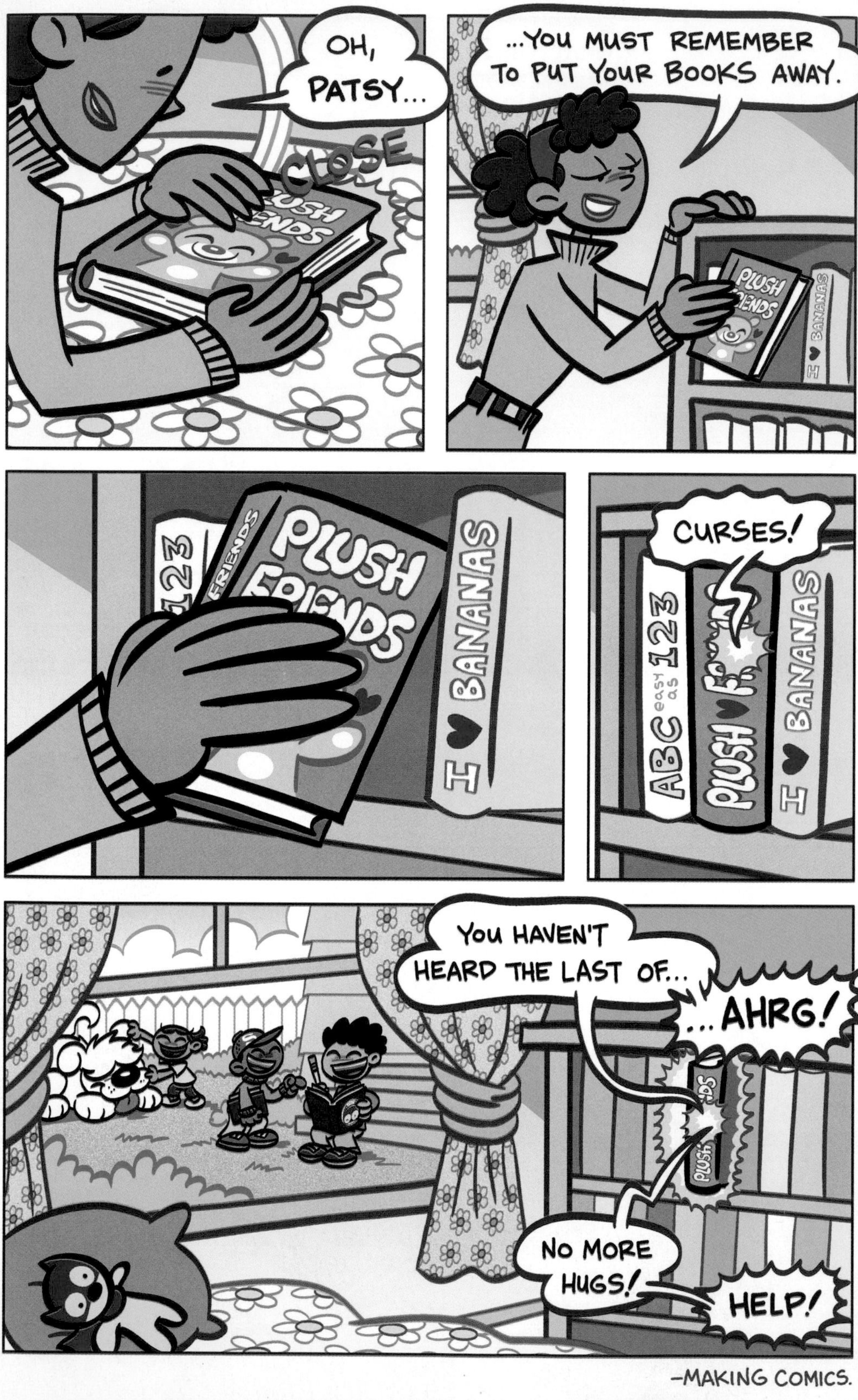
OH, PATSY...
CLOSE
PLUSH FRIENDS
...YOU MUST REMEMBER TO PUT YOUR BOOKS AWAY.
PLUSH FRIENDS
I ♥ BANANAS
123
FRIENDS
PLUSH FRIENDS
I ♥ BANANAS
CURSES!
ABC easy as 123
PLUSH ♥
I ♥ BANANAS
YOU HAVEN'T HEARD THE LAST OF...
...AHRG!
NO MORE HUGS!
HELP!

—MAKING COMICS.

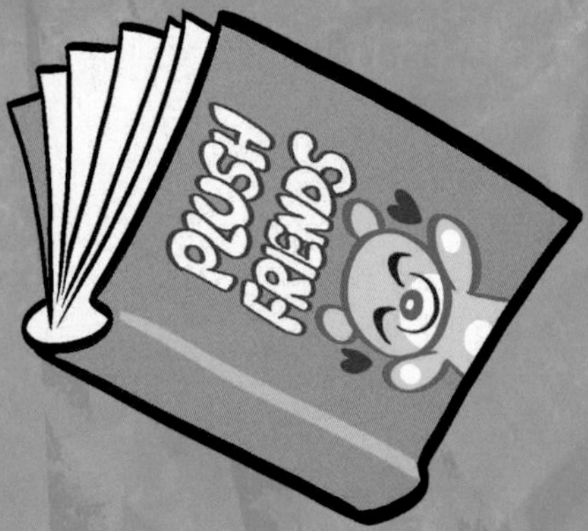
PLUSH FRIENDS

DISCOVER
EXPLOSIVE NEW WORLDS

Adventure Time
Pendleton Ward and Others
Volume 1
ISBN: 978-1-60886-280-1 | $14.99 US
Volume 2
ISBN: 978-1-60886-323-5 | $14.99 US
Adventure Time: Islands
ISBN: 978-1-60886-972-5 | $9.99 US

The Amazing World of Gumball
Ben Bocquelet and Others
Volume 1
ISBN: 978-1-60886-488-1 | $14.99 US
Volume 2
ISBN: 978-1-60886-793-6 | $14.99 US

Brave Chef Brianna
Sam Sykes, Selina Espiritu
ISBN: 978-1-68415-050-2 | $14.99 US

Mega Princess
Kelly Thompson, Brianne Drouhard
ISBN: 978-1-68415-007-6 | $14.99 US

The Not-So Secret Society
Matthew Daley, Arlene Daley,
Wook Jin Clark
ISBN: 978-1-60886-997-8 | $9.99 US

Over the Garden Wall
Patrick McHale, Jim Campbell
and Others
Volume 1
ISBN: 978-1-60886-940-4 | $14.99 US
Volume 2
ISBN: 978-1-68415-006-9 | $14.99 US

Steven Universe
Rebecca Sugar and Others
Volume 1
ISBN: 978-1-60886-706-6 | $14.99 US
Volume 2
ISBN: 978-1-60886-796-7 | $14.99 US

Steven Universe & The Crystal Gems
ISBN: 978-1-60886-921-3 | $14.99 US

Steven Universe: Too Cool for School
ISBN: 978-1-60886-771-4 | $14.99 US

AVAILABLE AT YOUR LOCAL COMICS SHOP AND BOOKSTORE
To find a comics shop in your area, visit www.comicshoplocator.com
WWW.BOOM-STUDIOS.COM

ADVENTURE TIME, OVER THE GARDEN WALL, STEVEN UNIVERSE, CARTOON NETWORK, the logos, and all related characters and elements are trademarks of and © Cartoon Network. A WarnerMedia Company. All rights reserved. (S19) THE AMAZING WORLD OF GUMBALL and all related characters and elements are trademarks of and © 2019 Turner Broadcasting System Europe Limited & Cartoon Network, WarnerMedia. All Rights Reserved. All works © their respective creators and licensors. KaBOOM!™ and the KaBOOM! logo are trademarks of Boom Entertainment, Inc. All Rights Reserved.